UNDER THE
SURFACE

ALSO BY DIANA URBAN

Lying in the Deep
All Your Twisted Secrets
These Deadly Games

UNDER THE SURFACE

DIANA URBAN

G. P. PUTNAM'S SONS

G. P. PUTNAM'S SONS

An imprint of Penguin Random House LLC
1745 Broadway, New York, New York 10019

First published in the United States of America by G. P. Putnam's Sons,
an imprint of Penguin Random House LLC, 2024

Visit us online at PenguinRandomHouse.com.

Library of Congress Cataloging-in-Publication Data is available.

ISBN 9780593625088 (hardcover)

ISBN 9780593857236 (international edition)

1st Printing

Printed in the United States of America

LSCC

Design by Alex Campbell

Text set in Calisto MT Pro

This book is a work of fiction. Any references to historical events, real people, or real
places are used fictitiously. Other names, characters, places, and events are products
of the author's imagination, and any resemblance to actual events or places or
persons, living or dead, is entirely coincidental.

The publisher does not have any control over and does not assume any responsibility
for author or third-party websites or their content.

Inspired by true events

For those lost in darkness.

Have hope.

Level One

this graffiti stood out

Michel-Entendu entrance

Pierre 1767

well

trapdoor

E

manhole

tricky gate

crawl space

crumbling stairs

A

camp night three

D

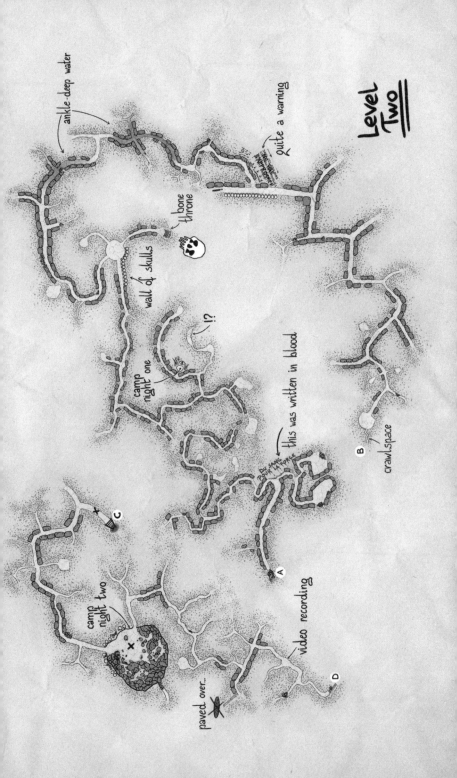

Level
Three

Basin de serpent

C

belly-deep water

bone pit with bone thrones

PROLOGUE

Ruby

I never thought I'd die alone in the dark under the City of Light.

That's what they call Paris. The City of Light. Makes sense when you think of the Eiffel Tower glinting in the sun or sparkling at night over the Seine. Or the vibrant paintings bedecking the palatial Louvre Museum. Or the glittering fashionistas strolling the Champs-Élysées. Or the dazzling boulevards with whitewashed buildings gleaming like pearls against the blue sky.

God, I'd kill for some of that light right now.

As I hurtle through the dark, cramped corridor deep underground, my phone's flashlight makes elongated shadows bounce and bob across the craggy walls like a chaotic, ghostly dance, and I have to stoop to keep my skull from slamming into the low, jagged ceiling.

There's no sign of the others.

Terror claws up my chest, and I try not to think of the crunching noises under my boots, try not to think how it's only a matter of time until my phone runs out of power, until my mouth parches, my stomach shrivels, and my legs give out beneath me. Then there'll be nothing to do but curl into a ball and wait for the darkness to become infinite.

Unless *they* get to me first.

No. That can't happen. I won't let it.

I turn a corner and slam my back against the wall, then toggle off my flashlight, plunging the corridor into pitch blackness. But hiding in the dark means my friends won't find me, either. I breathe hard, feeling like I could choke on the dank, humid air, and a sob scrapes my throat. I'm screwed. Undeniably, irrevocably screwed. But I can't spiral. Panicking got me into this mess to begin with.

Keeping my spirits up among six million corpses isn't exactly an easy feat. That's how many are entombed down here in the catacombs, their skeletal remains intricately arranged throughout this ancient labyrinth that stretches under the bustling streets of Paris like layers of rotted casserole squished under a decadent crust. My chest constricts, and it's like I can feel the crushing weight of all six million dead.

And that number's high enough, thank you very much.

A low, rasping growl echoes through the passageway. My heart jolts, and I clamp a shaking hand over my mouth to mask my heavy breathing.

But it's too late.

They found me.

Maybe there are worse things than dying alone.

1

Ruby

"Now's our chance," I whisper to my best friends, Sean and Val, under the shadow of the Eiffel Tower. "Let's go."

It's only our first day in Paris—the culmination of studying my ass off in French class and fundraising to death to go on the best trip in the history of ever—and I'm already trying to sneak away from our class.

"Go where?" Sean frowns and glances at our teacher, Mr. LeBrecque, who for some bizarre reason scheduled us to take in the sweeping views atop the Eiffel Tower while delirious with jet lag. He's gesturing wildly at the engraved names of French scientists and engineers under the first balcony while half the class is verging on a collective collapse and the other's bursting with adrenaline-fueled giddiness.

"To find that bunker." I look to Val for backup, but she's stuck in a stupor.

"I don't think we have time," says Sean.

"But it's literally *right there*."

The secret military bunker I read about—a secret no other travel You-Tuber has covered, as far as I know—is supposedly hidden beneath the south pillar. Which I can see from right here, at this very moment.

Not on my laptop screen. Not on my phone.

With my actual human eyeballs.

I asked Mr. LeBrecque earlier if we could scope out the bunker as a class, but he huffed, "I already squeezed the catacombs into our itinerary for you. This whole trip can't be the Ruby show." A jab at my channel, Ruby's Hidden Gems. As much as I respect the snark, it shattered any illusion that my teachers knew nothing of my online endeavors.

And if my teachers know, Dad probably knows, too.

Dad's not exactly sold on my jet-setting aspirations. But it's kind of hard to make it as a travel YouTuber when you can't, you know . . . travel. If it were up to him, he'd swaddle me for eternity—at least, whenever I'm not nursing his hangovers or waiting tables at his restaurant. He wants me to keep working there while I go to community college, and when I told him Val asked me to backpack across Europe with her after graduation, such a tormented expression crossed his round, bearded face that he looked gaunt. This week's as much a trial run for him as it is for me and, for once, I'm not the one most likely to fail.

I can't worry about that now. Not here at the Eiffel freaking Tower. I've daydreamed about this moment for too long to worry about anything except how quickly it will become a memory. I need to savor every minute. Film every nook. Explore every cranny. Even if it means sneaking away from our class for, like, 0.2 seconds.

I tug Sean's jacket sleeve. "Come on."

But Val's still zoning out.

"Val."

"Mm?"

"The bunker?"

"Oh, right, sorry." Val blinks furiously and adjusts her purple horn-rimmed glasses under her black bangs, a sharp contrast to her alabaster skin and vibrant hazel eyes. "Extreme hottie at nine o'clock." I look, but nobody stands out in the swarms of tourists.

Mr. LeBrecque's facing us again. I groan. So much for that.

It's not like Val to waste chances. She's an adrenaline junkie who craves—no, *demands*—attention at all times. Last year when she moved to Starborough, our sleepy suburb north of Boston, she burst into my life like the Tasmanian Devil, dragging me kicking and screaming from my comfort zone. Some of our exploits would give Dad an aneurysm, like breaking into the crypts under Old North Church, white water rafting in the Berkshires, and bribing this cute park ranger to let us camp overnight on Georges Island. But the more daring we got, the more my subscriber count jumped, so after a while I didn't need much convincing.

And look at me now, instigating the sneakage.

"LeBrecque told us to stick together, anyway." Sean motions to the twelve other seniors on this trip. We've distanced ourselves behind them in a futile attempt to keep them from videobombing my slow pans and zooms, oblivious as worms on wet pavement.

"But getting footage of that bunker would make my video pop," I argue. "Everyone and their grandma has posted about the Eiffel Tower."

"Not my grandma," he says, deadpan.

I snort. "You know what I mean."

"Well, we shouldn't."

Val rolls her eyes. "Way to have zero chill."

Sean crosses his arms. Stick a rulebook in front of him, and he'll have it memorized in an hour. He's JROTC and plans to join the military after graduation like his dad, and his towering athletic stature, broad shoulders, faded buzz cut, chiseled cheekbones, and perpetually furrowed brows sure make it easy to picture him in uniform.

And picture it I do. Often.

But getting that uniform will take him away from me.

"Now," Val whispers. "Now, now, now." Mr. LeBrecque's gesticulating at the tower again, and I nod, my fingertips buzzing with adrenaline as Val clasps them.

Sean shoots his hand into the air. "Sir?"

"What are you doing?" I squeak, swatting his cargo jacket's sleeve.

"Mr. LeBrecque, sir," he says, ignoring me as our teacher turns around. "Sorry to interrupt, but is it okay if the three of us head over there for a minute?" He motions vaguely toward the south pillar. "Ruby wants to grab some footage."

Mr. LeBrecque sighs, exasperated, and checks his watch. "Our tickets are for fifteen minutes from now. Be back here in ten."

"Thanks," Val calls back, already making a beeline for the south pillar.

Sean throws me a lopsided grin and steers me after her by the small of my back.

"Oh, shut up," I mutter.

His smile widens. "Didn't say a word."

He doesn't move his hand. I don't want him to. But I speed out of reach anyway.

The electricity between us has been amplifying for months, and now, in Paris, my blood seems to pulse with each fleeting glance, each time a smile curves his lips, like I'm perpetually tripping over a live wire. But I'm terrified to let him touch me, to let those sparks ignite. I can't risk letting him incinerate my soul.

Because that's how it would end.

That's how everything ends.

So I have to keep myself grounded.

As the three of us search for the bunker's entrance, Sean keeps scouting our class's position.

"Will you stop?" I motion to the iconic wrought-iron lattice pillars surrounding us. "You don't get to see this every day."

His steel-gray eyes flick to mine. "Oh don't worry. I'm enjoying the view plenty." Our gaze holds a beat too long, and my cheeks warm despite the chill in the air.

Sometimes he almost makes it seem worth getting scorched.

It's wild to think Sean used to intimidate me. He's basically had biceps since birth, and if resting asshole face were a thing, he has it. I could never tell whether he was shy or thought he was the shit until senior year, day one, when Mr. LeBrecque partnered us to make a video in French touring Starborough. We trudged to the grocery store after school to get it over with, timid as deer, but when I hit record, Sean brandished his arms and screamed, "Le boutique est grand et à des bananas," and I snort-laughed so hard it hurt. We tried to out-outburst each other in French all afternoon and barely had any usable footage to splice into a cohesive narrative, but he managed anyway— an impressive feat, considering. He's been helping me edit my videos ever since.

"Hey look," Val calls out, pointing behind Sean. "I think that's it."

We hurry over. A cage of rusted green bars blocks a cement staircase descending underground.

"This is it," I say. "I've seen a picture of the door that's down there." It's not visible from our vantage point, but I stick my lens between the bars, against the glass barrier, and film what little I can.

Val slinks under the green railing before the metal door and gives the handle a frustrated shake.

Sean chuckles. "What'd you expect? If any rando could get in, it wouldn't exactly be a secret bunker."

I back up a few feet. "Lemme grab some B-roll, at least."

Val grimaces. "You sound like my mom. *Honey? Grab me some B-roll.*" She snaps and points, imitating her singsong voice. Her parents have their own HGTV show and cart Val around the country to film in different regions year after year. "*Honey? B-roll.*" Snap and point.

"Sorry. I'll try to be less triggering," I say. She laughs, and I kneel to get some of the lattice in the frame and pan across the gate. "Sean, either get out of the shot or look at the stairs." He's watching our class like a hawk.

Distracted, he trips over the edge of the gate's frame and barely catches himself on the rail, then tugs down his jacket's hem. "No one saw that."

"Oh, they *will*." I tap my camera.

He groans. "Please delete that."

"Mm, I dunno. How much will you pay me?"

He laughs softly, his eyes glinting like the beams overhead until they float down to my lips and linger there.

My blood goes warm and tingly like I just downed a steaming café au lait. I slowly rise to my feet and lower my camera as he steps closer, studying my face like he wants to memorize every detail. Electricity sparks through me, and my breath shudders like the sky ran out of air.

"Can I . . ." he starts.

My nerve endings catch fire. This is it.

Our first kiss.

Under the Eiffel Tower.

It's so cliché, I press my fingers to my lips to keep from giggling. Sean sweeps a hand over his buzz cut and averts his gaze, then shoves his hands into his pockets.

Just like that, the moment's gone.

It's for the best. Besides, I don't want to make Val feel awkward—

Wait.

Val's gone, too.

I scan the crowd of tourists swelling under the nearby pillar but don't see her anywhere. Sean sees my expression shift and whips his head toward our class. "It's fine. They're still there."

"Not that—where's Val?"

"Oh." His eyes bounce around, then land back on me. "I don't know."

"Maybe she's trying to find another way into the bunker." Or she spotted something shiny and wandered off, as usual.

"Is there another way in?"

"No idea."

He checks his watch. "Our ten minutes is almost up."

"I know."

"I'll tell LeBrecque—"

I catch his sleeve. "Hang on. She must be close." I spin and race to the right, but there's only an old-timey ticket booth under the pillar, and no other doors or stairs.

"Ruby, wait—" Sean tries.

I veer left, expecting to find a gift shop or something around the corner, but there's nothing but a tall plastic barrier. "Dammit." Frantic, I rush into the crowd, weaving through swarms of tourists. "Val!"

I don't see her anywhere.

By the time I spin around to backtrack, I realize I've lost Sean, too. Crap.

I heave a sigh, then spot those familiar purple glasses.

Val's talking to some stranger. He's maybe a couple of years older than us, with striking features and tousled chestnut hair that flops across his forehead, and hint of stubble darkens his sharp jaw. Maybe he's the hottie she spotted earlier.

"Val," I call out.

She finds me in the crowd. "There you are." Like I'm the one who disappeared.

I grab her arm. "We have to go back."

"Hang on." She turns back to the young man. "Where should we meet later?"

My mouth falls open. Before he can answer, I shake my head. "Nuh-uh. Let's go."

"But—" Val tries.

"It's okay," the man says to Val, his accent clearly French. He brandishes his phone with a wink before disappearing into the throng. She bites back a grin, her cheeks rosy as a ripe apple.

"Did you already give him your number?" I ask.

She mashes her thin lips together, her eyes sparkling mischievously.

Oh geez. She should know better. But I don't want to pick a fight over this. Confrontation's my least favorite thing on the planet.

Besides spiders. Spiders suck.

"What?" she says, catching my judgmental expression. "I asked him for recommendations for any off-the-beaten-path sort of spots, and he promised to send me a list. And then—"

"*There* you are." Sean appears, puffing like he was sprinting hundred-meter dashes through the crowd. He scowls at Val. "What gives?"

"Donors," Val shoots back, then bounds back toward our class.

Sean furrows his brow, mouthing the word *donors* like it didn't click.

I laugh. "There's no point making sense of her, honestly."

"I don't know how you deal with it."

My heart sinks. Sean and Val have never exactly been close—if anything, they've been sniping at each other more than usual this past month. I'd hoped they'd finally bond on this trip. That's looking unlikely.

Mr. LeBrecque is lecturing our class in French as we reunite with them, oblivious that our little excursion went awry. On the other hand, Mrs. Williams, our librarian who volunteered to chaperone, gives us exaggerated side-eye as she hands us our tickets. She's cool, but I'd consider ourselves warned. Oops.

"Thanks to the tourist traffic, this is a hot spot for pickpockets," says Mr. LeBrecque. Cool tidbit. I start filming. "Who remembers what I said on how to avoid becoming a pickpocket's mark?"

Olivia Clarkson, as always, is first to shoot her hand into the air.

Mr. LeBrecque, as always, picks someone else. Even our teachers don't think she needs any more validation that she already knows everything.

But my gut curdles when he calls on Selena Rodriguez instead.

Salutatorian. Future astronaut. Queen bee. Girlfriend of the queenier drama club star.

And my nemesis.

She wasn't always, though. Until last spring, we were brooding besties, preferring stargazing over parties and NPCs over real people. We joined the swim team to pad her resume for college apps and chose swimming because you don't have to talk to anyone while holding your breath. I'm pretty sure she's faking her entire personality at this point, because you can't suddenly become an extrovert.

"Don't be loud, rowdy Americans," Selena recites in perfect French. "Don't keep your wallet in your back pocket. Keep your bag . . ." Good, she forgot the word for *zipped*. "Er . . . be vigilant in crowds and on escalators."

Sean scoffs, muttering to me, "Our class is toast."

Kyle drifts into my shot, staring at his phone, eyes shadowed by his Red Sox hat, proving Sean's point. We exchange a muffled laugh.

As Mr. LeBrecque herds us in line for the glass elevator that'll take us to the first level, Val loops her arm through mine. "God, that guy was hot," she whispers so Sean can't hear. Olivia's jabbering his ear off, anyway.

"I'll give you that," I whisper back.

She smirks. "He invited me to a party tonight."

"That was fast."

She releases my arm to brush back her glossy, shoulder-length hair and sets a hand on her hip. "Can you blame him?"

"Oh, get over yourself." I shove her, laughing. "You'd never be allowed to go."

"Obviously. We'll have to sneak out."

I gape at her. "No way."

She quirks her brow. "I snuck to that bunker with you."

"We didn't— That's different."

Her smile dissolves. "Why?" Even if Sean hadn't asked permission, slinking a few feet to the south pillar wouldn't put us on an early flight home.

"You know why." My voice rises. "If we get caught sneaking out at night—"

"Shh." She glances around, but nobody's paying us any mind.

Except for Selena.

Her eyes bounce away, but they've already plunged daggers into my chest. Twelve years of friendship down the drain over one fight. One mistake.

My mistake.

Guilt sours my stomach. It's my fault the girl I'd considered a sister is now my archenemy. I can't let that happen with Val, too.

I sling my arm through hers again and force a bright smile onto my face. "Let's talk about this later, okay? I can't believe we're really *here*." I squeak for good measure, and a genuine shiver of glee rushes through me.

Val's demeanor shifts, too, and she gives my arm a giddy squeeze.

Hopefully we won't have to talk about this later. Hopefully she'll forget that French guy altogether.

Otherwise I'll have to put up a fight, because there's no way I'll let either of us screw ourselves out of a week in Paris over one night of partying.

2

Sean

Val's hiding something.

As our class trickles into the lobby to head to Saint-Michel for dinner, she, Ruby, and I wait in line for the maître d' so I can report my hotel room feels like a furnace, and she's been texting someone nonstop. That's not weird on its own—it's how she keeps angling her screen away from Ruby whenever she gets close.

A small thing, maybe.

But after the crap she pulled at Olivia Clarkson's birthday party a few weeks ago, I don't trust her.

She wasn't so bad when she first moved to town. She's spunky and has a zany sense of humor, but then she put her daredevil antics on full display, and I'm not a fan. Then, the party. I don't know what the hell she was thinking.

Val notices me watching and dims her screen. "Maybe there's someone else who can help?"

"Chill." Ruby shifts her focus back from the drama club kids congregating near the door: Aliyah, Lisa, Alex, and Kyle. Selena's there, too, holding Aliyah's hand. "There's only one person ahead of us."

"Yeah, but we're leaving soon," Val whines, bouncing on her toes.

"Says the one who hogged the bathroom for an hour," Ruby teases, running her fingers through her damp blond waves to shake out the moisture.

Val chuckles. "Sorry. There was, like, no counter space."

"Don't worry," I assure Ruby. "Your hair looks great."

"Yeah, the *drowned squirrel* look is super in right now." But her cheeks go pink. I notice that happens whenever I compliment her, or whenever I so much as look her in the eye lately. It makes my heart go bananas.

I point at my buzz cut. "Hey, better than bald squirrel."

"Ha!" Ruby runs her fingers over the shortest strands near my nape. "More like fuzzy squirrel." She yanks her hand back and blushes harder.

Yeah. At this point, I'm 99.999 percent sure she likes me back. But whenever I try to hint at taking things further, she scurries away. Like earlier at the Eiffel Tower—God, I thought that was gonna be it. I could practically see the sparks sizzling between us. But I don't want to push it or do anything to mess up our friendship. I'll wait however long until she's ready.

Finally, the maître d' waves me forward. "Bonjour, comment allez-vous?"

"Je vais bien—"

"Vous avez déjà votre clé, non?" she interrupts, crinkling her forehead. *You already have your key, no?*

"Oui, madame. Je suis allé dans ma chambre mais j'étais trop chaud." *Yes, ma'am. I went to my room, but it was too hot.*

Her eyebrows arch as she stifles a snicker. I throw the others a look.

Val seems nonplussed, but Ruby covers her mouth like she's suppressing a laugh.

"What?" I ask.

"Uh . . ." Ruby lowers her hand, revealing her rosy cheeks. "I think you told her you went to your room but you were too horny."

Val lets out a loud crow.

Blood drains from my face so fast I'm shocked it's not pooling at my feet. The last thing I want is to make Ruby or this woman or anyone else feel uncomfortable.

"Oh, God, I'm sorry," I tell the maître d', mortified. "I mean, désolé . . ."

The maître d' smiles kindly. "You meant *mais il faisait trop chaud*, yes?"

"Yeah," I croak. French has never come easily to me. I'm not one of those people like Olivia who can absorb information like a sponge. I had to study real hard to make the cut for this trip. Only the fifteen seniors with the highest French GPAs got to go, and I couldn't miss out on a chance to see Paris with Ruby.

"The look . . . on . . . your face!" Val howls.

I pretend to laugh along, but inside I'm dying of death.

Ruby flicks Val's arm. "Get over it. You're one to talk, anyway. You totally cheated on the French midterm—"

"Shhh." Val clasps Ruby's wrist, but instead of denying it, she succumbs to a fresh fit of giggles.

"I'll have maintenance take a look," the maître d' assures me. "What is your room number?"

After she picks up the phone to place the call, Olivia wanders over from the group of drama kids. I bet she heard everything. I noticed her trying to catch my eye earlier, but I've felt awkward around her ever since that damn party. "At least you didn't say *je suis bon* instead of *je vais bien*," she says cheerfully. "That means *I'm good in bed*."

16

I cringe. "Is that really much worse?"

"No." Val wipes her eyes. "No, it's not."

Ruby throws me an apologetic look, still blushing, which ups my humiliation tenfold. I take a calming breath, trying not to let Val get under my skin.

But in this moment, I wish she never moved to Starborough at all.

3

Ruby

It's been over an hour since we got back to the hotel from dinner, and I only just noticed my wallet and camera are gone.

Gone.

I may or may not be on the verge of a nervous breakdown.

The camera cost me six months' worth of tips, but it's the wallet that has me breathing in short bursts as I paw at the bottom of my purse with shaking fingers. Nothing. I flip the bag upside down and shake its contents onto my bed: lip gloss, a stretchy headband, a hair tie, a pocket-sized notebook, a packet of almonds, and a few Métro tickets. All useless items that should be banished from existence for committing the atrocity of not being my wallet.

The worst part isn't losing the wallet itself. Credit cards can be canceled. A driver's license can be replaced. The worst part is Dad will murder me and drag me home, in that order.

Not that he's the murderous type. But he barely conceded to let me come to Paris and only caved after I made him a PowerPoint on how my first trip abroad would teach me independence and responsibility.

So far, I've been independently responsible for losing his credit card. The thought of disappointing him makes my throat constrict, but knowing he'll rebook me to an early flight home makes me feel like I'm drowning. Paris is my shot to prove to him that I can do this whole traveling thing. That he can be okay on his own. That we can do this *together*, even though we're thousands of miles apart. I'm not just letting him down. I'm letting myself down.

"Ruby?" Sean edges open my hotel room door, which I hadn't bothered shutting all the way. We'd been editing in his room, and I'd dashed back here to grab my camera so we could add footage from dinner in Saint-Michel. "Everything okay?"

My heart usually leaps whenever he enters a room, but it's already plummeted into my belly. "I can't find my wallet. Or my camera."

His thick brows shoot up. "What?"

"I'm pretty sure I said that in English." I instantly regret the jab.

Sean chuckles, though, and steps inside. "It'll be okay." He sets a comforting hand on my arm. Warmth spreads through me, but I lurch back, avoiding his touch as usual. He frowns.

"I'm sorry . . ." My voice wavers, and I press a palm to my forehead as I scan my side of the room I'm sharing with Val. She'd gotten bored while Sean and I edited and left to get hammered with the drama crew. I'd teasingly called her a traitor, though deep down I worry she's getting bored of *me*.

"Maybe Val borrowed your camera?" Sean suggests.

I tut. "For what? She's with Alex and Kyle for their booze, not their company."

Sean shrugs. "Maybe she wants to blackmail them for having it."

"Nah," I say. "She'd use her phone's camera." He laughs, but my smile fades. "Either way, she wouldn't have taken my wallet."

Sean drops to his hands and knees like he's about to give me twenty and scours the narrow space under my bed. "What does it look like?"

"A wallet."

"Helpful."

"Well, you know. A regular black wallet."

"Maybe you dropped it?"

I sink onto the edge of the bed, staring at my sad, empty purse. "No, it's obvious what happened. I got pickpocketed."

He stands and tilts his head. "When, though? When did you last use your camera?"

"At dinner." Before hopping into the shower earlier, I plugged my camera into my laptop to upload footage and charge it, then filmed with it during dinner, but only used my phone to take pictures on the walk home. That, at least, is charging on the nightstand. "It must've happened on the way back here."

"But your purse was zipped the whole time, right?"

I cringe. I'd been so intent on nabbing the perfect selfie with the Eiffel Tower glittering across the inky Seine behind me, I hadn't been paying attention. "I'm not sure . . ."

"Ruby. LeBrecque *just* went over this."

"I know." I sweep my hair back.

"He specifically said to keep your purse—"

"I *know*. But this isn't my fault. Some creep stuck their grubby hand into my purse, right under my arm, and stole my stuff." The hairs on the back of my neck prickle. I feel so *violated*.

Sean wipes a hand down his face. "I'm sorry. I didn't mean—"

"To blame the victim?" I finish for him, then clamp my lips. Panic is making me word vomit. "Oh God, Sean, I'm sorry. I'm being a total jerk."

"It's okay. You're upset. I get it." He steps closer and raises his hand, and I can swear he's about to cup my cheek. My breath catches, and I hold his gaze, wanting him to close the distance, even though I know

I'll pull away, anyway. But he rubs the back of his neck instead. "Do you need to call your dad?"

My stomach clenches. "I can't . . ."

"You have to," he says gently. "Did you have a credit card in there? A debit card? He has to cancel them—"

"I know. But he'll make me come home early. You know how he is."

Sean understands what it's like to have an overbearing father. But his mother is alive and well, so I don't know what *his* father's excuse is. I sigh.

"No, you're right. I have to call him." I shoo Sean to the door. "Let me get it over with, okay? I'll see you in the morning."

"I can let Mr. LeBrecque know what's up."

"No. Let's wait till tomorrow. I don't need any more lectures tonight."

He winces.

"I meant my dad, not you."

"Oh, right. Obviously." He hesitates, gripping the edge of the door as he gives me one last look, like there's something on the tip of his tongue. But all he says is, "Well . . . text me if you need anything."

Then he's gone.

I grab my cell to call Dad, but a series of WhatsApp messages from Val distracts me.

Where are youuu?

She sent this while Sean and I were raiding the vending machine down the hall, examining all the French candy options.

I left Alex and Kyle's room, they ran out of booze.
What a drag.

21

???

Listen, I'm going to that French boy's party after all. This is a once-in-a-lifetime thing, and I don't want to miss out. Don't wait up. LOVE YOU.

My heart jolts. She sent the last message fifteen minutes ago. Losing my valuables is one thing, but losing my best friend is another.

Frantic, I call her. No answer. I shoot back a WhatsApp message:

Where are you? Come back!!

Still on the train. Getting off at Luxembourg.

I wait a moment, and when she's clearly ignored my request, I say:

COME BACK!!!

No way! And DON'T TELL.

I let out a huff and pace the length of our tiny hotel room, biting my thumbnail. She could lose a whole week in Paris over this. Or something much worse could happen while she's out there alone with a group of strangers. I could kick myself for so adamantly avoiding an argument earlier. I should've shut this down right then and there.

Someone has to stop her.

If I tattle and tell Mr. LeBrecque, he'll send Val home early, and she'll never forgive me. But if something horrible happens to her, I'll never forgive *myself*. I eye the Métro tickets on my bed. Oh, hell.

I shoot off a message:

> I'm coming, too. Wait for me at
> Luxembourg?

YAYAYAY. But hurry! My phone's almost dead. And
wear boots and something warm.

I change into jeans and slip on my faux leather booties and puffer jacket. My hair's a tangled mess of blond waves and my jet-lagged eyes are bloodshot against my pale skin, but it doesn't matter—I'm going to grab Val and come straight back.

I scoop my banished belongings back into my purse, shoot off a quick email to Dad explaining someone stole my wallet and camera, then sling my purse onto my shoulder, take a deep breath, and crack open the door to peek into the hall.

The coast is clear.

My pulse races as I slink down the hall and scurry around the corner to the elevator. I press the down button and cross my arms, plucking my lower lip. There's only one tiny elevator in this hotel. I should take the stairs.

Before I can move, a nearby door opens and laughter and music flood the hall, then quiet with a *slam.* Someone rounds the corner.

She sees me and freezes.

Selena freaking Rodriguez.

We haven't exchanged two words since the incident last spring, glaring whenever we pass each other at school, like each of us can't believe the other has the audacity to exist. It's hard to believe that beforehand, she was like family. I'd go to her house whenever Dad worked nights, and the longest we'd ever been apart was her stint at Space Camp before freshman year. She was the one who got what it was like to grow up without a mom, the one with whom I spent countless hours watching movies and playing video games, the one I always texted good night to before bed.

Then we started to crack, and in my attempt to seal the fissures, I blew everything up.

She stares back with wide, russet eyes, her lashes so thick it always looks like she's wearing eyeliner. Her damp black tresses drape over her shoulders, and her agape mouth elongates her pointed chin. The memory of our last terrible encounter hovers between us like toxic fumes, and I almost can't breathe.

When the elevator opens with a friendly *ding*, her expression hardens and she sets a hand on her hip. Sneaking out yields a harsher penalty than partying, and she's sure to rat me out.

Holding grudges is kind of her jam.

"Where the hell are you going?" Her words slur a bit, and a hint of pink blushes across her tawny cheeks. She must've downed booze before Alex and Kyle ran out.

"I could ask you the same." I mirror Selena's hand-on-hip pose, trying to look blasé. "Isn't your room next to mine?" She's rooming with Aliyah, who I thought replaced me as her best friend until I found out they were dating.

Selena shakes her head. "Aliyah's sick. They moved me in case it's contagious—"

The elevator starts to close, but I whip my arm out, holding it open.

Selena narrows her eyes. "Where *are* you going, anyway?"

I let the door close. This is bad. As much as I suck at confrontation, I'm a downright miserable liar. Maybe if I'm honest about my rescue mission, she won't tell on me. "Val went out, and I think she might get into trouble," I say. "I'm going to bring her back."

Selena arches her brows. "Seriously?"

The elevator slides open, and Olivia tiptoes out wearing a long pink puffer coat, her springy golden-brown curls piled atop her head. I gasp. "Liv!"

If there's anyone less likely to break the rules than Sean, it's Olivia. She's like a walking encyclopedia that spews rainbows and sunshine, and her claim to fame—besides being our class valedictorian—is winning *Teen Jeopardy!* four times. We're not super close, but our social circles cross a lot. If you can call mine a circle. More like a straight line from point A to B, and I'm a dot chilling in the middle.

Her heart-shaped face instantly reddens, and she jumps so hard she fumbles a bulging bag from Monoprix, the French grocery store chain, then sees it's me and lets out a relieved chuckle.

"I forgot toothpaste," she explains, scooping up the bag. I notice the wary look she throws Selena. She doesn't know why we fell out, but she's clearly caught some disloyal vibes. "Nobody had the kind for sensitive teeth, so I went to buy some—"

A nearby door opens. We all go still.

A moment later, a loud knock.

"Turn that music down, would you?" Oh, no. It's Mr. LeBrecque. "Some of us need to sleep to educate you all tomorrow."

"Crap," Selena whispers, lunging into the tiny elevator. I follow, but Olivia lingers in the hall, eyes like saucers. I reach out and snare her coat sleeve.

"No—" she starts to protest, but I yank her inside. Her plastic bag rustles between us.

"Someone there?" asks Mr. LeBrecque.

Olivia blanches, and Selena pounds the ground floor button. I back against the wall and squeeze my eyes shut as if that'll make me invisible. I can't let him send me back to my room. I have to get Val.

The door slides shut.

"Did he see us?" I ask.

"Only if he has X-ray vision," says Selena.

"That man wouldn't have a superpower if it bit him in the ass."

Selena laughs with a mini-snort like she always used to at my jokes. A flicker of remorse crosses her face, and she looks away, clearing her throat. "What now?"

"We should book it," I say, "in case he checks the lobby."

"What's even happening right now?" says Olivia.

I sigh. "I'm going to grab Val before she goes to some French boy's party. And unless you want to get busted, you're coming, too."

4
Ruby

I'm going to kill Val. Assuming that French boy hasn't already murdered her.

"Where the hell is she?" I scan the crowds at the Luxembourg Métro stop as late-night revelers pass through the turnstiles and swarm the stairs leading to the platforms. Cold air bursts into the station each time the doors open, and I stuff my hands into my pockets. "She was supposed to meet me here."

"Do you think she went to meet that guy already?" Olivia asks. I feel bad for dragging her into this, but I'm glad she's here as a buffer between me and my nemesis.

"She better not have," Selena slurs, hugging her loose baby-blue cardigan closed. She didn't have a chance to grab a jacket. I'm surprised she didn't hang back near the hotel. Heck, I'm surprised she came to Paris at all. She'd drag her feet whenever she came to historical Boston sites with me to film, bored out of her skull. Paris must be shiny enough to have tempted her.

I navigate to Val's WhatsApp messages. "Dammit. She did go meet him."

She sent an address, so I tap the link. All we have to do is get her back to the hotel before anyone notices we're gone.

"All right," I say. "She's a few blocks away. Let's go."

We leave the station and cross the street toward the iron-barred fence lining the Luxembourg Gardens, which slashes across a moonless sky hazily aglow from light pollution. A few stars peek through like ghostly speckles above the bone-white buildings.

I hate how I automatically look for them, how the night sky always reminds me of Selena and her obsession with space and sci-fi. I quit the swim team to avoid her, but I can't exactly shut off the stars. Now here she is, all chattering teeth beside me.

"Is the party in someone's apartment?" Olivia's practically jogging to keep up, a head shorter than me.

"I'm not sure. Val said it's a 'once-in-a-lifetime thing,' whatever that means."

"You don't think it's in the gardens, do you? Or the *palace*?" It almost sounds like Olivia would be down to party. She's living proof that being a nerd and an extrovert aren't mutually exclusive. I've been to some of her game nights and themed birthday parties over the years and always need a day to recover afterward. Two people is my social threshold before my brain wants to explode.

Selena snorts. "Right. And at midnight, your clothes'll turn into rags, and these cars'll turn into pumpkins."

I glance at my map. "We're heading away from there, so probably not."

The farther we get from Luxembourg, the more the crowds thin, and once we cross another street and turn right, the sidewalks are nearly deserted. Our red-eye flight has made the last two days feel like one endless stretch, and the only thing keeping exhaustion from slamming into me like a pile of bricks is worry for Val.

"Rube!"

Speak of the devil.

Val's on the next corner, waving frantically under a red awning. Someone's leaning against the looming building next to her, his face obscured in shadow.

"What were you thinking?" I throw my arms out as she jogs over.

"You didn't come to ream me out, did you?" she teases, but her face falls when she spots Selena and Olivia. She pulls me in for a hug and whispers, "Why'd you bring *them*?"

I release her. "Because— Wait, is that my camera?" I point to the DSLR camera dangling from her neck.

She cradles it. "Yeah. I knew you'd want footage of this." Her eyes dance behind her glasses as she slips off the strap and hands it over. "Now you can get it yourself."

"Val, I thought someone *stole* it." I stuff it into my purse. "Did you take my wallet, too?"

She frowns. "No. Why would I?"

"Oh. So someone *did* pickpocket me—" I freeze as the boy in the shadows approaches.

He's as handsome as I remember. Strands of tousled chestnut hair flit across his forehead, stubble shadows his sturdy jaw, and his eyes glimmer under the streetlamps like sand under the midday sun. Weird outfit choice, though: he's geared up for a mountain trek in his taupe military jacket, black cargo pants, and muddied hiking boots.

His warm smile falters as he scans us over. Then he says to Val, "It seems your friend has multiplied!" in a French accent as his gaze settles on me.

I stay quiet.

Val slings her arm through mine. "The more the merrier, right?"

"We're not going with you," Selena says. Val pulls me in tighter.

I take a deep breath, steeling my nerve. "Yeah, we're not here to crash your party. We're going home. Now."

"*What?*" says Val.

"We're not getting expelled over some party," I whisper to her. The boy's gripping his backpack straps over his chest with a furrowed brow, looking low-key stressed.

"We won't get expelled," says Val.

"From this trip, we will."

She releases my arm and gives me a little shove toward the others. "You go back, then. I'm staying."

"I'm not letting you go alone." I grab her hand and tug her toward the Métro. She groans but lets me drag her away, and Selena and Olivia trail close behind.

"No, wait." The boy chases after us, a note of dismay in his voice.

I ignore him.

"Can I ask you something?"

"You just did," I call over my shoulder.

"Don't you want to party somewhere most *Parisians* never even get to see?"

"No thanks—" I still with a sharp breath. I know I should keep moving. I know I should ignore him. But capturing the little-seen corners of Paris for my channel is exactly what I want. The intrigue is too fierce, too tempting. A puff of steam escapes my mouth, dispersing in the cold air, and I slowly turn.

His lips twitch, his warm eyes glimmering with the prospect of adventure.

My pulse thrums. "What do you mean?"

"Let me show you." The corners of his eyes crinkle.

"Why would we go anywhere with you?" Selena asks.

"Yeah," says Olivia. "We don't even know you."

"How rude of me." The boy releases his backpack straps to offer a hand to Olivia, flashing a smile that clearly belongs on some billboard somewhere. "I'm Julien."

She turns beet red as she shakes it. "Olivia. But my friends call me Liv."

Selena warily extends a hand, but Val pulls me closer. "This is Ruby," she says giddily, like she's excited to show me off.

"Ruby." Julien repeats my name like he's savoring it on his tongue. "And what do your friends call you?"

Val calls me Rube, like life's too short for the extra syllable. "Just . . . Ruby."

"Just Ruby." Dimples crease Julien's sharp jawline as he grins, then shifts his gaze to Selena. "And you are . . . ?"

"Selena."

"There." He shakes her hand. "Now we are better acquainted, yes?" With a tip of his head, he beckons us to follow.

I want to, but the longer we stay out, the more likely someone back at the hotel will notice we're gone. I cross my arms, torn.

Julien claps his hands together as though in prayer. "I promise, you'll never forget this for as long as you live."

Val shakes my arm. "C'mon. You'll get so many subscribers from this. And it'll be way cooler than some old bunker under the Eiffel Tower."

"I'm going back," says Selena.

"Cool, bye." Val strides back to Julien.

Selena huffs, then says to me, "Are you seriously going to let her talk you into this?"

I narrow my eyes. "No. I *want* to see what he's talking about."

31

"You shouldn't do this, Ruby."

"You're not the boss of me, either."

"Yeah. We've established I'm nothing to you."

My mouth drops open. Like *I'm* the one who ended our friendship. Selena purses her lips, and Olivia's eyes ping-pong between us.

I take a steadying breath and turn to Val. "If anything seems off, we're leaving."

She nods. "Absolutely."

"See ya," I mutter to Selena.

"No, I . . ." She hesitates. "I'll come."

I'd rather she left but don't want to fight anymore. "Whatever. Liv?"

Olivia shrugs. "We're already out. Might as well." I'm surprised she'd want to risk smearing her record when I know she's gunning for Harvard. Then again, she was willing to risk it for toothpaste. Maybe being so far from home makes her throw caution to the wind.

We follow Julien down a narrow street nestled between a tall, archaic cobblestone wall and six-story Gothic apartment buildings. Thick iron bars cage the first-story windows, a deterrent to thieves. If only my own purse had such security features. Maybe then I'd still have my wallet, and my phone wouldn't be trilling with texts from Dad. My heart sinks each time it buzzes. Hopefully he'll think I fell asleep and give up until tomorrow.

Val leans over to whisper, "He's so hot, right?"

I muffle a laugh. Julien's close enough to hear. "How old is he?" I whisper.

"He said he's a sophomore at university."

He leads us past a graffitied mural of a toad dressed in pastels, fishing in a tiny pond while squatting on an upturned bucket. It's such a stark contrast to the ancient cobblestone wall across the street, I pause to snap a quick photo with my phone.

A bit farther down, Julien sets a hand on Val's shoulder. "One moment."

"Of course." Her voice is all silk and honey, somehow making those two words flirty. He smirks. I snicker, and she mouths *Shut up* with a sly grin. Maybe Julien's the one who needs protecting.

He slides off his bulging backpack and stoops to dig for something. "Here we go." After retrieving a small hook, he stands and slots it into a rusted drainage grate in the sidewalk.

"What're you doing?" I ask.

Ignoring me, he straddles the grate and lifts it with a grunt.

"What on earth . . . ?" says Olivia. We exchange a baffled look, and Selena seems ready to bolt back toward the Métro. But Val's grinning, bouncing on her toes.

Julien shuffles over and sets the rectangular grate onto the pavement with a soft thud. "All right, let's go." He kneels next to the gaping void and extends a hand to me as though to help me climb down.

He can't be serious.

Selena peers into the hole, then jerks back. "Whoa, that goes *really* far down."

Julien waves us closer. "We must hurry, yes?"

I scoff. "After you!"

"I have to go last to put that back," he says, motioning to the grate, as though I meant that literally.

I shake my head.

"Attends un peu." He clasps his hands, pleading. "Please. I'm sorry, we should have explained. I asked Val not to tell anyone she was going to a party in the catacombs—it *has* to be a secret—but we're so late—"

I gasp. "The *catacombs*? Like, the actual Paris catacombs."

His mouth curves into a smile.

No wonder Val's so excited. We've been dying to see the catacombs—

33

the intricate web of tunnels beneath the city where the skeletal remains of six million long-dead Parisians line miles and miles of passageways in artistic arrangements. It has to be one of the creepiest things you can see on the entire planet, which obviously means I *have* to see it. Mr. LeBrecque added it to our itinerary after I begged and pleaded, but we'd be visiting the small touristy section—the only bit open to the public. Most of the other entrances scattered throughout Paris have been sealed for ages, and the only accessible ones are secret from everyone except for—

"You're a cataphile, aren't you?" I ask, breathless.

Suddenly his outfit makes sense.

Selena sputters a laugh. "Did you just call him a pedophile?"

"A *cataphile*," Olivia pipes up. "It's what they call the explorers who meet up in the catacombs." Of course she'd know about them, too. "*Illegally*, I might add. Isn't it dangerous down there?"

"How's it dangerous?" Selena asks.

"It's not if you know what you're doing," says Julien, "and where you're going. And I do."

I've read up on the cataphiles' secret parties. Not many outsiders get to attend, so a video like "10 Secrets of the Paris Catacombs (Rare Cataphile Party!)" is exactly what could catapult Ruby's Hidden Gems into the stratosphere. I can wait to upload it till after graduation so we won't get in trouble, and if I manage to land a sponsorship? Holy crap. It could turn my channel into a bona fide moneymaker. Dad would *have* to see the opportunity there. Maybe then he wouldn't guilt-trip me so hard about traveling with Val. Maybe then Sean and I would have more videos to edit together. Maybe he'd even defer cadet training to travel with us.

"Come." Julien peers over his shoulder down the empty street. "We need to go before anyone sees us."

I dare a glance into the hole. Metal ladder rungs stretch down a narrow shaft toward an eerie orange glow below. I hadn't noticed the light peeking through the grate's narrow slats. That's how deep it goes. A chill sweeps through me, but Val's clasping her fingers under her chin, her shining eyes pleading with me.

"Listen," Julien says, "this will be the most unique experience you'll ever have. It's like an entire underground city. The history, the artwork—there's nothing else like it on Earth, I promise you."

He's speaking to my soul. I might not be great at existing around other humans, but seeing the feats they've achieved, the architecture they've built, what makes cultures tick . . . I crave it like a thirst I can never quench, stuck in one state my whole life. It's why I started my YouTube channel: to soak in as much of the world as I could and earn my way to exploring more of it.

And if Dad flies me home early because of the stolen wallet, at least I'll have *this*.

Excitement bubbles in my belly, and I nod. "Okay."

"Yes!" Val fist-pumps.

"You can't be serious," says Selena.

"You coming?" I ask Olivia.

"Uh, I don't think"—she clamps her lips and lets out a long breath—"No, you know what? I always do everything right, and it's never"—she closes her eyes briefly, then nods, resolved—"Yeah. Yes. I want to see it."

"Hell yeah." Val gives her a high five.

"But we're not wearing the right clothes. Or shoes," Selena tries, motioning to her wedges. "And we don't have the right equipment."

"There are lamps waiting for us down there." Julien pats his backpack. "And I've got extra flashlights—"

"I'll tell Mr. LeBrecque," Selena threatens, balling her hands into fists.

My stomach dips. "You'll get in trouble, too."

"Honestly," says Val, "if you're that scared, leave." Selena clenches her jaw, making her pointed chin even more pronounced. "Seriously, go back to the hotel. We won't judge."

"No. She should come." Julien puts an arm around Selena's shoulders. "You'll have fun, I promise." He quickly releases her.

Selena glances at me, conflict plain on her face. I don't understand why she won't just leave. She had no problem ditching me last year.

"The Métro's pretty close," I say. "You won't get lost—"

"No. It's fine," she says. "I'll come."

"Très bon." Julien motions for Olivia's Monoprix bag. "Give me that?"

"Uh . . ." Olivia hands it over, and he holds it over the opening. "Wait—" She tries to snatch it back, but her fingers catch air. A faint rustling noise reaches us as plastic hits stone.

"Trust me." He smiles. "It will be easier to climb down." Kneeling next to the grate, he waves me forward.

I extend my purse strap to wear it cross-body so he won't chuck it, and as I approach, he takes my trembling hand to help me down. His hand's calloused, like Dad's are from handling hot skillets, and I grip it tight as I turn, kneel, and lower one leg into the hole, feeling for the lowest rung I can reach with the tip of my boot while pressing my left palm into the gravelly sidewalk.

I can't believe I'm doing this, I can't believe I'm doing this.

My other foot finds the next rung down as I release his hand, and pebbles prick my palms. Whoa, this shaft is narrow. I glance up at the smattering of stars glimmering through the haze and take a deep breath. This'll all be worth it once we're down there—once I get to film a party in the catacombs with actual cataphiles.

Steeling myself, I reach down, clasp the top rung, and begin my descent. Step down, grab a rung. Step down, grab a rung. I got this.

The cramped shaft darkens as Selena follows, cutting off the streetlamps' glow, and the metallic rungs clang with each of our steps, getting slicker with dew the deeper we climb. I pause to wipe my hand on my jacket and angle my head to peer between my arms at the ground, still so far away. My toes tingle like I've stuck them in an electric socket.

Maybe this is a mistake.

Obviously this is a mistake.

I look up in time to see Selena's shoe nearly pummel my face. "Wait!" I shout.

She freezes. "Can you not stop right now?"

"You okay, Rube?" Val says somewhere overhead.

"I'm just—" I swallow hard as fear clenches my chest and grip the rung so tightly my fingernails dig painfully into the undersides of my thumbs.

"Come on, Ruby, go!" Selena yells.

"You're almost there," Val calls down. "You got this."

"I regret all my life choices," I call back.

Suddenly Julien shouts, "Go, go, go! Now!"

Selena scrambles down, forcing me to move. I pry my fingers from the rung to continue down, down, down toward the eerie glow below as the grate clatters back into place.

5

Ruby

When my feet finally touch solid ground, I fling myself back against the cool stone wall and clutch my chest as my heart tries to eject itself and scramble back up the ladder.

"Did someone see us?" I call up.

Julien hushes me.

Two gas lamps dangle from a rusted iron sconce next to the ladder, illuminating a narrow corridor so long it fades to pitch blackness in either direction. I'd half expected to see a pile of skeletons right away, but no one's here to greet us—dead or alive.

Stones jutting from the ceiling cast elongated shadows on the misshapen walls, some mix of limestone, cobblestone, and concrete. They're covered in graffiti—a jumbled mass of cartoon rats and mushrooms, of bubble letters and cursive scrawl. Cracks and crevasses slice the stone, forming a design of their own, like the earth has been warring its intruders for attention.

I wipe condensation from my hands onto my jeans. The cool air is so moist it presses against my cheeks, and goose bumps prickle my arms even though it's warmer down here than on the street. A peculiar smell makes me wrinkle my nose; not quite moldy or musty, but like the tangy odor of neglected books when they've been accumulating dust for too long.

Selena drops down and steps aside, clutching her knees. "Way to wimp out."

I can't tell if she's serious or teasing.

Val steps off the lowest rung and hugs me. "You okay?"

"Yeah," I say. "It was a long way down."

She chuckles, squinting as the humidity fogs her glasses. "How'd you survive when we jumped the fence at Six Flags?"

Selena's mouth falls open. Yeah, she's missed a lot. But so have I.

"You not taking *no* for an answer might've had something to do with it," I say.

Val grins as she takes off her glasses to wipe the lenses. "Hey, we had a blast that day."

Olivia hops off the ladder and scoops up her bag, the curls poking out of her bun already frizzing.

Selena raises her phone. "No signal." She's usually my height but seems taller now thanks to her wedges.

"Bad shoes for this," I say.

She tuts. "Told you." Val's Converse sneakers, my black booties, and Olivia's beige faux sheepskin boots make us only slightly better equipped.

Julien touches down and slaps dew from his hands.

"Did someone see us?" I ask again.

"A car turned down the street. But I don't think they saw." He unhooks the lamps from the sconce and gives them a little flourish. "Well, then. Welcome to the catacombs."

Val whoops, and the rest of us titter with nervous anticipation. He hands her one of the lamps. "Oh, they're electric," I notice. The designs only imitate old-school gas lamps.

Julien nods. "Easier to deal with. Sorry I don't have more—I wasn't expecting four of you. But these light the way plenty, yes?"

"Yeah." Val raises her lamp to eye level. "Wow. Feels like we're Indiana Jones."

"But without the treasure," Selena mutters, inspecting graffiti of a skull with keyholes painted where the eye sockets should be, encased in a frenetic mass of black swirls. An adjacent etching reads 1782.

"No," I breathe. "This place *is* the treasure."

"Absolutely." Olivia opens a bottle of water and takes a sip.

"Watch it." Julien points at the plastic seal she accidentally dropped. "What comes down must go up."

"Sorry, sorry." She picks it up, harried, not used to getting things wrong.

"These are sacred halls. Let's not disrespect the dead by leaving our trash down here with them."

The dead. I peer down the corridor. They're down here somewhere.

"Shall we?" says Julien. As we set off, he scrolls through his phone until a Taylor Swift song blares from the tiny speaker.

I smile on reflex—I'm a total Swiftie—but Val says, "Way to kill the ambiance."

"Cataphiles play music so you know they're coming." But he turns the volume down, stooping slightly to keep his head from grazing the jagged ceiling. "Anyway, we got a good turnout tonight. There's plenty of food, and, of course, it wouldn't be a party without wine."

But I'm not here for the wine.

I dig my camera from my purse and linger behind, adjusting the aperture for the darkness. The light from the lamps is fading fast. I take a quick video, then snap a photo, the flash illuminating the narrow, craggy passageway.

"Stop!" Julien shouts.

I gasp and back into the bumpy wall as he rushes toward me.

"Sorry, I'm a horrible guide, I'm not taking any time to explain. But I can't let you take photos here."

"For real? I can't come down here and *not* get it on camera."

"That grate used to be sealed. We don't want the police to realize it has been *un*sealed." He points to a blue plaque on the wall reading RUE MICHEL-ENTENDU, which wound up in my shot. That must be the street overhead.

"Oh. Sorry." I flush and power off the camera.

"I forgive you, Justruby. This time."

"No, it's just Ruby—" I stop short, realizing.

He winks, which only makes me blush harder.

I stuff my camera back into my purse and catch up to the others as he leads us ahead. Val flicks my arm. "Troublemaker."

I flick her arm back. "You're one to talk."

Selena puffs air between her lips.

"What?" Val asks. Selena only shakes her head. "Come on. Out with it."

The way Selena's eyes bounce between us, I can tell she's coming up with a lie. We're both crap liars. "Aliyah's gonna freak when she hears about this," she finally says.

"Who's Aliyah?" Julien asks.

"My girlfriend."

"I thought you were with Tyler what's-his-face?" says Val.

I tense. Tyler Russell. And quite the face he has, with his angled jaw tapering to a sharp chin and sky-blue eyes that pierce your soul. He's tall and lithe as a Tolkien elf and the star of each year's school play, and he's not on this trip since he takes Spanish, thank God.

Selena's expression tightens. "Why would you think that?"

"Because—" Val starts, but I make a slicing motion at my throat. I told her how Selena used Aliyah to get close to Tyler. How she thirsted over him from a distance until junior year when she joined Gavel Club, an extracurricular Aliyah started for practicing public speaking. Afterward, she and Aliyah hung out constantly—during lunch, after swim practice, at parties—and I would've admired her commitment to barging into Tyler's field of view if I hadn't been so crushed she barely had time for me anymore. After we fell out, she and Aliyah must've bonded for real, because they started dating in the fall.

"Oh—sorry, Selena," Val says instead. "I must've had the wrong impression."

"It's fine," Selena mutters.

Sorry, Val mouths to me, cringing.

I shake off the awkward moment and focus on our surroundings, skimming my fingers over the ancient wall flecked with sediments and shells—at least, I think those bone-white specks are shells. Graffiti coats most of the others with artwork and cartoons—familiar ones like SpongeBob and Darth Vader and foreign ones I don't recognize—and dates and words I can't understand, not because they're in French but because they've been scrawled over too many times. It's like the walls are oozing history, time, and the abstraction of the human mind. I wish we had more time. There's so much to see, and we're so lucky to see it. All thanks to a stranger.

"Do you come down here a lot?" I ask him.

"All the time." Julien grins at me over his shoulder. "You feel more alive here, yes?"

"More alive down here with the dead?" Val teases.

"There's more to this place than death," he says. "No internet to distract you from your thoughts, from conversations with friends. Here, your mind is free."

After several turns down similar passageways, Selena says, "I didn't think there'd be all this graffiti. Kind of sullies it."

"I think it's incredible," says Val, admiring a nonsensical mural, a riot of multicolored shapes and whorls that seem to dance across the serrated stone. "I'm surprised enough people have been down here to leave all this."

"Right?" I say. "So much for seeing an unseen corner of the world—"

My foot catches on something. I stumble and gasp sharply, then glare at the ground like I always do when I trip for no reason. But this time, there's a culprit.

A chill tiptoes down my spine. "Is that a . . ."

Bone.

A human bone, its narrow length knobbed at either end, browned with filth and age. A femur, I think.

"Whoa," says Val, "you just tripped over someone's *leg*."

Selena shakes my shoulder and points ahead where the corridor spills into a large chamber. I follow her finger to see dozens of eyes staring straight back.

No, not dozens. *Hundreds.*

The blank, vacant eyes of the dead.

6
Ruby

We follow Julien into the chamber, where grotesque displays of skulls and femurs interlace five tunnels branching out like spokes in a wheel. It's like a construction crew ran out of stones and mortar and figured human bones would do nicely instead, arranging them in artful criss-cross, zigzag, and swirling patterns. A tinny buzzing noise fills my ears. There are so many skulls, too many to comprehend, and I've never even seen a dead body before.

Not unless you count my mother. She died moments after giving birth to me, while I was in her arms. I can't remember it, obviously, but she recorded a video a week earlier saying she couldn't wait to look me in the eyes and tell me how much she loved me despite all the times I'd pummeled her spinal cord at 3:00 a.m. Apparently by the time I opened my eyes and looked up at her, she was gone. She never got to look me in the eyes at all.

And that sucks to think about.

Whenever I do, an oppressive cloud of sadness smothers my soul. Selena understands since she also lost her mom young, but I can't talk to her about it anymore. Val's too bubbly to broach such a heavy topic, and Sean—well, if I open myself up to him like that, I won't be able to break my fall. And since bringing it up to Dad sends him straight into a depressive episode, these days, I ride out the storm alone.

I shake the encroaching fog from my mind and step farther into the chamber.

The incandescent lamps cast an amber glow onto the skulls, their eye sockets blackened by shadow. Val stretches a finger toward one, but Julien snakes out his hand and grabs her wrist.

She gasps.

"Don't touch," he says softly. "We don't disturb the dead."

"My bad," Val whispers as he lets her wrist slide from his grasp. Even in the dim light I can see her pale cheeks flush.

Selena spins in a slow circle. "Paris must be absolutely cursed."

"We don't insult the dead, either," Julien scolds. "Without their strength, we'd be reduced to dust."

I tilt my head. "How do you mean?"

Julien rakes his hair back. "They are providing, how do you say . . . structural integrity."

Like bricks and mortar after all. "Would this room actually collapse—"

Julien's music abruptly stops, and he checks his phone, clucking his tongue. "Dead. We're almost there anyway. Come, we're late."

But we're all too transfixed. Selena's hand flutters to her throat. "Why'd they stack the bones like this?"

"It was the best option at the time," Olivia explains. "In the 1700s, the cemeteries throughout Paris were so overcrowded they were literally overflowing, so they started moving the bodies down into the old quarries. I think it was easier than cremating them all or shuttling them outside the city."

Julien throws her a lopsided smile, impressed. "So became the *king-dom of the dead*."

Val, on the other hand, throws her side-eye. "Dork."

"Okay, Indiana," Olivia smoothly retorts. Val laughs.

I hone in on a nearby skull baring its grin at me like it caught my gaze on purpose. My spine prickles. One of its browned incisors is chipped at a corner, like maybe it once bit down on a peach pit too hard.

Not *it*. *They.*

"My God," I say, my voice wispy. "This was a *person*. A living, breathing person, walking around Paris, going about their business."

Julien twirls his pointer finger. "They all were."

"Yeah, but if you stop and *really* think . . . maybe this one was a teacher. Or a stonemason. Or maybe they nursed people who were sick with the plague. They probably had a favorite food, a favorite drink. Maybe they were in love, or took care of their siblings, or had a fuzzball who curled up in their lap at night. But now this is all that's left. One skull among hundreds—no, *millions*—down here. Packed underground and forgotten." The enormity of it makes my head spin.

He puckers his cheeks. "It helps if you don't dwell on it too hard."

Selena gestures at the zigzagging skulls. "Why the weird designs, though? Why tear the bodies apart?"

"It wasn't like that," says Olivia. "They were skeletons already—at least, the ones they moved." She frowns. "I'm not sure about the ones who died in the French Revolution, though. They brought a lot of them straight here . . ." She trails off, leaving us to imagine how that might've gone down.

I recoil at the thought and step back, and the skulls surrounding this one fill my vision. Any one of them might've witnessed the Revolution. Maybe that one impacted in mud fought for freedom. Maybe that one with missing teeth built barricades in the streets. Maybe that one with the narrow nasal cavity stormed the Bastille. Any one of them—maybe *every* one of them—saw all that history go down with their own eyes.

Eyes now nothing but gaping voids.

There's no way to know. None of these people left videos behind. None agreed to be arranged like this, in these strange patterns, disconnected from the rest of themselves. A shiver rattles my own bones, and I grip my jacket tight around my torso. I knew to expect bones down here, have seen plenty of photos of the ones on the official tour route.

But seeing it in real life is nothing like seeing pictures on the internet. There's this grisly weight to the air, an ominous discomfort you can't shake, like every fiber of your being is innately aware of the wrongness surrounding you.

I catch Julien watching me. He averts his gaze. "Come, we can still catch the end of the party," he says low and husky, jerking his arm to the right. "This way—"

"Whoa," I say, catching the way the light from his lamp glints off some nearby graffiti. My exclamation reverberates through the chamber, bouncing off the bones. I lower my voice. "How's this paint still wet? It's two *hundred* years old."

"How do you know?" Val asks.

"It says so." Olivia points at the year 1787 scrawled under the name PIERRE. Above, a depiction of an ivy-wreathed cross looks as damp. "It must be the humidity. Paint back then was super oily, so it could stay slick a long time. Centuries, even."

Wishing I caught that factoid on camera, I pull it out and start filming. "This graffiti's over two hundred years old," I narrate. "And get this." I run a finger along the edge of a shiny letter and raise it to the lens, showing off a bit of black residue. "It's still damp! The humidity—"

My camera's no longer in my hands for the shot.

Julien has snatched it and is slinging the strap around his neck. I'm so surprised, I don't even grab for it.

"I told you we wanted to film down here," says Val.

"I'll give it back when we get to the party," he says, then turns to me. "Such passion for some old scribbles. Yet you were so quick to desecrate it."

I frown. "What?"

He motions to the edge of the letter I touched.

My cheeks burn. He's right. "Sorry. I'm sorry. I got excited."

He snickers. "Don't apologize to *me*. What's so exciting, anyway? It's only paint, no?"

"It's not about the paint." I consider the glistening scrawl, struggling to articulate my jumbled thoughts. "Pierre left this. *Created* this. He probably wasn't famous or written about in history books, but we're talking about something he did in this very spot, right here, right now, after so much of the world has changed—and it seems so *fresh*. It's like we're reaching through time itself."

Selena hangs back, arms crossed. As a sci-fi geek, she's always cared way more about the future than the past. But Olivia's eyes glimmer. "That's all so many of us want in the end. To leave some mark on this world."

I smile. "You get it."

"Yeah, deep stuff," says Val.

Julien's staring again—not at me, but past me, his dark brows knitted, eyes glazed, lost in thought.

"Well?" I ask. "Can I have my camera—"

Chattering, laughing voices float in from an intersecting tunnel—I can't tell which since this cavern's acoustics bounce the sound every which way.

Julien blinks, then glances over his shoulder and mutters a curse at his wristwatch. "We're really late. Come, I know a shortcut." He guides Val by the small of her back to the left, then strides down the corridor as the rest of us scurry close.

This passageway is danker and narrower than the first, forcing us to walk single file. It's so dark I can't tell if mold is coating the walls, but I'm wary to run my palms over them to keep my balance on the uneven ground. Some walls are crumbly, revealing dark cavities leading to other tunnels, other caverns, making the space feel claustrophobic and infinite all at once. We take several more turns, Julien confidentially guiding us without a map.

I check my phone. It's already midnight. "We're almost there, right?"

"Are we there yet?" Val says nasally, like a child in a back seat.

"The less we stop to sightsee," Julien says, "the sooner we'll get there."

I harrumph, but he ignores me and presses on.

"Did you know Robespierre is supposedly buried here?" Olivia chirps. "Or . . . piled, or whatever—"

"Who's that?" Val asks.

"*Who's that?*" Olivia repeats, affronted. "Only the most famous leader of the French Revolution. He got *thousands* of people guillotined? Ended up getting beheaded himself? We learned about him in history class a few years ago."

Val shrugs. "I've gone to seven different schools thanks to my parents' filming schedule. Never learned about it."

"Still," says Olivia.

I chuckle. "Not everyone can retain the knowledge of a four-time *Jeopardy!* champ."

"The trivia show?" says Julien, taking another turn. "You were on that?"

"Yeah," Olivia says with a bashful smile.

"Excusez-moi, I didn't realize I was talking to a celebrity."

She giggles. "That doesn't make me a celebrity."

"Makes her a mega dork." Val pokes Olivia's arm. "Are there any other *actual* celebrities buried down here? Besides Rob Pierre."

"*Robespierre*," Olivia corrects. "And yeah. There's Charles Perrault— you know, the author of 'Little Red Riding Hood' and 'Cinderella.'"

"I didn't know. But go on."

"Well, there are a couple of other writers, a composer, a bunch of famous revolutionaries, King Louis's mistress. None of it's confirmed, though. They didn't exactly mark the graves. And there are so many graves across so many tunnels—two hundred miles' worth."

"We're walking all two hundred to get to this party," Selena grumbles, limping slightly. "And I have at least two hundred blisters." She glares at me like it's my fault. Like everything's always my fault. I wish she weren't here to remind me.

"Hey, Julien, I thought you said we were taking a shortcut," I say.

He grins, stopping abruptly. "Here we are."

We gather around a cobblestone shaft even narrower than the one we climbed down from the street. It protrudes from the ground like a crumbly doughnut, a well without water, leading to a pitch-black void. An ancient-looking rusted ladder peeks out, gray crusted with brown, its stabilizers hooked over scabrous stone.

"How deep exactly is this party?" Olivia asks.

"One gallery down," says Julien. "Right under the cavern with the bones."

Selena bites her lip. "Maybe this isn't a good idea."

"Aw, but we're so close," I say. "Please? I really want to film this. Leaving now would be like getting to the peak of a roller coaster and then taking the stairs down." She's always loved rollercoasters and that g-force weightless feeling I hate.

She doubles down, shaking her head. "I think we should leave."

Val makes a noise in the back of her throat like she's suppressing a laugh.

Selena's big eyes become narrow slits. "What?"

"I *told* you to go back," says Val. "This kind of thing isn't for everyone. There's no shame in it. No one's judging." But she clearly is, the way she flicks me a quick, devilish look, a ghost of a smile on her lips. She's goading Selena for my sake.

"It's not that," Selena insists. "It's getting late, and we're not even there yet. I didn't think this party would be so far."

"So go back."

"What, *alone*?"

"Then come with us." Val shrugs. "I don't know what else to tell you."

"This is a shortcut, right?" Olivia asks Julien. "Can we go the regular way instead?"

"That's not the point," Selena bristles, looking to me for support. My skin prickles with discomfort. I hate picking sides. And I want to keep going.

Val folds her arms. "Seriously, it's okay to admit you're scared. It's dark down there."

Selena raises her voice. "I'm not afraid of the dark."

"Claustrophobic, then?"

Now it's my turn to suppress a laugh, more over the indignant look on Selena's face than the accusation. She's always wanted to be an astronaut, and darkness and small spaces are kinda part of the gig. She'd probably rather stick a bone in her eye than admit she's scared of them. She casts me a quick look, then raises her chin. "Even if I was, it's nothing to laugh at."

"Who's laughing?" Val shrugs. "Rube's not laughing. Neither is Liv—" She cowers as Selena storms over, like she thinks Selena's going to deck her or something.

Instead, Selena swipes her lamp and stalks to the well.

"Uh, I should go first—" Julien tries as I say, "Wait."

But Selena's got her legs over the ledge and is clambering onto the ladder, which wobbles and creaks under her weight, not fully secured to the stone all the way down. "Let's get this the hell over with."

"Selena, be careful," I say, peering down the well. She's already halfway down. The lamp dangles from the crook at her elbow, its orange glow lighting the corridor below.

I set my palms on the ledge, ready to boost myself up and follow.

Julien touches my wrist. "One at a time."

I huff, then spin to face Val. "Do you really have to rile her up like that?"

"How am I riling her up? I told her it's okay to back out."

I rub my forehead. "This is awkward enough—"

Selena gasps and curses, and a loud *clunk* ricochets up the shaft. I turn in time to see one of the ladder stabilizers break off with a *snap*, and Selena shrieks as she plummets the rest of the way down.

7

Sean

I drum my fingers on the tiny oak desk next to the window as I scroll through YouTube, my insomnia not giving a flying fart about jet lag. Every so often, I glance at the bed where the comforter's rumpled from Ruby sitting there earlier, cross-legged, editing our video.

She still hasn't replied to the WhatsApp message I shot over an hour ago:

> Hey, I'm sorry about before. Obviously it's not your fault you got pickpocketed. Let me know if there's anything I can do.

Maybe she passed out soon after I left.

Or maybe she's pissed at me.

Not that I'd blame her. I'd been a total asshat when really, I'd been mad at myself, not her. I should've noticed her purse was unzipped. I should've spotted someone pickpocketing her. I was right freaking there and I was useless as a box of rocks.

I rub my eyes. Catching feelings like this is a first for me. I've never so much as gone on a date before, always too busy studying or doing drills—Pop's orders. I'm *destined for service*, he always says. I'll be saving lives. Protecting our nation. Everything else is trivial.

Then Ruby snort-laughed at my sad attempt to say *the store is big and has bananas* while filming that video for our French class, and I was toast.

More like melted butter on toast.

And nothing about her is trivial.

I tab back to Ruby's Hidden Gems's YouTube dashboard but don't want to upload our video from tonight until she checks out my final edits. I'd dabbled with editing before making that French class video— mostly *Call of Duty* recaps that languished on my hard drive, unseen— but when Ruby captured our Podunk town like it was some vibrant New England hamlet, her amber eyes absorbing the beauty in the world most people are too distracted to notice, it inspired me to splice her footage into all these cool montages, flexing creativity muscles I didn't even know I had. And when she asked if I wanted to help edit her videos to get more practice, I was game. Working with her, hours slip away like moments.

I can't let too many hours slip away now. We have to be downstairs for breakfast at 7:30 sharp. I better try to get some shut-eye.

I go brush my teeth in the minuscule bathroom and slam my funny bone into the doorframe at least twice. Living spaces in Paris are way more compact than I expected, but at least I don't have to share a room. Though let's be real—I'll be sharing plenty once I ship off to military academy in a few months.

Shaking out my arm, I flop onto the bed, and something hard digs into my back. I pull out the offending object: Ruby's laptop, its lavender shell matching her cell phone case. It's been hiding under the quilt fold.

If she wakes up to discover it's missing, she'll freak. The last thing she needs is to think someone stole yet another one of her things.

I pull on a sweatshirt, grab my room key, and head down the hall. The floor's shaped like a long rectangle; Olivia and I each have our own rooms by the elevators, while Mr. LeBrecque and Mrs. Williams have theirs somewhere in the middle, and everyone else is paired up. Apparently there are other random tourists on our floor, too, but I haven't seen any.

There's no sign of the faint thumping bass I heard earlier, which probably means Alex and Kyle's little shindig is over, and Val's back in her room with Ruby.

I raise my fist outside their door, about to knock, but freeze. They're probably asleep. I hold my breath and listen for signs of life. There are muffled voices, but those might be coming from next door. I don't want to press my ear to their door like some creeper—

The elevator scrapes open down the hall, and Mr. LeBrecque rounds the corner.

Well, crap.

"Sean," Mr. LeBrecque grumbles, stopping in front of the neighboring door. He's wearing rumpled blue pajamas under a long peacoat and is gripping a shopping bag from the grocery store across the street. His graying brown hair's sticking up in the back, and purple half moons shadow his bloodshot eyes behind his rimless glasses. "What are you doing here?"

"I, uh . . ." I run a palm over my buzz cut and clear my throat. "Ruby forgot her laptop in my room earlier, sir. I'm just bringing it back."

Mr. LeBrecque raises a brow. "Ruby was in your room, hmm?"

"We were working on a video project, sir. She was back in hers by ten."

"Mm-hmm." He taps on the neighboring door; I'm pretty sure that's Selena and Aliyah's room.

The door cracks open, and Mrs. Williams peeks out.

"How is she?" Mr. LeBrecque asks.

"Poor girl's still vomming like there's no tomorrow," says Mrs. Williams. A retching noise follows, like Aliyah's trying to chime in from the bathroom.

Mr. LeBrecque passes Mrs. Williams the bag. "They don't sell Pepto-Bismol here, and the pharmacist left at ten. But I picked up re-hydration salt and ginger tea, and some crackers. You've got a coffee machine in there, right? For hot water?"

"Yup."

"And Selena's all right?"

"She was fine last I saw her—she's in Olivia's room for now. But listen, if Aliyah's not doing any better in the morning, I'm bringing her to the hospital." Mrs. Williams narrows her eyes at me. "What're you up to?"

"I was just—" I start.

Mr. LeBrecque waves me off, yawning. "Never mind, never mind. I'll see you in the morning, Monique. Thanks for looking after her."

"Thanks for the medicine run." She nods and shuts the door.

"Poor Aliyah." Mr. LeBrecque shakes his head. "Not the best way to spend your first night in another country."

"I'm pretty sure it's the actual worst way," I say.

He chuckles and motions to the laptop. "Why don't you give that to Ruby in the morning?"

"Yeah, all right." I glance at her door. "You should probably know that Ruby got pickpocketed tonight."

Mr. LeBrecque's shoulders slump. "You're kidding me."

"No sir. They got her wallet and camera."

"Why didn't she tell me?"

"She only realized later. She thinks it happened on the way back from dinner."

"Well, we'll deal with it in the morning." He shakes his head. "Why does it seem like everything's going wrong? And on the very first day, no less." He rubs the back of his neck. "Well, there's good news, at least."

"What's that?"

Mr. LeBrecque offers a tired smile. "It can only go uphill from here."

8

Ruby

"Selena!" I rush to the well's edge. Selena's sprawled on the ground below, the lamp on its side beside her, and I'm pretty sure my heart's down there, too, because it has fully evacuated my body. The ladder's dangling at a slant from the stabilizer still hooked over the well, but it's the angle of Selena's left leg that makes me gasp.

Julien's next to me with his lamp, swearing in French.

"Are you okay?" I call down. "Are you *alive*?"

"No," Selena replies with an agonized groan. So, yes, definitely alive, thank God.

As she shifts to sit up, she bends both knees to scoot back from beneath the precariously swaying ladder, so her leg's not broken after all. Her jeans are ripped, but since they were already distressed, I can't tell what's new.

"I'm okay, actually," Selena croaks, rotating both of her ankles, testing them, then hisses through her teeth as she brings her arm to her chest. She tugs up her torn sleeve and exposes a bleeding forearm. I take a sharp breath. Even from here I can see blood streaking from the gash down to her palm. "I didn't even feel it . . ." She whimpers. "It's really deep."

"We can't call for an ambulance," I say, frantic.

"Nope, no signal." Val waves her phone around overhead.

"That won't work," says Olivia. "The stone's too thick."

Julien leans against the well, muttering obscenities, clenching and unclenching his fists like he's trying to work out what to do.

"How'd this happen?" Val picks up the jagged bit of the ladder's broken stabilizer. Rust deteriorated the metal so badly the end that hooked over the stone snapped clean off.

Olivia swats Val's wrist so she drops it. "Don't. Haven't you ever heard not to touch a rusted nail?"

"It's not a nail."

"But it's sharp and rusted." Olivia calls down, "Did you cut your arm on the ladder?"

"I don't know." Selena shakes her head. "It all happened so fast. I tried to catch hold of something . . ."

"Have you gotten a tetanus shot?"

"I— Maybe?"

"Let's worry about that later," I say. "How do we get her back up here?"

"Can't she climb back up?" Val suggests. "We can hold the side that broke."

"It's too dangerous," says Julien. "She could fall again. Besides, the ladder doesn't extend all the way to the ground. We would've had to hop down from the lowest rung, and I doubt she can hoist herself up with her arm bleeding like that."

I rub my lips together, scrambling for a solution. "Can we brace ourselves against the walls"—I trace the well's circumference in the air—"and shimmy down?"

He tuts. "So, you have a death wish? Figures."

I scowl. Then I remember our initial descent down extremely sturdy rungs and how I barely clung on.

He's right. I'd break my neck.

"I don't know about the rest of you," says Olivia, "but I'm no Legolas."

"I can probably do it," says Val, peeking down.

"Absolutely not," says Julien.

"We should go back to the street and call for help," says Olivia.

"Are you kidding?" Selena cries.

Julien wipes a hand down his face. "That would take too long. We'd have to wait for help to arrive and bring them all the way back."

I imitate his tut. "You just don't want to give up your secret little entrance." He quirks a brow at me.

"No, please," Selena wails. "You can't leave me alone. *Please.*"

She left *me* alone.

My eyelids flutter shut. That doesn't matter right now. I snap my eyes open and ask Julien, "Do you have any rope or something?"

"She can't climb with her arm like that," he says.

"No, I mean, for one of *us* to climb down and wait with her."

He shakes his head again. "We'll have to go another way." He fishes something from his backpack and tosses it down to her. I think it's a shirt. "Here. Wrap your arm."

"What about the party?" I ask. "Can she get there faster?"

"Yeah," says Selena. "I can—"

"No." Julien jabs a finger at the ground. "She has to stay put." He looks down at her. "Selena, listen to me. *Do not move.* If you try to get to the party on your own, you'll get lost, and we'll *never* be able to find you. Do you understand?"

"Please don't leave—"

"*Do you understand?*" he repeats with such urgency his voice comes out all raspy.

"Y-yeah."

Julien turns back to us. "Let's go. Now." Bile leaps up my throat, but we all follow, leaving Selena bleeding and crying and alone.

The dewy passageways have turned into an obstacle course. When the compact dirt ground turns to uneven, slippery limestone, I come alarmingly close to twisting my ankle several times. And after Julien lifts some yellow caution tape (ENTRÉE INTERDITE) so we can descend a crumbly staircase barely the width of my hips, some of the steps are so severely corroded we have to basically surf down a pile of rocks while gripping the walls.

Now that the ground's flat and coarse and somewhat less perilous, we're practically jogging. Selena's all alone and she must be so scared, but I can't help but dwell on how she abandoned me last spring, leaving *me* all alone.

Granted, it was my fault. I was the one who screwed up at Tyler's Cinco de Mayo party. She didn't text me back all weekend afterward, her silence louder than anything she could've said, sending me spiraling into a full-blown panic. I was desperate to explain, to apologize, but when I found her in the packed cafeteria on Monday, she was sitting with Aliyah and her drama club posse. My brain always turns into cheese curds around them, so I froze. She spotted me anyway. Anger sparked in her eyes, and her whispers to the group hissed like a lit fuse. A heartbeat later, laughter exploded from their lips, and their stares were like shrapnel striking my skin.

Right then, I knew.

I was too late. Just like I feared.

Someone already told her what I'd done.

Julien curses, snapping me from my thoughts. We've reached the underside of the crumbly well.

The only sign of Selena is her blood. It splotches the ground like spilled ink.

"Selena?" I cry, gripping a painful stitch under my rib cage.

Val wipes a sheen of sweat from her upper lip. "Where'd she go?"

"I *told* her to stay put," Julien says as Olivia backs into the wall, breathing in rasping gulps. Short springy curls have escaped from her bun and fall into her eyes as she rifles through her purse, the plastic bag at her elbow rustling until she pulls out a red inhaler and raises it to her lips. Julien's brows pucker as he watches her suck in and hold her breath, letting the medicine seep into her lungs. "You okay?"

She nods, resting her hands on her knees. After a few moments, her wheezing softens. She straightens and widens her eyes at something over my shoulder. I turn. Large letters span a wide breadth of the opposite wall in deep red paint.

DU SANG POUR LA FORCE.

"Blood . . . for strength," Olivia translates between shallow breaths.

All four of our heads dip to the red blotches on the ground.

Goose bumps rush over my skin. The letters are written in blood.

Selena's blood.

"It means nothing," Julien says. "Just random scribbles like all the rest."

Of course. No one dragged her off and left this warning. She isn't possessed by some catacomb demon who forced her to scrawl it herself. My sleep-deprived imagination is running wild.

Olivia dabs one of the letters and rubs her fingers together. "Yeah, it's not wet."

Val rolls her eyes. "Obviously." She prods Julien's arm. "Maybe your friends found her. I bet they heard her crying and came to get her."

He wipes a hand down his face. "I don't know."

"Maybe *she* heard *them*," Olivia says, "and figured she could make it there on her own."

Julien sets his hands on his hips and stares at Selena's blood. Finally, he nods. "You're right. That's probably what happened. Come. We're going back up." Without waiting for us to agree, he heads back down the corridor.

"Shouldn't we make sure she made it?" says Olivia.

"What about the party?" Val asks.

"How can you know—" A moan cuts me off. It's coming from past the well, in the opposite direction from where Julien's surging ahead. I grab a strap dangling from his backpack. "Did you hear that?"

Julien stills. "What?"

"I didn't hear—" Val starts.

But there it is again. A girl's voice, faint yet familiar as my own heartbeat, which I hear reverberate in my pillow night after night as I lie awake rehashing our demise.

"Selena?" I yell.

"Ruby." She seems eerily far, but her voice echoes through the barren passageways, making her sound close at the same time.

My blood turns cold. "She's lost."

"Ruby!"

"This way!" I tug Julien's sleeve—I can't surge ahead without a lamp of my own. He resists, hesitating, then lets out a grunt and keeps pace beside me as we plunge into the darkness.

We traverse corridor after corridor and take turn after turn, following the sound of Selena's voice, but it's like playing Marco Polo in a god-awful maze where the echoes are endless. I keep expecting to hear the telltale signs of a party—music, chattering, bottles and cups clattering—but only our crunching footfalls permeate the space.

Selena's stopped answering.

Julien presses a finger to his lips after I call her name for the dozenth time. *"Shhh."*

"I can't hear her anymore," says Olivia.

"Me neither—" I start.

"Maybe if you stop blabbering, we could," says Julien. We hush up, our ragged breaths filling the air instead. "And stop *breathing* so hard."

I clamp my lips, listening for Selena's voice.

But it's a tomb of silence. It reminds me of swimming breaststroke at a meet, how each time my head dipped underwater, the babble from the bleachers would quiet, and my ears would feel clogged with all that water and nothingness.

I check the time on my phone. My stomach twists—it's nearly two in the morning. The night's leeching away.

"Maybe your friends found her first," Val says to Julien.

"Yeah, maybe." But the way he pinches his brow and takes slow, deliberate breaths isn't exactly reassuring. He considers the three of us, taking in our anxious faces. "Come. I'm taking you back up."

"No," I say. "Take us to the party. If she's not there, you can drop us off and keep looking—"

"The problem is," he says, "the party's probably over by now."

We agree to let Julien take us back aboveground once he convinces us it's the fastest way to find out if his friends really did run into Selena on their way back to the surface. We can't know for sure until we get there, too. But now it feels like we're walking downhill, delving deeper and deeper underground.

"Are you sure we're going the right way?" I ask.

I expect Julien to utter some cocky reassurance, but instead he stops to dig through his backpack.

"What're you looking for?" Val asks.

"My map. I must have forgotten it at the party before I went to pick you up."

The hairs on my nape stand on end. "Are we lost?" I hadn't tracked our route as we followed Selena's voice, and if someone offered me a million dollars to find the broken ladder, I'd remain dirt broke.

"No," he says. "I only wanted to double-check something. I think we took the last turn too late. Let's backtrack a bit, yes?" He zips his bag and slings it over his shoulder, then jabs a finger in the air like he's leading a troop of soldiers. "Onward."

"Backward," Val corrects.

"Backward." He catches my and Olivia's worried expressions. "We're fine. Trust me."

I don't trust him.

I barely even know him.

Still, we follow, having no other choice, and take the next right to course correct and speed ahead.

When we pass a small alcove I don't recognize, unease niggles the base of my skull. And when the long curved passageway beyond abruptly ends, dismay shudders my spine. I place my shaky palm on cool limestone where I'm sure an empty space should be. "I don't understand. We didn't even go that far."

"How'd we make a wrong turn already?" Val asks, her forehead scrunched with worry. None of our misadventures were ever this disastrous, not even that time the cops chased us clear across Castle Island, and I was sure they'd bust down my door the next day for trespassing.

Julien closes his eyes and presses his fingers to his temple, like if he concentrates hard enough, a map will appear under his eyelids.

"This is *bad*," Olivia croaks, her eyes misty.

"Shut up," Julien snaps, making her flinch. "Everyone just . . ." He takes a deep breath. "I'm sorry. Just be quiet. Let me think." He teeters his weight from his toes to his heels, then skims the wall with his fingertips as he strides back down the corridor.

When we reach the last junction, he motions to the left. "We came from there, yes?"

"Yes," Olivia replies as Val says, "No."

"What do you mean, *no*?" I say. "Yes, obviously, we just came from there."

"No," Val insists. "We passed this hall before—er, tunnel, whatever. We turned right farther down."

I look to Olivia for validation, but she's shaking her head, wheezing again.

"Oh God." I'm utterly disoriented, my fingers and toes tingling like my blood's gone fizzy with carbonation. I pull out my phone and navigate to my maps app. There's obviously no signal, but maybe the GPS works.

Nope.

I brandish my phone this way and that, but the usual blue dot showing my location won't appear. I switch to the compass app with trembling fingers—

"That won't work," Olivia rasps. "All the rocks and soil and whatever metal's nearby will interfere."

Val checks her phone. "Dead." She palms her forehead. "I can't believe I forgot to charge it this afternoon. Stupid, stupid . . ."

I squeeze my eyes shut, wishing I could rewind to the grate to drag Val back to the hotel, or better yet, to a few hours earlier when we were all at the Eiffel Tower, when Sean stepped close with that intense gaze of his and I could swear he was about to kiss me.

God, I'd give *anything* to go back to that moment.

"So what do we do?" I grip my neck. Panic has me in a choke hold. "Which way should we go?"

We stare at Julien, waiting for an answer, waiting for our guide to tell us how to get the hell out of here.

But he merely utters a curse in French and stares ahead, where the light from our lamp dims to a void of blackness beyond.

9
Ruby

"Let's stay calm, yes?" Julien sets a hand on my shoulder. He must feel me shaking—my legs are trembling uncontrollably as my heart tries to pulverize my rib cage. "We should rest in that alcove we passed. Get our bearings."

"No," I cry. "We have to keep going."

"Actually, he's right," Olivia says between ragged breaths, wiping her cheeks with the backs of her hands. "I go hiking with my dad a lot, and he always says if you ever get lost, you should stop in your tracks. If you panic and keep going for the sake of it, you'll get even more lost."

"We've already reached peak lostness," I say. "Could we really get *more* lost?"

"We'll be fine," Julien says. "I'm sure your friend is fine, too. We just need to stop and calm down for a moment."

"Okay," says Val.

I bite my lip, discordant, desperate to find that crumbly staircase, but I've already been outvoted.

A few minutes later, we're stooping through a low entryway into a small alcove. Barely an inch of it isn't coated in graffiti, which would be reassuring—at least people were here, people who *left*—but something about the art makes my skin crawl. It's not the hideous rats or warped faces, or the sinuous whorls shaping a demon's silhouette, or even the colossal eye on the back wall, dilated and staring—it's the frenetic energy of the overlapping scrawl that makes the walls seem to pulsate with life, almost like they're *breathing*.

And anything alive can decide you're not welcome.

Julien sets his lamp in the middle of the alcove and sits beside it. Val lets her purse flop next to him while Olivia sinks to the ground beneath the eye and hugs her knees to her chest. I poke Julien's shoulder and hold out my hand.

"What?" he says.

"Camera?"

He glances down, frowning. It's been dangling from his neck ever since that cavern of bones. "Sorry. Forgot I had it." He slips it off and hands it over.

Val *tsk*s. "If you'd been recording the whole time, we could've watched it and found our way back."

I groan. Julien offers an apologetic shrug, then pulls a flashlight from his backpack and switches it on and off, testing it.

I turn on the camera and hit record, more to soothe myself with the familiar act than anything. "We're lost in the Paris catacombs," I narrate, spinning in a slow circle. Olivia offers a half-hearted wave as the camera pans over her. "We're stopping here to make a game plan—"

"Shouldn't you conserve the battery?" Julien says as he slides in-frame. "If you want to track our route with it later."

"Oh. True." I stop recording.

"If your friends found Selena," Val says to him, "they'll come looking for us, right?"

A muscle in his jaw twitches.

"I'm sure she told them about us." Olivia rakes her teeth over her lower lip. "Unless she passed out from blood loss or something."

"No, that's not—" He shoves back strands of tousled hair, anxiety marring his features.

I kneel beside him. "Julien, please be straight with us. Do you think your friends found her? Do you think help is coming?"

He lets out a breath. "No."

"Why not?" I ask through the fear knotting my throat.

"I didn't hear music," he says. "Remember? Cataphiles play music when they're walking around so you know they're coming."

"Then why'd you want to leave—"

Val talks over me. "But when we didn't show to the party, they must've realized something's wrong. Would they really just go home without looking for us?"

Julien rubs his knuckles along his stubbled jaw. "They probably assumed you changed your mind, and that I didn't feel like coming back alone."

"So they don't even know we're missing." Olivia chuckles bitterly. "Jesus. I do *one* thing I shouldn't, and this happens."

I shiver from head to toe, stuck on one word.

Missing.

This whole situation is so surreal, it feels like I can hit Edit, Undo on some simulator to find myself back at the hotel with Sean. Val would've been better off if I never came after her, if we never took that shortcut, if Selena never fell. She would've been best off if she never left the hotel at all. I should've shut this down at the Eiffel Tower, right when she first met Julien, instead of avoiding a fight.

"Did you tell anyone where you were going tonight?" I ask Val.

"Just you. Did you tell Sean?"

I shake my head. "He went back to his room before I saw your messages." Olivia knits her brows. "No one will know to look for us tonight," I say, my eyes watering. "*No* one."

"We'll find a way out," Julien says. "I promise."

"You can't promise that," says Olivia. "We're literally in the world's biggest maze."

"Even if we don't find an exit," says Val, "I'm sure we'll run into someone."

"You're not grasping the scale of this place."

"But we're right in the middle of Paris. Cataphiles come down here all the time, right?" Val gestures around us. "Look at all this graffiti."

"It's been painted over *decades*. Centuries, even. We have no clue how far we walked."

"It couldn't have been that far."

Olivia raises her voice. "You can't rationalize your way out of this—"

"Girls." Julien raises his hands. "Let's stay calm, yes? That's why we stopped. Let's all just breathe a minute."

Olivia buries her head in her arms. I try to focus on taking deep, calming breaths, but another part of my biology distracts me.

"Julien?" I ask.

He finishes a great yawn. "Yes?"

"Are there any rules about, er, using the bathroom down here?"

"Où sont les toilettes?" Val chuckles.

Olivia snaps her head up. "Nothing about this is funny."

"Why are you being such a Debbie Downer?"

"Why are you being such a . . . a . . . Positive Pickle?" says Olivia. How she can say that with a straight face is beyond me, but she does, then bursts into tears.

Guilt sours my stomach. It's my fault she's in this mess. I never should've pulled her into that elevator.

Julien rubs his eyes. "Toilet. Let's see. The dead end to the right will be as good a spot as any, I think."

Val digs through her purse, then pinches a pack of tissues and shakes it like a sugar packet.

I sigh. "Good idea."

Val passes a tissue to each of us, and Olivia starts wiping her cheeks.

"That's not what it's—" Val starts.

"I know what it's *for*," says Olivia, though she switches to using her sleeve instead. "Sorry."

"It's okay," Val whispers, her eyes glassy, too, looking as remorseful as I feel.

Julien passes me a flashlight. "Ladies first."

I take it and head out alone.

Squatting in some dark, dank tunnel with my bare butt exposed was the last thing I expected to happen on my trip to Paris.

But here I am.

Squatting.

In the dark.

Butt exposed.

By the time I return to the alcove, Val's sitting cross-legged next to Olivia, tracing circles onto her back. It reminds me of that time I dashed into a restroom at school last May to sob my eyes out after Selena iced me out in the cafeteria. As I gripped the edge of the porcelain sink, tears dripping into it, someone touched my shoulder, making me gasp and my gaze leap to the mirror. It was Val. The new girl. I'd only spoken to her once before, after she discovered Ruby's Hidden Gems and asked to come to Boston next time I filmed. I never followed through, ever the introvert, but here she was anyway, drawing soothing circles onto my back.

"Was it a boy?" she'd asked. "A bad TikTok dance? Someone pee in your cereal?"

"Eugh." A raw laugh escaped my throat. "No."

"Well, spill. I won't judge."

Selena sure did. "My best friend *hates* me," I said through my tears.

"Why?"

Because I betrayed her. Tyler had sworn he wouldn't tell a soul what happened, but I should've known he was as trustworthy as the dust mites on his bookshelves. I blubbered the truth to Val, the whole truth, words spilling from my lips after squirreling them in my overstuffed cheeks for days. When I finished, she said, "There's nothing a heartfelt, handwritten apology can't fix." I was surprised I hadn't thought of it myself. Selena and I used to pass notes in class all the time, folding them into little origami envelopes and slipping them into each other's bags when our teacher wasn't looking.

So that's what I did. Filled three pages, front and back. Folded it like we used to.

But when I texted Selena to ask if she read it, she replied: Don't worry, I got your message loud and clear. You can fuck all the way off now.

Now she must hate me more than ever. I just hope she's okay.

Val crosses the dimly lit alcove, and I hand her the flashlight. "Watch out for the wet spot."

"Ew." She takes it and speeds out. When I sit beside Olivia, I can sense how hard she's shaking.

"Do you have anything to start a fire?" I ask Julien.

"No. Either of you have a lighter?"

We shake our heads.

"Ah, well. Let's see what we do have." He unloads his backpack, pulling out a baguette, Tupperware filled with cheese, and a bottle of wine. "Good thing I didn't unpack at the party."

I frown. "How long exactly do you think we'll be down here?"

"Not long." Julien pats his stomach. "I'm just always hungry."

"I've got more." Olivia crawls over to dump out her Monoprix bag, adding two bottles of water, a pack of pretzels, and a box of individually wrapped madeleines—mini cake loaves stuffed with chocolate cream. I fish the lone packet of almonds from my purse and toss it onto the bounty.

Val returns and sees the pile. "We're not making camp here, are we?"

Julien exhales like a horse. "Maybe we *should* try to sleep."

"You've gotta be kidding me," I say. In just a few hours, our class will realize we're gone. Mr. LeBrecque. Sean. *Dad. "Shiiiiiiiiiit."*

Val plops down next to him. "We'll have a better shot of running into someone in the morning," she says. Olivia purses her lips.

"It's more that I can't keep my eyes open." Julien rubs them. "It's, what, almost four in the morning?" He checks his watch. "Yep."

I mash my palms into my forehead. "My dad's gonna flip."

"Same," says Olivia.

"At least your parents will give a damn," says Val.

"Yours will, too," I say.

She snorts. "Nah. They'll be too busy filming their bogus house-hunting show to notice anything's wrong." Fair. Whenever I go to her place, they ignore us, glued to their editing bay or granite samples or whatever. Unlike Dad, who barrages my friends with bad puns and better meals he's testing for his restaurant. He might be overbearing sometimes, but at least he cares.

"How is it bogus?" Olivia asks.

"People fake considering multiple homes. They already know which one they're buying. The real estate industry funds the network, it's a total scam." Val sighs. "Anyway, at least people will know to look for us in a few hours when we don't get on the bus to the Louvre."

My throat constricts. "But they won't know to look for us *here*."

Val tugs Julien's sleeve. His eyelids have been drooping like he's about to doze off. "Won't your friends realize what happened when you're gone tomorrow?"

He blinks. "Ah . . . the people I come down here with, I don't talk to them every day."

"What about your family?" I ask. "Or your school friends?" Val mentioned he was a sophomore at university.

"My sisters will be the first to realize I'm gone." He slumps his shoulders, dropping his chin to his chest. "But they won't know where I went. They don't know I come down here at all."

"So we're truly on our own." Dread pools in my gut as I stare at the pile of food. Selena's out there somewhere with nothing but a lamp. I didn't even think to drop supplies down that well to her. I assumed we'd quickly reunite.

Julien lowers himself to his back.

I groan. "I'll never be able to fall asleep down here." Even at home, I can't fall asleep without a blanket. If my feet are exposed, I envision a shadowy hand stretching up from under my bed to snatch them.

"Same," says Olivia. At least her pink puffer coat is almost as big as a sleeping bag.

"Here, this might help." Julien grabs the wine bottle with a grunt, then pulls a switchblade from his backpack's outer compartment, flicks it open, sets the bottle down, and jiggles the blade straight down into the cork.

"You're gonna cork it," says Val.

"Your confidence is inspiring." Julien starts twisting. A sliver of beige peeks out.

Val smiles wryly, then eyes the supplies. "At least we won't starve to death."

"We'd thirst to death first," Olivia says matter-of-factly.

"La vache! Nobody's thirsting to death." Julien pops the cork as though to prove his point, then passes me the bottle.

Booze always makes Dad mopey and lethargic, and the one time I drank—well, I don't like to think about it. So I never have more than a few sips of the foul, cheap beer Val hands me at the parties she drags me to. But I take a swig, desperate to settle my nerves.

It's not bad. Deep red, laced with fruit and smoke, almost like I can smell the barrel where it fermented, and it warms my throat as I swallow. I'm surprised I like it.

Between the four of us, we drain the bottle quickly, each having a little more than a glass's worth. Once it's empty, Val puts her glasses in her purse and rubs her arms. "Should we spoon? You know, for warmth?" She casts Julien a come-hither look under her dark eyelashes, patting the ground between us.

"It's not that cold," I protest, averse to making a Julien sandwich.

Julien nestles behind Val, making her the little spoon, and they can go ahead and enjoy that, thank you very much. I curl into the fetal position a few feet away, facing Val and resting my cheek in my palm. My hip bone digs painfully into cold limestone no matter how I shift to find a fleshier spot, and I think of the lavender, polka-dotted sleeping bag I brought to the Harbor Islands last summer when I complained to Val I could feel pebbles and lumps of grass beneath me. I'd give anything for that sleeping bag now.

"Ready?" Julien hovers a finger over the lamp's off switch.

"Do we have to turn that off?" Val asks.

"We shouldn't waste power."

Unease prickles my skin. "How long do those last, exactly?"

Julien wrinkles his nose. "Something like sixty hours? Seventy? On low, though." He flips the switch a notch, making the alcove twice as dim and ten times as creepy. "Don't worry, we won't need them that long. Plus, I have three flashlights with fresh batteries."

"So can't we keep it on low?" Val asks.

"I'd rather play it safe. Imagine trying to walk around"—he switches it all the way off—"in this."

The darkness is oppressively black. I wiggle my fingers in front of my face, but my eyes might as well be closed. Even with my blackout shades back home, the streetlamps' light peeks around the edges and a tiny light in my headphones charger glows on my desk. But this darkness is stifling, the kind that creeps up your nose and down your throat and burrows in your bones, that siphons all hope you'll ever see light again. The silence filling my ears like wads of cotton isn't helping. I stare at the ceiling—at least, where I know the ceiling is—trying not to think about what could be lurking up there in the dark.

Not that I believe in that sort of thing. Selena does, though, which is odd for such a science nerd. Once we used a Ouija board during a sleepover, and she asked it if Tyler would ever kiss her. I surreptitiously nudged the planchette toward *yes*, and she couldn't fall asleep after until I put the board out on the back porch, no matter how much I assured her I'd moved it, that ghosts aren't real, that none would ever hurt her. Only the living can crush your soul.

Now in this suffocating darkness, as the cool, damp air sends shivers down my spine, it seems all too plausible that some ghoul with rotted flesh dangling from its decrepit bones could be hovering overhead, inches from my face, glowering at me through gaping sockets.

The mental image jolts my heart. I need to see *right now*.

I pull out my phone and brighten the screen.

Nothing's up there. Nothing but air and stone. I let out a rattled breath.

"You okay?" Val whispers.

"Yeah."

But I keep the screen brightened.

Sometimes when I can't sleep, I yank my phone from my nightstand and watch one of the videos my mother recorded while she was pregnant, all bubbly and excited and extremely unaware of her fate. She had Dad's sense of humor, babbling jokes to her belly (aka me) and sharing silly stories about her day. They must've been the most obnoxiously adorable couple on the planet. It's no wonder he never remarried—she didn't have the kind of shoes other people could fill.

I don't know why I watch her videos so often. They only make me sad.

I can't watch one now, anyway, so I stare at the screen's background, which I changed earlier to a photo of me and Sean at the Eiffel Tower shortly before our almost-kiss. That was close. Too close. I swore off loving anyone ages ago, after seeing firsthand how my mother's death destroyed Dad. I can't let anyone wreck me like that.

But I can't deny how seeing Sean's face on my phone brings me such comfort. Just from his photo alone, I can feel the reliable zip of excitement I get while filming together, the consistent thrill of amusement from his deadpan humor, the perpetual flutters in my belly from his presence. I soak in his image, remembering his warmth as he put his arm around me, how I savored his closeness, so close I could feel how sculpted his abs were beneath his coat, how I smiled so wide knowing we'd be spending an entire week in Paris together—

"Is that Sean?" Olivia whispers behind me. She can see my screen.

"Yeah."

"Huh."

I frown and twist to see her. She's propped on an elbow, pouting. "What is it?" I ask.

"Are you two together?"

My heart does a little somersault. I bite my lip, and even though it's way too dark for her to see I'm blushing, I can't help feeling self-conscious.

Before I can even answer, she says, "You said they were friends." She's looking over me. At Val.

"They are," says Val. I can only barely make out her silhouette, but she sounds defensive.

"Did I miss something?" I ask.

Olivia turns back over and curls into the fetal position.

"Forget it, Rube," says Val. "You should shut off your phone. You know, to save the battery."

"Right."

I imprint Sean's steel-gray eyes and those dimples creasing his sculpted cheeks to memory one last time, then power off my phone, plunging us into darkness once more.

10
Sean

Sitting alone in this hotel restaurant is extremely on-brand for me.

It's not that I don't like people. I just prefer solitude. It's peaceful. Serene. Way better than having orders barked at me. Perfect for reading and editing videos and observing the world.

The only person I'm ever happy to have join me on my island is Ruby.

I have no clue how long she takes to get ready, so rather than risk waking her, I brought her laptop with me to breakfast. Now I'm scarfing down my second croissant, watching my classmates chatter excitedly before we board the bus to the Louvre. Everyone was supposed to be here a half hour ago, but Ruby and Val are still no-shows.

I sent Ruby a WhatsApp message fifteen minutes ago: Hey. You guys coming down soon? And I'm not saying I've been staring at that message, waiting for those tiny dots to show her typing, but . . . okay, fine, that's exactly what I'm saying.

Damn, I've got it bad for this girl.

Every time I see Ruby, my heart flips out. Every time her eyes light up while delivering a ridiculous punch line—boom, heart. Every time she bites her full lower lip like she's lost for words—boom, heart.

Even now, catching a glimpse of someone walking in, my heart gets up to its bullshit.

But it's just Aliyah.

She ambles toward the buffet, off-kilter as she picks up a plate, unusually dressed down in a baggy sweatshirt and jeans, her jacket and purse draped over one arm. She's forgone her usual cat-eye eyeliner, too—I know what that is thanks to my little sister, Emily, who's addicted to makeup tutorials. Aliyah's beautiful without a lick of makeup: rich mahogany skin, big brown eyes, high cheekbones, and eyelashes so long they make little shadows on her cheeks. Ruby doesn't like her, which is weird, because Aliyah's always seemed perfectly nice.

Aliyah sinks down next to me and dumps her stuff on the floor. I quirk a brow, surprised. But then I see her friends' table is packed.

She moans as she eyes the meager pile of fruit salad on her plate.

"You picked wrong." I motion to the rest of the croissant on my plate. "Flaky on the outside, moist and fluffy on the inside."

"That's what got me in trouble yesterday, I think."

"You got food poisoning from a croissant?"

She shakes her head. "I have celiac disease. Can't eat gluten."

"Oh, crap. Sorry."

"I'm usually so careful, but everyone was having one, and they looked so damn good . . ." She gives me a tired smile. "I tried, anyway."

"That's gotta count for something."

"It doesn't. It sucks." She pops a cantaloupe ball into her mouth and makes a face.

"Sorry," I say again, feeling like the world's biggest tool. I check my phone—still nothing from Ruby. "Did you happen to see Ruby or Val upstairs?"

"No." She frowns, scanning the room. "Have you seen Selena?"

"Nope."

She snorts. "Where the hell is that girl?" She takes out her phone and brightens the screen.

Maybe jet lag's screwing with people. I'm used to my 4:30 a.m. wake-up times thanks to Pop's training schedule for my JROTC cadet challenge next month. Not that I need it; I'm already in the top percentile for curl-ups, pull-ups, and push-ups. But Pop insists I can always improve my one-mile run time. Though I bet even if I clock in under six minutes, it still won't be good enough for him.

I can forget about solitude once I start cadet training this summer, that's for sure.

I drum my fingers on Ruby's laptop—

Oh.

Maybe she hasn't come down yet because she's busy tearing apart her room, searching for her laptop.

Which I have right here.

I curse under my breath and stand fast, startling Aliyah. "Be right back."

"Sure," she says.

I bypass the rickety elevator and bolt up the stairs, taking them two at a time. By the time I reach her door, I'm slightly winded, so, okay, maybe Pop has a point. I knock on her door.

No one answers.

I knock again. "Ruby? It's me. Sean." I cringe. Obviously she'd recognize my voice. "I have your laptop."

Still no answer.

I press my ear to the door but don't hear anything, then check Whats-App once more. Something niggles at the base of my spine. It's not like Ruby to ignore me like this. We'd never even argued before last night.

I glance up and down the hall. Maybe she and Val went to visit someone. But I'm pretty sure the whole class is downstairs except for Selena, and Ruby would never go to her room—they're, like, mortal enemies or something. Which could explain why Ruby doesn't like Aliyah, since she and Selena are practically glued at the hip.

I tried asking Ruby about their falling-out once, but she didn't want to talk about it. I didn't press it—I figured she'd tell me when she was ready. And whenever she is, I'll listen. I'd listen to anything she has to say, really.

"Ruby?" I try calling once more. No dice.

I troop back to the dining room, where Mr. LeBrecque stands at one end, trying to get everyone's attention. "Clap if you hear me once," he says in French.

There's a smattering of claps, and the chatter simmers down. I scan the room, but Ruby and Val aren't here.

"Clap if you hear me twice."

Everyone claps twice, and the room silences.

I catch Aliyah's questioning gaze and shake my head. Selena still hasn't shown up, either.

Something's wrong.

"Good morning, everyone," Mr. LeBrecque says in French. "The bus is here, and we'll leave for the Louvre in ten minutes. So finish your breakfast—er, yes, Sean?"

I lower my hand, which I raised even though I'm, like, a foot from his face. "Sorry, sir, but a few of the girls—"

"En français, s'il vous plaît."

I grit my teeth and say in French, "A few of the girls are missing."

"Yes, Mrs. Williams just went upstairs to get them. They can take some pastries to go—"

"They're not upstairs."

"Pardon?"

"They're not upstairs," I repeat, pretty sure I said that right.

Mrs. Williams hurries in, her brow crinkled as she scans the room. She waves Mr. LeBrecque over to the door.

Aliyah watches them whispering together, too, ignoring her fruit, then mutters something and starts texting someone. Probably Selena.

Impatient, I approach our teacher and librarian. "What's going on?"

Mr. LeBrecque claps my shoulder. "Everything's fine, Sean. Please sit—"

"They're missing, aren't they, ma'am?" I ask Mrs. Williams.

She gives me a small smile. "Let's not get ahead of ourselves."

"Maybe they're showering," says Mr. LeBrecque.

"All four at once?" Mrs. Williams whispers.

"Wait, four?" I say. "There's Ruby, Val, Selena . . . ?"

"Liv, too," says Mrs. Williams. My stomach twists as I remember what happened at Olivia's party, but I shake it off. "Maybe they went out for coffee."

We aren't supposed to leave the hotel on our own, and I wouldn't put it past Val to break the rules, but not the others. I shake my head. "No, ma'am, I don't think so. Ruby and Val aren't exactly friends with Selena, and Liv would never sneak out. And Ruby's not texting me back."

Aliyah joins us. "Selena's not texting me back, either."

"Maybe we should have the maître d' check out their rooms," Mrs. Williams suggests.

Mr. LeBrecque nods, finally looking worried. "Yes. Let's."

Mrs. Williams heads for the front desk. I move to follow, but Mr. LeBrecque stops me. "Sean, please. Sit. I'm sure there's a simple explanation."

I feel too high-strung to sit, like my nerve endings might all spontaneously combust if I don't get answers in the next millisecond, but

I perch on the edge of the nearest chair anyway and watch Mrs. Williams explain the situation to the woman I accidentally told I was horny yesterday.

A minute later, the maître d' rounds the front desk, gripping a few keycards. "You'll head up?" Mr. LeBrecque asks Mrs. Williams.

"Yeah, I got it."

As Mr. LeBrecque turns back to our class, I rush past him and follow Mrs. Williams and the maître d' into the minuscule elevator. Knowing it'll take longer to convince me to scram, Mrs. Williams lets me smush myself into the corner and throws me side-eye.

The maître d' smiles, exposing a fleck of bright red lipstick on a front tooth. "Not to worry," she says in a thick French accent. "I'm sure they are fast asleep."

Upstairs, she leads us down the hall, her stiletto heels thudding on the burgundy carpet, and raps on Olivia's door first. "Bonjour?"

When there's no response, she opens the door and steps inside. She even checks the tiny bathroom. "Rien." Nothing.

There's no one in Selena and Aliyah's room, either.

Mrs. Williams and I wait with bated breath as she checks Ruby and Val's room, but when she reappears, her smile's gone, and the corners of her eyes crease with sympathy. "Désolée. No one here."

So where the hell are they?

11

Ruby

This isn't the first time I've woken to the sound of screaming.

Not that you ever get used to it. Dad's night terrors have jolted me awake ever since I was little, back when he'd feign ignorance and I'd dive-bomb under my covers thinking some ghoul was haunting our house. Once I was older and braver, I crept down the hall to investigate and found him hunched over in bed, clutching his forehead, unable to wipe away the fat tears rolling down his cheeks fast enough.

That's when he finally admitted the truth. After drowning his sorrows in wine, his brain would replay my mother's death in vivid clarity until he'd wake up screaming, and no matter how hard he tried, the vicious cycle kept on cycling. It explained why he spiraled so hard whenever I came to him with my grief. There's only so much you can buoy someone else up if you have no life raft of your own.

But Selena's the one screaming now. I'm having a night terror and can't open my eyes to see what's happening—

Oh wait. My eyes *are* wide open.

It's just so dark, I can't see a damn thing.

I jolt upright and my neck cricks painfully. My head somehow wound up on Val's abdomen, which wasn't a particularly supportive pillow. The screaming has silenced. Maybe I did dream it. "Selena?"

Someone knocks something over, fumbling in the darkness.

"Shut *up*," Val groans. Then reality sets in. "Oh God . . ."

"What time is it?" Olivia asks.

Julien's the only one wearing a watch. It blinks on in the dark. "Almost nine." I'm surprised we got as much sleep as we did.

"Welp, everyone must know we're missing—"

There it is again. A scream in the distance.

Not just a scream; a veritable *shriek*.

"Selena!" I scramble to my knees and dive for the lamp—at least, where I think the lamp should be—and crash into someone.

Julien grunts, and I tumble back onto cold stone, the wind knocked out of me in a whoosh as pain blooms up my shoulder where we collided.

"Are you okay?" He switches the lamp on low, filling the alcove with an eerie orange glow.

"I'm fine," I grunt, shaking out my arm. That'll bruise quick. I stand and loop my purse across my chest, grab a flashlight, and make for the corridor.

Julien stands and lunges for my wrist. "Hang on."

"Why?"

"We have to pack everything—"

Another scream.

There's no time. I try to yank myself free from Julien, but he holds firm.

"Why's she screaming like that?" I ask as Val and Olivia groggily gather our belongings.

"I don't know." His wide eyes and puckered forehead say otherwise. He's frightened.

"Who else is down here?" I demand.

"No one! I mean, maybe other cataphiles . . ."

Selena shrieks again, and I can feel every ounce of her terror reverberate in my own chest. No nerdy urban explorer would make her react like that.

I twist from Julien's grasp and race out into the corridor.

I can't lose Selena all over again. Like last year when she ditched me for her shiny new drama club friends, and I stretched through that dark loneliness to snatch her back. In my desperation to latch on, I made a terrible mistake.

The worst mistake of my life, until this.

Going to Tyler's Cinco de Mayo party made me feel like a butterfly packed in a cocoon that had fallen into a beehive. I sat alone on his couch nursing a Solo cup of fruity God-knows-what while Selena spread her wings, barely recognizable in a vibrant, colorful crop top and sultry eyeliner, gyrating her hips to the beat as Aliyah, Lisa, and their posse buzzed around her and Tyler played beer pong nearby. Selena had invited me, but clearly all she cared about was vying for his attention.

I wished I could ditch my comfort zone with such abandon and join her.

I wished she'd stop chasing social clout to get close to a boy.

But the fact that neither would happen made panic flutter through my chest. So I downed my drink and decided to play matchmaker, to hell with her roundabout strategy.

Mistake number one.

I bumbled over to Tyler, set on setting them up, but the music was blaring too loudly to think straight, let alone talk straight, and you can't exactly be subtle while screaming. I turned tomato red and nearly skulked away, but he was sweet as honey, not snobbish like I'd expected, and invited me upstairs to find reprieve from the noise. In his bedroom, the postcards lining the wall above his bed distracted me from my mission. London. Paris. Tokyo. Rome.

"Don't tell me you've been to all these places," I said.

He mashed his lips together, following my orders.

"You have! Tell me about Rome. Could you just *feel* the history seeping from the buildings?"

"Actually, yeah." He smiled, his words slurring a bit from drinking. "It's not like New York, where the historic shit's squished between modern buildings. There, everything's ancient."

"Wow. What about Tokyo? I'd give my left arm to see Japan."

His laugh lilted like wind chimes in a summer breeze. "Let's see. There's this pulsing energy to the city, and everything's so clean. And there's nothing like authentic sushi. The fish tastes fresher, more *buttery* . . . it's hard to explain."

I tipped my head back. "Ugh, you're doing great."

His grin widened. "And Paris?" He pointed to his Eiffel Tower postcard. "When you bite into a baguette, it's crusty on the outside . . ." I soaked in every word as he recounted his favorite foods in each city, and as I watched his energized face, I understood what made Selena swoon. Such sharp angles. Such bright, blue eyes. Such tantalizing lips . . .

He must've noticed my focus shift, because suddenly he was staring at *my* lips, trailing a finger along my cheek.

I basically stopped breathing. I'd never been kissed before, never imagined someone like him would want to, never felt this overpowering longing that curled up my spine. I knew it was wrong to kiss the boy my best friend liked. But I wanted to know what she was so willing to stomp all over our friendship to get. So when he touched his lips to mine, I didn't stop him. I even kissed him back.

Mistake number two.

A minute later, I got the sense to back away. But it was too late. I'd felt the way my lips parted, the way the tip of his tongue swept across mine, the way I'd clung to the back of his neck, holding him close.

Dizzy with regret and mortification, I hurtled from the room, down the stairs, and out the front door without a word to Selena, knowing how much this would hurt her, knowing if she found out from someone else, it would hurt even worse.

Mistake number three.

Tyler couldn't keep his mouth shut, so by the time I wrote my three-page letter begging her forgiveness, I was dead to her.

You can fuck all the way off now.

Now I'm desperate to get Selena back again, only this time I'm chasing her disembodied screams through the darkness.

Unlike last night, I'm leaving a trail. At each intersection, I tear two pages from my pocket-sized notebook and drop a crumpled ball on dry ground before and after the turn. If nothing else, I'll be able to find my way back to the others.

But now I can't hear her.

Fear blooms in my chest, and I listen for signs of a struggle, of life, *anything*. I hear Julien and Val arguing somewhere behind me, but besides that—

A crunch over pebbles.

A footstep.

Coming from ahead.

I slink to the next intersection, cautious now. Another crunch. I look left, where a faint glow emanates down the perpendicular corridor. It blinks off. On. Off again.

Selena, maybe?

Something stops me from calling to her.

There must be a reason she stopped screaming.

I hear no music, so it's not a cataphile—at least, not one who knows their protocol.

I crumple two pages and drop them, then follow the intermittent light. Hundreds of eyes stalk my steps—a floor-to-ceiling wall of skulls to the right. I swallow hard, trying not to think about the brittle crackling under my footfalls.

Bones.

Bile rises in my throat, but I press on toward that blinking orange glow until the passageway spills into a cavernous den with four intersecting passageways. The wall of skulls extends into this space to my right, their stares unyielding. The blinking light has stopped. I don't know which corridor it came from.

I pause and wait for one of the passageways to brighten again.

None do. Or maybe I can't tell.

With a sharp inhale, I switch off my flashlight. I don't hear Val and Julien anymore. I don't hear anything besides blood thundering in my ears. I'm holding my breath and can feel the ominous presence of death beside me, prickling my skin like someone's blowing icy air under my ear, taunting me.

A light blinks on. The tunnel to the right.

Could be Selena. Could be her attacker, summoning me into a trap.

I shudder and turn on the flashlight, darting the beam around to make sure I'm alone.

I am. Unless you count the skulls.

As I creep down the right-hand passageway, a subtle tang overtakes the corridor's damp and dusty odor until it's so putrid I have to cup my nose.

The light's not blinking off anymore, and I follow the curving tunnel ahead, the stench leeching through the cracks between my fingers.

There she is.

Still as a statue.

Facing away from me.

Frizz from her dark mane haloes her head, and the way she's standing there, deathly silent, as though she's melding with the labyrinth's shadows, makes a shiver curl up my spine.

"Selena?"

She gasps and spins. The motion makes her lamp flicker off. *"Ruby."* She lumbers over and clutches me tight.

Like the past ten months never happened.

I hug her back, eyes squeezed shut, hardly noticing the smell anymore, grateful, so grateful, not just that I've found her, but that even if only for a moment, it feels like I have my best friend back. I'm not sure what surprises me more: her reaction or mine—that I *want* her back. I've been so angry with her for ending us over one fight, one mistake, so angry I consider her my nemesis.

She's probably hugging me out of sheer relief, though. I'm reading too much into it.

I pull back. She's aggressively shivering, tucking her injured arm into her chest. Even in the darkness, I can tell she's paler than usual, her cheeks streaked with crusted mascara, her light blue cardigan caked with dirt and blood, especially her left sleeve above where she's wrapped her arm with Julien's gray shirt—

"Your *arm*." Blood has soaked through the fabric, darkening it to almost black.

"I know. It hurts—" Her lamp blinks on, then off. She jiggles it. "Something got loose when I fell, I think." It flashes on.

I gasp, catching sight of what's behind her, of what she'd been staring at before, and goose bumps coat my arms like a rash.

There, nestled under a low arch, is the most grotesque sight I've ever seen.

12
Ruby

I don't know why anyone would make a throne out of human bones.

But clearly someone has. They've fashioned hundreds of bones browned with age and dirt into an imposing chair, the backrest made of interwoven rib cages, the armrests of femurs wired into bulging curlicues, the legs of tibiae clustered in bunches, the seat of skulls packed tight, their smooth craniums like eggs in a square carton. Another five skulls crown the backrest, glaring down at us like an unspoken threat.

Only a nightmare of a person would want to sit on dead people.

"Is this what stinks?" I pinch my nose.

"I think so. It smells kind of like . . ." She shakes her head like she's not sure.

"Death," I finish.

"Yeah."

One time a mouse died in the wall between my bedroom and the bathroom, and I had to sleep in the living room until an exterminator came to clear out the nest. This smells like that. I didn't know bones could stink for that long. Maybe the dampness locks in death like perpetual rot, like how the paint could stay wet down here for centuries. I notice some nearby graffiti of a misshapen skull with distorted eyes. The black and red scribbles look dry to me.

Footsteps crunch behind us. We turn, and Selena grabs my arm with her good hand, her fingers digging into my flesh even through my puffer jacket, eyes wide as a skull's empty sockets. My heart races so hard I can hear it thudding in my ears.

Then they appear.

Julien, Val, and Olivia.

I let out a breath, and Selena releases my arm.

Julien rushes over. I think he's going to berate Selena or check her wound, but instead he makes a beeline for me.

He grips my head over my ears to get me to focus on him, his lamp dangling from an elbow. I'm so surprised, I don't even try to pull away. "Ruby, listen to me." His sandy eyes dart between mine. "Never do that again. If you run alone into the dark again, it's very possible no one will *ever* be able to find you. People die down here doing what you just did."

My voice is stuck somewhere in my throat, along with my breath, my heart, and all the rest of my internal organs.

"No matter what happens, you do *not* run off alone."

"I-I'm sorry."

"I need you to promise me you won't do that again."

"I promise."

"You promise *what*?"

"She gets it, all right?" says Val.

But Julien doesn't tear his eyes from mine. My face is pulsating with heat. He's right. Running after Selena alone was reckless.

"I promise I won't run off alone again."

He releases me, then snatches my flashlight, switches it off, and stuffs it in his pack.

"Good idea with the paper," Olivia says to me, tapping her bag. She collected the crumpled sheets.

"Thanks." At least I did something right.

Val wrinkles her nose at Selena. "Ew, you reek."

"Why would you think that's me?" says Selena. "It's that thing." She motions to the throne.

"Never mind that." Julien hands me his lamp so he can yank the blinking one away from Selena, and casts a wary glance at the menacing row of skulls staring down from atop the throne. Val sidles next to him to gawk at it. "Why didn't you stay put?" he asks Selena.

She clutches the knotted shirt around her arm, shivering. "I got scared waiting there alone. There was this super-creepy writing on the wall, and—I don't know, I freaked. I thought I heard voices. Your voices. I wanted to get to you faster. So I followed them, but then . . ." She bites her lip.

"Then what?" Julien unscrews the top of the finicky lamp.

"I don't know, exactly. I thought I saw something." She eyes the throne. "No, I don't know."

"What do you think you saw?" Olivia asks as Julien tightens the long bulb inside.

A shudder rattles Selena. "Skeletons."

Julien tenses, the bulb's steady glow starkly illuminating his alarmed expression.

"They're kind of everywhere down here." Val motions to the throne.

"No, I mean, two of them," says Selena. "Full skeletons. They . . . they ran after me."

My eyebrows rise. I know Selena believes in ghosts, but this sounds like she hit her head.

"Yeah, right." Val sneers.

"I'm serious. I ran for it, and at one point I turned, thinking it was a hallway, but it was a room. A dead end. I hid in the corner and turned off the lamp, and a few seconds later I heard them run past."

"That's impossible," says Olivia.

"I know," says Selena. "But it seemed so *real*."

"There's no such thing as ghosts," I assure her. "Or walking dead or whatever."

Julien screws the repaired lantern's top back on. His silence makes unease prickle my nape.

"There's always some other logical explanation," Olivia says. "A dream, a trick of the light, hallucinations—even mass hallucinations are a thing."

"Oh." I snap and point at Val. "Remember when we filmed that Halloween video in Salem? At the museum they said some bread fungus made the villagers hallucinate and think they saw witches in their fireplaces."

"Oh. Right," Val says, distracted, studying the throne again.

Olivia nods. "Yup, mass hysteria caused the Salem Witch Trials. I've read papers on this. There's zero scientific proof anything paranormal exists."

"Dork," Val teases.

"Thank you," Olivia says simply. "Anyway, I bet you fainted—blood loss and exhaustion can totally do that—and you had a bad dream. We'd just seen all those skulls in the upper gallery."

"Yeah, that makes more sense," I say.

"Ya think?" Val says.

"I guess." Selena rubs her forehead. "It *is* all kind of a blur."

"Why were you screaming just now?" I ask.

She drops her gaze. "I woke up in the dark and the lamp wouldn't stay on, and I lost it. I ran and wound up here, but then I heard footsteps, and I thought of those skeletons. So I stopped and stayed quiet."

"You didn't hear me calling your name?" I ask.

She shakes her head. "I didn't even think you'd still be down here."

Julien sighs. "Well, we stick together from now on, yes? No more rushing down ladders or tunnels or *anywhere* until I say it's safe."

Selena and I each mutter another, "Sorry."

"It's fine. Let's—"

"Can you imagine if that one's Robs Pierre?" Val interrupts. She's pointing at a cranium in the seat, right where someone's butt would be if they sat.

"*Robespierre*," Olivia corrects. I have a feeling Val's saying it wrong on purpose.

Julien swoops over like he's afraid Val will try to touch them. "Let's get away from this." He entwines his fingers with hers and guides her down the corridor. Olivia trails them.

Before I follow, I can't resist—I pull out my camera. The itch to capture something so bizarre on film is too strong. I record a quick clip, but as I lower the camera, queasiness rolls through my stomach. None of these people had any idea they'd be a throne someday. Like Robespierre had no idea he'd someday face the guillotine after putting thousands to the blade in the name of virtue. Like my mother had no idea she'd bleed out bringing new life into the world. Like we had no idea we'd get lost in an underground labyrinth when we giddily boarded a plane to the most glamorous city on Earth.

"Depressing, isn't it?" I say to Selena, who's lingered beside me for some reason.

"What?"

I shrug. "For all we know, that *could* be Robespierre. No matter how famous or powerful you are up there . . . in the end, we all wind up like this."

"A chair?" There's a hint of a smile in her voice. That surprises me.

"Not specifically a *chair*. Bones. That's all any of us are in the end.

A pile of bones." My lower lip quivers. Every friendship, every love, everything we've ever looked forward to—it all comes crashing down, and then we die, and that's it. All for nothing. "God, what's even the point?"

Tears sting my eyes, and I blink them away. I feel Selena's gaze on me, but if I look back, the floodgates will truly open, so before she can respond I whip around and stalk after the others. We quickly catch up to them.

"Do you know where we are?" Val asks Julien.

He sweeps his lamplight over a sign that says CIMETIÉRE. "This looks vaguely familiar."

"There must be dozens of signs down here that say that," says Olivia.

Selena frowns. "Do you not know the way out?"

"We got a bit turned around looking for you," Julien says. We enter the cavern lined with floor-to-ceiling bones. Unlike the zigzag and swirling patterns we saw in the upper gallery last night, these are stacked in lopsided rows.

"Are you saying we're *lost*?" Selena cries.

"Let's stay calm—"

"*Obviously* we're lost," Val interjects. "And no offense, but it's kind of your fault."

"Val," I say.

"Okay, fine, full offense."

"*Val.*"

"Well, what? If she stayed at that well like she was supposed to, we would've gotten back to the hotel by three. She could've said she slipped in the shower"—Val motions to Selena's injury—"and we all would've gotten away with this."

Selena jabs a finger at Val. "If you hadn't snuck out in the first place, none of us would've come down here."

"You could've gone back. No one put a gun to your head—"

Fwoomp.

Like a huge sack of rice hitting the ground.

We jerk our eyes toward the wall of skulls—it sounded like it came from behind it.

"What was—" I start.

"*Shhhh,*" says Julien. The color has drained from his face.

After a long pause, Olivia whispers, "Cataphiles?"

Julien shakes his head stiffly and raises a finger to his lips. A muscle in his jaw twitches. He's afraid. Selena and I lock eyes, and a chill snakes through me.

"The police, maybe?" Olivia whispers.

"Oh yeah," I say. "I've read they inspect the galleries—"

"*Shhhh.*" Julien hisses again.

Whispers fill the space.

Whispers from the skulls.

Impossible.

"You all heard that, right?" says Selena.

Val's laughter peals through the cavern.

"What?" says Selena as Julien shushes Val more harshly.

"You're being ridiculous," says Val. "It's gotta be the police."

"They don't come this far down," Julien whispers. "Now, *quiet*—"

Boom.

We all pitch back from the wall. I trip over Val's sneaker and land hard on my butt. The coppery taste of blood fills my mouth; I bit the edge of my tongue as I hit the ground.

Boom.

I scuttle backward into the middle of the cavern. "Come on," Julien whisper-screams.

Boom.

"What *is* that?" Selena cries as Julien hauls me to my feet by my hands.

Boom.

Boom.

Boom.

Like the beat of a drum.

Then dozens of skulls explode from the wall.

13
Sean

Apparently I suck at reading lips.

Our teachers are out in the lobby telling two French police officers about how Ruby and the others are missing, and despite my clear view from here, I can barely make out a word they're saying. Our class has been waiting in the hotel's dining room for the past couple of hours, and everyone's getting antsy. Aliyah pulled up a chair to squeeze between her friends at the packed table next to mine, and she's uncharacteristically quiet, tugging at her lower lip.

Beside her, Alex mutters to his friend Kyle, "I bet they went out for booze and got lost."

"Yup." Kyle adjusts his Red Sox hat. "Val was pissed when we ran out."

"This is obnoxious," says Alex's girlfriend Lisa on Aliyah's other side, tossing her platinum hair over her shoulder. "We're getting punished because *they* snuck out—"

"Yo, shut up," I snap.

"What's your problem, man?" Alex narrows his beady eyes at me.

"There's no way they went on a booze run," I say. "Have you even *met* Liv?"

The police come in then, a middle-aged woman with brunette hair swirled into a low bun and a few loose tendrils framing her face and a younger man with sideswept blond hair and an equally sideswept nose. It must've broken at some point. They're wearing navy coats with matching navy caps, almost like the US Navy might wear, and her coat has an extra white stripe on each shoulder.

"Hello, everyone," the woman says with a slight French accent. "I'm Capitaine Charlotte Debois, and this is my partner, Lieutenant Daniel Garnier." He nods, his expression friendly. She clearly isn't concerning herself with our French proficiency. Any other time, that'd make Mr. LeBrecque's head pop. "It will be faster to ask you all our questions at once, so let's chat, yes?"

We all nod. Even Alex, Kyle, and Lisa exchange worried looks. If the police are questioning us, this must be serious.

Capitaine Debois scrolls up on her tablet, reviewing her notes. "So . . . we have Valerie Moreau, Ruby Hale, Selena Rodriguez, and Olivia Clarkson. Are all these girls—excuse me, please stop recording."

Everyone looks at Aliyah, who's surreptitiously angling her phone at Debois. She mashes her lips together, guilty as charged. Mr. LeBrecque crosses the room to confiscate it. "But—"

"No buts," says Mr. LeBrecque, plucking it from her grasp.

"I would also ask," says Debois, "that you all refrain from posting *anything* about this online."

"Why?" Aliyah asks.

"Because we don't know what we're dealing with."

"This one time, we had a case," Garnier chimes in, his accent so strong *this* sounds like *zis*. "Missing girl, same age as you. A friend thought she ran away, so she posted her picture online, started a Facebook group, pleading if anyone had seen her. It went . . . how do you say . . ." He makes an exploding motion with his hands.

"It went viral?" Lisa says.

"Oui. The kidnapper saw this, and he panicked. In two days, she washed ashore of the Seine."

I can feel the blood drain from my face, and Aliyah clutches her throat.

Debois frowns at her partner. "But there's no reason for *us* to panic. For all we know, the girls went out for croissants and got lost."

"No way," Aliyah mutters under her breath.

"So," says Debois, "these four girls . . . they are friends with each other?"

"No, Madame le Capitaine," I say. Alex and Kyle chortle, probably at my formality. But ever since I was a kid, Pop drilled into me to address authority as such. "I mean, Val and Ruby are, but—"

"Selena isn't friends with any of them," Aliyah cuts me off. "This doesn't make any sense."

"Let's stay calm, yes?" says Debois. "What are your names, please, the two who spoke up?"

"Aliyah Harrison," she answers breathlessly. "I'm Selena's girlfriend." Debois nods, tapping out notes.

"Sean McIntyre. I'm friends with Ruby. And Val. Sort of." I shift uncomfortably.

"And what about Olivia?" Debois asks. "Who's closest to her?"

A bunch of us shrug, and after a long pause, Aliyah says, "She's nice and all, but none of her best friends are on this trip."

"Ah, I see. Well, when did you last see each of the girls?"

A bunch of us chime in—Lisa recounts when Selena and Val each left Alex and Kyle's little shindig, and I explain how Ruby got pickpocketed on the walk home after dinner, and that I last saw her in her room, about to call her father. Nobody can pinpoint when they last saw Olivia.

"Did any of them mention plans they had later in the night?" Debois asks. "Perhaps someone they wanted to meet?"

Nobody has an answer.

"Or this morning? Any plans to get food, to meet anyone?"

More silence. Debois notes something down, her expression blank. "Did any of the girls ever mention wanting to leave the group and go off on their own? Perhaps not go home at the end of the week?"

I furrow my brow. "You mean, did they want to run away?"

"No," says Aliyah. "Selena would never."

"Liv neither," says Lisa. "She's wanted to go to Harvard since forever."

"I heard she didn't get in," another girl whispers.

"Are you serious?" Lisa whispers back.

I shake my head. "I really don't think that's it."

When nobody else chimes in, Debois leans forward. "Do any of you have any reason to believe anyone wanted to hurt these girls?"

A couple of people inhale sharply, but nobody speaks.

"No? Good," says Debois. "There's no need to worry—just being thorough. Did anyone notice anything unusual yesterday? Any strangers trying to speak with them? Or with you?"

"No," a few people murmur. I spent all day with Ruby and Val and didn't see them talking to anyone suspicious. Then again, I didn't notice someone swipe Ruby's wallet and camera, and that happened. Maybe I'm not as vigilant as I'd like to believe.

"Uh . . ." Aliyah darts a worried glance at me. I frown.

"Is there something you'd like to say?" Debois asks.

She shakes her head.

"Aliyah?" Mrs. Williams says encouragingly. "Anything might help."

"It-it's probably nothing."

"Sometimes the smallest detail helps," says Debois.

"Well . . ." Aliyah rubs her lips together. "When I was in the bathroom last night . . . I heard Ruby and Sean fighting through the wall. In Ruby's room."

My face goes hot as everyone swivels their heads to stare. "We weren't fighting." Ruby hadn't raised her voice for more than a moment.

"And maybe Val was in there, too, I don't know . . ." Aliyah rambles.

"She wasn't." I wipe a hand down my face. "Ruby was freaking out about getting pickpocketed. That's it—"

"She sounded mad," says Aliyah.

"Yeah, at the pickpocket." I bristle. "And, well, there was one point when I might've accidentally blamed her, and she got a little mad at me. But that's it. It wasn't even an actual argument." Both cops narrow their eyes at me. My stomach falls. "I'd never hurt Ruby."

But even Mr. LeBrecque gives me a wary look—he saw me outside Ruby's room after eleven.

I swallow hard, tightening my grip on Ruby's laptop.

Well, crap.

14
Ruby

I race down the corridor after the others, imagining those shattered bones reforming into disjointed, mangled skeletons staggering after us, stretching their cracked fingers to claw at me, strangle me, tear me apart. Absurd. Impossible. But the way Julien keeps rasping, "*Quiet,*" isn't exactly reassuring. I want answers, but I want to die less, so I follow without a word.

Olivia tightens her grip on her plastic bag to keep it from crinkling, but there's not much we can do about our steps. The puddles dotting the corridors are so wide we have to slosh through them. Cold water splashes my jeans and seeps into my boots as shadows from our jostling lights bounce across the craggy walls.

With each turn, I snap a quick photo. Digital breadcrumbs. But dread leeches through my veins when the battery meter shows only half power remaining. We're seven or eight stories beneath the city, a distance I can feel in my bones, and the more of our devices that die, the more severed our connection feels from the city above, like they're all that's tethering us to the real world. Like once they're gone, we'll be trapped down here for good.

It doesn't make sense, but terror slices through rationality like an executioner's blade.

At least we found Selena. Being so afraid for her made me realize that despite how much I resent her, I miss her.

Fiercely.

Val's friendship is as exhilarating as white water rafting, but Selena's was so *easy*, like bobbing along a lazy river, soaking in the sun as your fingertips graze cool water. I miss gabbing with her for hours about nothing and everything without needing to recover after, like I do with Val. I miss lounging by her pool at night watching travel vlogs as she futzed with her telescope, content in each other's quiet company. I miss confiding in her about Dad's binge drinking without worrying she'd ever stop giggling at his terrible puns. I miss feeling her gently squeeze my hand whenever I'd clam up around other people.

In the months since our falling-out, I've hated her for throwing away our friendship over one craptastic night. For holding such an unwavering grudge against me for kissing Tyler. For casting me aside like some slut-shamed pariah. The memory makes mortification smother me as tightly as it did back then.

But when she hugged me before, relief filled my chest like fresh air streaming through a fissure.

It makes me wonder if I've really hated her at all.

I'm the one who tried to cling on as she rocketed up the social ladder but bashed my own fingers and sent myself hurtling through space. And I've regretted it ever since. *Despised* myself ever since.

How can I expect her to forgive me when I've never forgiven myself?

A rumbling noise permeates the limestone walls, steadily increasing to a menacing roar like a cacophony of ghouls. It's so loud I can feel the stone vibrate under my feet.

"What *is* that?" I ask.

"Must be the Métro—" Olivia starts.

Julien hushes us, though it's been clear for a while nobody's chasing us. Maybe by the time whoever made it through the wall they knocked down, they didn't know which way we went.

"Please, I have to stop." Selena steadies herself against the wall, clutching her injured arm. "I just need a minute." Before anyone can argue, she drops to the ground and slips off her wedges and socks to stretch her toes, hissing through her teeth.

My stomach turns to see how raw and red her pinkie toes and heels are. "Looks painful."

"It is," she grunts. "My blisters have blisters."

Julien glances behind us and seems satisfied with the nothingness there. "All right. Quick break."

Selena rests her head against the wall and licks her chapped lips. "I'm thirsty."

"Here." Olivia unseals a water bottle and hands it over.

"Thanks." Selena takes a sip. Her eyelids flutter in relief. "How many of these do we have?" She raises the bottle to her lips again.

"That's it." Olivia shakes the empty one. A look of trepidation passes between us. Selena caps hers without drinking any more.

"Better than nothing," Val says too high.

"Good thing you needed toothpaste," I say to Olivia.

She winces. If she hadn't, she wouldn't be here at all.

I turn to Julien. "So what's the deal? Who was that back there?"

He rubs his shoulder above his backpack strap. "I don't know."

"With all due respect," I say, "bullshit."

"With absolutely no respect, bullshit," Val says.

His shoulders tense. "I *don't*."

"Then why make us run for so long?" I ask.

"Clearly, they are trouble, yes? Who in their right mind would desecrate the dead like that?"

"It was like they were *inside* the wall," says Selena, "trying to get out."

Olivia frowned. "No, there had to be another tunnel behind there. Maybe they heard us talking and were trying to reach us."

"Dude," Val says to Julien, "did we just run from people trying to help us?"

I hadn't considered that, too startled by the aggressive *boom, boom, boom* and the wall's macabre composition to do anything but flee.

Julien sweeps his hair back. "No cataphile would damage bones like that. And I don't have the highest opinion of the police, but I don't think they would, either. They would have called to us."

Val seems unconvinced. "We should go back."

He sets his hands on his hips and stares down the corridor like he's considering it. His Adam's apple bobs, and he mutters a curse in French.

Selena groans. "You don't even remember the way, do you?"

"Wait, I took pictures." I turn on my camera and switch it to preview mode to scroll through the images. Icicles spear my chest. After the video I took in the alcove last night, each photo is a dark, pixelated blur. I've taken night shots before without a flash, but I must've been moving too fast for these to come out. "Useless. We're *really* lost now, aren't we?"

Another deep groan resounds along the corridor as though the labyrinth itself is trying to answer. It increases in intensity until the roar quickly dissipates.

"Yeah, that's gotta be the Métro," says Olivia. "Sounds like we're right next to the tracks."

"Maybe there's a way into the Métro tunnels," I suggest. "We could follow the tracks to a station."

"And get smooshed?" says Val.

"Any entrance would be sealed, I'm sure," says Julien. "Most are paved over with concrete. I don't know about any of you"—he pats his backpack—"but I don't have a jackhammer in here."

Someone's stomach growls like they have one. Olivia grips hers, then passes each of us an individually wrapped madeleine cake she bought at Monoprix. I have no appetite, but Olivia stuffs an entire loaf into her mouth, then sits cross-legged next to Selena and motions for her arm. "We should clean that." The cake muffles her words.

Selena cringes. She's always been squeamish about blood. One time she fell in my backyard while we were playing tag, took one look at her skinned knee, and lost her entire mind, hyperventilating so hard she struggled to breathe. She only calmed down after Dad came outside with a box of Mickey Mouse Band-Aids and antibacterial gel and asked her why Mickey went to space. She mulled it over until he smoothed down the Band-Aid's edges and said with a grin, "To find Pluto."

Now she stoically extends her arm so Olivia can untie Julien's shirt from her forearm, averting her gaze from the grizzly wound. There's so much dried blood crusted on her shredded skin, it's hard to tell how big the gash is. Selena watches me to gauge my reaction. I try to keep my expression neutral.

"Does anyone have a tampon?" Olivia asks.

Val peers at Julien, her mouth full of cake. "I do, but . . . uh, I kinda need it."

"Oh no," I say with a stab of sympathy, though odds are at least one of us would be on our period.

She swallows and wipes the corners of her mouth. "It's almost over, though, if you really need it."

"Hang on." I don't use tampons since I find them uncomfortable, but fish out the spare pad I keep in my purse's inner compartment. "Here."

"Perfect," says Olivia.

Val chortles.

"What's the problem?" Olivia says coolly, looking Val dead in the eye.

Val's cheeks flush. Her reaction's the only shameful part of this. I'd gladly walk around with a pad on my arm if it kept me from losing the limb. Even I know infections from that kind of wound are no joke.

Olivia pours a bit of water on a clean edge of Julien's ratty shirt and wipes dried blood from Selena's arm, and Selena winces whenever the fabric passes over the wound. Once her skin's as clean as Olivia's going to get it, it's apparent the gash is mostly clotted, and a bunch of smaller scrapes are clustered alongside it.

"I think maybe you scraped it against the wall," says Olivia, "not the ladder."

"Is that better?" Selena asks.

Olivia nods. "I have no idea."

We all chuckle lightly.

"I need something to tie this to your arm. Something clean—oh." She unloops her floral scarf from around her neck.

"No, wait," I say, digging through my purse. "She can wear that to keep warm. Use this." I pass her my stretchy headband.

"That'll work." As Olivia unwraps the pad, Julien stuffs the dirty shirt into his backpack.

"Ew, don't keep that," says Selena. "My blood's all over it."

"I don't want them to find—" He cuts himself off. "What comes down must go up."

I watch him zip his bag and sling it over his shoulder. "You *do* know who's back there, don't you?"

His eyes snap to mine like magnets. "No I don't."

I stand to meet his gaze more levelly. "Who's *them*?"

"What?"

"You were about to say you don't want *them* to find your shirt."

He folds his arms, leaning against the wall with a smirk. "If I knew, why wouldn't I tell you?" He's playing at casual but keeps flitting his gaze past me, down the corridor. Checking.

"You tell me. You're freakin' *terrified*," I persist, unable to help how my cheeks flush. His smirk decays. "Selena saw them last night, didn't she?"

"No, I—" Selena stutters as Olivia ties a knot over her arm. "I must've dreamed that." I don't know if that's what she really believes, or if she doesn't want to endure more of Val's mockery.

Either way, Val's focus is fixed on Julien, not her. "You saw that video, didn't you?" She crosses her arms, mirroring him.

His jaw clenches.

I'm confused. "What video?"

Val pokes her cheek with her tongue, waiting for Julien to dish. When he doesn't, she says, "They found someone's camera down here recently and uploaded the footage online. *Supposedly.*" Her tone is clipped. Annoyed.

Julien blows air between his lips and rubs his stubbled cheek. "He never should have come down here alone. Only the most experienced cataphile ever should, and even then . . ." He brandishes his arms, indicating how he got lost himself.

Olivia and Selena look perplexed, but Val tuts. "Oh geez."

"Wait, I'm so lost," I say. "Who was this? What happened to him?"

"A documentarian," Julien says. "He disappeared down here."

His words seem to rattle the air, making me shudder. "Why didn't you show me this video?" I ask Val.

"Because it looked like some cheesy *Blair Witch* remake. I thought it was a hoax. Still do."

"It was no hoax," Julien says.

Val rolls her eyes.

"What was on the video?" Olivia asks.

"Not much." Julien hikes his backpack straps farther up his shoulders. "He didn't narrate or anything. Maybe he meant to add voice-overs later, or he was doing research, I don't know. Either way, he just roamed around for a while, until . . ."

"Until *what*?" I ask.

Julien shoots Val a frustrated look. He didn't want to share this. "He was filming some graffiti until the light from his flashlight bounced around like he was looking for something, and he started to run. The camera was too shaky see anything, and after a few minutes he dropped it. It fell facing him, so you could see his legs run off." He mimes running with two fingers. "It kept filming for fifteen minutes or so, I guess until it ran out of battery or memory. That's it."

"Oh c'mon," Val says. "Why leave out the freakiest part?"

He puffs air between his lips, shaking his head.

Selena's eyes widen. "What was the freakiest part?"

"Did someone follow him?" I ask.

"You couldn't see anyone, but . . ." Julien says. "Before he ran, there was this terrible scream in the distance. People downloaded the video and tried, how do you say, making the sound clearer—"

"They enhanced the audio?" I guess.

"Sure, yes. But you couldn't make out any words. Just that *shriek*."

A shiver coasts down my spine.

"I read once that someone got mugged down here," says Olivia. "They took all his stuff and left him to find his way out alone. Maybe something like that happened."

Selena makes a face. "Who would ditch someone in the middle of a two-hundred-mile-long, pitch-black maze?"

"People ditch each other all the time," I grumble. She parts her lips like she's about to say something, then clamps them.

"I don't even think it was that," says Val. "It was a hoax. Pure and simple. And you fell for it like an anvil." She pokes Julien in the chest. "Then you went and got us even more lost, running from absolutely nothing. Maybe from our *rescuers*. All because you saw something stupid on the internet and believed it."

"Je jur," says Julien. *I swear.* "It wasn't a hoax. I swear on my parents' graves." A jolt of grief makes my heart tumble. His parents are dead. I know what that feels like.

"What," says Val, "did you know the guy?"

"No."

"Did your friends?"

He wipes his upper lip. "No."

"So all you've got to go on is that video. Don't you know how easy those are to fake? That scream was like something out of a C-list horror movie. It was probably added later."

"Why bring it up if you think it's fake?" he says.

"Because it *proves* it. Whoever posted that video made it as creepy as possible, clearly after views."

He grits his teeth. "Most people don't think it was fake."

"Who's *most people*?" says Val. "Some randos in the YouTube comments?"

"That's how people get brainwashed so easily, actually," says Olivia. "Just because 'most people'"—she makes air quotes—"believe a thing or say a thing doesn't make it true."

Julien's eyes narrow. "Tell that to his wife. She reported him missing."

Nobody has a rebuttal to that.

"Maybe she was in on the hoax?" I suggest.

"Well, according to her, he never came home," Julien says. "I don't know what else to tell you."

Val rubs the back of her neck. She clearly didn't know that part.

"You think he died down here?" I ask Julien.

He nods. I feel dread burrow deep in my bones.

"And you think whoever chased him is chasing us?" Selena asks.

He nods again.

"If you really believe this," I say, clenching my fingers into fists, "why hide it from us?"

"I didn't want to scare you," says Julien. "I just want to get you out of here."

Anger simmers in my veins, bubbling over the fear. "How could you bring us down here *at all*, knowing this? Why would you even want to come down here yourself?"

He mashes his lips together, then sighs. "You never think lightning is going to strike twice until it does."

15
Sean

"Did you find anything, Madame le Capitaine?" I stand as Debois shuts the door to the maître d's tiny office, where she told me to wait until she and Garnier finished surveying the missing girls' rooms. I've been passing the time by wondering what I ever did to make Aliyah think I'd hurt anyone, let alone the girl I'd throw myself in front of a bus for.

"You can drop the formalities, Sean." Debois sets her cap on the desk and takes the manager's cushioned seat, then absently motions to the spindly wooden chair across from it without looking up from her tablet. "Please."

I perch on the edge of the seat, clutching Ruby's laptop, and ask again, "Did you find anything?"

"Ah," she says, still reading, "so you'll be conducting this interview, I see."

"Interview?" The prospect of her grilling me makes my blood sizzle and pop—not for fear for myself, but because she's wasting time when

she should be searching for Ruby. "Do you really think Ruby raising her voice at me for, like, three seconds means I went and *murdered* her? Then, what, I killed three other girls in my class just for kicks?"

Debois finally lifts her gaze, her finger frozen on the screen.

"I mean, c'mon," I go on, "there's no way I could've single-handedly dragged them all out of here. There's someone at the front desk twenty-four seven, right?"

She plops the tablet on the desk and folds her hands over it. "Are you finished?" She looks more amused than annoyed.

"Uh, yeah." I'm not usually the blubbering type, but my worry for Ruby's making me go all wackadoodle.

"I know you didn't murder anyone, for *kicks* or otherwise. The hotel's security footage shows the girls leaving of their own accord—Val around nine-thirty, and the others, together, around ten."

My mouth falls open. "Ruby, Selena, and Liv?"

"That's right."

"Why aren't you out there looking for them?"

"Out *where*? Paris is a big city, no? They could be anywhere." Debois temples her fingers. "That's why I must ask. Did Ruby tell you anything about where they might have gone?"

"No, Mad—no." I rub my forehead. "I would've said so before. She didn't mention any plans to leave at all."

"Well, if you please, can you take me through your last conversation with her?"

I tell the capitaine everything I can remember. She jots notes the whole time, though I don't understand what can possibly be so noteworthy, then asks me to repeat it. Once she finishes typing, she grips her armrests as though to stand. "Thank you, Sean—"

"Wait," I say. "What happens now? Will you hold a press conference?"

She sinks back into her seat with a small sigh. "That may be how things are done in America, but that is not how we do things here. We still don't even know they're in trouble."

My brows draw together. "You think they ran away."

"To be honest with you, that's exactly what it looks like."

"All *four* of them?"

She nods. "This sort of thing happens all the time. Kids run away from home—or a school trip, as the case may be—but usually come back once they lose their nerve, and everyone has panicked over nothing."

"Usually?"

She bites the inside of her cheek. "Usually."

"I *know* that's not it," I insist. "Can't you trace their phones?"

"Unless we have proof of criminal intent—"

"Ruby's still seventeen. Liv, too. You're allowed to track minors."

Debois's eyebrow twitches. She's clearly trying to keep her expression neutral.

But I know my logic is flawed. If Ruby's lost and her phone's trackable, she would've gotten in touch. She's smart—if she had no cell service, she'd find the nearest McDonald's or something to use their Wi-Fi. If her battery ran out, she'd borrow someone's phone. She'd at least have her dad's number memorized, and her dad would call Mr. LeBrecque.

Unless someone's stopping her from getting in touch.

My spine prickles. "Maybe someone kidnapped them."

"All *four* of them?" Debois imitates my tone, then chuckles softly.

I grip Ruby's laptop tighter. "Doesn't Paris have those CCTV cameras everywhere? Aren't you recording, like, every street?"

"Not *every* street. But many, yes."

"So why aren't you checking those?"

The corner of her lips quirks. "Do you want to be an inspecteur someday, Sean?"

My eyebrows shoot up. "No. I'm gonna join the military. At least . . ." I trail off.

"At least what?"

I shift uncomfortably. What does this matter right now? "That's what my father wants."

Until this year, I'd had tunnel vision, never even considering other careers. But then Ruby came into my life, and it was like she slid a ladder down so I could climb from the tunnel and see the whole sky's boundless expanse. But Pop will always drag me back in and drive me toward that one singular point in the distance. Feels useless to fight it.

"He wants you to follow in his footsteps?" Debois asks.

"How'd you know?"

She shrugs. "People are predictable."

A staticky voice blares from her radio. I can only make out one word: *muertre. Murder.* My gut clenches. She raises the radio to her lips, brow pinched, and tells them she's on her way.

"Was that about the girls?" I ask.

"No." She stands and put her cap back on.

"Wait. You're gonna look for them, right?" Desperation laces my voice. "You're not just gonna wait and see if they come back, are you?"

Her radio goes all staticky again, and she sighs. "I must go. Why don't you stay here for a few minutes? Cool off a bit, yes?"

I don't need to cool off. I grit my teeth so hard I think my molars might crack—

Okay, fine. I need to cool off.

She leaves before I can say anything else, anyway.

I collapse back into my chair and stare at Ruby's laptop. No one asked for it—they must've assumed it's mine, that I really like the color lavender. And Mr. LeBrecque must've forgotten I had it.

I bounce my knee, wondering what the detectives' next move might be. Hopefully not wait and see.

I thumb the edge of Ruby's laptop, thinking of how I got sketchy vibes from Val in the lobby yesterday as she texted someone nonstop. Maybe she texted something to Ruby later about where they were going. If Ruby has WhatsApp installed on here, and the messages synced . . .

No way. That'd be a terrible invasion of privacy.

But if Ruby *is* in trouble, and I can help, she'll forgive me for snooping on her laptop.

And if she *isn't* in trouble, she'll probably want to whack me over the head with it.

An acceptable risk.

I open it and snort at the password prompt. The first time I saw Ruby type one letter four times and hit enter, my eyes nearly boinged from their sockets. I tried explaining the security risks, but she refused to change it to something more complex. I think she likes to see me squirm each time.

Ruby has a zillion tabs open. I ignore them and pull up the search bar to type *WhatsApp*.

Not installed.

Next, I open her Messages app. This feels dirty. I hate prying and wish I could automatically block anything irrelevant from my eyeballs.

My name's right up top. I was the last person Ruby texted nearly two days ago, right before she got to the airport. We've all been using WhatsApp ever since.

I notice her laptop's offline; it hasn't synced any new messages. I click the Wi-Fi icon, select the hotel's guest Wi-Fi, and wait for it to connect.

A blue dot appears next to one name. *Dad.*

Those messages are useless, though. It seems she emailed him about her stolen wallet sometime around 9:45 p.m., and he texted her about fifteen times afterward—

A new window pops up.

A file of photos. It's syncing from the cloud.

One new photo appears: the only one highlighted, the most recent, appearing ahead of the others from last night—mostly selfies of us in front of the glittering Eiffel Tower across the Seine as we walked back from dinner in Saint-Michel.

It's graffiti on some random wall of a toad squatting on an upturned bucket, fishing in a pond. I don't remember seeing anything like that.

Then again, I didn't notice her get pickpocketed, either. I remember walking next to her with vivid clarity, though, the way her lavender-scented shampoo wafted my way in the crisp breeze, the way my heart thrummed in my chest as I considered reaching for her hand.

Either way, she must've taken this sometime afterward. I close the photo and right-click the file, navigating to its properties.

Holy hell.

Ruby took the photo at 10:34 p.m. last night.

My posture straightens, and I'm breathing fast. She left the hotel around 10:00.

I scroll through the properties, fingers buzzing, searching for something, hoping it's there.

Yup. There it is.

The geo stamp showing the latitude and longitude.

I know where Ruby went.

16
Ruby

I didn't expect to feel parched this fast. We polished off the water a few hours ago after Olivia convinced us *it's better to hydrate and maintain cognitive function longer than to ration and start dehydrating sooner,* but now the water's gone, and we're still spectacularly lost. I smack my paper-dry lips, imagining the tangy flavor of my favorite lime electrolyte drops back home.

Val hears me. "Same, I'm so thirsty." She's been sticking to me like glue, slowing her pace to force back anyone else who winds up beside me. I passed her my lamp at one point, thinking she wanted to be near the light, but she's still clinging. "How long does it take to die of thirst?"

My stomach twists. I'd expect Selena to know from all the videos she's watched about deep space survival, but she stays silent, her face a mask of concentration as she sidesteps sharp rocks, having abandoned her blister-inducing wedges a while back. Olivia and I keep offering her turns with our boots and jackets, but she waves us off like she has something to prove.

"Depends," Olivia says.

"On what?" Val asks.

"The environment. How much you're exerting yourself. Like, we'd thirst faster under the scorching sun in the desert, but we'd thirst slower if we were just lying around instead of doing all this walking—"

"Nobody's dying of thirst," Julien assures us. "You'll be home soon."

Home. Home seems a universe away. These tunnels feel infinite, indistinguishable except for any discernible artwork—eyes, skulls, hieroglyphics, pop culture memes. The artists have spoken a language of their own, painting shapes that aren't quite letters or numbers, leaving nonsensical messages for the darkness to decipher. We've passed no street markers today. Maybe those only exist in the highest gallery.

"There's plenty of water down here, anyway," says Val.

"You mean from the flooded tunnels?" I ask. We're on dry ground, but we've had to trudge through ankle-deep water that went murky as our steps swilled silt. "That can't be safe."

"It's spring water, no?" says Julien.

"Liv?" I ask.

"No clue," says Olivia, "Could be sewer water for all I know."

Val clasps her chest. "Good lord, she doesn't know something."

"I'm not a walking encyclopedia," Olivia bristles.

"To be fair," I say, "you *are* the smartest person we know."

She snorts. "Tell that to Harvard."

My mouth falls open. "You didn't get in?"

"Nope," Olivia says quietly. "Found out last week."

"But you're our valedictorian by a *long* shot," says Selena. She's always been up there academically-speaking, too, so she keeps track of that sort of thing. I've long since accepted I'm a straight B student.

"Sometimes doing everything right still isn't enough," Olivia says, then sighs and softens her tone. "There are only so many spots and so many other valedictorians."

"You got into UPenn, though, right?" I ask.

"Yeah, but I wanted Harvard. My grandma lives right in Harvard Square; she's a neurosurgeon at Mass Gen. She's kind of my inspiration. I was going to move in with her and everything." She shrugs. "Oh well, I guess."

"College is a scam, anyway," says Val.

"Not if you want to be a surgeon," Olivia snaps.

"*You're* in college, right?" I ask Julien, batting the tension away like Whac-A-Mole.

"University."

I catch up to him and match his stride, curious about this mysterious, adventure-seeking Parisian whose life we upended. "Which one?"

He smirks. "One you wouldn't have heard of. Nothing like *Harvard*."

"What's your major?" I dig.

"I haven't picked one yet."

"Oh. Is your school in Paris?"

"Yes."

"Did you grow up here?"

"Yes."

"How old are your sisters?" I persist. I've gotta get *something* out of him.

He side-eyes me. "I told you about them?"

"Last night. You said they'd be the first to notice you're missing."

"Ah, right. Well, they're sixteen and eleven." He'd also mentioned his parents are dead.

"They don't live with you, do they? You're not, like, their guardian?"

"I am," he says softly.

"God, they must be worried sick. *You* must be worried about *them*. Why didn't you say anything?"

"What would it help? Chelsea can take care of Francesca for now—" His voice cracks, and he clears his throat. "They'll be fine. Anyway, let's not talk about such stressful things." But his forehead remains crinkled with anxiety. I feel bad for bringing it up.

"Okay." I run my tongue over my teeth, brainstorming how to cheer him up. I'm no good at small talk—not with strangers, anyway. "So, what's your favorite spot in Paris?"

He grins. "Oh, easy. There's this little crepe stand right beside Notre Dame. I get one with strawberries and Nutella, so warm and gooey, the edges so crisp, *ugh*, it is perfection." He clasps his stomach. My mouth would water any other time, but after breathing in stale air that reeks of damp dust for hours, it feels dry and gritty. "I like to sit on a bench right there with that magnificent view, early in the morning, when the sky is clear and it is not so busy. There is no better place, not in Paris, not in the world."

"I love that," Val says, but I scoff.

Julien peers at me again. "What?"

My cheeks warm. His answer reminds me so much of what Tyler told me about Paris that night in his bedroom. "It's just— That sounds so cliché. So touristy."

He gives me a little shove. "Look at you, judging me." The corners of his eyes crinkle. "Locals can enjoy what the tourists do. That's how it becomes a tourist attraction to begin with, yes? The most appealing spots become the most popular." Julien brandishes his arms. "And up until yesterday, *this* was my favorite spot."

"Sorry we ruined the death maze for you," Selena mutters, heaving a sigh. "We're never going to find a way out, are we?"

"Not with that attitude," says Val.

Selena narrows her eyes. "It's not like we can manifest ourselves out of here."

"That would be convenient," says Julien. "Imagine closing your eyes and thinking of your favorite place in the world, et voilà!"

"That's not how manifesting works," says Olivia. "We'd have to envision ourselves finding a ladder or something."

"Teleporting would be much easier, yes?" he says. "Where would you think of?"

Olivia rolls her eyes, but answers, "My grandma's lake house in Vermont. We go almost every weekend during the summer—my whole family, even my cousins. We have s'mores and play assassin, and it's just very fun and wholesome, you know?"

"Can you see the Milky Way up there on clear nights?" Selena asks.

"Nah, it's not far enough north. There's still too much light pollution."

Julien nudges Val's arm with his lamp. "What about you?"

Val shrugs. "I don't really have a favorite place. I'm dying to see the ocean, though—like, tropical waters, not that brown New England sludge."

"So why haven't you?"

"Never had the chance. My parents aren't into tropical vacations. Or any vacations, really. I've never even been swimming before. But I'd love to go scuba diving. Not just in a pool. In the ocean. Where the water beneath you fades to the blackest blue, and you don't know how far it goes, and anything can be down there. It's wild how we still don't know what's at the bottom of the deepest parts of the ocean, and—I don't know. I want to *feel* the vastness of it."

"God, that's exactly how I feel about space," Selena says, a bit breathless. "I want to see that infinite expanse with nothing in the way. To be one step closer to the absolute unknown."

Val offers a slight smile, surprised. "Yeah. I get that."

Seeing them relate is surreal—like two of my universes colliding.

But then Val ruins it. "When we graduate," she says, looping her arm through mine, "we want to travel together and see the Great Barrier Reef."

Selena's smile fades.

So does mine. Unless I land a sponsorship or something, Val will have to stuff me into her suitcase. The paltry monthly revenue my channel has finally started generating won't cut it—

Julien stops short, cursing in French.

I lift my gaze—I'd been staring at the ground, but ahead, the corridor abruptly ends with another wall of skulls. "Crap," I say. "A dead end."

Val chortles. "Literally."

It takes me a moment to realize. "Obviously, no pun intended."

"Mm-hmm," says Selena. "Apple, tree."

My chest tightens. She always used to tease me for having Dad's sense of humor, even though his puns annoy me. Thinking of him makes my eyes mist. He must be worried sick.

"It's not a dead end, though," says Olivia. "It's another hall, see?"

She's right; there's a perpendicular corridor ahead. Swirling graffiti coats the walls on either side of us in dense blacks, whites, and reds—skulls and scrawls, stick figures and signatures, an unintelligible mass of scribbles.

"Hey, look!" I skirt past Julien, who raises his lantern to better illuminate dozens of red arrows next to a cartoon skull, all pointing to the right. "Let's go that way," I say.

Val nods as she raises her lamp, too, but Julien quirks his brow and says, "If there was a sign with arrows pointing off a cliff, would you follow it?"

My cheeks heat. "No," I mumble.

"Only if it was pointing away from you," says Val, flashing me a devilish look.

Julien scoffs. "They could be pointing the wrong way on purpose. Many of the street signs in the upper gallery have been switched around, too."

"Why?" Selena asks.

"Why does anyone ever prank anyone?" Julien says with a lopsided smile.

Farther down the corridor, I find a mess of black arrows, this time pointing down with the message NE PAS S'APPROCHER sprayed underneath. "Stay away," I whisper, translating aloud. The same words in large, streaky black scrawl cover a red-painted message. I squint to make out the partially concealed words. "Dans ces couloirs, ceux qui sont oubliés protègent ceux qui ont oublié. I think that means *In these halls, those who are forgotten protect those who have forgotten.*"

Julien crunches over gravel as he rushes over. "You know French?"

"To varying degrees." I have reading, writing, and comprehension down pat, but no amount of studying will make me suck less at speaking.

Olivia lightly touches one of the letters. "I wonder how old it is."

"It's gotta be old," says Val. "People don't talk like that."

"They do if they're being cryptic."

"I have a bad feeling about this," says Julien. "Come, let's go back—"

"Wait, why?" says Selena.

Julien's nostrils flare. "We should heed the warning."

"We don't know it's a warning," says Val. It sure looks like one to me.

"If it is, they're only warning whoever not to go down," Olivia points out. "Nobody covered the red arrows."

As they debate it, I approach the junction to search for more directional clues. Skulls stacked in floor-to-ceiling rows line the far wall, but the inner wall is bare stone. It's so dark, I can't tell if anything's scrawled over it. I think to snap some photos with the flash on; then I can inspect the pictures and zoom around on-screen. I switch on my camera and fiddle with the settings, adjusting the aperture, then point it at the wall—

Something crunches over gravel to my right.

Startled, I jump and press the shutter button.

The flash brightens the passageway for a split second.

My heart plummets. I want to shout, but my voice sticks in my throat as I struggle to process what I illuminated with the flash.

A skeleton lurking far down the corridor.

I stare into the darkness at the neon green afterimage imprinted on my retinas, terror locking me in place like someone's bound my ankles and superglued my boots to the ground. Selena thought she saw two skeletons chasing her but brushed it off as a dream. Maybe it wasn't. But they couldn't be *alive*, obviously—they were simply propped up, a macabre display like all the other artistic arrangements down here.

Yes, that must be it. She saw something like this and bolted.

I chuckle more to relax myself than because I'm amused. The others are still arguing, but I'm impatient to take another look, so I slip my phone from my pocket and power it on, then toggle on the flashlight.

I gasp.

It's closer now.

Feet away.

Bone-white and spindly, its eye sockets hollow like graves gouged into the earth.

But it's not a skeleton. It's a person wearing a skull mask. A headlamp is strapped around their mask's cranium, but it's off. My light's the only one that glints off the knife in their grip.

This must be who smashed through that wall of skulls. They found us. And they're not here to help. They were trying to sneak up on me.

They want to *stab* me.

They lunge forward, blocking me from the others.

"Run!" I scream as I do just that.

17

Ruby

Running away from problems is kinda my go-to.

I quit the swim team so I wouldn't have to see Selena's judgy face at meets. I scurry from Sean's touch instead of telling him why I'm scared to take things further. I storm off to my room whenever Dad sets an absurd curfew instead of levelly negotiating or explaining that I feel stifled.

So I know I have a problem.

A running problem, specifically.

But when someone in a skull mask lunges at you with a knife eight stories beneath the streets of Paris, you don't stick around to talk things through.

You freaking *run*.

Julien warned me not to run. Made me *promise* not to run. But thinking of those pits for eyes and that blade tearing my flesh makes me run like the wind, right, left, right again, stooping to keep my skull from slamming into the low, jagged ceiling as my ears ring with adrenaline.

I run even though I'm getting separated from the others.

I run even though this could be the death of me.

Oh God.

I never thought I'd die alone in the dark under the City of Light.

A low, rasping growl echoes through the passageway. My heart jolts, and I clamp a shaking hand over my mouth to mask my heavy breathing.

But it's too late.

They found me.

Maybe there are worse things than dying alone.

Since I've switched off my phone's flashlight to hide, I can't see them coming in the pitch blackness, but squeeze my eyes shut, anyway.

Crunching footfalls grow louder. Running footfalls.

Yup. I'm screwed.

I take mental inventory of my belongings, scrambling for what I can use to defend myself. Would my camera make a good weapon? Anything can if you slam it hard enough into someone's skull. Maybe not a pillow—

Someone whispers my name as the insides of my eyelids brighten, and panic slices through me like a guillotine. I snap my eyes open.

"Val," I gasp.

Her cool fingers latch on to my wrist. The sensation calms me, grounds me, like I'm somehow siphoning her strength. She's always so brave, with fire glimmering in her gold-flecked hazel eyes. For months I've swept aside the feeling that one day that fire would blaze out of control. But I was right. And now we might burn.

"Did you see—" I start.

Julien covers my mouth and raises two fingers. *There are two of them,* he mouths as my pulse thrashes wildly. *This way.* He releases me, keeping his lamp on low as we scurry through the passageways, quiet as mice. After taking a series of turns, we follow a long corridor that seems to stretch for miles, until—

Julien hisses a curse.

There's a dead end ahead. For real this time.

Val leans against the wall, breathing hard. "Did we lose them?"

"I think splitting up confused them," Selena whispers.

"Where was the other one?" I ask.

"Behind the one that went after you," says Selena. "It was like they couldn't decide who to go after, and that one tripped and bit it."

"They had a knife," Val adds.

"No they didn't," Julien says, low and husky.

"The one I saw definitely did," I say.

"What do they want?" Selena asks.

"*To murder us,*" Val hisses.

Julien wipes a hand down his face and turns. "Come on—"

"Wait." Olivia squeezes past us to the end of the rounded alcove, then crouches to peer into a squat, craggy crevasse that looks like a creature clawed out the bottom of the wall. "I think this opens up to something, but I can't see." Val tries passing her the second lamp, but Olivia waves her off. "Can I have a flashlight?"

Julien clenches his jaw, a sheen of sweat on his brow.

I edge around to his backpack.

"I got it." He unslings his pack to dig one out.

Olivia takes it and angles the beam down the cleft. "Yeah, there's a room down there."

I kneel beside her to see. It's a jagged, downward-slanting crawl space about the length of a school bus, and it spills into a wide-open cavity. "I see skulls. What if it's just a pit of bones? Another dead end?"

"We can hide in there," Val says frantically.

"No," says Julien.

"Why not?" says Val. "We can turn off our lights and wait them out. They'll never think we squeezed through there."

The message scrawled under those downward-facing arrows flashes through my mind.

Ne pas s'approacher. Stay away.

My skin crawls, like the very molecules in my flesh are warning me against this.

"No way," says Selena. "I'd rather fling myself at whoever's back there than go another level deeper."

"Cool, bye." Val lowers herself like she's about to dive into the cavity headfirst.

I reach for her hand. "Val—"

She yanks her arm back. *"Rube."*

I wince, curling into myself like a pill bug.

Val lowers her voice. "I'm not getting sliced open down here because *she* can't hold it together for, like, thirty seconds." She jabs a finger at Selena. But if anything, Val's the one panicking.

Selena stiffens. "If we go any deeper underground, we'll be trapped for good."

"Not necessarily," says Julien, torn. "Sometimes you have to go down to go up."

"See?" Val looks to me for support.

I know she expects it after giving me hers last night, when I wanted to take Julien's shortcut but Selena didn't. That was different. That was before we knew how wrong everything would go and what was really down here. I cross my arms, plucking at my lower lip.

"C'mon, Rube," says Val. "Back me up."

I can't. Selena's right. I shake my head.

Hurt fills her eyes. "Some friend you are."

"Oh, like *you're* such a great friend," Olivia says. Before I can ask what she means, she looks at me and spews, "She's been trying to set me up with Sean."

The revelation is so abrupt, so jarring, I take a step back.

I don't know what to say. Val's mouth has formed an *O* of surprise, like she's trying to catch the ball Selena's and Julien's eyes are ping-ponging between us.

"I'm sorry, I—" Olivia chokes out. There's no time for this, but whatever she's been bottling up is exploding. "I thought you two were a thing. But she swore you weren't. She said he liked me but was too shy to make the first move." Humiliation's plain on her face, the way it's so red even in this low glow.

"Did *you?*" I can't help but ask.

She nods. "At my birthday party. We kissed."

My heart goes into free fall, and my eyelids flutter shut. I was there. I had no idea.

"He stopped it, though," says Olivia, "made some excuse about needing to focus on getting into West Point. But she's had me going for *weeks*, telling me not to give up, that he's just shy."

You said they were just friends, she'd said to Val last night, after she caught me staring at the picture of me and Sean on my phone.

"I didn't mean to—" Val stutters. Like she never expected Olivia to say anything. "I only wanted to help—"

"*You know I love him!*" I shout, then cover my mouth. It's the first time I've said it out loud. The first time I've admitted it to myself.

Then I catch Selena's stare. I knew she liked Tyler, and I kissed him anyway.

Hypocrite. The unspoken word sours the air between us.

Voices rasp somewhere in the distance.

Julien swears. "They're coming."

I let out a choked sob, terrified, mortified, wishing I could dissolve into a puddle and seep into the cracks in the limestone. I do the next best thing—I swipe the flashlight from Olivia, clamber onto my stomach, and hurl myself into the squat crawl space, not giving a damn whether anyone follows.

I contort my spine to squeeze under the rough rocks that scrape against the back of my skull, and part of me is rooting for the layers of stone overhead to collapse and smoosh me so I'll match my pancaked heart.

Val's betrayal is making me reel, but I'm even more floored the thought of Sean with any other girl is crushing me so deeply. I promised myself I'd never let myself fall for him, not completely. Not after Dad loved my mother so much her death wrecked him for decades. Not after the one time I kissed a boy I lost my best friend over it. None of it seems worth the pain.

Plus, as Val keeps reminding me, Sean and I have an expiration date. Sure, we can technically date long-distance, but if he joins the military, I don't think I can handle the constant low-level fear of him being in perilous situations day in, day out.

But when he looks at me, when he makes me feel like the room's been sapped of oxygen and all I need is him to breathe, he almost makes me forget to be careful.

Apparently, me and Olivia both.

She's hurting, too. Puzzle pieces are snapping together that I didn't know should ever fit, like how red and puffy Olivia's eyes were halfway through her birthday party, how she's been so awkwardly bubbly around him lately, how he's been stiff and quiet around her, how she's been frigid toward Val since last night—

A sudden rancid smell yanks me back to reality.

I freeze just shy of the opening to the cavern beyond, but the downward slant is so steep, I slip and have to dig my palms into stone to keep from sliding forward.

The sound of rustling plastic behind me quiets. "You okay?" Olivia asks.

Behind her, Selena whispers, "Keep *going!*"

"Sorry, I—" I gag, catching another wave of that stench. "God, what's that smell?"

"The sewer?" Olivia guesses.

"I don't think so." This doesn't smell like rotten eggs; it's far more putrid. It reminds me of the throne of bones we stumbled across this morning, of the decaying mouse in my bedroom wall.

"Ruby, move," Julien whispers. He's right. We have to hide and shut off our lights before those masked people reach that dead end and spot the glow.

I squirm to the edge of the ridge, breathing through my mouth. It's not just a pit of bones. It's an enormous cavern as big as the one from last night. Rows of skulls and femurs line the opposite wall, and a column of them rises in the center of the space. Another cimetiére, I guess.

I peer over the edge, shining my light down to see how far the drop to the ground will be, and let out a bloodcurdling shriek.

18
Ruby

I cover my mouth, but it's too late—I've already made a sound that could wake the dead. Those knife-wielding freaks will surely find us now. Everyone behind me demands answers, but all I can do is clamp my eyes shut and hope that when I open them, the dead body will be gone.

That I only imagined it.

That the past eighteen hours have been nothing but a nightmare.

Something brushes against my leg, and I yelp, trying to punt it off.

"It's me, it's just me," Olivia says, gripping my ankle so I won't kick her in the face.

I let out a shuddered breath. "Sorry, sorry."

"What happened?"

I have to look again. There's no other choice, nowhere else to go. I peek through my eyelashes and angle the flashlight down.

Still there.

"There's a dead body."

The person died in the fetal position and seems to be dressed in men's hiking clothes: cargo pants, boots, and a black nylon jacket, all covered in some sort of white mold. And his head—oh God, what happened to his *head*?

No. I can't look, can't even think of it, otherwise I'll be sick.

"News flash," Val whispers, "there are lots of dead bodies down here."

I can't with her snark right now.

Neither can Selena. "Obviously she means a more recent one."

"It's blocking the way," I say. It's one thing to crunch over bones, but another to step through gore. This is unfathomable.

"Ruby," says Julien, "you're going to have to climb over it." The urgency in his voice tells me that if I don't, we'll all wind up like this guy.

I'm too high from the ground to slide out headfirst—if I do, I might break my neck—so I bend my knees to spin around and wriggle from the crevasse feetfirst. The crawl space is only just wide enough to manage it. The dead man's not centered directly below me, his legs extending too far to the right to reach empty space, so I'll have to aim for the left of the muck.

That's all that's left of his head.

Muck.

I balance the flashlight on the ridge so its beam points into the cavern, then shimmy my butt to the edge, legs dangling out, and take a deep breath—

Ugh.

On second thought, no deep breaths. Just go.

I launch myself to the left of the body.

As my feet hit the ground, I tumble forward and do a sort of off-balanced somersault, putting pressure on the shoulder I hurt this morning when I collided with Julien in the dark. Despite the pain, I scuttle back from the body like a crab.

"You okay?" Olivia whispers.

"Yeah." I scramble to my feet and shake out my arm, clamping my lips as I swallow a dry heave.

Olivia wiggles to the edge.

"Don't look down—"

"Too late." She grimaces.

"Give me those." I stretch over the body on my tiptoes and grab her bag and the flashlight, then shuffle across the cavern and toss them next to the wall of bones. Somehow, that's the safe side. The flashlight rolls, pointing left, but I'm already rushing back to help Olivia, who looks unsure how to swivel around like I did.

"Give me your hands," I say, "I'll pull you out over it."

She does, and as I yank her out, she kicks from the wall to vault over the body, knocking me back and landing directly on my hip bone. The breath I've been holding puffs out in a whoosh, and I stifle an agonized yelp, avoiding making more loud noises.

"Sorry," she grunts, scrambling off me.

We help Selena together, then Val, both landing like we did in a jumbled heap. As soon as Val clambers to her feet, she tugs me away from Olivia and whispers frantically, "Rube, I'm so sorry. I tried setting them up because I didn't want him to hurt you—"

"Not now," I whisper, covering my nose.

"I thought you'd get over him faster if—"

"We are *not* doing this now," I say firmly as Selena and Olivia help Julien down. He's the only one who manages to catch his footing, and as soon as he does, he switches off his lamp and hushes us. I dive for the flashlight and turn it off, too.

Darkness envelopes us once more.

Selena whimpers.

"Shhhh." Julien, I think.

Not even a minute passes before voices float through the crevasse. It faintly glows from their lights. We cut it close. So close. I can't make out what they're saying, but I think they're talking in French. Olivia and Selena skulk behind the column, and I see Julien's faint silhouette beckoning me and Val to join him against the wall next to the body.

I slink over, crouching low as someone scrapes and scuffles overhead. My chest constricts. They're checking in here.

Val reaches for my hand. Despite my anger, I latch on anyway. My heart's jackhammering my rib cage so hard I'm convinced whoever's up there can hear it.

Eventually the light fades and the voices peter out. Still, we cower in the dark next to the dead for what feels like hours.

"I think they're gone," Olivia finally whispers.

"I think so, too." Julien switches his lamp back on the lowest setting, and we scramble back from the body and join the others next to the column of bones, brushing mud and silt from our filthy clothes. Olivia thought to put on a KN95. Good idea. I find mine in my purse's inner compartment and put it on, too, wishing I had extras for the others, who cover their noses with their shirts or jackets.

Julien gapes at the corpse and mutters, "Bordel de merde."

Olivia's transfixed. "What happened to his *head*?"

"I don't want to know," says Selena.

"Looks like a purge," says Val. "The gasses in his stomach probably built up and pushed his organs—"

I tear off my mask and stumble to the only corner of the cavern free of bones or bodies to—well, talk about a purge. Val follows, pulling back my sandy waves, but I swat her away. She steps back, dejected.

"How do you even *know* that?" Selena asks.

"Haven't you ever fallen down a Wikipedia rabbit hole?" says Val.

"Dork," Olivia quips.

"Thank you," says Val, reversing their earlier exchange.

The moment of levity doesn't last. As I straighten and wipe my mouth, Olivia shifts away from Val, whose brow crinkles with regret. If she was telling the truth before, she used Olivia as a pawn to help me get over a boy. Which doesn't even make sense.

"You okay?" Selena asks as I plod back to the group.

"Yeah. Sorry about that."

"Nothing to be sorry for." She seems genuinely concerned, though I'm not sure whether it's over my retching or my kerfuffle with Val. Maybe both.

"You don't think this is the missing documentarian, do you?" I ask Julien.

He nods, rubbing the back of his neck.

"Or maybe it's the person he heard scream," says Selena.

"It sounded like a woman in the video," says Val. "Either way, that's some coincidence."

Julien quirks a brow. "Still think it's a hoax?"

Her gaze shifts back to the extremely real body. She doesn't answer.

"How long ago did he go missing?" Olivia asks.

He blows air through his lips. "A month or so."

Selena's brows pinch. "But this guy's still so . . ."

". . . squishy," Val finishes. Another wave of nausea hits me.

"How do you think he died?" I ask.

"Looks like he was getting the crap kicked out of him," says Val. "Or maybe they stabbed him. Looks like he's protecting his gut."

"I don't see any blood," says Olivia, "other than his head. And look, he was using his backpack as a pillow. I think he died in his sleep."

"Maybe he got lost and starved to death waiting for help," I say.

"More likely he thirsted to death, but yeah. And I think that's his flashlight." She grabs the one I'm holding, turns it on, and points it at him.

"*Whoa*," Val gasps.

"Holy—" says Selena.

We hadn't seen it in the dim glow from Julien's lamp, but the flashlight has illuminated a vibrant mural of Paris above the dead man. It surrounds us, covering the misshapen ceiling and spanning the entire cavern except where stacks of bones hide the walls and two squat archways on opposite ends lead to other passageways.

Olivia pans the beam along a jagged fissure stretching from the floor up to the cavity we crawled through, which has been incorporated into the mural as a storm cloud from which a giant bolt of lightning is splitting the city in two, forming a wide crack in the earth. Graffitied skulls beneath the disproportionate skyline stretch all the way to the actual skulls lining the wall behind us, and stars are sprinkled across a swirling night sky. Fairy lights encircle us, secured to the ceiling with thick strips of duct tape.

"Like those lights you had in your room," Val whispers to me.

When Selena and I were ten, her stepmom helped her decorate her room like our solar system, with fairy lights strung around the perimeter and lining the bookcases, planets dangling from yarn, and glow-in-the-dark stars and comets stuck all over the ceiling. I loved it so much, I talked Dad into letting me decorate my room like that, too. After Selena told me to fuck off, Val helped me peel off the stickers and tear down the lights, going off on this whole tirade about how Selena was a social-climbing, slut-shaming asshole I was better off without.

Now I ignore her, searching for the wire's end. "What do these lights hook up to?" When they're illuminated, the ceiling must look like a shimmering galaxy.

Julien finds the outlet plug dangling beside the archway. "Here. It must plug into a generator."

"I don't see one," says Val.

"My friends usually bring portable ones—"

"Check out the buildings." Selena points, an edge to her voice.

I examine the monuments lining the Seine. The lightning bolt has caused a seismic event that's knocked the Eiffel Tower askew like it's about to tip into the fissure. One of Notre Dame's gothic towers is crumbling. The Louvre's collapsing into a cloud of smoke behind its cracked pyramid. Sacré-Coeur's dome is tumbling off its hilltop.

"Looks kind of prophetic, doesn't it?" says Selena.

"Apocalyptic, sure," I say. "I don't know about prophetic—"

"Lightning can't literally break a city apart," says Val, racing to agree with me.

Selena rolls her eyes. "Obviously. It's symbolic."

"Either way," says Olivia, "Paris isn't on a fault line. This wouldn't happen. Although . . ."

"What?" I ask.

"Paris did actually split open like this once."

"Yeah, right," says Val.

"No, it's true," says Olivia. "A mile-long trench opened up one afternoon—December 1774, I think—and all the houses on that stretch collapsed into it. They called it the Mouth of Hell."

"But if there are no fault lines . . ." I trail off.

"It wasn't an earthquake. It was actually because of this place. The catacombs." She tilts her head. "Only, they weren't *catacombs* yet. They were originally mines. They took a ton of limestone from down here to build the city, even buildings like Notre Dame, but they didn't properly fortify these tunnels afterward. So buildings started collapsing into them."

"It wasn't until they started moving the dead into the tunnels that the city stabilized," says Julien.

"Yeah, that's around when they started bringing down all these bones." Olivia motions to the column. "The fortification work reminded them *Oh, hey, there's all this empty space right under our feet; perfect place to dump the bodies from the overflowing cemeteries.*"

It must've taken so much effort to fortify this endless maze of tunnels. I've always marveled at humanity's mind-boggling constructions—the interstate, vast skylines, cliffside castles, colossal monuments—but here, six million people are buttressing a city long after their deaths, a feat they had no say in. The thought is disturbing.

"Hey, look." Val points overhead. "Those aren't stars. They're skulls."

Olivia sweeps her light over them. Dozens of black swirls each encircle a skull, the swirls blending into a riotous night sky like a van Gogh painting. The skulls' eye sockets are bulbous and elongated, which looks oddly familiar. "What's up with their eyes?" I ask.

But Olivia's distracted. She approaches the column of bones. "This thing looks kinda like a pulpit, right?" She slices her hand through the air, indicating how it comes up to her chest.

"Is it my imagination"—Selena's hand flutters to her throat—"or does this room seem awfully cultish?"

The hairs on my nape rise. I look to Olivia, expecting her to refute that with some other factoid.

But she grimly says, "It's not your imagination."

"Oh my God," I say, my nerves sizzling. "Those people. Those *masks*."

Selena nods. "We just climbed into their den."

"Holy—" says Val.

Only one of us remains silent.

Julien's still staring at the body, pinching his shirt collar above his nose.

"Julien?" I say.

He blinks. "What?"

"Those people chasing us . . . are they in a cult?"

"A *cult*?" Julien dismisses the thought with a wave of his hand. "No, there's no cult."

"But this artwork is so strange."

"All the artwork down here is strange."

"True. But their *masks*." I gesture to the skull artwork surrounding us. "And they're obviously violent."

"Are all cults violent?" he asks. "No, I think they're a bunch of depraved sadists who've decided it's fun to scare people. The masks just fit the vibe, no?" He motions to the real skulls.

"They want to hurt us," I insist. "One of them lunged at me with a *knife*."

His eyes dart to mine, then slide back to the body. Finally he says, "That, I agree. Whatever they're doing, it's become more than just a prank—"

Loose stones tumble from the cavity onto the corpse.

Plop.

Plop.

Plunk.

I gape at the crevasse. Maybe it's nothing. Maybe we jostled those stones loose while climbing through.

Something scuffles against stone.

None of us have moved.

Julien raises a finger to his lips and points at one of the two arched exits.

We follow wordlessly, leaping over a large puddle as to not make a sound.

I'm the last one out. Before stooping under the archway, I throw one last look at the crevasse. And before I tear my gaze away, I can swear I see the edge of a skull peek out.

19
Sean

I don't get what's so special about the *Mona Lisa*.

All I see is a small, muted portrait of some slightly amused lady—at least, from the bits I can see around the bulging mass of tourists crowding her. She's dwarfed by the enormous palatial room she occupies, and everyone ignores the other vibrant pieces lining the walls, craning their necks to catch a glimpse of the painting they've already seen a billion times on the internet.

Yeah. I don't get it at all.

If Ruby were here, we'd be laughing about it together. Jesus, I miss her. I miss her smile, her giggle. She's the one person I can be my silliest self with. Pop's got such a stiff upper lip and Mom's so self-conscious, we never goof around or tease each other. Even my sister, Emily, texts me her snarky remarks instead of saying them out loud. I'm always on edge at home, wary to dip a toe out of line and get an earful about how I need to take myself and my future more seriously. But with Ruby, I want to burst from my shell like a turtle with a jetpack.

Our class only has a couple of hours to explore before the museum closes, and we're all soaked from waiting in the line that wrapped around the courtyard's iconic glass pyramid while it poured. We were originally supposed to break into teams of four for a scavenger hunt, but Mr. LeBrecque insisted we stick together, God forbid anyone else evaporate into thin air. I'm trailing behind the group, lost in thought despite his efforts to keep us occupied, wondering if Capitaine Debois is doing anything with the photo I found on Ruby's laptop. She'd sent some lackey to pick it up, and I wish I could be a fly buzzing around her head right now.

"Why d'you think they left together?"

I jump. I didn't notice Aliyah sidle beside me.

"Sorry." She tucks one of her braids behind her ear.

"Whatever." I'm still pissed she suggested I'd hurt Ruby.

The truth is I'd do anything to keep Ruby from getting hurt. Even if it meant keeping a secret about that two-faced friend of hers. I hate that Olivia got caught in the middle of that. I never wanted to hurt her, either. Guilt claws at my insides. I didn't handle any of that well.

"So why d'you think they left?" Aliyah presses. The museum staff made everyone stuff their wet umbrellas into long plastic bags, and she keeps spinning and unspinning hers by the extra plastic at the end.

"Hell if I know."

She inhales sharply at my icy tone but persists. "It's not like they're friends anymore. Selena and Ruby, I mean."

I shrug, watching our classmates pose for selfies near the *Mona Lisa*. Earlier they scarfed down a late lunch at the museum's cafe while I stared at a banana, appetite nonexistent. They're either exceptionally good at pretending nothing's wrong or genuinely don't give a crap.

"And Selena actually kind of hates Ruby," Aliyah goes on. "I know for a *fact* they'd never sneak out together."

That kind of talk about Ruby makes my stomach sour. "Clearly you're wrong. Because clearly they *did*."

She sighs at my clipped tone. "I'm sorry, okay? I didn't mean to accuse you of anything."

"Then why did you?" I finally meet her gaze.

She's short, maybe five one, and peers up at me from under her long, dark lashes. "The police asked if we'd noticed anything unusual, and you two arguing *was* unusual. It was the only thing I could think of." Her bold expression withers. "And I'm just so worried about Selena."

I get that. I'm worried about Ruby, too.

All right, I can't hold on to this grudge. Aliyah's the only other person I can relate to in this whole mess, and I'm itching to theorize with someone.

"Okay, so," I say, "I don't know how Ruby, Selena, and Liv wound up together. But Val sneaking out first tracks."

Aliyah leans forward. "Does it? I don't really know her."

"That girl can't sit still for a minute. She's gotten Ruby into trouble before. Like last month, she convinced Ruby to sneak into some historic fort at night, and a bunch of cops chased them out."

"So you think the others met up with her?" she asks. Mr. LeBrecque's corralling everyone into the next room. We hang toward the back.

"That's my guess." I pull up Ruby's photo from last night, explaining how I texted it to myself from her laptop. "Look, Luxembourg Palace is right over there." I zoom in on Google Maps. "I bet Val wanted to sneak onto the grounds. Ruby probably found out and went after her."

Aliyah tugs at her lower lip. "But why would Selena go with them?"

"That, I don't know. Liv going is bizarre, too. And I don't know why Ruby didn't tell me about it, either—"

Mr. LeBrecque's cell trills.

He answers and throws Mrs. Williams an anxious look before slipping into the hall. Is that Capitaine Debois? Aliyah and I exchange a glance and try to follow.

"Sean. Aliyah." Mrs. Williams waves us back. "Stay with the group, please."

My jaw tightens, but I'm not one to disobey. Aliyah follows me back to the class, and we both keep a close eye on the door. When Mr. LeBrecque reappears, we corner him immediately.

"Well, sir?" I ask. "Was that the police?"

He hesitates.

"What'd they say?" Aliyah prods.

"Please, sir," I say, "we're really worried."

He sighs. "They looked into that photo you found."

"And?"

"They searched CCTV footage in that area from that time," he says, "and they found them on there." I inhale sharply, and Aliyah touches her fingers to her lips. "Apparently Ruby, Selena, and Olivia met Val outside a café, and there was someone else, too."

Shock locks my jaw.

"They haven't been able to identify him yet." *Him.*

"What did he look like?" Aliyah asks. "How old—"

Mr. LeBrecque shakes his head. "She didn't tell me anything about him."

"Did they go in the café?"

"No. They went down the street, and there are only so many camera angles, but the police haven't been able to find footage of the girls *leaving* that street."

That doesn't sound good. "Are they searching it now?" I ask.

"I don't know. The capitaine seemed to think they might've gotten into that man's car—"

"Dorian?" Mrs. Williams calls, noticing Mr. LeBrecque has returned.

Mr. LeBrecque claps a hand on my shoulder. "Let's not get ahead of ourselves, hmm? The police are on it, and you've helped a lot already." With that, he strides to Mrs. Williams to fill her in. Alex, Kyle, and Lisa give Aliyah questioning looks, and she goes over to give her friends a recap. The rest of our class joins the huddle to listen, finally interested.

Mrs. Williams claps her hands as Mr. LeBrecque rushes off again, probably to call our school district and the missing girls' parents. "Don't you worry," she says. "I'm sure the girls are fine. Let's focus on all this incredible art, okay?"

She leads us into the next gallery, trying her best to keep us busy, but now everyone's fully distracted.

About damn time.

Their whispers hiss through the old palace halls like snakes.

"—why would they meet some rando—"

"—talked to Liv yesterday; she didn't mention anything—"

"—who do you think that dude was?"

I'm lost in my own thoughts. Time is ticking—I once read that your chances of finding a missing person drop significantly after seventy-two hours. We're already eighteen hours deep.

As we explore the museum, an antsy, helpless feeling gnaws at my gut, making me want to scramble out of my own skin. I can't stand around and stare at art. Ruby needs me.

Mrs. Williams leads us into the museum's basement, a cool, dimly lit space housing the remains of the medieval Louvre castle. I consider the green SORTIE sign indicating the nearest exit beside a partially collapsed stone wall. Pop will straight-up murder me if I eschew my teachers' orders to stay with the class.

But Ruby's amber eyes flash through my mind, and I forget how to breathe.

If I'm overreacting, fine—Ruby and the others will eventually come home, and everything will be okay. But if I never see her again, I'll look back at this exact moment and regret doing nothing.

Mrs. Williams has her back to us, directing everyone's attention to an archway from the original fortress. "Looks kinda like Roman ruins, right? Well, fun fact: some of this stone was mined from the quarries under the city they turned into ossuaries, like the Romans did . . ."

Now's my chance.

I start down the dimly lit hall.

Someone grabs my coat sleeve. Aliyah. "Where're you going?"

"To look for them," I whisper.

"Where?"

"Where they went missing."

"What d'you think you'll be able to do? It's not like he's hiding them behind a bush or something."

"Obviously."

"Well, you won't be able to get into any of the buildings."

"I know. But I have to do *something*." My voice comes out low and raspy.

Her expression softens. "There has to be another way to help."

I don't have time for this. I have to take advantage of our teachers being distracted. Without letting Aliyah get another word in edgewise, I turn on my heel and stalk out alone.

20
Ruby

"Where's all this water coming from?" I ask. We've been plodding down a long corridor through ankle-deep floodwater that's been creeping higher up our calves, forcing us to slow our pace. The masked menaces haven't caught up to us, which is strangely unsettling considering our loud sloshing and junction-free route. We're not exactly hard to find.

"It's still Monday, right?" says Olivia.

"What, is that when someone waters the plants down here?" Val asks beside me, her lamp off to conserve power.

"There was supposed to be a huge storm starting early Monday morning."

Oh right. My weather app had forecasted a 10 percent chance of rain until yesterday, when it shot up to 100 percent. I groaned about it to Sean at dinner, saying I hoped the storm would pass before our Versailles trip on Wednesday so we could search the grounds for Hameau de la Reine, a tucked-away hamlet where Marie Antoinette used to take refuge from court—perfect fodder for Ruby's Hidden

Gems. He then plunged his fingertips into his water, dribbled some onto my hand, and pretended to type on his phone, *Melting absent. Subject remains solid.*

"So it's been raining all day," says Julien.

"Pouring, probably," says Olivia. "The Seine might've flooded again."

"These lower galleries flood even when the Seine doesn't. It's been happening more and more lately—but look, we're in luck." He speeds to an intersecting stairwell ahead.

"Does it lead to the upper gallery?" Val asks hopefully.

"I don't know. Careful, it's steep and slippery."

He's not kidding; each tall, rough-hewn step juts out at a slanted angle. When he reaches the top, he crunches on something and freezes.

"Whoa," Val exclaims. I hurry up beside her, but Julien sticks out his arm, blocking me. It's a dead end, anyway—another alcove. Actually, *bone pit* would be more accurate. I can't tell how deep it goes, but mounds of them cover the ground like a macabre ball pit at a carnival, and all four walls are rows of glaring skulls. Two thrones like the one this morning stand side by side against the far wall as though erected for a king and queen. The air is stale and musty, but at least it doesn't reek.

I'm already getting numb to the sight of so much death, but Julien wavers on his feet, making his lamplight bow across the bones. I worry he might faint, but then he turns to squeeze past us, back out into the flooded tunnel, and leans with his palms flat against the opposite wall, dipping his head between his arms as he sucks in air like he's trying not to be sick.

I follow him. "Are you okay?"

He nods. The lamp sways gently, dangling between his thumb and forefinger.

"Did those masked people make these thrones?" Selena asks.

He shuts his eyes, shaking his head. "I don't know."

"That other throne smelled like a nest of dead mice," I say.

"I don't know what those smells are." Julien pushes himself off the wall and continues down the corridor.

"Wait, *smells*?" I jog to catch up, splashing water up my jeans. "You've smelled that stink of death down here before?"

"Yes. But there's never a body. Not until that man before. Now I don't know what to think."

Selena sloshes after us in her socked feet. "What *did* you think?"

He rubs his lips together, then sighs, exasperated, and says without slowing, "For a while, we thought another group of cataphiles was playing pranks. They'd leave odd messages, make strange noises, pop up with those masks and disappear, like jump scares in a movie. We even started to think up pranks to play in return. But then—that man's video. The smells. Now a body? This is no prank."

"Has anyone reported this to the police?" Selena asks.

"And risk them adding security? Sealing more entrances?"

I raise a brow. "Better than risk getting hacked to death by masked sadists."

"You don't understand," he says, low and husky. "Coming down here . . . it's like a drug. An addiction. The rush of exploring the unknown, of finding rooms nobody has entered in centuries—there's nothing else like it. It's been bad enough avoiding this gallery."

I shoot him a confused look.

He scrubs a hand along his stubbled jaw. "This is where they've been spotted the most."

Ne pas s'approacher. Stay away.

Dread curdles my stomach like sour milk. It was a warning after all.

"You said it's been flooding down here more lately, right?" says Olivia, sounding winded.

"Yes," says Julien.

"I wonder if it's something like a turf war. If they *are* a cult—"

"They're not," he insists. "People can be evil without being organized about it."

"Okay, fair. But *clearly* they're separate from the cataphiles. Isolated groups of any sort can get fanatical over time. If they feel like they're losing their home base because of all this flooding and have no choice but to move up to the higher galleries, they might feel like you're encroaching on their territory."

"It's not *theirs*," he says. "It's not anyone's. It belongs to no one—to *Paris*."

"Yeah, but they might not think that."

"You don't think they live down here, do you?" I ask Olivia.

She shrugs. "I don't know. It's just a theory. But it sounds like things have escalated. They tried to scare the cataphiles away, and when pranks didn't work, they turned violent—"

"Hang on." Julien halts and raises his lantern, better illuminating how the ceiling slants down ahead. "Stairs here. The water's about to get deeper."

"How much deeper?" I ask through chattering teeth.

"I can't tell. Wait here." He slowly descends, carefully toeing each step down until the water rises to his knees, then stills and shines the flashlight down, sweeping it forward until he says, "There's the end. Short flight, at least. It will come up to my stomach. Higher on you."

"How do we know it won't get even deeper?" I ask.

He peers ahead, then turns back to us and says grimly, "We don't."

A sudden realization makes me gasp. "That's why they're not chasing us. They know it's too flooded ahead. They know we'll have to turn back." This corridor has been one long stretch since the den of death. There's been nowhere else to turn. No other route to try. Turning back means facing them.

"We can't go back," Val says.

"Maybe they won't hurt us," says Selena. "If we explain we're lost and *want* to leave, maybe they'll let us go."

"Do you think we could reason with them?" Val asks Julien.

"I'd rather not risk it," he says.

"Oh, so you'd rather risk *drowning*?" I say.

"Actually," says Olivia, "I think Julien's right. If they're really killing people, they probably want to hurt us to make an example of us. Letting us go would make them an empty threat to the cataphiles—"

"Okay, okay. But what do we do with all our stuff?" I say, thinking of my camera.

"And the food," says Selena.

Olivia grips her jacket tight around her abdomen. "I'm more worried about getting hypothermia. It's bad enough our pants and shoes are soaked. If the rest of our clothes get wet, and we have no way to dry off, no way to start a fire, and we're still stuck down here . . . that's *bad*."

"How bad?" I ask.

"I mean, you can die of hypothermia. This water's cold enough."

"But you just said those freaks might hurt us if we go back."

"There's not exactly a good option here," says Olivia.

"Great," Val huffs. "So which is less bad?"

We all look to Julien to decide. He's the one who has the best idea of how big a threat those masked sadists really are.

He swings his backpack around to his chest, not even hesitating. "This is waterproof. Put anything in here you don't want to get wet."

We scramble to rejigger our belongings. The technology gets priority, so we seal my camera and all the phones (even though three have bitten the dust) in the Tupperware that contained the cheese; wrap the

Tupperware, cheese, and other food in Olivia's Monoprix bag; then stuff the bundle into Julien's backpack.

The flashlights go in my purse since Julien says they're waterproof. So are the lamps, supposedly. I'm worried that's not true. Once we lose all our light sources, we'll reach our final stage of utterly screwed.

"I'm running out of room," Julien says, jamming Val's jacket into his pack.

"I don't know if my bag's waterproof," says Val, "but it zips, at least." Unlike Olivia's tote, which is huge but only snaps shut with a magnet. Useless. Val holds hers wide open.

I feel the nylon lining inside. "That might work—" Something familiar inside catches my eye, and I grab it. "My wallet!"

She frowns. "No, that's *my* wallet—"

I flip it open and show her my driver's license.

"Oh." She rifles through her purse, befuddled, then picks out another wallet. "Weird."

"How'd you have both?"

Val shrugs. "I was rushing on my way out; I was afraid you'd come in and stop me. Must've grabbed yours by mistake." Her eyes shine with tears. "Now I wish you did stop me." She turns away, like she doesn't want me to see her cry. I've never seen her cry before.

As I wriggle out of my jeans and wring out the bottoms before shoving them in Val's purse, Olivia unbuttons her sweater, eyeing Julien bashfully, cheeks pink. I, on the other hand, am already disrobed, my dignity first to get chucked overboard as our chances of survival sink. "Pretend we're in our bathing suits," I whisper, scooping my waves into a high ponytail. She gets even redder.

We quickly trudge on. I suck in a sharp breath as we descend the stairs and water rises to my abdomen, and my steps soon get stiff and jerky from how cold it is.

I can't even imagine how comical we'd look to anyone who runs into us now. Julien's wearing nothing but boxers and boots, leading the way with his lamp and overstuffed backpack, followed by four girls in bras and undies. We all keep our shoes on (except Selena) since they can't fit into our bags and are too cumbersome to carry; we need our hands free to break our fall if we take a bad step on slippery stone in the murky water.

If it means not freezing to death, I'll gladly be a laughingstock.

As it is, I can't stop shivering from the cold, from anxiety, from fear, and my head hurts from how hard I'm clenching my teeth to keep them from chattering.

Soon after the water reaches my bra's underwire, the corridor curves and spills into a tear-shaped cavern, widening at the far end where the jagged ceiling slopes like a shallow dome until it intersects with the water's surface. No tunnels branch out from here. Julien pans his flashlight beam across the sunken pond, making the water glitter.

My stomach drops, and I curse. "We're trapped."

"Not exactly," says Julien.

"*Yes* exactly." I brandish my arms at the zero pathways available to us.

"No. I know where we are."

We all gasp.

He nods. "I've been swimming here with my friends before. We call this place basin de serpent. It's a pool shaped like a snake."

"Looks more like a poop emoji to me," says Val. I agree. What might've been an underground oasis to a bunch of cataphiles is now a prison of inky blackness.

"Well, the bend is submerged now, yes?" He raises his lamp higher, but it's so dark under the surface I can't see anything. "We're at the tail, and it curves to its head." He draws an *S* in the air. "That's where the ladder is. Like a fang. And I know the way out from there."

"Are you sure?" Olivia asks. "I don't see an opening."

"Flashlight?" Julien shows me his palm. I hand him one, and he switches it on and points it down into the water, revealing a sudden drop-off ahead of us. "See? That's usually the edge." He raises the beam to the far wall, where I now see a submerged void darker than the surrounding stone. "There. That's the opening. It goes pretty deep, even when it's not flooded. But it's a moot point. We have to go back."

"What? *Why?*" I demand.

Julien motions to Val. "She can't swim."

My heart deflates. That's right. Dammit.

"Yes I can," Val says.

"You said yourself you've never swam before," says Julien.

"I said I never *have*, not that I never *could*. Don't all mammals have some innate ability to swim?"

Olivia clamps her lips, clearly stopping herself from correcting her. But if we try to swim for it, ignorance won't be bliss. It'll be a death sentence.

"You're thinking of dogs," I say. Val looks baffled.

"Well, some dogs," says Olivia. "Lots of mammals can instinctively swim, but humans aren't one of them. It's a learned skill for us. And you'll have to hold your breath the whole time. Right?" she asks Julien.

"Unless you'd like to drown, yes," he says.

Val's eyes widen, but she insists, "Whatever. I can do it."

Julien grips the lower half of his face, considering her. I bet he wishes he never met her at all. He never would've gotten lost if he hadn't left the party to meet her. If Selena hadn't rushed down that well and fallen. If I hadn't raced ahead to find her.

But we did this together, and now we're in this together.

"Can the rest of you swim?" Julien asks.

"We're on our swim team," Selena motions between the two of us. Well, I *used* to be on the team. But the technicality doesn't matter; Val's inability to swim is a nonstarter.

"What about you?" he asks Olivia.

She nods. "I swim at my grandma's lake house—"

"Wait," I interrupt. "We're not doing this."

"Yes we are," says Val.

I stare across this death trap, fear roiling in my gut. No matter how angry I am that she went behind my back to hook Sean up with someone else, I can't lose her. I *can't.*

"I know you're being brave," I say to her. "You're always so brave. But that doesn't mean you'll magically know how to swim. This isn't a straight shot across a well-lit pool. You'll have to hold your breath in almost complete darkness for—how long, exactly?" I ask Julien.

"I don't know," he says. "I can check it out first and see."

My lower lip trembles. Even if it's not far, there's an enormous chance she'll panic and choke. If that happens, I'll never forgive myself.

Julien doesn't wait for us to reach a consensus—he clips his lamp to his backpack, trudges ahead, and pushes off the shelf to swim with long, graceful breaststrokes across the cavern, then flattens a palm against the ceiling where it intersects the water and spins to face us. I squint against his flashlight beam.

"If I don't come back in ten minutes," he says, "*go back.* Tell them you got lost; it's the only reason you're still down here. Don't mention me. Deny ever meeting me. Beg for their mercy."

Val curses. I nod, letting out a shaky breath.

His gaze settles on each of us in turn. "I'm so sorry." I can't make out his expression, but anguish drips from his voice. "I'm so fucking sorry."

It's the first time he's apologized to us.

He turns back and takes a deep breath, then sucks in one last gulp of air and dips under the surface. Val switches on the other lamp, letting it bob in the water in front of her, and we watch the glow from his lights dim as his dark form recedes.

I keep count in my head since Julien's the only one with a watch. *Nine. Ten. Eleven.*

Without him, the cavern seems darker, creepier, shadows stretching toward us like elongated fingers. Val checks an invisible watch on her wrist. "Should we take bets?"

"Yeah," says Selena. "I bet you're the one who bets he drowns."

Val scowls. "I meant how long he takes to get back—"

I hush them. "I'm timing him."

Twenty seconds. Twenty-one. Twenty-two.

Olivia's cheeks puff out like she's practicing. All is silent except for the sound of water gently lapping against the stone walls until Val notices my lips moving and starts counting aloud with me.

"Thirty-eight. Thirty-nine. Forty—"

The underwater glow is already getting brighter. Julien's coming back. A moment later, he surfaces.

"That was fast," says Val. He replies in coughs and sputters as he swims to the nearest purchase to stand, clutching his scalp.

"What happened?" I ask.

"I thought—" He coughs again. "I thought I saw a break in the surface, but it was a boulder or something. I hit my head."

"Do you think you were close?" Selena asks.

"I don't know. I panicked and turned around."

"What now?" Val asks.

"I'll try again." He rubs his crown. "All right. Take two." He swims back out, and after several deep breaths he plunges underwater, leaving ripples in his wake. They expand like the shock waves of an atomic bomb, and I shudder violently as they disperse at my chest.

"How long was he under before?" Selena asks.

"Just under a minute." I restart my count.

"That means there's nothing by the thirty second mark," says Olivia.

"We're going to get stabbed to death, aren't we?" says Val.

Nobody answers.

The seconds wear on even longer than before, and this time Julien's light disappears entirely, the black void enveloping him.

Ninety seconds. Ninety-one. Ninety-two.

"How long can someone hold their breath?" Val asks.

"The world record's twenty-four minutes and thirty-seven seconds," says Olivia.

"I don't mean the world record, obviously. How long can a *normal* person hold their breath?"

"Oh," says Olivia. "Uh . . ."

"A minute or two," says Selena. "Some people can stretch it to three minutes, sometimes more."

"Yeah, with training," I say, trying to maintain my count. I haven't done the breathing exercises Coach Ventura taught us since I quit the swim team.

"And that's if you stay still," says Olivia. "Exerting energy makes you use oxygen faster."

One-seventy-nine. One-eighty.

"He just passed three minutes," I say.

"So either he got there . . ." Selena trails off.

Or he drowned.

Focusing on counting isn't keeping the panic at bay. It surges through my veins and shakes me to the core as the implication of losing Julien becomes all too real and far too overwhelming.

But another possibility slams into me like a tidal wave. "He took his backpack."

"So?" Val asks.

"Why would he bring it? Wouldn't that make the swim harder? And the way he apologized like that . . ." My stomach turns, and I clutch my neck as bile rises in my throat.

Selena gasps as she follows my train of thought. "No way."

I assumed he meant he was sorry for everything that's happened so far, not for what he was *about* to do.

Val starts laughing, cold and bitter. "That prick."

Yeah.

Maybe Julien just drowned.

Or maybe he made it to the other side and doesn't want to risk a return trip.

Maybe he never planned to come back for us at all.

21
Ruby

"Eight minutes." I stare into the depths where Julien disappeared like if I stare hard enough, he'll burst out with a great splash. But there's still no sign of him.

I bite back a sob.

If he did drown, I'll hate myself for standing here mistrusting him while he experienced the most horrific pain of his life as his lungs took in all that water, knowing we'll soon succumb to the same fate or worse.

If he didn't, he's a spineless coward who abandoned us.

Either outcome massively sucks.

"What do we do?" I croak, not bothering to count anymore.

"He said to wait ten minutes," says Olivia. She's been clasping her hands under her chin, her lips moving like she's praying.

"So he could get a head start," says Val. "Wonderful."

I shiver so hard, more concentric rings widen around me and collide with the others.

After another minute or so, Selena says, "The water's rising."

"Don't be dramatic," says Val.

"It is, though," says Olivia. "I've been watching over there." She points at graffiti to our right, only the top visible—a wide, red upside down *U*. I take a flashlight from my purse and point it into the water. It's another painted skull, the water's refraction warping its eye sockets.

Selena prods my arm. "We *have* to go." She sounds more determined than panicked.

I return my gaze to the spot where Julien disappeared, tears burning my eyes.

We'll never survive without him. Even if we don't run into those masked people, we don't know the way out. Julien took all our food, our phones, most of our clothes except for what's bulging in my and Val's purses, two flashlights, and a lamp that'll probably die soon. We'll never find a way out before succumbing to thirst or hunger.

I raise a shaky fist to my lips, trying not to break. *He left us.* I don't even know why I'm surprised. Everyone always leaves me, one way or another. The person who brought me into this world left moments later. Anyone I trust betrays me. Any mistake I make, they give up on me. Now the person who promised me adventure took us deep into a dark abyss and left us to rot.

Worst of all, I betrayed myself. I snuck out to get Val because I had a feeling she was in danger. I knew to walk away from Julien. I knew this was too dangerous. And I came down here *anyway*. I abandoned my own good judgment because I wanted views for my channel. I wish I could take it back, take it all back, but I can't, and now we're trapped with nothing but death ahead or behind us, and there's no way out of it. A fierce helplessness claws at my insides, ravaging me until I can't contain it anymore, and I let out a harrowing shriek.

"I'm sorry." I sob as Val wraps her arms around me and tears streak down Olivia's cheeks. "I'm so, so sorry." I should've hauled Val to the

Métro by her ankles if I had to. I knew something bad would happen. I knew, I knew, I *knew*.

"Are you kidding?" says Val. "This isn't your fault."

Over her shoulder, I see Selena touch her trembling fingers to her lips like she doesn't know what to say.

"I knew better," I say. "I literally *knew* better, and I let him talk me into this anyway . . ." Tears overwhelm me, choking off my words, and it feels like a vise is squeezing my chest.

Olivia sloshes over and hugs us both, and Selena joins our embrace, too. The four of us cling together, terror and compassion trumping any blame or grudges.

A gentle glow appears underwater.

I gasp. "Look!"

We break apart and watch the light grow brighter and brighter, until Julien emerges with a splash, sputtering and hacking.

He checks his watch with a grunt, then paddles over.

I squelch the urge to lunge at him, wanting to hug him and punch him in the face all at once, and instead back up to give him space to stand beside us. "Are you okay?"

"Yeah," he says between gasping breaths, then rubs his eyes and blinks rapidly. "Okay, so . . . I have good news . . . and bad news."

"Good news first," says Val.

"The good news is I was right—" He coughs again. "The ladder's where I remembered. It's secure, I checked, and the tunnel it leads to is dry." He's not wearing his backpack. He must've left it and the lamp behind.

"And you know the way from there?" I ask.

He nods. "I know the way from there." Val pumps her fist. But relief only briefly flutters my heart. He doesn't seem happy.

"And the bad news?" Olivia asks with trepidation.

"I timed it. You'll have to hold your breath for a minute and thirty seconds, give or take."

My stomach sinks, and I shoot Val a look as her smile disintegrates. That's a long time, even for me and Selena. For someone like Val, who doesn't know how to swim? Forget it.

She mutters a curse, knowing it.

"I wish we had rope or something," I say. If we did, Julien could secure one end to the ladder so the less experienced swimmers could pull themselves through the bend.

Julien wipes his face. "I know—"

Voices echo behind us. Men's voices.

"No freakin' way," Val says hoarsely as Olivia blanches.

They followed us after all.

"We have to go," Julien whispers as he switches off the lamp bobbing in the water.

Selena grips Julien's sleeve. "You go first." She says it low and calm, her expression hardened. Determined. "Get to the other side as fast as you can and point the flashlight at us so we have something to aim for."

He nods, but motions to Val. "I should help her—"

"I've got her. *Go.*"

Selena speaks with such authority, Julien raises a brow, but follows her orders, throwing Val an uneasy look before threading his arm through the lamp's handle and paddling back across the pool.

"Give me your purse," Selena whispers to Val.

Val scrunches her nose, confused, but hands it over. Selena loops it over her own body, under her arms, then twists the strap and loops it over herself once more. Then she shimmies it down and around so the purse hangs from her lower back. Across the cavern, Julien flattens a palm against the ceiling, takes a couple of deep breaths, and pushes himself under.

"Hold on to this the whole time." Selena passes Val the purse. "This way, my hands will be free to swim. All you have to do is kick."

My breath hitches. I never would've thought of that.

"You'll pull me the whole way?" Val asks. "Won't you kick *me*?"

"I'll be careful," says Selena. Taking on the burden of another person—someone she doesn't even like—is a massive risk to her own life. But she's not even hesitating.

"Maybe I should do this," I say, tightening my ponytail. "Your arm—"

"I'm the stronger swimmer," says Selena. "There's no time to debate this."

Val's gaping at Julien's fading light, visibly shivering.

Selena grips her shoulders. "Listen to me. Before you hold your breath, take a deep breath in, and exhale everything. *Really* push out any CO_2 buildup; that's what makes holding your breath painful. Then take a deep breath in, as deep as you can manage, and hold it."

"Okay." Val's not cracking jokes for once. She takes off her glasses and slips them into her purse, her expression as fierce and determined as Selena's. Olivia flaps her hands, hyping herself up, and my heart's pounding like it's trying to murder my lungs before this water can.

"You got this," I say to Val, and to Selena, "May the force be with you." We always used to say that before heading into scary situations like a roller coaster or a crowded cafeteria.

"May the force be with you," she says back, a ghost of a smile on her lips.

This better not be the last time I see them alive.

As they dog-paddle across the cavern, Val struggles to keep her head above water, and when her chin dips under, she takes in a mouthful, then spits and flails. "Oh God—" she sputters. "I-I don't got this!"

Selena swims closer. "You *do*. Just hold on—"

"I don't want to die." Val paddles frantically, wasting energy.

The splashing behind us is getting louder.

I push off the underwater ledge and swim to Val. "Look at me." I clasp her shaking shoulder with my free hand. "You're not going to die. You're a badass bitch. And once we get through this, we'll be one step closer to home." Olivia swims up beside me, nodding her encouragement. "We're in this together. And we'll be right behind you."

"Promise?" says Val.

"I *promise*."

"Okay, I— Okay. Let's go." Val hurls one last frantic look at me. I'm probably a blur without her glasses on. "Love you."

"Love you, too," I say.

Then they're gone.

"You next." I tell Olivia, wiggling my flashlight. "I'll light the way behind you."

"Not too close." She glances behind us. "Don't want to kick you—" Her purse strap slips off her shoulder, and she flounders to secure it.

"Maybe leave that."

"No, I got it," she says once it's back in place, then takes a deep breath and disappears.

Just like that, I'm alone. But if I don't move fast, I won't be for long.

22
Sean

I pull up my hood as I climb the steps from the Luxembourg Métro stop. As dusk settles on Paris, the rain that drenched our class while we waited in line for the Louvre has turned into a downright deluge.

The street where Ruby went missing is only a seven-minute walk away, but I double-check Google Maps after a couple of blocks, wishing I brought an umbrella so I wouldn't have to wipe my screen every two seconds. By the time I get there, I'm soaked to the bone. It barely phases me—Dad had me start taking ice showers each morning a couple years back like he did as a Navy SEAL to keep my body at peak performance. At first it was torture, but I quickly got used to it. Now I'm glad for it.

Strips of yellow police tape cordon off the street, and two cop cars are parked in front of the café—probably the one CCTV captured the girls next to—its red awning stretching around the corner. The chairs inside are piled atop the tables. Maybe it's been closed for a while, or it's closed on Mondays.

I duck under the police tape and head down the street, then start filming so I won't have to etch it all to memory, trying to maintain a stable pan like Ruby does so the footage will be crisp. Any detail might be important—

My phone rings.

Dammit. It's my father.

Steeling myself, I answer. "Hey, Pop."

"Why haven't you picked up?" Some greeting. I must've missed his calls on the Métro.

"I just did."

"Watch your tone."

"Sorry, sir—"

"Never mind. Care to explain why your mother had to hear from a *phone chain* that four of your classmates are missing?"

Mom's voice screeches in the background. "Tell him he's coming home tomorrow. I'm looking at flights now." My stomach drops.

"Ginny, calm down," says Pop. "Sean, tell me what happened."

I scramble under the nearest doorframe to escape the rain and fill him in. He listens patiently. Even though he's an entire ocean away, knowing he's on the other end of the line is reassuring. He retired from the navy years ago to work in the private sector and is now a VP at a tech company developing robotics. As an intimidating hard-ass, he's never exactly been a comforting presence, but growing up I always thought he could fix any problem. I'm not sure why I didn't call him right away. I guess I figured, what could he possibly do from there?

"Has the US Embassy been alerted?" he asks when I finish blabbering.

"I'm not sure. I think Mr. LeBrecque was in touch with the school administration and the girls' parents."

"All right. I'm going to make some calls."

"Thanks, Pop."

"There's an Air France flight at eleven tomorrow," I hear Mom say.

"No," I say. "Pop, I'm not leaving Ruby."

"Ruby isn't *with* you," he says. "There's nothing you can do. The police already questioned you without a lawyer present—you need to get the hell out of there and back on US soil."

"But they know I didn't do anything. I told you, the footage showed—"

"You'll do as you're told."

That's how he always signals the end of an argument. Don't want to go to bed at 9 p.m.? *You'll do as you're told.* Don't want to quit the hockey team to join JROTC? *You'll do as you're told.* Don't want to apply to West Point? *You'll do as you're told.*

And I always do.

But this time is different. This time, it's not about *me.*

"I'm sorry, Pop. Thanks for making those calls, but I'm not running away. I won't leave her here."

I hang up.

Oh man. I really did that. I hold the phone to my lips, inhaling deeply. I've never ignored his orders before. But I have to do this. I have to take control and do whatever it takes to help find Ruby.

Once I get a grip, I trek down the street and film an ancient-looking cobblestone wall as fat, cold raindrops assault me. The street ends at the next perpendicular one, so I cross it and head back, trying to capture all the details: the parked row of compact cars, the Gothic apartment blocks with barred windows rising six stories high, the graffiti scrawled over—oh, damn. The graffiti from Ruby's—

"Oof." I trip over something and nearly bite it, then spin to glare at the offending object. A drainage grate. I quickly pan over it, then rush down the block to the graffiti.

Yep, this is it. Ruby photographed this colorful toad sitting on an upturned bucket. I press my palm to it, as though Ruby's recent presence might've imprinted some clue I could siphon from the cement.

But that's ridiculous.

Being here is ridiculous.

Aliyah was right. There must be dozens of apartments on this street. I can't search them. I'm not even sure the cops will be allowed to search them. But if Ruby's not here, if that rando drove her off to God-knows-where . . .

I never cry, but my throat burns with the threat of tears. I've never felt so helpless before.

"Sean."

I turn to see Capitaine Debois speed walking toward me, a large black umbrella shadowing her face. Busted.

"What are you doing here?" she asks.

I raise my chin. "Have you found anything?"

"What are you *doing* here?" she repeats.

"I didn't think you were looking . . ." I hesitate, then ball my hands into fists. "They're still gone, and I—"

"—thought you could do a better job than us?"

I shift uncomfortably. "You thought they ran away."

"And I still think that may be."

Heat ripples through my veins. "No. There's no way—"

"But we're looking into it, yes? We looked into that photo you found. We found the girls on CCTV. We're here, sweeping the area."

As she tallies off all they've done today, it's clear they aren't simply brushing this off. I stuff my hands in my pockets, embarrassed. "I had to do something."

She scoffs gently. "You Americans are so impulsive; you think the world revolves around you. Do you know how many people go missing in this city every *week*? Many of them in situations you cannot even imagine—" She cuts herself off, sucking on her front teeth. Finally, she shakes her head. "Go back to your hotel, Sean. Have dinner with your friends. Let us do our jobs, yes?"

Before I can protest, she takes me by the elbow and guides me back to the police tape, then lifts a segment and motions for me to go under. I glance back down the street.

"Go," she says. "I'll let your teacher know if there are any updates."

I stoop under the tape and give a small, apologetic wave, and as I head back to the Métro, one word reverberates in my brain.

If.

23

Ruby

I used to think I knew what it feels like to drown.

No matter how the air gets sucked from your lungs, whether you get caught in a riptide, or kicked in the gut, or bombarded by a panic attack, or abandoned by your best friend, I was convinced it all feels the same.

That's how I felt when I read that awful text from Selena: *You can fuck all the way off now.* I hunched over at the sight of those words as my chest compressed and I gasped for air, thinking, *This must be what it feels like to drown*, because in that moment it felt like I was dying.

I'm about to find out if I was right.

Pressure swells in my lungs as I follow Olivia's blurred, frenzied form around the bend. Her movements are clumsy and uncoordinated, arms flailing wildly, legs kicking haphazardly. The flashlight in my grip makes it hard to slice through the water with my usual fluid strokes. I have to kick hard to keep up and regret wearing my purse across my chest. It tugs at me with each paddle like a toddler nagging for attention, but I'm too afraid to slow and take it off.

There's a sudden disturbance in the water in front of Olivia, and my heart thrashes against my rib cage. The blurry mass of bubbles and motion is too far to tell what's happening.

When the disturbance finally settles, it gets darker.

Too dark.

Only my own flashlight illuminates the water now.

I make a high-pitched noise in the back of my throat that peals through my skull, though I'm probably the only one who can hear it. It doesn't seem like Olivia can as she swims under a wide, flat boulder jutting from the ceiling where the tunnel curves. I bet that's where Julien bashed his head.

I follow her, trying not to imagine swimming over a corpse, eyes wide from fright, lips parted from that last watery gasp.

Suddenly a dark blob drops from Olivia's form and sinks to the ground, and her arms splay out like she's trying to catch it.

Her purse. She dropped her purse.

I hope she'll leave it behind and keep going. But she swims to the ground, pawing at the darkness.

Dammit, Liv!

I point my light at the ground to give her a better view. Her bun has come loose, and air bubbles swirl around her billowing hair as she fumbles for the bag, scattering stones beneath her. The strap is looped around her arm again, but she's still clawing at the ground.

A light points toward us again.

I swim down and grab her arm. She resists, panicking, but in my desperation, I kick hard off the ground, propelling us both toward Julien's flashlight.

Now I can see the flat surface where the bend spills into a larger cavern.

I release Olivia, my tortured lungs overruling any instinct to help her. I can do this. I *have* to do this.

I never cared much for competition at swim meets, never was the fastest or most agile, but I always enjoyed swimming. I found serenity in it, the way the crisp water caressed my skin, the way I'd feel weightless as I glided through it with smooth strokes.

But down here, the water's turning on me.

It turns into flames, making my lungs burn and my muscles sear in agony.

I have to keep pushing.

Have to keep fighting.

One more stroke.

One more kick.

One more moment before I cave to that fierce desire to breathe.

Almost . . . there . . .

So close . . .

. . . yet so far.

I kick hard . . . harder . . .

. . . grinding my teeth . . .

. . . clamping my lips . . .

. . . my throat raw with thirst for oxygen . . .

. . . and stretch . . .

. . . stretch . . .

. . . stretch toward that flat plane with my fingertips . . .

I break the surface and suck in greedy gasps of humid air.

Olivia surfaces next to me.

My vision is fuzzy as I paddle toward Julien and the ladder, breathing hard, so hard, queasy and lightheaded, my ears buzzing.

"You made it," he's saying. "You *made* it."

I latch on to a rung and dangle there, spitting and sputtering, then get so giddy with relief I start hysterically laughing even though Olivia's still hacking up a lung. She grabs hold of the rung next to me.

"Ruby!" Selena's poking her head out from the tunnel above. "Are you—hey."

Val shoves her aside to peer down instead, her glasses still off. *Everyone* made it. Everyone's alive. "Oh thank God—"

Olivia's loud coughs cut her off.

"Liv?" I say. "Are you okay—"

She loses her grasp on the rung and falls back into the water.

"Liv!" I cry as Julien dives in after her.

He pulls her back to the ladder, and she grabs for it, clinging on, her breaths wet and wheezing between coughs.

"She must've taken in water," I say to Julien.

"Let's get her up to solid ground," he says. I release the ladder and discover I can stand; there's a ledge here, too, like the cavern we just came from.

Julien hoists himself up on the rung beside Olivia. "I need you to climb," he tells her. She stretches for the next rung, water seeping from her purse, weighing her down.

I nudge her. "Give me that."

She lets it slip from her arm, hacking, and I take it and spill out the water before slinging it onto my shoulder. As she starts to climb, relief spreads through my chest. She's okay. We're going to be okay.

But halfway up, she freezes, coughing wildly, clinging on for dear life. Julien manages to scramble around her up the ladder, and once he reaches the top, he turns and stretches down. "Take my hand." She does, and he hauls her the rest of the way up.

Val's waiting to help me at the top. I clasp her hand and let her pull me over the ledge. "Thanks—oof." I stand on woozy legs, and Val pulls me into a hug. I can feel how hard she's shaking.

"I'm sorry. I'm so sorry."

"Hey, it's okay," I say. "You never could've known any of this would happen—"

"Not just this. All of it." Water's dripping down my shoulder, and I can't tell if they're her tears or water leaking from my ponytail. Maybe both. "I never wanted to hurt you." Oh. She's talking about Sean and Olivia, too. "You're the best friend I've ever made."

I don't know what to say. I don't want to lose her and want to understand her, but this conflict is the last thing on my mind right now.

And I can't say it back. Not when the best friend I've ever made is standing feet away.

My gaze flicks to Selena. She's still breathing hard, her brow knitted, fingers clenched into fists. I pull back from Val. "What's wrong?"

"She's full of it, that's what," says Selena. "She almost killed me."

"What?" I say.

Val scowls, batting at her cheeks like her own tears annoy her. "I *said* I'm sorry. I panicked, okay?"

"You pushed my head underwater," Selena shoots back.

"I was trying to stay afloat and I grabbed on to whatever." That must've been the disturbance I saw ahead, a blurry mass of bubbles and flailing limbs.

"The ladder was *right there*," says Selena. "You could've grabbed on to—"

"Like I said, I couldn't see anything, and I was confused."

"Your eyes were wide open—"

"I can't see without my glasses!"

"Stop cutting me off!"

Olivia's coughs are getting more desperate, more frantic. She keels over, bracing against the wall and clutching her throat. Julien watches, raking his hair back like he has no idea how to help.

As the girls squabble behind me, I approach Olivia. "Maybe you should lie down—"

But she's already on it, lowering herself onto her butt. I kneel beside her.

"What can we do?" Julien asks.

She points at me. At her purse. Then another coughing fit consumes her, and she clasps her chest, trying to suck in air, but her throat makes this awful dry wheezing noise like nothing's getting through.

"She needs her inhaler." I fumble through her purse. "Is it in here?"

Olivia shakes her head, but I fish through it anyway, trying to focus with Selena's and Val's bickering voices slicing my brain like daggers.

"Will you both shut up?" I shout. "Your petty bullshit doesn't matter right now. Don't you see what's happening?"

They quiet. But I still can't find that damn inhaler. I dump the purse's contents onto the ground and riffle through it all with shaking fingers. Nothing. I unzip all the inner compartments, having flashbacks to searching for my missing wallet, which Val had all along. I shake the thought away. "Where is it? When did you last—"

A sharp realization makes me gasp.

"What?" Julien asks.

Olivia dropped her purse underwater. I remember her fumbling at the ground even after she recovered it, stones scattering beneath her.

Those weren't stones.

They were her belongings. Including her inhaler.

"It fell out of her purse."

Olivia's eyes bug as she wheezes desperately, drowning on her own swelling throat.

No. I can't let this happen.

I stand and drop my own purse next to hers, then turn and race back to the ladder.

"Ruby!" Julien calls after me.

"Wait—" says Selena.

But I'm already hitting the water.

24
Ruby

I can't find Olivia's inhaler.

Even after three dives. Everything's so dark and blurry underwater, and I have to keep resurfacing to breathe.

I can't give up.

Masked sadists may be chasing us, and Julien may have brought us here, and Val may have instigated this whole misadventure . . . but I'm the one who grabbed Olivia's sleeve and pulled her into that elevator. I could've left her there, doe-eyed and confused for Mr. LeBrecque to find with her bag of snacks and toothpaste.

And if she dies . . .

No.

That won't happen.

It won't happen because I won't let it.

I sweep my flashlight's beam across the ground for what has to be the twentieth time. She's used her inhaler a couple of times down here. It's bright red, and you'd think that'd make it easier to spot, but underwater visibility isn't like it is in the movies, with those crisp, well-lit night shots of the hero easily locating and yanking their costar from a submerged car in a lake. In real life, without goggles, all I can see is one gigantic dark blur with indistinguishable blobs here and there.

We'd almost reached the ladder when Olivia dropped her purse, so the inhaler can't be far. Or maybe it can. Maybe our frenetic kicks created a current that pushed it farther along the curving pool. I'll have to dive again because my lungs are already on fire. I swim back to the surface and gulp in air.

"Did you find it?" Val yells from atop the ladder. The terror in her voice tells me things have gotten worse.

"Not yet," I sputter. "I'm going again."

"Hurry," says Val.

I don't need telling twice. One deep breath later, I'm back underwater. This time I swim farther and deeper before scanning the ground, so the indistinguishable blobs are bigger indistinguishable blobs, and—

There. A flash of red.

I swim over and scoop it up, then angle my flashlight to examine it and make sure the medicine canister hasn't fallen out of the plastic holder. But there it is, its silver tip gleaming.

I resurface and latch on to the ladder, clutching the inhaler in one fist and the flashlight in the other, and start to climb. As I pass the rung I leapt down from before, someone lets out a tortured sob. Selena.

"Liv, hold on!" I yell, climbing faster. "I found your—"

The flashlight fumbles from my grip.

I reflexively move to catch it, losing purchase on the ladder entirely. Sparks burst through my heels as the flashlight splashes below, and I start to fall—

Someone grabs my wrist.

Julien.

My abdomen careens into a rung, and air whooshes from my lungs.

"I got you," he rasps. Water drips from his dark, shaggy hair, his eyes hard with determination.

I scramble to grab hold of the ladder again, still clutching Olivia's inhaler. My legs tremble wildly, but I get a foothold, breathing hard. "I'm okay." I hold up the inhaler. "Here."

He won't let go of my wrist.

"I'm fine," I say. "Take it."

But his mouth contorts into a frown, and his eyes scrunch like he's holding back tears.

No.

No.

I must fly the rest of the way up the ladder or something, because the next thing I know, I'm hurtling toward the girls. Selena and Val are hunched over Olivia.

"I found it," I cry.

Val holds her flashlight askew, and Olivia's face is obscured in shadow. I uncap the inhaler and shuffle close.

"Ruby," Selena says in a shaky voice, setting a hand on my arm.

I recoil, swatting her off. "I got it. I got her inhaler."

Val adjusts the flashlight, illuminating Olivia's face.

She's so pale she can pass for a porcelain doll, except for her lips, which are a bruised, purplish color, and her eyes—wide, glassy, and bloodshot as hell. I raise her inhaler, but her eyes remained fixed on nothing.

This makes no sense.

She's supposed to be a neurosurgeon like her grandmother. She's supposed to graduate at the top of our class, to go camping with her dad, to tumble down Wikipedia rabbit holes, to win lots of trivia nights. She's supposed to resent Val for leading her on, to meet someone who eagerly kisses her back, to dance with her friends at prom, to feel her stomach sink whenever she spots Harvard's logo. She's supposed to experience joy and anger and love and disappointment and heartbreak and everything in between.

Not this.

Not an immobile heap of bones and flesh.

Not *nothing*.

"Wait," I say. Her face blurs as tears overwhelm me. "I got your inhaler. I *got* it . . ."

Like I can reason air back into her lungs.

This can't be happening. It can't. I found her inhaler. I did the thing. We should be able to save her now.

Val stares at Olivia, her glasses back on, her sallow jaw hanging slack like she's in shock. Sobs consume Selena as she watches my reaction. "Did you try CPR?" I whisper.

"Yeah," she croaks.

"I got her inhaler—" I say again, my voice breaking, my soul breaking.

"It doesn't matter if she can't breathe it in," says Val, a tear slipping down her cheek.

Julien kneels and clasps my shoulder. "I'm sorry. I'm so sorry. But she's gone."

25
Sean

Researching recent missing persons cases in Paris feels like trying to piece together a jigsaw puzzle when half the board's missing.

I've been camped out in the hotel's dining room for hours, too jittery to seek out my usual solitude, though I had to close the curtains so the reporters outside couldn't creep on me.

Yup. Reporters.

Apparently Aliyah posted a TikTok about all this, then quickly deleted it, but too late—the cat's out of the bag. There are only five reporters out there, but still, I got the surprise of my life when they swarmed me. I'd been head down, hood up, lost in thought in the pouring rain and hadn't noticed them clogging the narrow sidewalk under the hotel's awning until it was too late and they were shoving mics in my face.

"Are you with the class from America?"

"Do you know the missing girls?"

"What do you think happened to them?"

I'd frozen, gaping at all those lenses. I hate being on camera, always thinking my arms look scrawny, or I'm slouching all weird, or I'm not packing as much weight as Pop wants me to. It's a total mind fuck. Fortunately Mr. LeBrecque noticed the commotion and came out to save me, then reamed me out in the lobby for ditching our class at the Louvre.

"I know you're worried about Ruby," he said. "We all are. But if you run off like that again, I'll have no choice but to send you home. And this isn't a three-strikes-you're-out situation; this is your *only* warning. Got it?"

An empty threat. I'm eighteen, and if my parents can't force me to come home, neither can he. Still, I grunted, "Yes, sir. It won't happen again."

So I hunkered down to research.

Debois wasn't exaggerating—between forty and seventy-five *thousand* people are reported missing in France every year (and five hundred thousand in the US—I had no idea). Any local anecdotes I've found have been scattered and useless: a girl disappeared outside her school and washed ashore of the Seine, a woman was thought missing until she flew home from a spontaneous tropical getaway, a producer of some urban explorer documentary vanished and only his camera turned up, a boy went missing riding his bike and was found dead in a trunk. On and on it goes, story after story, and nothing Debois wouldn't already have in her database.

I only spot one pattern, or lack thereof: no *groups* have gone missing. There's the rare story about two teens going missing, but four?

Not a thing.

I wish I could crowdsource help on Reddit or something, but I want to heed the detectives' request to keep this off social media. I couldn't live with myself if my actions sent Ruby to her grave.

What the hell was Aliyah thinking?

I glare at her over my laptop screen. She recently came down with her friends and is sitting with them across the room, looking sullen, her bag of M&M's ignored on the table. I pull up her TikTok, but she's gone private. Maybe she left the video up, though. I follow her.

She must see the alert because her eyes dart up and rove the room until they settle on me.

Instead of following me back, she strides over. "Well?"

I guess she didn't notice me till now. "Didn't find anything," I grunt.

She sits next to me. "No shit, Sherlock. You done trying to be Ruby's knight in shining armor?"

"All right. I get it. I shouldn't've gone over there. But what's your deal?" I hold up my phone with her TikTok profile on-screen. "Trying to start a media circus?"

She crosses her arms and sinks back in her seat.

"What did you even say in it?" I ask.

"I—It doesn't matter."

"Oh, c'mon."

She blows air between her lips. "I shared Selena's photo and asked if anyone in Paris has seen her. And that freaking award was in the background." She points at a framed certificate next to the mounted flat-screen boasting the hotel's four-and-a-half-star Tripadvisor average.

"And what, it started blowing up?"

"Yeah. That cop noticed real fast." Her lower lip trembles, then she screws up her face and covers her mouth, trying not to cry. My chest tightens. I can relate to feeling so powerless, to acting rashly because you have to do something, *anything*, to help.

"It probably wouldn't have helped anyway," I try consoling her.

"Exactly," she says hoarsely. "Maybe it *hurt*. What if you're right? What if they *are* in trouble, and that guy kidnapped them or something, and I just totally screwed them over?"

A chill runs down my spine. "What changed your mind?"

"Because of how the cop noticed my TikTok *so fast*. And the way LeBrecque yelled at me to take it down." I glance at him across the room. He's been sitting at a corner table with Mrs. Williams all night, making calls. Aliyah holds a fist to her lips. "God damn it."

I let out a shaky breath. "Maybe they're just being cautious."

"Maybe."

We sit in silence with our fear until Mr. LeBrecque stands and encourages everyone to head upstairs to bed soon.

Aliyah rubs her eyes, then nods toward the teachers. "Bet they won't go upstairs till we do. And I sure could use a drink."

I eye the soda machine. "It's right there."

She gives me a look. "Not that kind of drink."

"We're not allowed, though." Even though the legal drinking age is eighteen in France, and I'm pretty sure Aliyah's eighteen, we're supposed to stick to the rules from home.

"So straight-edged." Aliyah snorts. "I don't wanna get trashed. My stomach's a minefield, anyway; I couldn't even drink much. I just need some help falling asleep so my mind doesn't race all night."

"Oh." Rules are rules, though, and I've always been a stickler for them.

Then again, I broke the rules to sneak away from our field trip and go play cop.

So who the hell am I to judge?

26

Ruby

This wasn't supposed to happen. None of us were supposed to die. No matter how dire our circumstances—the injuries we've racked up, the thirst gnawing our throats, the masked menaces chasing us, the putrid rotting corpse—I assumed we'd ultimately get out of here. All of us.

Maybe that's what happens when you barely survive your own birth. As early as I can remember, people called me a *miracle baby*—like Dad and I hadn't lost my mother in the process. But when you're told over and over that you're a miracle, you start to feel a bit invincible. Like no matter how much you suffer or spiral or feel alone in this world, you'll stick around to face whatever comes next until your inevitable demise at a ripe old age.

But sticking around is never a guarantee.

And there are no such things as miracles.

"Are w-we supposed to close her eyes?" Val asks.

Selena only sobs in reply. Julien bows his head, rubbing his arms for warmth. I don't know what to say. I don't know what's right.

Eventually, Val stretches and brushes her quivering fingers over Olivia's eyes, closing them, then yanks her arm back with a fierce shudder like Olivia's skin shocked her.

I can't stop staring at her lifeless face, can't let go of her cold, limp hand. I wish Val hadn't closed her eyes because that means it's forever. I wish these craggy walls weren't the last thing she ever saw. I wish I never wanted to see the catacombs.

I wish, I wish, I *wish*.

"Now what?" Val asks.

The thought of leaving Olivia alone in this dark tunnel sends a sharp stab of pain through my chest. But we have no choice. We can't carry her all the way out. Water drips from my ponytail down my bare back, making me shiver harder. I'll probably never feel warm again.

"Guys, w-we should—" Val tries.

"Give us a *minute*," Selena grits through chattering teeth.

"But what if they swim—"

"Don't you give a damn about her at all?"

"Of course I do," says Val. "B-but if they catch us anyway, she dies for nothing. We have to keep going f-for *her*."

"Don't pretend like you care."

"How *dare* you—"

"Enough!" I shout, covering my ears. "S-stop picking fights with each other. I can't t-take it anymore." Even as anger burns in my belly, I hunch over, crossing my shivering arms over my chest, cold, so cold.

"I-I'm not the one who keeps picking fights," says Val.

"You've instigated plenty," I say.

Val winces like I've slapped her.

Maybe she deserves it.

"Val's right, though," says Julien. "We have to keep moving." He dumps out his backpack into one big pile. "Hey. It all stayed dry."

Trembling, I pluck my puffer jacket from the heap, unstuff it from its own pocket, shake it out to fluff it, and clutch it to my chest. It's dry except for the tips of the sleeves that didn't escape the splash zone earlier. So is my sweater. *Good thinking, Liv.* A rock lodges in my throat.

As I tug out my ponytail and shake out my hair so it can dry faster, Selena forlornly eyes Olivia's pink jacket. "Should we dress her?"

Val picks up Olivia's leggings, rubbing the waistband gently. "Her clothes won't do her any good now." My stomach churns.

"We can't leave her like this," says Selena.

I pick up Olivia's jacket and hold it out to Selena. "She'd want you to have it. We can put the rest back on her."

Val makes a *tsk* noise as she empties her purse.

Julien sweeps back his sopping hair. "I hate to say it, but Val's right again. Liv's clothes are no use to her anymore." He kneels beside Olivia and wiggles off her faux-sheepskin boots. "You should put these on, too."

Selena clamps her lips but accepts them with a nod.

"Uh—" Julien hesitates "—hang your undergarments from your purse straps or belt loops to dry. I'll go get that flashlight and refill the bottles while you change. Maybe this water's cleaner than what's flooding the tunnels. Where are they?"

I'd stuffed them into my purse when we rejiggered everything, so I dig them out and hand them over. Julien heads back to the ladder.

Val uses Olivia's T-shirt as a towel, but Selena and I can't bring ourselves to—instead we shake our arms out and slap any lingering droplets from our skin with our palms. Selena grimaces as she unties my headband from around her arm, lifts the soaked pad, and inspects the gash underneath.

"How does it look?" I ask. She lowers her arm to show me. It's not bleeding, but the skin around the gash is an angry magenta color. I'm worried it's getting infected. "Do we have anything clean you can cover it with?"

"Here," says Val, rummaging through her purse. "I didn't need that tampon after all."

"Thanks." Selena takes it.

"I got it." I unwrap the tampon, then remove the cotton part from the plastic insert, unroll it into a square, and lay it across Selena's wound. She holds it in place as I secure it with the headband, tying it above her forearm so the knot doesn't put pressure on the wound. It's the best we can do for now. "We'll get you to a hospital in a few hours."

Once I'm back in my clothes, commando and braless, jacket zipped to my chin, my shivering quells a bit. But my toes are numb, puckered prunes, an unsettling shade of purple.

"Is it better to go barefoot?" I ask.

"I wouldn't." Selena peels off her stained socks, exposing raw, angry blisters underneath. They look so much worse than this morning. "I've stepped on way too many jagged things."

"But my feet are so cold."

"Pick your poison, I guess." She wrings out her socks, then puts them back on and squeezes into Olivia's too-small boots. Olivia would know what's best. *I'm not some walking encyclopedia.* I stifle a sob and glance over.

Val's kneeling beside her, filming. With my camera. She must've opened the Tupperware with the electronics.

I leap up. "What are you doing?"

Val looks up but keeps filming. "It's for her parents."

"Oh." A fresh wave of anguish washes over me.

"D'you think someone will come back for her body?" says Selena.

"Yeah," I say. "I'm sure Julien will tell the police how to get here."

"What if he doesn't really know the way out?" she whispers.

"He says he does."

"He says a lot of things."

My stomach turns. If Olivia's parents can't bury her—if they can't visit her to grieve—this will be even more painful. I think of Dad, of how when I was little, the morning after one of his ghoulish screams, I found him hunched over a memory box. He noticed me standing there and beckoned me over to show me his photos and keepsakes, including a lock of my mother's golden hair. It was soft and fine, maybe a shade lighter than mine, and almost seemed like it could've just been snipped from her head. I thought it was kinda weird, even back then, but maybe it helped him feel close to her, helped keep her memory alive.

Maybe Olivia's parents would appreciate such a token. It's the least I can do. Just in case.

Julien has that switchblade, the one he used to open the wine bottle. I kneel beside his backpack to dig through the front compartment and find the blade under a crumpled sheet of paper and—

"He has spray paint?" I pick up the can of paint and peer back at the ladder. "I didn't know he graffitied."

"Me neither." Selena swipes it. "We could've used this to mark our path."

"I bet he was afraid those masked freaks would track us down," says Val.

"Ah, true." I grab the switchblade instead and kneel beside Olivia, pinch one of her wet curls that's already spiraling, and slice through it. Val films it. I'm too tired to argue.

"What're you doing?" Selena asks.

"It's for her parents, too," I say. "I'm sorry," I whisper to Olivia as I close the knife and slip it into my pocket, then tuck the remaining lock of hair behind her ear and kiss her forehead. "I'm so, so sorry."

Tears burn my eyes as I pinch her curl between two fingers and stand. "Where should I keep it? I don't want to shove it loose into my pocket."

Val empties the Tupperware. "Is this too big?"

"Yeah, it'll go everywhere."

"Use this." Selena hands me a crumpled piece of paper from Julien's backpack. "You can fold it up like the notes we used to pass to each other." That's right—our origami envelopes.

"Hey, Rube, your phone survived," says Val.

"Turn it off," Selena says. "We might need the flashlight later."

"Geez, calm down."

But I'm too busy gaping at the paper, my pulse thundering in my ears. I raise the flashlight over it to get a better look, to make sense of the hand-drawn scrawls.

It's a map.

The map Julien said he left at the party.

He's had it this whole time.

27
Ruby

Something crashes behind me.

I spin to see a water bottle roll across the ground and bump into the wall. The other follows. I rush over as Julien's head crests the ledge and brandish the crumpled map in his face. "You've had this the whole time?"

"What?" His eyes settle on the paper and widen.

"What is that?" Selena asks.

"A *map*," I say. "A map of the freaking catacombs."

Val plucks it from my grip to examine the crooked lines representing intersecting passageways, some sections circled, others labeled with messy scrawl, the ink too blotchy to decipher.

Julien leaps up the remaining rungs and snatches it away. "La vache. Where was this?"

"In your bag," I say. "The outer compartment."

He scans it over, and his panic-stricken expression dissipates. "Merde. This is a different map." He wipes his dripping face and chuckles.

"What do you mean?" I ask.

"It's from another section I went to a few weeks ago, much farther south. Useless to us."

"Oh," says Selena, and Val rolls her eyes. They both turn back to the pile, organizing the last few strewn-about items.

"Not that it makes any difference," Julien mutters. "I'll already never forgive myself . . ." He crumples the map, but it's the way his face crumples that makes me think guilt is murdering him from the inside. I feel terrible for thinking he ditched us while testing the length of the swim. He'd wanted to give us a once-in-a-lifetime adventure in Paris, and what we got instead was a nightmare. He's misguided for sure, but he's no prick.

He presses his fist to his lips with a rattled breath, then gives me a long, watery stare before approaching to cup my face, needling his fingers through my hair. "I'll get the rest of you out of here. Je te le jure." *I swear to you.*

Tears prickle my eyes again. "You better."

He cracks the most imperceptible of smiles.

"Hey, you wanna put pants on?" Val tosses over his muddied cargo pants.

He releases me and shoots her a look, shaking his head, then plods down the corridor, wet feet slapping on limestone, and turns away from us to drop his boxers and pull on his pants. I avert my gaze, cheeks aflame, and busy myself tucking Olivia's lock of hair into the wrapper from Val's packet of tissues we'd used up earlier. Selena gingerly slides on Olivia's coat as though she has sunburn and the motion pains her.

"Are we ready?" Julien asks a minute later, zipping his pack.

I glance at Olivia even though the sight of her only makes this horror more real, and none of this can possibly be real. Leaving her alone down here is unfathomable. But somehow, it has to happen. Somehow, we have to put one foot in front of the other and walk away. And I want to get these first steps over with.

"Yes," I say.

The others nod.

"All right." Julien adjusts his backpack straps. "Let's get you home."

I stare blankly at the cave-in ahead, silent with defeat and exhaustion. Why did I let myself have hope? It seems so foolish now, so obviously foolish.

"No." Julien rushes toward the enormous mound. "This is impossible."

We've been following an expansive corridor dotted with iron sconces and coated in so much graffiti I expected it to bleed into a beating heart of cataphile dens. We've reached a den, all right, but a blockage of dirt and boulders has cut us off from any tunnels ahead, having spilled from a yawning chasm in the ceiling. Skulls and femurs line the walls to our right and left and disappear at a slant as the mound of debris rises and fills the entire back half of the cavern like a tidal wave petrified in stone.

"I'm starting to think there are more dead ends down here than people," Val mutters.

"It's not a dead end." I motion to a narrow corridor branching off to the left.

"But that's not the way," says Julien. "*This* is the way. When the hell did this happen?"

Obviously none of us have an answer.

He clambers up the pile of debris, backsliding on loose stones as he raises his lamp toward the gaping hole overhead. Even if we could reach it, there's nowhere to go.

"So we're lost again," says Selena.

"We're lost again," I say dully.

"Can we stop for a sec anyway?" She plops down on a fallen boulder that had rolled to this side of the cavern, her cheeks drawn, hugging her injured arm to her chest.

So much for thinking we'd get her to a hospital tonight. The last time I asked Julien for the time, it was almost five a.m., and God knows how much longer it'll take now. Val slouches against the one bone-free wall, pressing her forehead into the back of her hand. I lean beside her.

My body feels alien, uncomfortable—my muscles ache from shivering so hard, and my legs are tender from rubbing against my scratchy jeans where they'd soaked through. Silt scrapes my feet with each squelching step, even though I shook out my boots and socks before putting them back on. And I'm thirsty. Lightheaded. All I've had to drink since dinner in Saint-Michel is about one cup of water, not counting the wine—and doesn't wine dehydrate you? A foul taste coats my tongue, my throat's raw, and my stomach rumbles obnoxiously.

We're going to die down here.

The thought streaks through my mind like a lightning bolt, searing my nerves and jolting me from my stupor.

If I die, I'll be leaving Dad all alone. His worst fear come true. I've rolled my eyes at him too much, haven't appreciated him enough, raising me all on his own like he has. All he's ever wanted is to keep me safe.

No. I can't think like this. If I do, I'll come undone. None of us can fall apart. None of us can panic. We have to take this one step at a time. Our lights still work, and it's too soon to thirst to death. We just need to gather our strength.

"We should camp here," I calmly suggest. Julien clambers off the mound, then turns to face it, setting his hands on his hips.

"That's not what I meant," Selena says. "We can't spend another night down here."

"The night's almost over anyway," I say. "If any of us faints or something, that's the worst-case scenario. Let's eat something and rest. Get some energy back. Then we can look for another way out—"

Julien kicks at the debris and lets out this frustrated, strangled cry. It reminds me of how I lost it earlier, back when we thought he deserted us. He clasps his fingers behind his head and swears at the enormous pile, then squats and temples his fingers at his lips, shaking his head, muttering to himself in French.

A worried look passes between Selena and me. He needs to hold it together most of all. We need him to find a way out. Val's brows vanish under her bangs until she averts her gaze and puckers her lips like she's secondhand embarrassed, then preoccupies herself cleaning her glasses with her shirt's hem.

I take a deep breath and go kneel beside Julien. "Hey. You okay?"

He rests his elbows on his knees and chuckles ironically. "I'm not the one you should worry about." Raking back his mussed hair, he swears in French again. "I must have no soul."

"Of course you do. You never *meant* for this to happen."

He tuts.

"I'm serious. Bringing us down here was a mistake, yeah, but there's not a human on this *planet* who hasn't made a mistake. Except newborns. Obviously."

"Not one that killed someone," he says miserably, scrubbing a hand down his face.

"It's not like you held her head underwater."

He casts me a look of disbelief. "How can you be so forgiving?"

I shrug and pick up a stone, running my thumb over its rough surface. "I'm the one who pulled her into that elevator in the first place—" The words stick in my throat. I clear it. "It's as much my fault as it is yours."

"That's not true."

"It is. But lots of other stuff went wrong, too. Her inhaler falling out of her purse. The storm, the flooding. Those people chasing us."

Life's too intricate a web for a single snipped mooring thread to unravel it. Like with Selena. Our friendship ended with an apology too late. After a kiss that never should've happened. After a setup I never should've attempted. After *she* ditched *me* to climb the social ladder. *Snip, snip, snip, snip, kerplunk.*

Julien slumps forward, holding his head. "Trust me. You should hate me."

Desperation squeezes my chest. I need this boy to hold it together. So I can get back to Sean. To Dad. So Selena can get back to Aliyah, to her parents, work for NASA someday. So Val can wreak havoc on the world, swim in the ocean, burn brightly again.

If Julien unravels, we unravel with him.

I set a hand on his knee. "Julien . . . yes, you messed up. So did I. And it's good that you acknowledge it. You're a good person. But right now, we *need* your help. We need you to get us out of here. And I really, really would like to use an actual toilet. So can I ask you to save all this moping for when we're back aboveground? I promise you, when that happens, I'll get you into as much trouble as you think you deserve."

He raises his head, a hint of a gleam in his eye. "Oh? Will you call the police on me?"

I tense. I was mostly kidding, but Mr. LeBrecque must've reported us missing by now. The police must be involved. Whatever consequences Julien will face won't be my call. But it'll be better than dying down here. So I keep my tone light. "Oh yeah. I'll get you arrested so hard."

He chuckles, clasping his hands, and appraises me wistfully. "You know, you remind me so much of my sister."

"Which one?"

"The older one, Chelsea. Olivia reminded me of Francesca—bookish, loves being outside, under the trees. But you? Chelsea. She loves people unconditionally."

"I don't—" I start reflexively, but it'd be weird to say *I don't love people*. That's not even true. It's more that I don't like who I become around other people—uneasy, afraid to say or do the wrong thing and embarrass myself. It's rare to find people I'm truly comfortable with. Selena was one. Val almost is; she doesn't care how awkward I am as long as I'm up for an adventure, but I'm always afraid to disappoint her. "I'm no extrovert," I finally say.

"I mean it like . . . she has this strange, unwavering *faith* in people. Always so curious, always asking questions, but only ever sees the good in them." His lips curve into a frown.

"That's a good thing, right?"

"It's incredibly naïve," he says sharply.

My breath hitches. I'm shocked by his harsh change in tone.

He nods toward the others—Selena on that boulder with her head in her arms, Val watching us with a miserable pout. Her gaze flits away when I glance over. "Those two have betrayed you, yes?"

He's been paying closer attention than I thought. I don't answer.

He takes that as a *yes*. "Yet you haven't confronted them. You're so desperate to see the good in them, you let them hurt you."

"They're not—" I swallow hard. "I hate confrontation," I say honestly.

"Confrontation isn't bad. It can stamp out the bad in someone before it's too late."

I get the sense he's projecting. "Was there someone Chelsea should've confronted?"

He bunches his lips, anguish plain in each line of his crinkled forehead.

"Was it your parents?"

He bows his head, his hands clasped so hard his knuckles shine. "She told me she knew something was wrong. I never saw it. But she did. And she said *nothing*."

My breath catches. "How did they die?"

"I don't want to talk about it."

"I'm sorry," I whisper. Maybe he'd been there. Maybe he'd seen it. I shouldn't have asked.

"Don't apologize," he says. "You didn't kill them."

"I killed mine."

His eyes meet mine, glassy, alarmed. Mine would be waterfalls if I had any tears left.

"My mother," I explain. "She died giving birth to me."

"Mon Dieu." Sympathy etches more lines between his brows. "That's not your fault."

"If I never existed, she'd still be here. My dad would be happy." Dad never once blamed me. If anything, losing her made him love me more, protect me harder, cling to me tighter. I'm the only part of her he has left. But seeing his persistent grief, I can't help but blame myself. That's why I've felt so guilty about the prospect of leaving him to travel with Val. It's my fault he's lonely to begin with. How dare I make him lonelier?

"Bullshit." Julien palms his knees. "What was it you said? Newborns don't make mistakes?"

I rub the back of my neck. "I did say that, didn't I?"

"See? You know. You couldn't help what happened. That's not on you."

I nod, a tear sliding down my cheek after all. He's right. Of course he's right. But I've made other mistakes. Mistakes I want to fix. I can't control how I was brought into this world. But I can control what I do while I'm here.

And I'm still here.

Hopefully my web still has a few mooring threads left.

28
Ruby

We sit in a circle with a lamp in the middle, Val and Selena on either side of me as Julien passes us each a hunk of the baguette and cheese. Selena squeezes her hands through Olivia's tentlike jacket's collar to nibble on hers, hugging her knees to her chest inside.

My tongue feels like a wad of cotton as I munch on stale crust. I put on lip gloss before in an attempt to feel less parched, but all that did was make my lips sticky. I stare longingly at the bottles Julien refilled from the water we swam through.

The water that killed Olivia.

Nobody's touched them.

Val follows my gaze. "Do you want some?"

"I wouldn't risk it," says Selena. "Getting sick down here would be rancid icing on this crap cake."

"I wish we could boil it," I say, rubbing my bare toes. I'd taken my shoes and socks off to dry.

Selena pinches the edge of Olivia's scarf and holds it up to the lamp.

Some light filters through. "We can try filtering the sediment out with this. The real problem's bacteria. For that, with no fire, we'd need to drop in a purification tablet."

"I think it's safe," says Julien. "It's like water from an underground spring, yes?"

Selena sighs. "Your funeral—" She cuts herself off, and her lower lip quivers.

Val squeezes my hand, and I nod, silently agreeing to risk it together. We each grab a bottle. I uncap mine and take a small sip. The murky water tastes stale and reminds me of clay. What else touched this water? I think of those blobs that were Olivia's fallen belongings. Had any bones littered the ground, too? The thought makes me swivel and spit it out.

"That bad?" Selena asks.

"I dunno." I wipe my mouth and ask Val, "What'd you think?"

She smacks her lips, squinting. "Don't love it. Better than nothing, though." She dares another sip and passes the bottle to Julien, who takes a longer swig, then gets up and grabs another flashlight to examine the cave-in again, like he can't believe it's really there.

I clench my teeth, gritting on sand. "Ugh, I'm crunching on something." I gnaw on bread to mask the sensation.

Val holds out Olivia's tube of toothpaste. "Wanna brush your teeth?"

"With what?" I ask. She wiggles her pointer finger.

"You can do like the astronauts do," says Selena. "Swish with water, then swallow it."

"Gross," says Val. "You can eat toothpaste?"

Selena cracks a small smile. "Not a lot, obviously. But a tiny bit's fine."

Val swirls toothpaste over her teeth. "You're not gonna drink your own pee, are you?" Her tone's mocking. "Don't astronauts do that, too?" She takes a sip of water.

"After it's been heavily filtered," Selena says, then smirks. "Technically they're drinking each other's pee, too. And the condensation from their exhaled breath."

Val pauses mid-swish, looking a bit green. Then she grabs another flashlight and dashes down the corridor behind us to use the "bathroom."

Selena chuckles, then sighs and hugs her knees to her chest, resting her chin on her forearm and staring into the distance. She's barely touched her bread and cheese.

My stomach ties in knots. She should've spent the day soaking in artwork in the Louvre with her girlfriend, not stuck down here with us. I nudge her arm. "You okay?"

"Obviously not," she says.

"Sorry, that was a silly question . . . I-I only meant—"

"God, can't I get a *minute* to myself?" she snaps.

I take a sharp breath, remembering the first time she snapped at me like this. January, junior year. I'd been waiting at her locker after final period to head to her house since Dad was working that night, but when she arrived, she said, "Actually, I'm going to Gavel Club today."

"Isn't that for practicing public speaking?" I couldn't think of a worse way to spend the afternoon, but my only other option was taking an extra shift at Dad's restaurant. Even though I was sixteen, he still didn't want me home alone.

"It'll be good for me." She spun her combination lock, tense, avoiding my confounded stare. "I'm tired of my brain going blank during presentations."

"I've never seen you flub a presentation." If anything, that was *my* MO.

She grabbed her hairbrush from the top shelf and ran it through her thick hair. "You're not in all my classes. You don't know."

"You don't need Gavel Club to get better—"

"God, can't I get *one* afternoon to myself?" she snapped.

Just like now.

I edge away to give her space and pick at a chipped fingernail, watching Julien chuck some debris, like he's trying to find a way around the cave-in, but it's hopeless. That's how I felt about Selena after that little tiff. Hopeless. She bonded with Aliyah at Gavel Club, then wheedled into her clique as I spiraled, day by day. I thought she was trying to get close to Tyler, but maybe she did want more friends. I always thought the more you have, the more who can hurt you. *Leave* you. So I clung to her, only her, the one person I was sure would stay forever.

I was too clingy. I didn't see it then. I see it now.

"I'm sorry," she whispers.

"Don't be," I say, smoothing out my rough nail. "If there's anyone who understands needing introvert time, it's me." The tremble in my voice gives me away, though—more over realizing I used to be a clingy nag than her snapping at me.

Her expression softens, and she shifts closer. "So, you and Sean, huh?"

Something flutters deep inside me, and my cheeks warm. "Yeah."

"You never mentioned him . . . before." Her own voice wavers, like she's sad she missed this. That's how I feel about her and Aliyah. I don't know how it happened, when they started hooking up, where they went on their first date. I missed all her firsts.

"I didn't get to know him until school started this year." Now I can barely stop thinking about him. His face is the first thing I see behind my eyes when my alarm blares each morning, the last I imagine before drifting off to sleep. I tell her about the time he made me snort-laugh over bananas at the grocery store, and she chuckles. "I think part of me knew I'd fall for him right then. Weird how you can change your mind about someone in two seconds flat."

"It was gradual with me and Aliyah. I was stuck on"—her smile fades—"well, Tyler. For a while. Even after he asked me for your phone number."

My heart jerks. I didn't realize that's how she found out; I assumed he bragged to his friends that we'd hooked up. Whenever I ran into him at school after, I'd bolt in the opposite direction, so he must've quickly figured out I wasn't interested. Wary to broach the subject with Selena, I swivel to something happier. "How'd you and Aliyah get together?"

She bites her lip. "You're going to think it's the dorkiest thing in the world."

"Are you kidding? The dorkier the better."

Her mouth curves into a smile. "She played *Mass Effect* over the summer. For me." Selena's favorite video game series, a space opera where you play a commander trying to save the galaxy. "She picked the same love interest, and I didn't even steer her ahead of time. Liara." Yeah, I remember the poster of the sexy blue alien in her bedroom. Playing those games helped her realize she's bi. "The fact that she took the time to play, how she gushed about the same romance . . . she *moved* me. I love how strong she is, too. She has these stomach issues—celiac, and other stuff; she never knows whether it'll be a good day or a bad day."

"Wow, I had no idea."

"Exactly. She doesn't let it stop her. Like with acting. She does it anyway, even though she could get sick during a performance, and a couple of times, an understudy stepped in. But it's better than not doing it at all. And she's so self-assured, so comfortable in her own skin, even though it's like her own body tries to sabotage her some-times. She inspires me every day."

I've never felt comfortable in my own skin, and for a long time I don't think Selena did, either. I can see how someone like Aliyah would embolden her to be the strongest version of herself.

"I love that." My voice cracks. It feels so good to be talking again, even though we're both beating around the bush, unwilling to address why we stopped.

She sighs. "God, I couldn't wait to play the next *Mass Effect* game. But now—" She hiccups, and a tear streaks down her cheek.

"You'll get to. We'll get out of here."

She shrugs, cracking her knuckles. "I keep imagining Aliyah playing someday and being sad I can never find out what happens next. Same with the next Star Wars movie, and whatever the Webb telescope captures next . . ."

Morbid thoughts have flitted through my mind, too—like how if we die down here, I'll never get to explore the world, to see all the places I've soaked in on YouTube in the flesh. But I hadn't even considered the media I won't see, the sequels I'll miss, the cliff-hangers that will last forever.

"That really sucks about dying," I say. "I mean, besides everything. But not getting to see all the cool stuff that happens after—what people invent, how society evolves, where humans end up. I want to see all of it. Well, assuming we don't blow ourselves up—"

"I'm sorry," Selena whispers. "I'm so sorry."

My breath catches. "For what?"

"For running last night." She retracts her arms into Olivia's jacket like a turtle, hugging her knees to her chest inside and rocking back and forth. "I should've listened to Julien. I should've stayed put. I don't know why I panicked like that."

Oh. For a moment I thought she was sorry about *us*.

I worry at my lip. "I panicked, too. I ran after I saw that person with a knife."

"Yeah, but they had a *knife*. They were obviously dangerous. How am I ever going to be an astronaut if I can't handle being alone in a freaking tunnel?"

"That's totally different."

"Is it? Astronauts need to stay calm through all sorts of life-and-death emergencies."

"But you'll get *years'* worth of training before you even step foot in a simulator, let alone a real rocket. You had no prep for this."

She meets my gaze. "That's true."

"And the way you took charge before we swam? You stayed calm when the rest of us were freaking out. You saved Val's life."

"But not Liv's," she whispers. "I didn't even think of her asthma; I was so focused on the fact that Val can't swim."

It suddenly feels like boulders from the cave-in are smooshing my rib cage. "Same."

She wipes her cheeks. "Listen, I know it's not my place. But I don't think she's good for you."

I raise my brows. "Val?"

She nods.

My blood cools. "You're right. It's not."

"There's something I think you should know."

Something in my chest twinges, but she glances to the right and purses her lips. Val's heading back, crunching over debris, and when she sits beside me, I almost want to tell her to scram again.

What the hell was Selena about to tell me?

29
Ruby

"Aren't you going to lie down?" Val asks Julien as we nestle along the only wall not lined with bones or buried under the cave-in. Maybe she's hoping he'll spoon her again.

"No," says Julien, sitting on the boulder Selena perched on earlier. "I'll keep watch—well, keep an ear out. In case they come."

They. The masked knife-wielders. I'm closest to the entrance we came from and lean over to peek down the long corridor. There's nothing but darkness beyond where our lamp's glow extends. I shift back. "Should we keep the lamp on?"

He shakes his head. "I don't know if there's much juice left, and that one's finicky." He gestures at the one that fell down the well with Selena. "I'll hear if anyone's coming."

"Should we take shifts?" says Val. "You should get some rest, too."

"I've pulled plenty of all-nighters down here. You girls rest."

I let Val spoon me instead, and after Julien flips the switch, someone starts sniffling. Selena. Between her injured arm and feet, she must be in so much pain. I wish she'd join me and Val, but she clearly wants space, so I don't pressure her. I hate that she blames herself for chasing those voices last night. None of this is her fault. I'm the one who pressured her to come down here.

On second thought, no I didn't. Val and I encouraged her to go back to the hotel. I don't know why she came with us. Maybe she was drunk. Maybe she hated how Val chided her for being scared. Maybe she thought she had something to prove. Either way, if anyone's to blame, it's those masked freaks. If they hadn't scared her—*chased* her—she never would've gotten lost.

"Hey Julien?" I say into the darkness.

He grunts.

"Can I ask you something?"

"You just did," he says. I snicker. That was my line, back when we first met.

"Why would those masked people hide their victims?"

A long pause. "What do you mean?"

"You said you smelled that stench of death before, but you never saw a body. So they must be hiding the bodies, right? But why?"

"Why wouldn't they?" he says slowly. "Don't most murderers hide the evidence?"

"Yeah," I say, "but if their whole schtick is scaring people away from the catacombs, wouldn't they leave the bodies in the open to freak people out?"

"We don't really know what their schtick *is*," says Selena. "That was Liv's guess, but who knows, really?"

"True," I say. Olivia was so smart, I accepted her theories as facts. *Was.* Holy hell.

"Hey Julien?" says Val, rolling away from me onto her back.

He grunts again.

"Can I ask you a—"

"Oh, just ask."

I hear her breath catch. Then she says in a small voice, "Are we going to die?"

My skin prickles. Her optimism earlier helped ground me, however much it annoyed Olivia, but the fear in her voice now is unnerving. And the fact that Julien doesn't answer makes terror grip my throat and squeeze tight, nearly choking me.

It only loosens its clutch at the sound of Selena's voice. "Should we pray?"

"Oh Jesus," Val mutters. "No pun intended."

"What?" Selena sounds hurt.

"You really believe some God's gonna help us out?"

I've never believed, never prayed—not after all the times Dad said there couldn't be a God because God would never take a perfectly healthy young mother from her newborn for no reason. I've always liked to think my mother's up there somewhere, though, watching over me, waiting patiently to meet me someday. But I'm not sure an afterlife can exist without God and all the rest of it. You don't get to pick and choose what's real.

"I don't know," says Selena. "Maybe."

"Is your family religious?" Julien asks.

"No," says Selena. "My mom was, but she died of breast cancer when I was four. My dad kept taking me to church on Sundays, I think because he thought it's what she would've wanted, but when he remarried—well, my stepmom and stepbrother are Jewish, and we never loved going to service, so we stopped. We celebrate Christmas and Hanukkah, though." A smile touches her voice. "Ruby, remember that year we tried to catch Santa in the act?"

"We were, like, eight, binge-watching Star Wars," I say. "Josh, too."

"My stepbrother," Selena explains.

"Yeah," I say, "and your parents were getting real nervous we'd never pass out. So your stepmom brought us cookies and milk at, what was it, four in the morning?"

"Yup," says Selena. "And then she dropped the whole tray."

I laugh. "Literally every glass broke. I think half the milk wound up on the cat."

"It did. All so Dad could get those presents under the tree. Sneaky bastards."

"Sounds real spiritual to me," Val says.

Our laughter halts.

"So, what, you believe in nothing?" Julien says, obviously to Val.

"Of course," she says. "How gullible can you be?"

"How faithless can *you* be?" says Julien.

I hear the scrape of Val sitting upright. "Just because I'm a skeptic doesn't make me a bad person," she says.

"Being an asshole about it does," Selena mutters.

"Screw you—"

Julien groans. "Oh, here we go."

"What's your problem?" Val says.

"All the squabbling," he says. "Don't you ever get tired of it?"

"You patronizing son of a bitch," she says. I can imagine she's gone red in the face. "You think we're just a bunch of ridiculous teenage girls, don't you?"

Pebbles crunch as Julien shifts. "If I thought that, I never would've—" The end of that sentence never comes. "It has nothing to do with your age. Or your gender. It's your attitude."

"Okay, *Dad*." So much for her little infatuation. "I never should've trusted you."

I can't help it—I snort. "You're one to talk."

She inhales sharply. Crap. I didn't mean to say anything. I didn't want to talk about this down here.

Now we have to.

Maybe it's for the best. Avoiding honest conversations with Selena ended up destroying us.

I steel myself. "Why'd you try to set up Liv and Sean? Why'd you think that would *help* me? And how could you do that to Liv?" My voice shakes. "It's not like Sean would suddenly like her just because you told her so. That's not how feelings work."

She doesn't answer any of it. All she says is "I'm sorry, Rube."

"It's *Ruby*. I hate when you call me that."

"Why didn't you ever say so?"

"You *knew* I liked him." She's not the only one who can ignore questions. "Why'd you really do it?"

"Isn't it obvious?" says Selena. "She didn't want to be your third wheel." I wonder if she's thinking of my letter where I explained I meant to ask Tyler out for her. I wasn't afraid to be her third wheel, I was only afraid she was replacing me with new friends. Fake friends.

"You stay out of this," says Val. She sniffles, wet and sloppy. I stay quiet. I'll wait for an answer. Finally, she catches her breath. "Rube— Ruby, I swear, that wasn't it. I really did think I was helping. I mean, I've told you before; if you date him, it'll hurt so much worse when he ditches you for the army. And Liv obviously liked him, and she's Ivy-bound anyway, so I thought . . . two birds, one stone. Save you the heartache, and they could hook up for a bit. Win-win. I guess I didn't realize how much Sean *really* likes you."

My pulse spikes. "What do you mean?"

"Apparently when Liv kissed him at her party, he basically shoved her away, and she got all embarrassed and blabbered that she went for it because I *told* her he liked her." She sighs. "He found me after and reamed me out."

I sort of remember when that might've happened. I'd gone to the bathroom for the umpteenth time, more for an introvert break than to use the facilities, and when I came back, Val was storming away from Sean, red in the face. I figured she was flushed from drinking too much—it was a dry party, but she'd brought a flask—and that maybe he'd commented on it.

"What did he say, exactly?" I ask.

"He said he only has eyes for you. He promised not to tell you what I did only because he didn't want to hurt you, but said if I ever pull that kind of shenanigans again, he'll tell you what an awful friend I am."

He only has eyes for me. I clasp my chest. It feels like my heart's been set on fire while simultaneously crumbling into a million pieces. If I die down here, neither of us will get to tell each other how we feel. Both of us will have wasted this.

"After," Val goes on, "I felt terrible about Liv. I thought he'd go for a hookup; I didn't think it'd be such a disaster. That's why I kept egging her on. I knew she wouldn't try such a bold move again, but I was afraid to admit I lied to her and hurt her feelings, so the lie just sort of kept spiraling. I wanted her to have hope. Hope is better than crushing disappointment."

"No, it's not," I croak. "Nothing's worse than *false* hope."

"I'm sorry," says Val. "I'm so sorry. Oh God. I'll never get to tell Liv how sorry I am . . ." Sobs consume her. After a moment, I shimmy over to draw circles onto her back until finally, she snorts a juicy sniffle. "Can you forgive me?"

I want to. I really do. She's the one who pieced me back together after Selena sliced me in half, who tore me from my hardened cocoon, who encouraged me to see the world through my own eyes instead of a screen. She actualized my dreams of adventure.

But I can almost *feel* Julien listening, his eyes on me in the dark. *You're so desperate to see the good in people, you let them hurt you.* Whatever.

217

I won't let this break us. Chalk it up to a lesson we both learned the hard way—I tried interfering in Selena's relationships and that went sideways, out the door, and over the guardrail. But it doesn't always have to end that way.

"Promise you won't do anything like that again," I say. "My relationships are *my* choice; I don't want you trying to pull the strings like that. Or leading anyone on like that."

"I promise," says Val.

I fumble in the dark. "Where's your hand?"

She lets out a wet laugh. "Hang on, I just wiped my face." There's a swipe of skin on fabric. Then her fingertips find mine. "I'm really, really sorry."

"It's okay."

Selena huffs. This is one thing she can't relate to.

All of us make mistakes. But not all of us drop our friends for making one.

30

Sean

It's another cold, dreary morning as our class waits in line for a catacombs tour in the torrential downpour. Aliyah groans, huddled under
an umbrella. "The last thing I want to do right now is look at dead
people."

Mr. LeBrecque's determined to keep us busy and away from those
prying reporters outside our hotel, even as the missing girls' parents
arrive to meet the US Embassy liaison. I saw them briefly, their eyes
puffy and bloodshot, worry and exhaustion plain on their faces—it's
bad enough taking a red-eye flight when you're not soaring over the
Atlantic in a state of sheer panic.

"Nah, it'll be cool to see all the old bones," says Kyle, punching her
arm lightly as water drips from the rim of his baseball cap.

She wrinkles her nose. "I'd rather fling myself into the Seine."

"You wouldn't even get wetter," Alex mutters, hands stuffed in his
pockets. His girlfriend, Lisa, and another classmate are flying home
early at their parents' insistence, so our numbers have dwindled to

nine, plus Mr. LeBrecque. Mrs. Williams stayed back at the hotel with the parents.

I woke to a text from Pop, who'd clearly disregarded the concept of sleep. He got in touch with a buddy at the US Embassy who confirmed they're assisting with the search and assigned that liaison to the case, but they won't interfere in any local authorities' ongoing investigations. If red tape keeps us from finding the girls, I'll blow a gasket. At least Pop talked Mom out of switching me to an earlier flight. I'm glad for that, but know I'll get an earful later.

"Have you heard from Debois?" I ask Mr. LeBrecque.

"Not since you last asked five minutes ago," he says. "Let's assume no news really is *no* news, hmm? Though, honestly, I'm not sure she'll tell us anything in case you kids plaster it all over TikTok."

Aliyah clamps her lips.

A sprightly, hooded man hurries over, scanning a clipboard under an umbrella. "This is the Starborough High School class, yes?"

"That's right." Mr. LeBrecque shakes his hand.

"Come, come." He waves us into a tiny, forest-green shack resembling a toolshed with a ticket booth. As we cluster in the stark-white lobby inside, sopping wet, he bounds in front of us and pushes back his hood to expose a weathered face and gray, shoulder-length, straggly hair.

"Welcome!" He claps gleefully and bares a row of yellow teeth. "My name is Guillaume, and I'll be your guide. Who's excited to see the infamous Paris catacombs?"

I blink.

Someone coughs.

A boot squelches on tile.

"Whaddup, Gill?" Kyle finally says. Alex chuckles awkwardly.

"Guillaume, please." He launches into a spiel of the catacombs' history, and I don't catch a word. All I can think is how Ruby begged Mr. LeBrecque to add this to our itinerary—she even offered to tutor freshmen for free. From the downtrodden look on Mr. LeBrecque's face, I bet he's thinking of that, too.

Suddenly we're moving.

"I must warn you," Guillaume says as we follow him down the hall, "it's a hundred and thirty-one stairs to the bottom, so take your time and mind your step. And there's no cell service below, so get your last doom-scroll in now."

We troop down the narrow spiral staircase single file, the white-painted walls cracked and crumbly. He wasn't kidding—it seems to stretch down forever, like in a video game I once played where you climb a staircase infinitely if you haven't earned enough stars to access that level. It makes me feel strangely unsteady. In front of me, Aliyah keeps a death grip on the metal rail while running her other palm against the cement stability column.

"You okay?" I ask.

"Yup! Just some light vertigo, no biggie." But her voice squeaks.

When we finally reach the bottom, we gather in a dimly lit tunnel. The air is cool and damp, and maps and pictures of archeological digs line the grayish-brown stone walls.

"Welcome to the catacombs." Guillaume motions to the largest map. "Can anyone guess how long this network of tunnels spans?"

If Olivia were here, she would've shot her hand into the air. But no one's in the mood to play know-it-all in her stead.

"Three hundred kilometers," he says. "Only this small section's open to the public." He traces a circle around a small highlighted area. "The rest is illegal to enter since it's so dangerous. There are cave-ins, flooding . . ."

He rambles on as he leads us down a narrow, downhill corridor, our shoes crunching over gravel. I bury my hands in my pockets—it's warmer than outside, but the chill down here sinks bone-deep.

"Did anyone notice this black line?" Guillaume asks.

I'd vaguely noticed it winding through our route along the scabrous ceiling, reminding me of the red brick Freedom Trail back in Boston, so I absentmindedly raise my hand.

Always a mistake.

He calls on me. "Do you know what it's for?"

"Uh . . ." I stiffen, hating getting put on the spot. "Is it . . . so people don't get lost?"

"Very good," he says. I relax my posture. "It's called the *lifeline*. When the catacombs first opened to the public in the eighteen hundreds, none of these lights were installed yet, and you could easily take a wrong turn into an enormous, pitch-black maze. Back then, grifters would bring people down here and threaten to leave them to find their way out alone . . . unless they paid a price." He rubs his fingers together, eyes glinting.

"Yikes," says Alex.

People can be awful to each other.

After we pass a large castle sculpture and reach a doorway where the lifeline ends, Guillaume turns to face us. "We're about to get to the part you've all been waiting for—"

"Yes," Kyle hisses.

"—but to understand how the catacombs were created, we must go back to the origins of the city."

Kyle groans.

Aliyah pokes his arm. "Don't be rude."

Guillaume launches into it: The Romans conquered the city and settled along the Seine, blah blah blah, these tunnels were mined to construct great Parisian architecture, so on and so on, as the population boomed and plague spread the church built mass graves, yada yada yada . . .

I can't believe how much information this dude's memorized. Despite my best efforts, I tune out, wondering where Ruby is now, what she's thinking, what she's feeling, whether she's feeling anything at all . . .

"—rained for a month straight, and the shop basements next to the cemeteries caved in and filled with half-decomposed corpses."

That makes me tune back in.

"Gross," says Kyle.

"Indeed," says Guillaume. "The cemeteries shut down since they were a public health hazard, but the bodies had to go *somewhere*. Around the same time, they discovered this huge abandoned quarry system"— he gestures around us—"because buildings above were collapsing right into it. As they fortified the tunnels, they decided to move the bodies down here."

"Must have been an interesting time to live in Paris, hmm?" Mr. LeBrecque chimes in.

"No kidding," says Alex.

Guillaume chuckles and points to a phrase chiseled in stone above the doorway. "Now, can anyone tell me what this means?" ARRETE! C'EST ICI L'EMPIRE DE LA MORT.

"Stop," Aliyah reads. "This is the empire of death."

Mr. LeBrecque nods. "Good, Aliyah."

"Before we go in," says Guillaume, "I must remind you . . . each of the bones within belonged to a human being. Touching them is *strictly* forbidden. Understood?"

We nod, and it seems like we're all holding our breath apprehensively.

Guillaume beckons us into the ossuary, his dark eyes glimmering.

We meander through the caverns, taking it all in. I'm not squeamish, but a queasy feeling ripples through my gut. There must be *thousands* of bones in this one section. A bulging column of them rises from the center, and countless skulls zigzag across the walls. Farther down, more skulls are arranged in the shape of a heart nestled into hundreds of stacked femurs. It's gotta be the least romantic thing I've ever seen. Empty eye sockets stare back wherever I look, gaping voids over a permanent grimace. I can't believe each pair belonged to an actual living, breathing person. There are just so *many*.

Kyle poses next to the enormous bone column to snap a selfie, but Mr. LeBrecque stops him. "Please," he whispers, "respect the dead."

I pause to peer through an iron-barred gate that doesn't seem to be able to open. The corridor beyond intersects with a perpendicular path. I grip the bars and press my forehead to the cold metal, thinking of those grifters who'd abandon their marks down here. It'd be terrible to get lost in these tunnels—dark, damp, filled with the dead. Goose bumps prick my arms.

Guillaume pops up next to me.

I jump.

"See anything down there?" He pulls a water bottle from his coat's large pocket.

"No, sir." I shake off the startle. "Why, where does it lead?"

"To the halls we're not supposed to see," he says slyly.

I cross my arms. "Have you seen them?"

"When I was young." He pauses for a sip. "These days, I'm not quite so adventurous. But there are explorers who wander the tunnels, have secret parties, play cat and mouse with the police. Cataphiles, they're called."

I eye the sealed gate. "How do they get in?"

He smirks. "If I told you, I'd have to kill you." He lowers his voice and motions to a nearby pile of bones. "We can always add to the collection."

Oh, brother. This guy would get along great with Ruby's dad.

"What, are there secret trap doors in people's basements or something?"

He nods. "In a city this old, there are all sorts of ways in. Sewer grates, ventilation shafts, crevasses in the Métro tunnels. Just last week, the police sealed an entrance under a bridge . . ."

His voice fades as a tinny buzzing noise fills my ears.

Sewer grates.

I tripped over one on the sidewalk yesterday.

Four girls walked down a street and vanished.

Not into thin air.

Not into a car.

Underground.

"Thank you, sir," I say. Guillaume nods and moseys off. I whip out my phone, pulse racing, and play the recording I took on the street where they disappeared. I'd panned over the cobblestone wall, then turned to film the cars parked in front of the apartment buildings, pausing when I spotted the graffiti from Ruby's photo. Then the footage goes all shaky when I tripped.

There it is. The grate.

I pause the video and squint at it. The slats are too narrow to see what's underneath, and it's too dark, anyway. It appears to be flush with the sidewalk, but I distinctly remember how it felt, how my toe had caught the edge of metal.

No way. That'd be too big a coincidence.

Then why does it feel like every nerve ending in my body's caught fire?

Those explorers—cataphiles or whatever—have parties down here.

Val can't resist a party; the riskier, the better. And it'd be so easy to get lost in this enormous labyrinth—

"Sean?" Aliyah approaches. "You look like you've seen an actual ghost—"

"I think I know where they are," I whisper.

Her eyebrows shoot up. "What?"

"They weren't kidnapped. They're here. In the catacombs. The off-limits areas."

She gapes at the bones. "That's nuts."

"Is it?" I recap what Guillaume said. "Maybe that guy was taking them to a party or something, but then, I dunno, something happened—maybe a cave-in—and they got trapped. Check this out. I took this on the street where they disappeared." I show her the clip and point out the grate.

"I don't see anything—"

"That grate, right there. I tripped over it. I don't think it was closed all the way." I thumb at Guillaume. "He said some of the entrances are old sewer grates. What if *that* leads *here*?"

"I dunno. It's so much more likely they got in that guy's car—"

"That theory makes no sense. Ruby would know better than to get in some random dude's car."

"Oh, but she wouldn't know better than to climb into a freaking hole in the ground?"

I scrub a palm over my buzz cut. "I know Ruby. Seeing this place was on her bucket list. And Val would totally instigate this . . . it tracks with how she left the hotel first."

I'd guess Ruby had second thoughts, then went after her later. If I'm right, I could *kill* Val. I'm still pissed she told Olivia I liked her when I *know* she knows Ruby and I are—well, whatever we are. But *this*? This is absurd. This is life-and-death.

"But I know Selena," says Aliyah, "and she'd never come down here." But there's an edge of uncertainty in her voice.

"Val has a weird way of talking people into things." I think of Olivia, of that earnest, hopeful longing in her eyes before she closed them, leaning close and tilting her face up. She really thought I was into her. Val managed to convince her, even though I never gave her any signals—at least, not intentionally. My heart's been set on Ruby for months.

Aliyah covers her mouth, her eyes darting back and forth.

"We have to tell LeBrecque," I say.

She nods. "Okay."

We swarm him, and I launch into my theory, but when I try showing him the video, he waves me off. "Sean, I really think you need to let the police do their jobs."

"But, sir, it'd take them only a few minutes to see if this grate leads anywhere. Can't you *please* call Debois and run this by her?"

He wipes a hand down his face. "There's no signal down here—"

"Then let's get out of here."

"I can't leave the class."

"Then give me her number, and I'll run back up there."

Stress lines burrow across his forehead. "You're not going anywhere alone. And that's final." He turns from us, as though that settles it.

I glance at Aliyah. "You coming this time?"

"Abso-fucking-lutely."

Then we bolt.

31
Ruby

Images of Olivia's lifeless face consume my thoughts as I try to sleep—bloodshot eyes staring at nothing; purple, swollen lips; curls that would dry into tight spirals one last time. Finally my thoughts flit to Sean, as they do many nights as I lull myself to sleep.

Most nights, my script stays the same. I tell him how I feel—eloquently, of course, no stuttering or endless yammering—and he cups my cheek, needling his fingers through my hair, so close I can feel heat radiating off him. And he asks me gently, holding my gaze, "Can I kiss you?" and I say *yes*, wanting it so badly. A pleasant sensation tingles my spine, and I let my eyes flutter shut as he tilts his face, his nose barely brushing against mine before our lips touch . . .

Next thing I know, someone's ripping my hair out by the roots.

That can't be right.

But my scalp sears in pain as I jerk awake. I'm not on the ground. I flail and kick, my bare toes scraping stone as someone hauls me to my feet by my hair.

There's cold steel at my throat.

I don't have time to cry out. But I don't need to—the scuffling wakes Val and Selena. Whoever's got me, they have a light, and its beam bounces all over the girls as Val scrambles for a flashlight and Selena shrieks. Their grip on my hair forces up my gaze, and I can't look down to find Julien. My cheek is pressed against some ridged latex material.

The skull mask.

Its sharp cheekbone juts into mine.

My heart goes into free fall. I can't struggle with a blade pressed into my neck, so I clutch their arm, desperate to relieve the pressure. Their coat sleeve is damp.

"Où est-il?" they growl, low and deep, slightly muffled behind the mask's teeth. A man's voice. "Où est-il?" *Where is he?*

"Let her go!" Val cries.

This guy's going to snap my neck if he tugs my hair back any further. I strain to lift my head, and he responds by pressing the blade deeper into my skin. A sharp burning sensation sears across it.

This is it.

This is how I die.

I squeeze my eyes shut and hold my breath, bracing for a final flare of pain.

"Où est—*Oof.*"

I feel a jolt and suck in a gasp of stale air as the man's grip slackens. I yank his arm down by the sleeve and skuttle from his grasp, clutching my neck. Selena and Val catch me as I vault toward them, and I turn to see Julien behind the masked man, holding a large stone slab. He'd snuck over and bashed the stranger's head from behind.

The man doesn't go down—his grotesque mask's cranium covers his own like a helmet—but he wobbles on his feet, shocked by the blow. He's wearing a headlamp over his mask, and I raise a hand to block the sharp light.

Val beams her flashlight into his face. He raises a hand, too, and while the mask conceals his expression and those bulbous sockets shadow his eyes, I can see him squint back. His outfit is the color of bones—a taupe military jacket flecked with brown, matching utility pants, beige hiking boots, even beige gloves. It's like he's trying to blend in with the dead.

Julien hesitates. He could easily land another blow and knock the man out, but he's not a violent person. The stranger's cold eyes rove over us as he tightens his grip on his knife.

"Julien!" I cry out.

Too late.

The masked man spins and swipes at Julien, who barely sidesteps the blade. Julien raises the rock like a shield, protecting his chest as the man launches a flurry of slashes, but his attacks are so lumbered and uncoordinated, he slices nothing but air. As Julien keeps darting nimbly out of reach, my heart races like a jackrabbit, and I scan the ground for anything I can use as a weapon. I don't see anything.

Julien gasps and trips over the lamp next to the boulder, then lands in a crumpled heap. "Argh, ma cheville." *My ankle.* Val swears, and Selena squeezes my hand hard. I didn't even realize she was holding it.

Before any of us can help, the masked man surges forward. Julien scrambles to his feet, limping heavily, and before the stranger can strike, he swings the rock with a growl, slamming the guy's wrist so hard his knife goes flying and clatters over stone. He cries out and clasps his wrist, then gapes at Julien, taking shallow, rasping breaths. "Idiot," he snarls. "Que fais-tu—"

Julien clobbers him in the face with the slab, flinging off his headlamp.

The man staggers in our direction, mask askew. We scramble out of the way as he careens into the wall of bones beside us. He stays on his feet somehow, then adjusts his mask to see out the sockets and fumbles for something. A femur. He yanks hard, dislodging it from the wall, then spins and wields it like a sword.

I clasp my mouth. This can't be happening.

He lumbers toward Julien, whose eyes bug in horror as he says, "Ne le fais pas—"

Julien dodges too late.

The man swings the femur and clubs Julien's shoulder, but the bone shatters, ancient and brittle. Fragments rain down around Julien as he yelps and drops the slab, which lands with a loud *thud*.

The stranger teeters off-balance but braces himself, clutching the remaining jagged end of the bone. Julien grips his ankle, propped on one knee, defenseless as the man steps closer. I'm frozen in fear. It's like I'm seeing all this in slow motion, helpless to stop it.

No. Not helpless.

I can't watch this man sink bone through Julien's flesh.

When he's done, he'll come after *us*.

I can hardly believe what I'm doing as I slide another femur from the wall, one right next to the small empty cavity he left behind. *Forgive me.* My fingers tremble, but I clasp it tight and surge forward. Our attacker doesn't see me coming; his peripheral vision must suck in that mask. As he winds back, rearing to stab Julien, I swing the femur at the exposed skin of his nape as hard as I can.

Thwack.

The bone doesn't break.

He goes down like a rag doll, flopping onto his knees and sucking wind.

For the briefest moment, Julien and I gape at the intact femur in my grasp, breathless, and our eyes meet in disbelief. Then he shifts his focus back to the stranger and punches him in the throat, making him topple back onto his bulging backpack, legs splayed beneath him at a strange angle. I scuttle out of the way.

Julien throws himself on top of the stranger and tears his mask off. I think he's about to demand answers, but instead he pummels his face, alternating fists, letting out a gravelly growl with each wallop. The man's head snaps back like a punching bag, propped up by his pack, and Julien's rage possesses him, visceral and raw. I can feel waves of it coursing off him as he delivers blow after blow.

Maybe he's thinking of Olivia lying dead in that passageway.

Maybe he's thinking of how we're thirsty and starving on his watch.

Maybe he's thinking of how these freaks have tormented his friends.

Either way, I can't look. I press my cheek into Selena's shoulder and squeeze my eyes shut, waiting for it to end.

It doesn't take long.

The cavern goes quiet.

I peek up at Selena. She hasn't looked away, but she's covering her mouth with both hands. Val's jaw hangs open, brows raised, like she's fascinated. Impressed, even.

Julien's slumped over the man, staring down at his own bloodied knuckles.

"Qu'est-ce que j'ai fait? Qu'est-ce que j'ai fait?" *What have I done?*

"Help me," I whisper to the girls before rushing to him. I set down the femur to grab his arm as Val takes the other, and we haul him off the stranger.

One glance at the man's face, and I know he's gone.

"Good riddance," Val mutters.

We drag Julien to the boulder, and he shimmies back against it, legs sprawled out, staring at his bloodied hands. "Qu'est-ce que j'ai fait?" *What have I done?*

I kneel beside him. "Tu m'as sauvé la vie." *You saved my life.*

"No—" His eyes flit up to mine, then widen. "Your neck."

My hand automatically rises to the cut there. It stings, and my fingers come away slick with blood.

He starts to reach for me, then stops, remembering his own hands are covered in blood. "I'm so sorry. I went to relieve myself"—he motions to the other side of the cavern beside the cave-in—"and I only used the light from my watch to see. Next thing I knew, he had you."

Selena bends close to me with another flashlight, inspecting my wound. "It doesn't look bad. Just a thin cut." She unloops Olivia's scarf from around her own neck, then grabs one of the bottles of water and starts to uncap it. I touch her wrist with my clean hand. "Don't waste it."

"Are you sure?" says Selena. I nod, wrapping the scarf around my neck. Good enough.

"We have to go." Val grabs the lamp Julien tripped over. "Weren't there two of them?"

Julien starts climbing to his feet and gasps. I whip around, afraid he saw the other masked sadist, but no one's there. "My ankle," he grits through his teeth, clutching his left one.

"Is it broken?" I ask.

"Yeah." Val flips the lamp's switch back and forth. Nothing happens.

"His ankle, not the lamp," I say, exasperated.

Julien slowly rotates his ankle, then hikes his pant leg up. "I-I don't think so? Twisted, maybe. It's swelling." His face contorts in agony. "I need a minute— Don't touch that."

I follow his gaze to Selena. She's picked up the dead man's mask. The headlamp is several feet away, pointing up, lighting the space.

"Look at its eyes," she says, angling the mask toward us. It's so lifelike, the way a coronal suture stretches across the frontal cranium, the way its nasal cavity is ridged and uneven. But unlike real skulls, this mask has elongated eyes—a rectangular notch juts down from each bulbous socket, a bit uneven, like they were carved out by hand.

"They're like keyholes," I say.

Like the skull we'd seen graffitied near the ladder we first descended.

Like the one next to those dozens of red arrows, and the one near that putrid-smelling throne of bones. Like the dozens decorating the chamber over that rotting corpse, sprinkled across Paris's night sky like stars while the stone wall's fissure split the city in two. Not just elongated. Keyholes.

Is it my imagination, or does this room seem awfully cultish? Selena had asked.

It's not your imagination, Olivia had responded.

"It *is* a cult," I say now.

Julien says nothing, staring again at the red on his hands, at the stranger's blood mingling with his own.

Val prods Julien, panicked. "Get up. We have to go."

"I don't think his buddy's coming," I say, picking up the femur I'd set down.

"How can you know that?" Val asks.

"His sleeve was all wet." I return to the wall of bones. "I think they swam after us."

"So?"

"*So,* I think the other guy didn't make it. Why else would he fight alone when it was four against one?"

Maybe five.

I study the femur. Not even a crack. The one our attacker wielded is scattered beside him in hundreds of tiny fragments. I lift my gaze to the row of skulls above the small cavity. They're all watching me. Expectantly. *No.* They're only bones. Calcium and proteins. Nothing more.

But as I slide the femur back into the cavity, I whisper, "*Thank you.*"

Selena's breath rattles. "Why are those people so determined to catch us they'd risk that swim?"

"I don't know," says Julien.

My stomach twists, thinking of that intricately decorated cavern. "There are probably more than two of them."

Julien nods. "There will be more. Help me up." As Val and I haul him to his feet, Selena picks up the fallen headlamp and switches it off. "Take his backpack, too. He'll have more lights. And food, maybe."

It's a team effort to lift the man, loosen each backpack strap, and slide them down his arms. Val's the one to carry it, and Selena takes her lighter purse. We don't even discuss where to go. We can't return to the flooded, snake-shaped pool. And if we try to claw through the cave-in, more boulders might collapse and crush us.

Suffocate by water or suffocate by stone.

There's only one other choice: the narrow tunnel veering off to the left.

So really, it's no choice at all.

32
Sean

Yes.

I admit it.

I considered Hulk-smashing the sidewalk open.

That would do no good, though. I need Capitaine Debois to take me seriously, and she already chased me off that street once. Taking it upon myself to tear up the sewer grate probably isn't the smartest move.

Plus, no superpowers.

Dread twists my gut as we pull up to the curb outside the hotel. Despite the police force's efforts to squash all media attention, the crowd of reporters has swelled like a balloon. And once that thing pops, the circus will begin.

"Ready?" I ask Aliyah.

She nods as she finishes paying the cab driver. We take a deep breath, then dive from the cab and hurtle past the reporters' incessant questions into the lobby. Debois is supposed to be giving the parents a briefing right now, so I head straight to the dining room, which has basically turned into our war room.

No Debois.

Just a bunch of parents looking utterly overwhelmed. I recognize Selena's and Olivia's parents from years of school concerts and science fairs, and Val's parents from HGTV (Mom always has it on), which is kind of weird. Selena's stepmother wraps Aliyah in a hug. I don't see Selena's stepbrother anywhere, and I think Olivia has a kid sister Emily's age, but maybe they don't have passports yet.

Ruby's dad, Jeff, is sitting alone at a table holding his head in his hands. He has the same blond hair as Ruby, the same amber eyes, but his face is rounder behind his graying beard. I've been over to dinner a few times when he's had off from work, and he's always seemed like a good dude. She's complained about how overbearing he is, though. Relatable.

He must be losing it.

"Mr. Hale?"

Jeff slowly raises his gaze. "Sean." He wearily stands to shake my hand. "I hear you're the one who figured out where they went. Thank you for that."

Maybe more than he knows. A rock lodges in my throat, and I swallow hard. "Where are the detectives?"

"They left a little while ago," he says. "It's just the embassy liaison here now." He nods toward a bald man in a suit sitting across from Olivia's parents.

"Did either of them give you their number?"

Jeff frowns and fishes a business card from his coat pocket.

Before he can hand it over, Mr. LeBrecque hurtles into the room. "Sean. Aliyah. With me. Now." He's out of breath; he must've followed us out of the catacombs and left our class with the overenthusiastic guide.

Aliyah and I exchange a tense look and follow him into the lobby.

"I'm sorry, sir, but—" I try.

"No *but*s. No excuses. I've already been in touch with both of your parents."

"What?" We both exclaim.

"I warned you last night. Your parents are switching your flights now."

My stomach sinks, and Aliyah's eyes widen. "Wait, mine, too?"

"Yes."

"But I didn't get a warning—"

"TikTok was your first strike," he says, then rubs his eyes behind his glasses, the lenses splattered with raindrops. "Listen, I get that you're worried. But Mrs. Williams and I already have our hands full. We can't be chasing you two down every few hours."

Aliyah grabs my arm to steady herself. "Please don't make us leave."

"You can't," I tell him. "We're both eighteen. We're adults. You can't force us to go home." But the way I'm trembling doesn't make me feel like an adult.

"And where will you stay, hmm? You're on the school's reservation."

I sort of want to call bullshit—I overheard him on the phone last night arguing with someone over the insurance company's resistance to cover costs for early return flights for the remaining students, and I doubt he'd get refunds for our rooms—but instead I say, "We'll figure something out."

He sighs, frazzled, patting down his hair in the back that's sticking straight up.

"Hang on," I say. "I have to tell Capitaine Debois about that grate." I pull up the video I tried showing him in the catacombs and hold it up.

Mr. LeBrecque frowns at the screen. "What's this?"

"I took it last night at that street the girls disappeared down." I explain my theory again, how Ruby was so excited to see the catacombs, how I think she and the others went down there. "I tripped over the edge of this grate; I think it was ajar and I kicked it back in place by accident. And if that's true, the cops might not've noticed it at all."

"That's quite a leap, Sean."

"I'll tell you what," I say. "Tell Debois about this, and we'll pack our stuff right now and go home."

Aliyah inhales sharply. "We can't leave them, Sean."

I know how she feels. But this other feeling—this overwhelming sense that I'm right—takes precedent. If leaving Ruby is the biggest way I can help her, I'll do it.

"Please, sir. Call her, and I'll get outta your hair. I *promise*."

Mr. LeBrecque regards me, folding his arms.

"Fine," he finally says. "But I can't promise she'll listen."

33

Ruby

"Want some pretzels?" Selena looks back at me and jiggles Olivia's Monoprix bag, our remaining lamp dangling from her good elbow. My stomach just grumbled so loudly she probably heard it. Julien has one arm over my shoulders as he walks with a heavy limp, and Val's straggling behind us; she's had to pause several times to be sick. Her cheeks have gone paper white, her thin lips chapped, and I don't want to say Selena told her so, but . . . Selena told her so. Julien's stomach seems fine, though, and he drank the same pool water, so who knows?

"Just one, maybe?" I whisper. I'm afraid to speak louder than a whisper, terrified more of those masked sadists will find us.

Selena hands me a pretzel. All I've eaten today is one of those madeleine cakes. I slide it into my mouth, letting the salt and yeasty flavor coat my tongue, but then remember that man's pulped face again and barely manage to choke it down.

Now my mouth's even drier. Dammit.

Selena offers me more, but I shake my head, focusing on taking slow, deep breaths instead of how my tongue feels like a mound of sand pressing on my gag reflex—

I spot something ahead.

A glint of metal against stone.

"Do you see that?" I rasp to Selena.

"What?" she asks, then gasps, seeing it, too.

Ladder rungs.

We hobble over. The rungs are cemented into stone and ascend into a well. About ten feet above us, rotted wooden slats cover half of the opening, leaving only a narrow semicircle to squeeze through. I can't tell how far the shaft extends past it.

Julien peers up beside me, arm still slung over my shoulder.

"Do you think it goes all the way up to the street?" I didn't expect to find a way directly to the surface from two levels down, but if we just found one, my God. This could really be over.

"I don't know," he says.

"Can we fit through there?" Val asks, gripping her stomach.

"I think so." I have the widest hips of the group, and I'm sure I can. Between Selena's arm, Julien's ankle, and Val's stomach, I'm in the best shape to scope it out, anyway. "I'll take a look." I sidle from Julien's side, sling off my purse and hand it to Val, then grasp a rung.

"Wait." Julien grabs my wrist. "I should go." Dried blood cakes his knuckles.

"Your ankle's shot." I point out how he's putting all his pressure on his right foot.

He redistributes his weight. "It's fine." But his jaw clenches. It's not fine. "This could be dangerous."

"I can climb a ladder."

"You don't know what's up there."

But I can see the truth written all over his face—he wants to be the one to deliver us to safety. Like maybe that'd assuage his guilt for everything that's happened.

I tighten my grip on the rung. "If you fall and break your neck, we won't be able to carry your ass through this place."

"If I fall and break my neck, I'll probably be dead."

"So you have a death wish?" My cheeks burn, but I hold firm, matching his challenging stare. Maintaining eye contact feels important, like if I don't, he'll see the fear roiling under my skin like a brewing storm. And I don't want him risking this.

After a moment so long it bends the rules of physics, his nostrils flare, and he backs off. "Fine."

I take the lamp from Selena, sling my arm through the handle, and let it rest in the crook of my elbow to free up my hands to climb. But when I reach for a higher rung, the lamp slides up my arm and whacks me in the chest.

The corners of Julien's lips quirk. "No rush. Take your time."

Ignoring him, I hand the lantern back to Selena and circle behind Julien to grab the dead man's headlamp, the only thing of his we kept besides a bag of beef jerky. All his flashlights were dead, and there was nothing else useful in his pack. I strap it around my head, switch it on, and shoot Julien a look. But instead of making some other condescending remark, he offers a tight-lipped, encouraging smile. My stomach wobbles. *He killed a man to save me.*

I nod in return. Then I climb.

"May the force be with you," Selena calls after me.

"You got this," says Val.

I thought the rungs would be slick with dew like the first ladder we descended, but they're coarse and bumpy with rusted brown spots. I quickly reach the wooden barrier and nestle close to the rungs to squeeze past it. Once I climb farther, it gets brighter, and I peek down to see Julien shining up a flashlight to give me a better view.

I tilt my head back, which makes the cut at my throat sear. I grimace and lower my gaze, willing the pain to subside, then steel myself and carefully peer back up. "Whoa." It's a *long* way up. The ancient-looking shaft rises at least five stories high, and jagged, cracked slabs jut this way and that, further constricting the narrow space. My nerves sizzle.

"What's up there?" Selena asks.

"Not sure yet. It goes really high—"

I gasp. There, at the top, far but clear, is a circular plate.

A manhole cover.

A way out.

"Oh my God. It's a manhole. I think it leads to the street." I climb faster, breathing hard, eager to feel cool metal under my palms, to lift it and suck in the fresh air above.

The circle grows larger in my view. I'm close enough now to see the rough cover is rusted orange and flecked with black paint.

"Careful," Julien calls up. "It will be heavier than you think, and there could be cars driving over it."

"Okay—"

Something scuttles over my right hand.

I yank it from the rung, then yelp when my left foot slides and tighten my grip with my other hand, barely clinging on. An electric current shoots up my legs, and my fingertips go numb.

"Ruby!" Selena shouts.

"What's wrong?" says Julien.

I grasp the rung with both hands again, my grip slick from the sweat coating my palms. My legs tremble uncontrollably as my heart races, and I shut my eyes, breathing slow, trying to calm down.

"Are you okay?" Val asks.

"Yeah. I thought I felt something . . ." I peer through my eyelashes and catch sight of a radial crack the size of my palm splintering the stone beside the ladder. One of the fractures twitches—

Twitches.

No.

Oh no.

Every nerve ending in my body catches fire. That's no crack.

That's a spider.

The world's largest spider.

Everyone keeps asking me what's wrong, but my voice fully malfunctions as I stare at it, my skin crawling so severely it makes me want to slither out of it and flop down the shaft as a skinless, boneless blob.

"Just come back down," says Julien.

Just. Like moving even a smidge is a simple task right now. "I can't—"

My voice must startle the spider or something because it zooms up the wall, past my face. I scream.

The girls shout my name, and Julien cries, "I'm coming up!" Someone points a flashlight every which way, the beam of light exposing different sections of the shaft, all covered in what I'd assumed were radial cracks.

Spiders.

All spiders.

I'd been so focused reaching that manhole cover, I hadn't realized. Now I'm surrounded.

Julien lands back on the ground with a thud and a pained grunt.

I can't move, can't speak, can't *think*. Scuffling noises scrape beneath my feet and it sounds like Selena and Val are bickering over which of them will climb, but I can't hear much over my pulse thrashing in my ears. The rational part of my brain is screaming at my muscles to move, to climb, to reach the manhole cover and escape, but right now I'll do anything to avoid feeling those hundreds of spindly legs scurrying over my body—even if it means simply letting go and plummeting to my death.

Okay, wait.

I've faced far worse than this down here.

These spiders can't hurt me. I've never heard of a venomous spider infestation in Paris. I have to be strong. To breathe. To keep going. I'm close, so close to a way out, and that's all that matters.

But I think I feel something scuttle over my jeans, and fear stifles all logic. I kick, trying to hurl it off, and my other foot slips.

My yelp turns into a shriek as I start to fall.

34
Ruby

My abdomen crashes into the rungs as I cling on for dear life, feeling like my arms are about to tear from their sockets.

Something clamps down hard on my ankle.

"Hold on!"

"Selena," I sputter, stunned she's the one who climbed up this ladder to help me, despite her injuries, despite having fallen from a ladder herself, her own trauma be damned.

"Are you okay?" she asks.

"S-spiders—"

"No, they're just some friendly crickets."

"Crickets?!" Don't crickets chirp? I stare at the closest one. Oh. It was an antenna that twitched, not a leg. And their bodies are too narrow, their legs too wiry to be spiders. Still, they're humongous, bigger than any crickets I've ever seen. And there are so *many*.

Hello, new cricket phobia.

"They won't hurt you," says Selena.

"Easy for *you* to say." She knows I have arachnophobia. If a spider ever appeared while we were hanging out, she was the one who'd capture it and bring it outside, and once on a class trip to a wildlife preserve, she was first in line to hold a tarantula while I tried to dissolve into the nearest tree trunk.

"I don't think anyone has ever died by cricket."

"They're so gross." I cringe away from the closest one.

"The feeling's not mutual. That one's probably wondering how some hot girl wound up in his living room. He's like, damn, that's a ten. Haven't seen a ten in a while."

My laugh comes out as a gurgle.

"You got this?"

"Yeah." I gain a foothold on the closest rung, no longer dangling like a rag doll. "Hey, Selena?"

"Hey what?"

"Now you're not the one who freaked out the worst." I'm still breathing hard.

She squeezes my ankle. "It's okay to have phobias. Chris Hadfield—you know, the astronaut?—he's afraid of heights, and this one time, he lost his vision on a space walk because something irritated his eyes and he teared up. So there he was, dangling above Earth with his purge valve open to evaporate his tears, listening to air hiss out of his space suit. Scariest shit in the world—well, galaxy. But he didn't let that fear take over. He controlled it. He knew he wouldn't actually fall. He knew his team was giving him the right instructions. You know these crickets can't hurt you. *You* can control this."

For some reason, that makes me want to cry. I wish I were so brave. I press my forehead against the rung and blink rapidly, holding back tears. The last thing I need is for *my* vision to go all blurry right now.

"Come back down," Julien calls up. "Take it slow."

Selena lowers herself to the rung below, but I glance up. There are only ten or so rungs above me. *So close.* "I'm going up."

They're just crickets.

I can be stronger than my fear. I can reach the surface anyway. I can do this.

Selena stills. "Are you sure?"

"Yeah. You can go back."

"No, I'll be right behind—er, below you."

I nod, bracing my shaking legs, adrenaline raging in my veins. I can control my body. My fear. My fate. One rung at a time. I take a deep, grounding breath, then stretch up.

Grasp a rung.

Step.

Stretch.

Grasp.

Step.

Stretch.

Grasp.

Something tickles over my fingers.

My eyes flutter shut, and I swallow hard, but I don't flinch. I don't fall. I'm in another cricket's living room, that's all.

I angle my head back to better illuminate the rusted manhole cover. Almost there.

Finally, it's mere inches overhead. I reach up and press my palm to the cool, bumpy, rusted metal, and push hard, as hard as I can.

Nothing.

"Dammit," I grunt. "Can you hold my ankle again? I need both hands."

"Got it." She grips it firmly, and I use all my upper body strength to heave against the cover, straining to shift it even a millimeter.

But it's like trying to shove Notre Dame into the Seine. It won't budge.

"Please." I slap the plate with my open palm. It makes a dull *thud.* "Help!" I scream, banging on it with my fist. "Help us!" More dull thuds, like there's something thick and heavy behind it.

Selena joins in, and we shriek at the top of our lungs, desperate for anyone to hear us.

"It's no use." Julien's voice floats up here. "It must have been paved over."

"No . . ." I let out a frustrated growl, then fumble for my phone in my jacket pocket and turn it back on. Maybe I'll get a signal this close to the surface.

"Come back down," says Julien.

"Hang on," I say. It takes seconds to power on but feels like millennia.

Once it does, I stare at the space next to the battery meter, willing a signal to appear. My gaze drifts down to the photo of Sean and me. He always hates being on camera, but in this shot, he looks so happy, so comfortable, holding me close, his gray eyes shimmering in the sunlight, so sharp they slice through the screen.

A sob scrapes my throat. For a moment, I can feel the crisp breeze that tousled my waves as Val snapped the photo. I can feel Sean's arm wrapped around me, can feel his warmth as I nestled close, can feel how safe I felt, how excited I was for the week ahead, a week in Paris, a week with *him*. I'd give anything to feel his arms around me again. I have to get back to him.

But there's still no signal.

Selena waits with bated breath as I raise my phone and position it flat against the metal plate. "Maybe it's just slow," she says. "It took forever for my phone to connect to the French provider when we landed."

Nope.

No bars.

"Dammit," I choke out.

I navigate to my map app to try for a GPS signal and hold the phone to the plate again, a tear slipping down my cheek as I wait for a blue dot to appear, or for the map to shift to our location. *"Please."*

But nothing happens.

Nothing.

"Let me try your phone," I say.

"Yeah." She takes it from her pocket and presses the power button. The screen remains dark. "It's dead . . ."

No. So close. So damn close.

A bustling city street is mere inches away. Commuters hustle home from work, breathing in the crisp air, clutching baguettes under their arms while others speed by on mopeds or rest their toes on the pavement as they wait for a traffic signal to change. Locals crowd the cafés lining the sidewalk, sipping espressos or spritzers as they idly watch groups of tourists flock past. Pigeons strut the sidewalks, angling for scraps, taking flight whenever a leashed dog comes too close.

Sean's somewhere up there, too. I wonder what he's doing right now, at this exact moment. Is he thinking of me? Worried for me? Trying to find me? Somehow, I believe so. But he has no way to know I'm trapped beneath his feet.

I let out a strangled cry and flatten my palm against the cool plate.

They're all up there, right now, right above my head.

But they might as well be another world away.

35
Ruby

"I'm Val Moreau, and this is Ruby Hale and Selena Rodriguez, and we're on day three of being lost in the catacombs."

We stand side by side, me in the middle, staring into my camera lens as Julien films. My heart sinks to hear those words spoken aloud. I can't believe we've been down here that long, yet it feels like we've been down here for a lifetime.

"We were going to a party with—"

The red light blinks off as Julien lowers the camera. "Since there's so little battery, maybe just say what you want your families to hear."

"We at least have to explain what happened to Liv," I say.

Filming this was Selena's idea. In case we don't make it. She wants to be able to say goodbye to her family. My camera's been useless in the navigational department, anyway.

I just hope nobody stumbles across it later and uploads the footage of three of the dead teenagers who went missing in Paris weeks earlier.

Julien starts recording again. Val doesn't bother wiping her tears as she explains what we've been through, how we're thirsty and hungry and nearly out of food, how we lost Olivia to an asthma attack. "We tried so hard to save her. Selena tried giving her CPR." I glance at Selena, who keeps her eyes downcast. I didn't realize she'd been the one who tried. We got training on the swim team; I should've known. "And Ruby dove back into the water to find Liv's inhaler."

Tears brim my eyes. "I-I was the one who ran into her at the hotel and pulled her into the elevator so our teacher wouldn't catch us sneaking out. I'm sorry. I'm so sorry."

Val leans close and whispers, "She *wanted* to come down here."

I'd assumed she'd been bottling up her own guilt. But maybe she's been rationalizing it away. It's true, though. We did all choose this.

Selena huffs beside me, but I don't respond to Val. Instead I go on, "She loved her family. She told us how much fun she had going to your lake house, and going on hikes with her dad. She wanted to go to Harvard and live with her grandma. She was always so helpful, and so damn smart. And she'd want you to know how much she loved you. She really, truly did."

Selena sniffles, tears dripping from her chin onto Olivia's coat.

"Our stuff now?" Val asks. I can tell she's eager to get this over with.

I nod. "Go ahead." I want to go last. I'm bad at winging speeches and usually write out scripts for my voice-overs ahead of time. It's impossible to sum up everything I should have a lifetime to say. If word vomit's the last thing Dad and Sean will ever hear from me, I at least want to do a practice run in my head.

"Thanks." Val clears her throat and fluffs her matted bangs. My own frizzy waves are beyond fixable. "Mom, Dad . . . oh God." She screws up her face and covers her mouth. I put my arm around her.

"Maybe stop recording?" Selena says to Julien.

"No, I'm fine." Val wipes her eyes, then pulls down an invisible zipper in front of her face and blows out air. "Okay. In case we don't make it, I want to say goodbye. Coming down here was— Ugh, I really shit the bed on this one, huh? What else is new?" She shakes her head. "All I ever wanted was to make you proud, and all I ever did was the opposite. Well, I'm going to miss you—or not, because I'll be dead. At least there's that, right? No pain once this is over. Anyway. I'm sorry and I love you. Oh God, that was awful. Can I re-record that?"

She rushes to Julien, who stops recording. "I don't know how to—"

"Here." I join them, angling for my camera. "We can delete that one clip."

"It was fine," Selena says.

The battery meter has one slice left, blinking red. I switch to preview mode and see the recent clips' thumbnails—

My chest tightens. "Holy crap. They're gone." I scroll back and forth through the thumbnails with trembling fingers. The last image before the clip where Val introduces us is a clip from dinner in Saint-Michel. "All the photos and videos from down here—they're all gone."

"Are you sure?" says Val.

"Did your camera get wet?" Julien asks.

"No." I'd been careful to keep my purse above water before we transferred the camera to the Tupperware. "If the memory card got wiped, everything would be gone. But the stuff from our day in Paris is still here." I rub my brow. This makes no sense.

"Those pictures weren't helping, anyway," Val says.

"I don't understand how this happened," I say.

"Should we bother recording more if the memory card's not saving anything new?"

"I still want to record," says Selena. "It saved what you just recorded, right?"

"Yeah," I confirm. "There's only a little power left. Let Selena record, okay?" I say to Val. "If there's still time after, you can redo yours."

"But—"

"*Please*," I say, strained. "I don't want to argue."

Val pinches her lips but nods.

We resume our positions. Selena takes a deep breath, and the red light blinks on.

"Hi Daddy, Mom, Josh . . . I don't know if you'll ever see this, but I wanted to say I love you all so much. I'm sorry for coming down here. I don't want you to blame yourselves at all. It was a mistake, but . . ." She hesitates. "The truth is, I wanted to make sure my friend would be okay." She clasps my hand. "And Jeff, I know she's not going to say it, but that's why Ruby's here, too. She went out that night to find her friend and bring her home. One thing led to another, and that sucks, but she had the best intentions, and I hope that makes you proud."

My jaw hits limestone.

I thought she came down here because she had something to prove. Because Val accused her of being scared. Not because she wanted to protect *me*.

Val stiffens beside me. Selena's just thrown her under the bus.

"And I want you to know," Selena continues, "how much you all mean to me. Daddy, you always made me feel like a princess no matter what you were going through, and Mom, you were as much of a mother to me as if you'd given birth to me yourself. Josh, thanks for making me watch you play *Mass Effect*." She chuckles. "I love all things space thanks to you. I'm so grateful to you all and love you. I'm sorry you're all probably going through hell right now."

A swell of emotion bursts in my chest. I can picture Dad sitting in front of his laptop, watching this video, a palm pressed to his mouth the way he always does when trying to stifle tears in front of me, trying to be strong for me. I wish he believed in an afterlife. Maybe then he could find comfort in believing I've reunited with my mother. Maybe soon I really will get to meet her. If I do, I'll make sure to tell her how much Dad still loves her, if she doesn't already know, if she hasn't already been watching.

But then I'll be leaving him behind, all alone, his greatest fear turned reality. This will destroy him. Nothing I say will make him feel less terrible. Maybe I could tell him what I've just been thinking, that I'll find peace with Mom and that I'm excited to meet her.

Tears streak down my cheeks as Selena continues. "Aliyah, I love you. I'm so happy I got to experience what love is with you, and for every moment we got to spend together. And I want *you* to be happy. I'm not alone down here, and I don't want you to be alone up there."

She glances at me, but I signal for her to keep going. I'm still gathering my thoughts. I wish I could say something so eloquent to Sean. This could be my last chance to tell him how I feel. That I love him. That I have for months. That he gives me something to look forward to each day. That all the times I recoiled from his touch were out of fear—fear that we'd meld perfectly, only to face a day when he'd never touch me again. But there will be no gauging his reaction. No takebacks if I say something too mushy.

". . . just please don't be sad for too long, okay?" Selena's saying, "I love you and—"

Julien lowers the camera before she can finish her thought. "I'm sorry . . . It shut off."

My stomach bottoms out.

No. My chance is gone.

I should've said what was in my heart instead of worrying it'd come out all wrong. It was all right there, right inside my head.

Now I'll never get to say goodbye at all.

36
Sean

I hunch over my desk and hover my thumb over the *Publish* button.

"You sure about this?" Aliyah asks, cross-legged on my bed.

Each of our parents booked us return flights in the morning, but I won't give up. I have no clue whether Mr. LeBrecque relayed my catacombs theory to Debois, or whether she'll take it seriously or laugh it off. Several police officers were here a few hours ago to inspect the girls' rooms again, which seems pointless beyond belief.

"Yeah," I say. "I can't do *nothing.*"

The hardest part's already done. I set aside my discomfort and filmed myself explaining the situation, then added footage of that grate from the other night and some Google Maps screenshots of the area. I'll post it from my TikTok account and Ruby's YouTube channel (since I'm an admin), and posting it there will probably make the biggest splash—her subscriber count shot up when the media started covering the girls' life stories, branding each with some cheesy attribute: Olivia, four-time *Jeopardy!* teen champion; Val, daughter of HGTV's *Fix It or*

Nix It stars; Selena, aspiring astronaut; and Ruby, budding travel influencer.

Aliyah takes a long draw of water, polishing off her third bottle in as many hours—she's been hydrating extra because of her celiac flare-up the other night—then swallows loudly. "What if Debois is right, and we freak out the guy who took them?"

"I don't think he took them. He's probably stuck down there with the rest of them."

"He's not *probably* anything. This whole grate thing is a wild guess."

"I don't think it is."

"Listen, I know how you're feeling—"

"No you don't."

"Um, yes I do." She goes stiff. "You're not the only one whose girlfriend's missing."

"Ruby's not my—" I stop myself. What Ruby technically is to me doesn't matter. All that matters is getting her back. "That's not what I meant. I know you love Selena."

"Then what *do* you mean?"

This guilt has been clawing at me for days. Maybe I should get it off my chest. I take a deep breath. "I knew Val was trouble. And I did nothing."

Her lips curve down. "I thought y'all were tight?"

"Not really. I kept this from Ruby, but . . ." I wipe my upper lip. "Last month, Val told Liv I liked her even though I *know* she knows Ruby and I—we're not together, exactly, but—"

"You're into each other."

"Yeah. I think so. On my part, definitely." I don't meet Aliyah's gaze but sense her posture relax. Still, I shift uncomfortably, clenching my fists on the desk. I don't confide in people much. Whenever I'm upset at home, Pop gives me a *Buck up, son,* and that's that. "Anyway,

Liv told me everything, and when I confronted Val, she made me swear not to tell Ruby. I don't know if I was being paranoid or what, but the guilt on her face—she knew it would hurt her. It was like she was *trying* to."

"Huh," says Aliyah. "That is weird."

I nod. "I didn't want to mess up their friendship or whatever, but if I was straight with Ruby, maybe she wouldn't have gone chasing Val, and she never would've gotten into this mess."

Aliyah leans over to cover my fist. "You don't even know that's what happened. And you can't blame yourself for this. Heck, I admire that you didn't interfere. You wanted Ruby to make her own choices about her friendships."

"But she should've at least had all the information, right?"

She sighs. "I don't know. Maybe."

"Either way, I have to fix this. I have to post this video."

"But what if you're wrong?"

"Then the cops will pull up the grate and see it leads nowhere. At least they'll quickly rule it out." And I'll probably seem like I've lost my goddamn mind, in an extremely public manner. Plus, I'll earn disapproval from Pop, from my teacher, from the police.

I've always played by the rules. Never taken big risks.

But right now, I have to trust my gut. And my gut's *screaming* I'm right.

So I steel myself and hit Publish.

37

Ruby

Rustling plastic haunts our steps as we plod down the corridors. I keep thinking I'll turn and see Olivia trailing us, but it's just Val carrying Olivia's bag. Each crinkle sends a stab of sharp pain through my chest.

Thirst torments me as fiercely as my grief. My mouth and throat are arid wastelands, and I'm getting real close to chugging that last bottle of pond water, to hell with the consequences. It feels like if I don't drink *something* soon, I'll die before any microbes have the chance to feast on my innards.

"How can you still not know the way?" Val's accusation comes out low and hoarse. We've reached the highest gallery yet seem no closer to an exit.

"Like I said," says Julien, "I usually come with a group. And I've never been to this section."

Selena whimpers and slows, gripping the wall. "I—I can't. I'm sorry. My foot . . ." She slides to the ground and takes off one of Olivia's too-tight boots. Blood's seeping through her sock.

I kneel beside her. "Did you cut your foot on something?"

"I don't think so." She rests her head back against the wall as she scratches at the headband securing the cotton to her arm wound. Her teeth chatter aggressively, her full lips as dry and cracked as mine feel. "The blisters got irritated or s-something."

"Come on." Val's eyes are bloodshot from exhaustion. "We have to keep going."

Julien stoops beside us. "We can't stop. Not here." Like it makes a difference whether we stop in the middle of a corridor or at a dead end or past an impassable pool. Those masked freaks can clearly find us wherever.

"I'm sorry," says Selena. "I *can't* . . ."

"Let's rest for a bit," I suggest. "It's late anyway, right?"

Julien checks his watch. "Almost two in the morning."

"Do you still have Liv's shirt?" I ask Val.

Val hands it to me, then sits against the opposite wall as I use it to wipe dirt off Selena's foot. She winces with each gentle swipe. Then I make a long rectangle, folding in the dirty parts, and tie it around her foot. "That okay?"

"Y-yeah . . ." She clutches her arm, her teeth chattering so hard it's a wonder they don't all crack.

"Maybe I should check your arm, too?" I say.

She shakes her head. "I don't want to see."

"But if it's infected—"

"What could you do? N-nothing."

She's right. We have no medicine, no more forms of sanitary gauze. I scoot back to sit against the wall beside her, and she lies down and sets her head in my lap.

Like the past ten months never even happened.

Julien sits beside Val, mashing his face into his palms as I feel Selena's forehead. She's warm, but not feverish. Not yet, anyway. A tear slips down her cheek, like she knows as well as I do that's what's coming. I stroke her long, black hair, a bit oily at the crown and matted at the ends, but soft otherwise. I've always been envious of her thick, shiny mane, and she of my fair, bouncy tresses. The grass is always greener.

"Hey, Selena?" I say.

She sniffles. "Hey what?"

"Where do books sleep?"

"Wh-what?"

"Books. Where do they sleep?" Everyone remains silent. Val stares like I'm sprouting antlers. After a few awkward moments, I say, "Under the covers."

Val groans.

But Selena lets out a dry chuckle. She always laughed at Dad's puns, even the ones I'd roll my eyes at. He'd save them up for whenever she was around.

"Do you know any others?" Julien asks.

"Yeah," I say, detangling a knot in Selena's hair. "What has two butts and kills people?"

"Aw," says Selena, "I already know that one."

"A serial killer," says Julien. "Wait, do two butt cheeks not count?"

"That's not it," I say.

"What else has a butt?" Val snaps her fingers. "Oh! Cigarettes. Those have butts and kill people."

"Does a cigarette have *two* butts?" Julien asks.

"N-no," Selena chimes in. "It's, like, one continuous butt." I laugh.

"Hmm." Val reconsiders. "Oh, I know. A soldier. The butt of his gun, and his own butt. And he kills people."

"You're overthinking it," says Selena, her voice steadying, teeth chattering less.

"No way, that totally fits," says Val. "What's your answer, Ruby?"

"You give up?" I say.

"No, my answer's right. What's *your* answer?"

"An assassin."

A moment passes.

Val gets it. "Oh my *God*."

"Wait," says Julien, "I don't understand."

"Spell out the word," I say.

"Ohhhh."

"That's *such* a dad joke," says Val.

"That's the point." My heart clenches. I wish I laughed more when Dad told them—

Julien shuts off the lamp.

"Wait," Selena says as I blink into the pitch blackness and Val whines, "Not yet. I'm so hungry. Can't we eat some pretzels before lights-out?"

"Turn it back on, Julien," I say.

He clears his throat. "I didn't turn it off."

38
Sean

I didn't think I'd go viral this fast.

Four million views in four *hours*. I didn't even know that could happen. It's nine at night in the US right now, so I guess it made for prime-time entertainment. Some locals have already wandered over to see ground zero for themselves, despite the fact that it's three in the morning here, and I'm getting tagged in their videos left and right.

"I bet Debois's head's exploding," Aliyah says as we watch the most recent one. It seems the downpour has let up, and a small crowd has gathered where the police tape's cordoning off the street.

> Are you packed?

Another text from Pop slides over the video. He texted my new airline ticket for tomorrow morning—well, technically *this* morning—hours ago. I haven't replied. The adults aren't the only ones who can dole out the silent treatment.

My phone rings.

It's not Pop. I don't recognize this number, but it starts with 33—a French number, I think.

"Hello?"

"Sean? This is Capitaine Debois."

My mouth drops open.

"What?" says Aliyah. "Who is it?"

I clear my throat. "Hello, ma'am—uh . . . Madam—uh, Capitaine." Aliyah gasps.

Debois must be calling to make me take down my video. It'll do no good, though; once something's gone this viral, there's no stopping it.

"I'm sorry to call so late," she says, "but I had a feeling you'd be awake, and some news is about to break. I wanted to tell you before it does."

My heart goes from sinking to a total war zone.

Ruby's dead.

"What is it?" I choke out.

"You were right."

I straighten. "I was . . . wait, what?"

"About the grate. It's not a sewer grate; there is a shaft underneath leading to the old quarry tunnels. It's very old, and it looks like someone dug it up after it was paved over."

I grip the chair's armrest. "Are you serious?"

"Of course. Why would I kid about this? And that's not all—we swept the ladder rungs for fingerprints and were able to match them to prints we took from the girls' hotel rooms."

My lungs freeze.

"That's where they went, Sean."

My heart stops.

On all accounts, I should be dead.

"What is it?" Aliyah swats at my sleeve. "Put it on speaker."

But I can't move. Can't breathe. Ruby's trapped down there, somewhere in those long, dark tunnels.

"You should know," Debois's tone goes stern, "we were already analyzing the prints when you posted that video. There was no need to turn this into a spectacle."

"I, uh—" I swallow hard. "I wasn't sure if you'd look into it, or if my teacher even told you—"

"Comme ci comme ça. What's done is done."

I let out a breath, my legs shaking like tree branches in a storm. "So what now? What happens now?"

Aliyah looks like she's about to pop.

"We're immediately launching a search and rescue operation," says Debois. "I'm going to be honest with you, Sean, I can't make any promises about what we'll find. But I promise you we're going to do *everything* in our power to find them."

The subtext of that promise is clear: *Stop interfering.*

But all that matters now is that they're one step closer to finding Ruby.

39
Ruby

Selena won't wake up.

I frantically shake her shoulder as Julien points his flashlight at us. "Selena? Selena, please, wake up."

Her breathing is shallow, her skin warm and clammy to the touch, and she's trembling furiously. She passed out after we all split the dead man's beef jerky by Julien's flashlight, and the rest of us decided to try to get some sleep, too. But maybe she actually fainted. And apparently the warmth from us curled up beside her wasn't enough.

Water splashes Selena's face and my hands.

I recoil with a gasp, and Selena sputters awake.

"There we go," says Val. I turn to see her holding one of the water bottles. Selena wipes her face as her wide eyes dart around, looking horribly disoriented.

Julien takes the bottle and offers it to Selena. "Here. Take a sip."

Selena moans as I help her sit up. "I can't."

"You have to," Julien insists. "You haven't drunk anything in so long,

UNDER THE SURFACE

and your body needs water. I really do think it's safe—safe *enough*, anyway."

"Tell that to my gut," Val grumbles.

"It hasn't made me sick," he says.

A crackle echoes down the corridor, and I whip my head around. But the passageway behind Val is empty. It must've been her plastic bag. Olivia's bag.

After a bit more cajoling, Selena relents to take the tiniest sip, grimacing until she succumbs and takes a long, slow draw. Then we pass the bottle around until we drain it, sighing in relief as though we've stumbled across an oasis in the desert, not caring what it tastes like. If it does make us sick, we'll get sick together.

Not that that'll make it much better.

Our thirst momentarily quenched, we put our socks and shoes back on, clamber to our feet, and head out. Val takes the lead with Julien this time while I walk beside Selena, ready to try to catch her if she collapses. Exhaustion and exposure have dug purple rings under her eyes, like someone's punched her in the face, and she looks frail inside Olivia's humongous coat.

I can't let us die down here without mending the gash between us. She came down here for *me*. To make sure I was okay, even when we were nemeses, her loyalty stretching beyond whatever pettiness had torn us apart. Maybe she finally accepted the apology in my letter. Or maybe she just misses me as much as I miss her.

She was the closest thing to a sister I ever had, and I wanted her to myself. That was my biggest mistake. Bigger than kissing Tyler. I tried to stifle her like Dad always stifles me, trying to protect *us*. Maybe being so afraid of losing the people we love most is exactly what drives them away, like some self-fulfilling prophecy.

My heart cracks for Dad. I never understood him before, never got why he's always so overprotective. Now I do. And it's too late to tell him so. A dead battery might be keeping me from telling him and Sean what's in my heart, but Selena's right here, right beside me. All I have to do is open my mouth.

"Hey, Selena?" I whisper awkwardly.

"Hey what?" she croaks, staring at the ground like each step requires immense focus.

I take a deep breath and spit it out. "I'm sorry about what happened with Tyler, and for running away after." The truth probably cut deeper when she heard it from him instead of me. "I know writing you that letter wasn't enough. I should've said it all in person—"

Her bitter chuckle cuts me off. "What, so you could blackmail me to my face instead? Don't worry, it wouldn't have been any better that way."

"*Excuse* me?" In my letter, I apologized profusely, begging for her forgiveness. I scramble to remember what she could've interpreted as blackmail. "I-I never blackmailed you," I finally stutter.

"Yes you did." Her voice rises, anger energizing her. "You said if I ever talked to you again, you'd tell all my new friends I was using them to get to Tyler. Which wasn't true."

I never wrote that.

Yes, that's what I thought she was doing at the time, but I *never* said it out loud or in writing. In my letter I barely even touched on her new friends, embarrassed to admit I felt abandoned.

"Whoa, what's going on?" Val says, turning to face us.

"I swear to God," I say, ignoring Val, "I'm in some alternate reality or something—"

Val gets between us. "Will you both stop it?"

"Come on," says Julien, "I thought we were getting along."

I swat Val aside, focusing on Selena. "I swear on all six million skeletons down here I never said that."

"Ruby, I read it with my own two eyeballs." Selena waggled her fingers between them. "It was in your handwriting. You wrote *horrible* things."

"What horrible things?"

Selena grimaces in disgust. "You're seriously going to make me re-hash it?"

I tug at my tangled waves, helpless. I can't explain what I wrote if I don't understand what she thinks I wrote.

She sighs and braces herself against the wall. "You bragged that you hooked up with Tyler. You called me a slut-shaming, social-climbing asshole. You accused me of dropping you for them; said you were tired of sucking up to such a user and poser, anyway. I'm pretty sure you threw a 'selfish narcissist' in there somewhere, too."

I frantically shake my head. I wrote none of those things. I never, *ever* would have.

Then the truth hits me like an avalanche of skulls spilling from the walls.

I jerk my gaze to Val.

She's gone deathly pale, eyes wide behind her smudged glasses.

Those were Val's words: *slut-shaming, social-climbing asshole.* When I blubbered what happened after she found me crying in the restroom, I told her I thought Selena was using Aliyah and her friends to get to Tyler. I forgot about that. She's the one who gave me the idea to write that letter. She's the one who offered to give Selena my note when I didn't want to hand it to her and run away like an awkward fool. And after Selena sent me that *fuck off* text, Val was right there to assure me I was better off without her.

My entire body goes numb.

"You switched the notes," I rasp.

My accusation hovers between us like a decrepit ghoul. At first, Val relaxes her expression, trying to mask her panic. But her glassy eyes betray her guilt, and after a long pause, her face crumples.

"I thought I was doing you a favor."

40
Sean

The world's attention has snapped to Paris like Sauron's eye to Mount Doom when he senses his ring's about to hit lava.

Not that I'm surprised this has blown up. Four American teenage girls lost in the Paris catacombs with a mysterious stranger is clickbait for the ages. It's the *speed* at which it's become a global phenomenon that floors me.

Helicopters circle over Luxembourg like vultures over a dead carcass, while Parisians and tourists brave the rain to rubberneck at the fringes of the cordoned-off area.

Reporters camp outside our hotel, eager to catch a glimpse of the worried parents, while the girls' faces are splashed all over the internet and every broadcast news outlet.

A CCTV image of them meeting the mystery man is circulating far and wide, Reddit threads and TikTok chains trying to identify him, but the image is too grainy, his face too shadowed for anyone to make a definitive hit.

#CatacombsRescue is trending on every major social media site, offering updates, analysis, conspiracy theories, and plenty of thoughts and prayers.

But as dawn broke over Paris, something else became apparent.

People want to *help*.

Rescue workers' white tents have sprouted up throughout the city where there are entrance points to the catacombs.

Our buddies Debois and Garnier and the French police have joined the French National Gendarmerie, French civil defense, and American embassy to coordinate ground teams with canine units and thermal imaging technology.

Cataphiles have come out of the woodwork in droves to assist with the search, knowing the layout of the subterranean labyrinth best, sacrificing their anonymity to help.

Experienced cave divers from across Europe have started flying in with their gear to search the flooded areas in the lower galleries in case the girls went down that far.

Locals are dropping off food, water, and supplies for the rescue teams and huddle near the tents, eager to run errands and help any way they can.

The presidents of the United States, France, and several other nations, and so many celebrities I can't even keep track, have already conveyed their well-wishes and support.

Campaigns have sprouted up online soliciting aid for the rescue efforts and the girls' families, and people across the world are donating.

I hope it's not all for nothing.

I hope wherever the girls are, they haven't lost hope.

I hope they know, somehow, that the entire planet is rooting for them to survive.

41
Ruby

I hope I'm hallucinating. There's no way Val just admitted to sabotaging my life. No way she's been parading around as my bestie for months after switching my sincere, handwritten apology to Selena with a friendship-eviscerating attack. No way I fell for it.

"You thought you were doing me a *favor*?" I repeat. The words burn my tongue, my thirst and hunger and everything else blinking out of existence because all I can see is red.

Val's lower lip quivers. "She was treating you like crap, Ruby."

Ten months of thinking Selena hated me.

Ten months of hating myself.

Ten months we'll never get back.

I'm not the kind of person who blows up at someone, but right now every strand of DNA in my system is vibrating.

"Wait." Selena shakes her head, baffled. "I don't understand."

"Val did this." I clench and unclench my fists, but my fingertips won't stop buzzing. "*She* wrote those awful things. I had no idea."

"How . . . ?" says Selena.

I take a steadying breath, then explain, "She found me crying in the bathroom at school the Monday after that Cinco de Mayo party. That weekend, I wanted to tell you everything that happened with Tyler and apologize, but I chickened out, and when I realized you already knew, I panicked. I lost it. I told her *everything*—I felt so alone, and she was right there, and I had to tell *someone*. Then she gave me the idea to write you a letter. And she offered to give it to you." I let out a growl and barely resist kicking the stone wall.

How foolish it seems now, trusting a stranger over my best friend.

"She never gave me anything," says Selena. "I found your note in my backpack."

"It wasn't *my* note."

"But it was folded just how we used to." Selena's watery eyes dart between mine. "And the handwriting . . . I'd swear it was yours."

I glare at Val. "She did a good job faking it."

She denies nothing.

"Fils de chien," says Julien.

I jump, startled. I'd almost forgotten he was there. He's leaning against the wall, ankles and arms crossed, observant as ever. His eyes lock on mine, filled with sympathy. *Confrontation isn't bad. It can stamp out the bad in someone—before it's too late.*

Oh, I'd say it's too late.

"What did your note say?" Selena asks me. "The one you actually wrote?"

"I apologized for kissing Tyler." I clasp my hands under my chin. "I *begged* you to forgive me. When he took me upstairs, I never meant to kiss him. I never wanted to hurt you. I only wanted to ask him out for you."

Her eyebrows rise. "For real?"

"I swear. But then we started talking, and he was so nice, and when he leaned in to kiss me . . . oh, I don't know. I wanted to know what it felt like. I wanted to feel *wanted*. Because the truth is . . ." I hesitate revealing the most broken part of me. But it's exactly what I should've told her from the start. "The truth is, before that party, I was lonely for months. You were spending so much time with Aliyah and Lisa and all of them, and it felt like you were replacing me. It really hurt my feelings. And when Tyler leaned in, I thought, well, at least *someone's* picking me—"

A sob-hiccup cuts me off. I can't believe I admitted that.

"When you stopped talking to me," I go on, "when you sent that last text, I figured it was because you hated me that much for hooking up with him."

She lowers her hand that's been clasping her mouth. "No. It was because of the letter. I was mad about Tyler, but I wouldn't have hated you. I-I'm sorry you felt so lonely. I won't deny it, I did want to make more friends. But I never wanted to replace you." She casts her gaze down and rubs her lips together. "*My* truth is, I did know you were upset. It's just . . . sometimes it felt like I couldn't *breathe*. It was just the two of us for so long, I didn't know how to be *myself* around other people."

I swallow hard. I was too clingy. That much I realized on my own.

Ten months.

We could've had this conversation ten months ago.

I wipe my damp cheeks. Somehow, I have tears left for this. "That's why you joined Gavel Club, isn't it?" Not to get closer to Aliyah or Tyler. "You knew I wouldn't join."

She crinkles her brow. "I needed my own thing. But so did you. You were starting your channel, and you kept asking me to come to Boston to film, and I thought, actually, it'd be good for us to have our own activities. Healthy, even."

"Oh, please," Val pipes up. "What you're really saying is she wasn't enough for you."

"No I'm not," says Selena. "Don't you dare put words in my mouth." But Val's put plenty in mine.

"I'm not. You just said ditching Ruby was *healthy*. My parents pull that crap all the time. *This show we work on twenty-four seven will pay for your college education, Valerie. We're doing this for* you, *Valerie.*" She scoffs. "I don't even want to go to college. It's gaslighting one-oh-one."

Selena scowls. "So that makes it okay for you to make Ruby think I would've slut-shamed her and iced her out? To call me those awful things?"

"How could you be so cruel?" I ask Val.

She blanches, steps toward me. "No, Ruby—" I recoil from her, and her face crumples. "I was trying to *help* you. I got you out of a toxic friendship fast. And you've been so much better off without all that drama. We've had so much fun together."

"Our friendship wasn't toxic," says Selena.

"You ignored Ruby for days," Val cried. "You ditched her all the time, abandoned her when she needed you, and for what? To climb the social ladder? To be Miss Popular? Oh, boo-hoo, you couldn't even *breathe* in her company? Bullshit. If anything, you're the cruel one here."

"That's not what I meant at all," Selena rasps, clinging to the wall like she's struggling to stay on her feet. "Stop twisting my words around."

Val looks back at me, eyes pleading. "You have to see it. I only sped up the inevitable."

"I stopped talking to Ruby based on a *lie*," Selena shouts. "If you hadn't interfered, we would've had a fight, aired out all our crap, and fixed our issues. And yeah, maybe that would've meant giving each other more space, but we would've figured it out together and stayed friends forever because we were like *sisters*."

I don't even know how to react. I've never felt more validated and alive and have never wanted to dissolve into the ground and die so hard at the same time.

"Were you, though?" says Val. "She believed you slut-shamed and ostracized her. And *you* believed she would've blackmailed you. So how close were the two of you, really?"

Her question's like a record scratch.

It sours the air and sticks in my throat, and I can't help but admit there's a kernel of truth to it. We fell for her deception so easily. Too easily. We caused each other pain and were both in denial. Selena wanted to pop our introvert bubble and make new friends. I wanted to get our heads out of the stars and explore what our own planet had to offer. The cracks were already spreading—all Val had to do was stick some dynamite in one of the fissures.

But drifting apart was one thing. Being blown apart is another.

I shake my head. "You tricked me from the start. You keep saying you were trying to help me—switching the notes, setting up Liv with Sean. Talk about gaslighting." I turn to Selena. "You were going to tell me something yesterday; you said she wasn't good for me—"

Selena palms her forehead. "That's right. Your wallet."

Val startles. "What about it?" I ask.

"She knew she had it," says Selena. "When we were drinking in Kyle and Alex's room, she ranted about how we should be allowed to drink in France since we're all eighteen. I told her *you* weren't yet, and she pulled out your driver's license to prove me wrong. But I was right, obviously." I turn eighteen next month. I met Val after my last birthday; we never celebrated one together. "I figured she was holding your wallet for you or something, but then she made up that whole thing about grabbing it on her way out by accident."

"Why didn't you say anything?"

She shrugs. "I thought maybe I was overthinking it."

"Why'd you really take my wallet?" I ask Val.

She bites her lip, and a tear rolls down her cheek. "I thought you'd be mad at me for meeting Julien. But I"—she glances his way—"I was so intrigued. I wanted to go so bad. So I was going to *find* your wallet the next day so you'd be happy with me again."

"God," says Selena. "Don't you see how manipulative that is?"

But my heart twists. All the time Val and I have been friends, I've been so afraid to let her down. Afraid she'd get bored of me. I had no idea she was so desperate for *my* approval. "Actually, that's just really, really sad."

"Well, *I'm* sad," says Val. "All the time. You know how many times my parents have made me switch schools? Seven times. *Seven.* You know how hard it is to start over seven different times? To make friends and have to say goodbye, over and over again? Everyone always promises to keep in touch and DM you and stuff, but no one ever does."

I motion between me and Selena. "But why sabotage us? Why *me*?"

"I found your channel. You seemed quirky. Fun. Down for travel, for heading to the city and stuff. I knew we'd get along." She lets out a hybrid chuckle-sob. "And we have, haven't we? We've had a blast."

Selena tuts. "And you wanted her all to yourself."

Like I wanted Selena to myself. I wonder if, deep down, that's the crux of my and Val's friendship. Our fear of abandonment. Our desire to be wanted. When I poured my heart out to her in that damn bathroom, she saw *herself* in me. She spotted an opportunity and snatched it.

"That's why you really tried to set up Liv and Sean," I say.

Val shakes her head. "No. Yes. Maybe? I don't even know. I really did think I'd be doing all three of you some good. But maybe . . ." Her shoulders slump. "You'd been spending so much time with Sean, and you two were majorly flirting at Liv's party, and you're my only real friend in Starborough. I thought everything would change if you two hooked up."

I grimace. She tried to take both Selena *and* Sean away from me.

She looks up and sees the disgusted look on my face. "Listen, I'm sorry, all right? I'm sorry I swapped the notes. I'm sorry I tried to hook up Sean with someone else." Her voice rises. "I'm sorry I took your wallet. I'm sorry I ever wanted to be your friend, because clearly you hate me now, just like everyone else—"

Crunching noises like footfalls over gravel echo down the corridor.

We all gasp and spin.

"Do you hear that?" Selena whispers.

The steps grow louder and louder.

Light illuminates from a tunnel far down this passageway, past where the light from Julien's flashlight reaches, glowing brighter by the moment. My insides go numb, and it feels like the ground has vanished from beneath my feet.

"Someone's coming," Val whispers.

For a moment I let myself believe they're cataphiles. Just a moment. I let myself believe we'll survive this. That we'll drink water, *clean* water, and breathe fresh air. That I'll scarf down Dad's famous chicken parmigiana and laugh at his silly puns. That I'll see Sean and wrap him in my arms and never let go.

But they're not playing music.

Two figures round the corner, each carrying lamps like ours that died, each wearing bright headlamps. I squint against the starbursts haloing in my vision, their faces obscured in shadow.

They must've heard us bickering. We'd become complacent, focusing on our petty drama instead of who could actually destroy us.

The shadowy figures switch off their headlamps, and I get a clearer view. But I already knew what I'd see.

Hollow eye sockets.

Sunken cheeks.

Gaping cavities where noses should be.

Rows of teeth bared in a permanent grimace.

And now it's too late. We have no strength to run.

42
Ruby

I stagger back and bump into Julien, who grips my arm to steady me, but the shorter stranger lashes out and latches on to my wrist, yanking me away from him.

"Let me go," I cry.

The man speaks over me in furious, rapid-fire French to Julien. I'm not fluent, but understand *What were you thinking, idiot?* His mask's skeletal jaw hinges up and down with each word, horrifically lifelike.

The taller man strides forward, exuding authority with his confident posture and strong stance despite the absurdity of his attire. He raises a hand, calling for silence, and the shorter man immediately obeys. Holes in his mask's shallow sockets reveal dark eyes as he studies us, then fixes his sharp, commanding gaze on Julien.

"Explain," he says softly in French.

I dart my eyes to Julien.

"Please," Julien says in French, too. "Do you have water—"

"Explain." He doesn't raise his voice a single decibel. He doesn't need to.

Julien audibly swallows. "We got lost."

"Marion and Paul saw you in—" I can't understand the next word. "You were so very, very close." His voice is like silk. Entrancing, somehow. I want him to keep talking so I can hear more of it.

But I'm confused.

Julien never told us he'd talked to these masked people before. If he knows some of them after all, maybe he can convince them to let us go. Hope springs in my chest.

"One of them wanted to film something," Julien says. Me. My cheeks warm. "We got off course, and my map was wrong. I did not think it would take so long to find the gate. I'm sorry. But thank you for finding us."

Wait. *What*?

I gawk at Julien, my brain rejecting the truth like a dam blocking a deluge of pain.

The tall one makes a satisfied humming noise and turns to his compatriot. "There, see? I knew it." He approaches Julien and grasps the back of his neck. "As I've told you, you're like a son to me," he says low, his hollow nose an inch from Julien's. But then his silken voice coarsens. "I knew a boy of my own heart would never betray me."

Julien lets out a breath. "I'm honored you'd search for me yourself."

"You should feel *ashamed*," he rasps softly, their foreheads touching. "Your *parents* would be ashamed. You left me no choice. There are too many eyes down here; I could only risk sending le cercle restraint."

It takes me a moment to understand the last bit: *Inner circle.*

I gasp.

I can't help it.

The tall one twists to look at me, releasing Julien, his eyes narrow slits behind those bulbous sockets. Eyes like keyholes.

It's a cult after all.

This tall one is clearly the leader.

And Julien is one of them.

No. Impossible. Denial engulfs my senses, making my vision blur as I sift through the past few days like one of Sean's montages. One memory surges to the surface: Julien beating one of them to a pulp. He killed a cultist to save me.

Or so I thought.

My heart thrums wildly as I gape at Julien, who has the gall to stare back, forehead crinkled, lips downturned. He fooled me like Val did, but worse, so much worse. But I'm too stunned to shatter, too confused to condemn him. Nothing he's told us is true. Nothing he's done makes sense.

Val's frowning like she has no clue what's going on, but Selena seems to understand, her jaw hanging slack like she's just seen someone guillotined.

The short man tightens his clutch on my wrist so hard sparks of pain leap up my arm. I let out a strangled cry and try to twist free, but that only makes him grip harder.

"Release her," the tall one commands, his voice smooth as satin slipping around the short man's neck.

The short one flicks me off like a gnat. I topple against the rough stone wall, lightheaded from thirst and hunger.

"Luc," Julien protests.

Luc, the shorter man, spits, "Sa mère." An insult.

I itch to flee, but we're evenly matched at three versus three, and these men could easily overpower us in our weak and weary states. Even if we run, Julien has the headlamp and all the flashlights. Except one. I surreptitiously reach into my pocket for my phone, and my fingers curl around Julien's switchblade instead.

I forgot I had it.

"Tell me," the leader drawls, "what were you thinking, bringing *four*?"

"It was only supposed to be her." Julien motions to Val as I find my phone instead and press the power button. "But when she brought the others, I saw an opportunity *de les assimiler*"—I can't translate that—"to make us more secure—"

"That's enough," he warns, then scans us over, briefly settling on the bloodstained scarf around my neck and the wrapping covering Selena's arm. We've clearly been through hell. "Where is the fourth?"

Julien visibly swallows. "Dead. We had to swim through basin de serpent—"

"She drowned?"

"It was an asthma attack," Val pipes up in English. But when the leader's biting stare settles on her, she shrinks back.

He turns back to Julien and whispers, "L'avez-vous assimilée?"

"Of course not," says Julien.

The leader mutters a curse. "We can't let them find her."

Julien's eyes go wide. "Who?"

"The police," says Luc. "Everyone. They got you on camera, genius."

My pulse quickens. People know we're here. I bet we made the news. Maybe that's how the leader knew there were supposed to be four of us—that, or his cultists who spotted us. He also said there are *too many eyes* down here. Others, searching.

"They know who I am?" Julien asks, looking queasy.

"No," says the leader. "They haven't identified you. *Yet.*"

That gives me an idea. I edge my phone from my pocket enough for the lens to poke out and tap the spot on the screen where I know the camera icon is to start recording.

"With respect," Luc says to the leader, "I disagree. If the police can't find them, they'll never stop hunting *him*." He motions to Julien. "Let them keep thinking it was an accident. All of them." He says the last part so quietly I barely hear him.

The leader sighs and shifts his weight on his heels, like he's struggling with this decision. Julien's breathing is ragged beside me. Finally, the leader nods.

"No." Julien's eyes are wide, looking as scared as I feel. "Please."

"Don't think this pleases me, my son." The leader cups Julien's cheek. "Our numbers are dwindling. You know this better than most. But I cannot allow the police to connect you to us."

"There must be another way." Julien's voice rises. "*Please*, Stefan—"

The leader—Stefan—slaps Julien, then shoves him into the wall with such force I can feel the slam reverberate in my rib cage. He towers over him, pressing his forearm into his neck.

"Stop!" I can't help shouting, then clamp my lips as Stefan's eyes drift to me, glinting in those sockets. He clucks his tongue mockingly. "How sweet. She doesn't want to see you get hurt. Have you been playing with your lambs?"

"No," Julien chokes out.

As Stefan admonishes Julien some more, I dart a frantic glance at Selena.

They want to kill us, she silently mouths.

Yeah. I picked up on that.

I don't know much about cults, but apparently they're losing members, and Julien said he brought all four of us "de les assimiler" to make them more secure. That must mean *to recruit*. I bet he was bringing us to some sort of recruitment or induction party, but then we got lost, and now they assume their usual brainwashing process won't work on us anymore.

We have to convince them otherwise.

We have to make Stefan *believe* we want to join them. Then when they bring us back to this gate of theirs, we can get aboveground and try to escape from there.

I wish I could communicate my plan to the others, but that's not exactly possible right now. Selena's frozen in fear, and Val looks bewildered, like she hasn't grasped a word. I'll have to do this myself.

Cripes.

Olivia mentioned something about brainwashing, but I can't remember. I'll have to wing this. Which I'm bad enough at doing under normal circumstances.

The men are still arguing, but I take a deep breath and interrupt in French, "Let us join you." My cheeks catch fire as everyone looks at me, and Stefan and Julien go quiet. I can swear Stefan's gaze is glimmering with amusement.

Better to be amusing than dead.

"I mean it," I go on, trying to keep my voice steady and earnest. "We've gotten to know Julien these past few days, and we want to help. We won't tell anyone about you—*us*. About us. I promise."

Stefan tilts his head at me, releasing Julien, who slumps back against the wall and clasps his neck. "You know French," Stefan says.

"They're here with their French class," says Luc. "Obviously they know some."

Stefan whacks Luc upside his head, knocking his mask askew.

"Gah." Luc briefly removes his mask to dab his lip and check for blood. He looks like he's in his midtwenties, and his stubble, the color of mud, makes his narrow, pale face look dirty.

"What's going on?" Val finally asks, frustrated.

Stefan's dark eyes bore into mine as he steps closer. "Why do you want to join us?" He switches to English, maybe for Val's sake. "Do you even know our purpose?" A challenge. A test. *Why should I believe you?*

My face blazes like a furnace. I'll only have one guess. Guessing wrong could mean death. I rack my brain, images from the past few days flashing through my mind.

The mural above the corpse: skulls dotting the night sky like stars—no, like *angels* guarding Paris while a fissure cracks the city wide open and buildings topple into it, like the Mouth of Hell Olivia told us about where a street collapsed into mines in the 1700s.

Julien, snaking his arm out to stop Val from touching the bones: *Without their strength, we'd be reduced to dust.*

A message, scrawled in red: *In these halls, those who are forgotten protect those who have forgotten.*

I flick a glance at Julien, and he stares back with such intensity it's like he's trying to beam the information through my skull. I inhale sharply, my nerves sparking with trepidation.

"You protect the dead—" My voice sticks in my throat.

Selena steps close enough for her arm to brush against mine. "And the dead protect *us*." She's connected the dots, too. We clasp hands—both of ours are shaking.

Julien's eyes flutter shut in relief but snap back open when Stefan rounds on him. "You told them about us."

"No." Julien raises his hands defensively. "I never told them anything. I swear it."

Stefan returns his glare to us. "Truly?"

We nod like bobbleheads. But Julien's done worse than talk. He *killed* one of them. And led another to drown, we suspect. Stefan must not know. He might not have a way to know. The cultists' phones wouldn't work down here, either. For all he knows, his people are still searching. For all he knows, we haven't been running from them all along.

I bet that's why Julien killed that lone cultist so quickly. The man knew Julien, knew he was avoiding them, and Julien didn't want him revealing the truth to us. But *why*?

After a long pause, Stefan asks us, "The dead have spoken to you as well?"

"Uh . . ." Selena falters.

Dismay jolts my heart. He thinks it's possible to commune with the dead. If we say we can, too, maybe he'll spare us. But if he's faking his powers, he'll know we're lying, too. Catch-22.

Let's be real. He *has* to be faking.

Though I think of the lone cultist, of how the femur in his grip shattered while mine stayed intact, almost like the dead chose to help me and not him. But that makes no sense. It sounds completely delusional.

And yet.

"No," I finally say, unwilling to risk it. Unwilling to believe it.

His shoulders slump like he's disappointed.

"Have the dead talked to *you*?" Val asks. I want to elbow her, but she's standing out of reach.

"Do you doubt me?" he asks.

"No," I say quickly, "of course not. I always wished for that. My mother died giving birth to me, and I've always wanted to speak to her and tell her how much I wish she were here." A tear slips down my cheek, more from fear than the sentiment. Though I wish my mother *were* here, protecting us somehow.

Stefan steps before me, scrutinizing my face, then trails a gloved finger down my cheek, tracing the streak my tear made. My heartbeat's so intense, my fingertips are pulsating.

"I wish I could reach her for you," he murmurs. "But I can only make contact through their essence."

Like bones, I imagine. I think of Olivia's hair in my purse but know testing him would be foolish. Instead I bow my head like I'm disappointed, too.

That seems to win him over. He lifts my chin so I look at him, his gloved fingers satiny under my skin. "You're right. We are *Les Gardiens des Morts*; we guard the dead, and the dead guard us. They have told me their strength is diminishing, and if they lose their strength, their *power*, the earth will swallow the city. If we fail to protect the dead, Paris will fall."

Selena tightens her grip on my fingers, and I have to gnash my teeth to keep my expression neutral with his eyes so damn close to mine.

But Val bursts out laughing.

Stefan steps back. I try to signal for Val to shut up, but she doesn't see me. And when nobody else joins in, she goes even harder, clutching her belly and pressing a palm to the wall, her pealing laughter scraping my ears like nails on a chalkboard.

"Wow." She finally settles down, raising her glasses to wipe her eyes. "I'm sorry. It's just, we've been lost underground for three days, and our friend died, and now we meet the leaders of a *doomsday* cult? It's like . . . Jesus. What can possibly happen next?"

Stefan sweeps around me and stands directly in front of Val, his silence more terrifying than anything he's said yet. Her expression falls, and her hazel eyes widen in fear.

Then he chuckles lightly.

Her posture relaxes, and her lips curl into a slight smile.

Without warning, he grabs the side of her head and slams it hard into the stone wall, knocking her glasses clean off her face.

Her skull makes a sickening *crack*, and she crumples to the ground.

That's all it takes. She's dead.

43
Sean

"Pop, I'm not getting in that car." I scrub a hand over my face without peeling my eyes from the mounted flat-screen showing coverage of another canine rescue unit heading underground. All the parents are here watching, too, along with Alex and Kyle, who've insisted on staying to support Aliyah even though most of our class is heading home early. I guess they aren't such tools after all.

Aliyah and I also refused to go to the airport, because of course we did. But instead of canceling my flight like a normal human being, Pop booked me on yet another one this evening and sent a car service to pick me up. But what's the driver going to do—wrestle me outside? He's chilling in his car letting the meter run, because Pop's paying for it one way or another.

"Sean, you need to leave this mess to the professionals." Pop's booming voice blares through my phone. Aliyah and Ruby's father, Jeff, sit on either side of me throwing sympathetic looks my way. Meanwhile, my phone buzzes at my ear—probably another text from Emily, who's been sending me live updates of our parents' freak-out. I bet she's doodled devil horns on Pop's head again.

I press my fist to the table. "I told you, I'm not getting involved anymore. But I have to be here when they find them." I watch Val's mother pass by and offer Jeff a glass of wine, but he turns it down with a quick headshake. Ruby once mentioned he binge drinks when his grief is too much to bear, but he's not an alcoholic—he's not chemically dependent on booze. I'm guessing he wants to stay alert. For her. Dark rings shadow his bloodshot eyes, and his beard looks extra scraggly.

"What good will that do?" says Pop. "If they're alive, they'll take them right to the hospital."

"It's not about that." I lower my voice and glance at Jeff, whose glazed eyes have shifted back to the flat-screen, one arm crossed over his chest while cupping his bearded face. "I gotta be here for the girls' parents. This is a *nightmare* for them."

Pop sighs. "I get it. You're a good kid. I know you want to help. But *you're* my main concern, and I want you on that plane—"

Aliyah plucks the phone from my ear.

"Hey—"

"Hi, Mr. McIntyre. This is Aliyah, Sean's friend. How ya doin'?" She chews her gum extra hard, and there's a long pause before Pop's baritone voice replies. "Mm, I've been better, to be honest. Not sure if you've seen the news, but my girlfriend's lost in the catacombs. They're these underground tunnels—oh, you've heard of them? Fantastic." I stifle a tense laugh. "Anyway, the only thing keeping me sane is your son over here. Did you know he's the reason anyone even knows they're in the catacombs?"

I shift uncomfortably, unused to praise, and open my laptop to have something—anything—else to focus on. The email I got yesterday from Emerson College fills the screen. An acceptance letter. They even granted me a partial merit scholarship for their film program. It hasn't even registered with everything else going on. I tab away from it to scroll through the latest #CatacombsRescue chatter.

After a few minutes, Aliyah hangs up and sets my phone down. "He's canceling your flight."

"Freaking miracle worker," I say, checking my texts. Yup. Devil horns. Pop's face is almost as red, a vein bulging in his square jaw.

Aliyah flips her braids over her shoulder. "I do what I can—" She sucks in a sharp breath, seeing Debois stride in. I sit straighter, and we exchange a tense glance as Debois gets everyone's attention.

But her update's more of a non-update: there's been no sign of the girls yet, and no sign of a cave-in or other obstacle near their access point.

"I assure you," she says, "we're moving as fast as we can. Unfortunately, there is significant flooding in the lower galleries." I'm surprised our catacombs tour yesterday hadn't been canceled, but maybe that tourist section's outside the flood zone. "But now that the storm has subsided, we're hoping the water levels will go back down quickly so those areas will be easier to search."

My stomach tightens. What else would they expect to find in previously flooded areas besides—nope, can't think about that.

"I want to be there when they come out," says Olivia's mother, motioning to the coverage on TV.

"When we find them," Debois says patiently, "we won't have much, if *any*, notice of which access point they'll come through, since the walls are too thick for our radios to work down there."

"*If* you find them," says Val's mother. She and her husband were last to arrive and are the only ones I haven't seen burst into tears yet.

Jeff crosses his arms over his stomach. "They'll find them."

291

"You don't know that," says Selena's father. "It's been three fucking days." His shoulders slump, and his wife puts a consoling arm around him.

"There have been underground rescues that took longer," Aliyah pipes up, motioning to her laptop; that's what she's been researching while I've been keeping an eye on the social media chatter. "It took eighteen days to rescue those kids in the flooded caves in Thailand, and those Chilean miners were trapped under the mine collapse for over two *months*."

Olivia's mother moans.

"That must've sucked," says Kyle.

"The point is," says Aliyah, "they all survived. Every one of them."

"*Those* times," says Selena's father. "What about all the times people didn't—"

"Enough," Jeff rasps, slapping the table. "I have to believe they'll find them. Otherwise I'll lose my goddamn mind . . ." His voice shakes and he clasps his mouth, and the look on his face guts me. Ruby's an only child. He'll be all alone if she doesn't make it.

Debois's tense expression melts, the curve of her lips softening. "Don't lose faith. Not yet."

His eyes mist. "I don't do faith."

"I don't either," she says simply. "But there's plenty of hope yet."

Ruby told Emily and me how her dad lost his faith, back before Christmas when she came over to help decorate our tree and Emily asked why she didn't have one. "He hasn't celebrated since before my mother died. Almost like in protest, you know? But I love it. I always went to Selena's, before—well, I love the movies, the peppermint, the sparkly lights, the presents. One time we stayed up until four in the morning trying to catch—" Her eyes got glassy, like her father's now. "Anyway, the holidays are so reliable. A cozy blanket you can curl into every December, no matter who you're with, or how crappy everything else is."

Ruby might not have grown up having faith, but she always has *hope*. No matter who won't—or can't—spend the holidays with her, each year she finds joy and comfort in them and believes she will again next year. We can have hope in anything. In each other. In new friendships. In ourselves. In our future. In the kindness of strangers.

Twelve boys in Thailand and thirty-three men in Chile survived against inconceivable odds.

And I have hope Ruby will survive, too.

I have hope I'll see her again.

44
Ruby

Blood pools around Val's head faster than it can soak into the ground. She died with her eyes wide-open, like Olivia did, staring blankly at her broken glasses resting inches from her nose.

Val believed nothing came after death. No pain. No confusion. No suffering. But no peace, either. No relief from her thirst or hunger. Just. Plain. Nothing.

It hasn't even fully sunk in how she manipulated me and Selena apart. Not twenty minutes after admitting it, she's gone. *Gone.* The girl who taught me to be bold and fearless, who embraced silliness and made me laugh, who desperately wanted someone with whom to share life's misadventures, plucked from this world in an instant. I don't know what kind of punishment she deserved—maybe in her own misguided way, she really *had* been trying to help me. But it's not this. It's not this.

Selena makes this gurgling sound as she suppresses a sob, and I squeeze her hand, hoping the cultists somehow won't notice we're shaking like leaves in a hurricane. We have to stay calm. We have to pretend we believe in whatever crock Stefan's shilling.

Otherwise we might be next.

Julien clasps his forehead. "What have you done?" Even Luc shakes his head in shocked disapproval.

Stefan mutters a curse, sounding more annoyed than remorseful, and tugs his glove further up his wrist. "I didn't think that would kill her."

But his intention doesn't matter. There are no backsies for this. No Edit, Undo.

"What if someone finds her?" says Julien.

Stefan huffs like this is all a terrible inconvenience. "On devrait l'assimiler." *We should recruit her.*

That can't be right. *Assimiler* can't mean *recruit*. She's already dead.

"There's that cemetery back there." Luc jabs a gloved thumb in the direction they came from.

Stefan nods.

"And what about us?" Julien nods at me and Selena.

"That depends."

"On what?"

Stefan doesn't answer. His eyes shift to mine, and a shock of fear courses through me.

"Please," says Julien. "Let them join. They *want* to." Maybe he's only trying to save his own skin. But at least he'd take our skin along for the ride.

Stefan points at Val. "That one clearly didn't."

That one. Like she wasn't even a person.

"No," I sputter, desperate. "But we do. We want to help you."

Stefan studies me with narrowed eyes. Skeptical eyes.

Luc leans close to him. "Let's get this over with."

Stefan nods and loops off a backpack strap to dig for something. A gun. He has a gun. The soles of my feet spark like they did when I lost my foothold on the ladder while clutching Olivia's inhaler. Like when those crickets fluttered over my fingers. Like when I peered at the ground from the Eiffel Tower's summit while Sean took my hand to steady me, but I slipped my fingers from his, scared, always too scared.

All for nothing. Scared for nothing.

What a waste.

I clamp my eyes shut, quaking as I clutch Selena's hand. I can't bear to look and want it to be over before I feel any pain—

Something hits my chest.

Something . . . cool?

I open my eyes. Stefan shoved a water bottle into my chest. No gun. Just water. I take it and let out a shaky breath as he passes another to Julien. "This will go faster if they help," Stefan says to him. "Then we can decide."

Help with what? I'm afraid to ask.

Julien chugs his entire bottle without pausing for breath, and Selena and I pass ours back and forth until we drain it. Stefan takes the empties and stuffs them into his backpack. *What goes down must come up.* I've read that's a real cataphile rule. Maybe there's some overlap. Or maybe Julien knew how to fool us. He'd talked like he was a real cataphile, addicted to coming down here, to the rush of it. Maybe he started as one before getting swept up in all this. Then again, anyone could research as much as I did about the cataphiles online.

"Pick her up," Stefan tells the men, motioning to Val.

Julien hobbles over to her and kneels. "We should wrap her head. Keep the blood from dripping everywhere."

"Good," says Stefan. "Do it."

Julien's the one to wrap Val's head in her own jacket. Afterward, they lift her, Luc gripping under her arms while Julien holds one ankle on either side of him, facing forward. Her head lolls back near Luc's gut.

Stefan kicks some gravel onto the blood, which has finally seeped into the compacted dirt, then takes me and Selena by the arms.

"Tell me," he says in English as we follow the others. Despite their sluggish pace between Val's weight and Julien's limp, Selena struggles to keep up. "If the dead didn't speak to you, how did you know they protect us?"

"We came across one of your murals," Selena says without missing a beat. "Julien didn't tell us what it meant, but he mentioned Paris only stabilized when they brought the dead down here."

That's right. I never would've guessed he meant the bones had actual protective powers.

"And your masks," I add. "They're like those skulls in the mural watching over Paris."

"A lucky guess, then," he says.

"An educated guess," Selena corrects.

Panic zips through me. I know she's trying to impress him: We're critical thinkers. An asset. But maybe critical thinkers aren't as easy to brainwash, and that would make us useless to him.

Stefan only chuckles. Minutes after murdering Val, he *chuckles*.

I swallow the bile singeing my throat. "How do bones protect Paris, anyway?"

His fingers dig into my arm. "How does any angel protect their charge?"

"Oh, of course." I meant to sound intrigued, but he clearly took it as a mockery. "Obviously that's not what I—"

"You said they're losing their power," says Selena, diverting his attention. "Why is that?"

He grunts. "Tourists, for one. Those *cataphiles*"—he spits the word—"keep bringing them here, and they don't always respect the bones." Strange. His people knocked down a whole wall of them to reach us. Then again, two of them were willing to risk swimming through that snake-shaped pond to reach us. Maybe Stefan instructed them to find us—and his surrogate son—at any cost, desperate to keep their cult a secret.

"But flooding is causing the most damage," he continues. "Over time, waterlogged bones deteriorate."

"And the more the bones deteriorate," I say, "the weaker their powers become?"

He nods, loosening his grip on my arm. "The bones are vessels for their spirits. Once they weaken, so does their protective energy and their ability to commune with me." A silken luster threads his voice again. "The flooding this week shows how dire the situation has become. The dead couldn't warn me until it was too late, and we couldn't move our supplies fast enough."

Sounds more like a meteorology problem to me.

"So how can we fix the damage?" Selena asks. *We.* Smart.

"One way is prevention. The quarries' pumps and drainage canals have been failing, so we must maintain them."

Seems awfully banal for a cult. But Selena nods along like this makes perfect sense. Aliyah's acting skills must've rubbed off on her.

I can't contain my bafflement. "Wouldn't the city handle that?"

"You'd *think*. The bureaucracy is in denial. They can't grasp what's at stake; they're too enmeshed in their own corruption to care what happens to some old bones. Trying to get them to accept the truth is like trying to convince a cat to take a bath. Well, when our monuments topple, and homes collapse while people sleep, and the earth swallows entire arrondissements, they'll wish they listened." He tuts. "Even seeing Notre Dame nearly fall *with their own eyes* wasn't enough."

"I read a cigarette or short circuit caused the fire," I say, then add, "Propaganda, I'm sure."

"Indeed," says Stefan. "Yet *I'm* the one they call a charlatan, a crook, a paranoid deviant."

True, true, and true.

Before Stefan can explain any other methods for fixing the damaged-bone situation, we reach a cimetiére—another wall of them.

Stefan bounds ahead to scan the space, moving with such fluidity you'd think he was wearing a cape. He strides several yards past the bones and motions to a divot in the opposing wall. Julien and Luc set Val's body flush against it, and the three men huddle, murmuring as Stefan draws lines in the air around Val. Luc pulls a large spool of wire from his backpack, but Stefan says, "There is no time for that."

I almost grab Selena's hand and run for it, but Julien and Luc double back and start removing skulls from the top of the wall next to us. Shock freezes me.

They're going to bury Val in bones.

"You." Stefan waves Selena over, commanding her to help him create a frame around Val's body while I (on my uninjured feet) shuttle the bones Julien and Luc extricate from the wall down the corridor.

This can't be real. This absolutely cannot be real.

When Julien hands me the first skull, it feels like a thousand tiny spiders are crawling over my skin. I'm holding someone's head in my hands. An *actual* person's head. Through this they drew breath and ate and blinked and spoke and heard music and—

"*Go*," says Julien. He avoids my stunned stare, shame plain on his face.

If he knows to be ashamed, I don't understand why he would be part of this.

Soon we have a system, and before I know it, I've piled so many bones down the corridor that Luc switches to helping Stefan and

Selena stack the bones in careful rows around Val, building something like a coffin around her.

I flash back to that ghastly throne of bones Selena found, reeking like the dead mouse in my bedroom wall, like the bloated corpse we'd stumbled across. Oh God. The truth floods in, taking my breath away. That's where they've been hiding the bodies of the people they kill. Inside the *thrones*.

Stefan said when the bones deteriorate, their protective powers diminish.

Julien told Stefan bringing all four of us would make them more secure.

Stefan called us Julien's lambs.

Yeah.

We were never meant to be recruits.

Our bones are fresh. We were meant to be *sacrifices*.

45
Ruby

Julien nudges my arm to hand me another skull.

As our eyes meet, fury bubbles in my belly, hot and thick. He lured us down here to murder us. Olivia and Val are dead because of him. And God knows how many other innocent people these freaks have killed.

But one gigantic puzzle piece isn't fitting. Julien brought us here to die, yet made us run from his fellow cultists the entire time.

I shuttle the skull down the hall, and when I return, he's chiseling hardened mud from between two more. I don't see a point in feigning ignorance with him—he'll likely share our fate, whatever it is.

"Can I ask you something?" I whisper.

"You just d—" Julien starts on reflex, then shakes his head and keeps chiseling.

"What does l'assimiler mean?" I ask anyway.

He sighs softly. "Assimilate." Not *recruit*. I should've guessed it translates how it sounds.

"So what, you *assimilate* fresh bodies with the old bones to amp up their protective powers or something?"

His brows rise. He's surprised I've figured it out. I'm disgusted to think of the times I reassured him he's a good person. No wonder he's been questioning it. But his self-awareness gives me a smidgen of hope. Maybe he's not fully lost.

"How haven't the cataphiles noticed?" I ask. Especially the reeking corpses.

"Some have, I think," he answers in as few words as possible.

I shake my head, confounded. "And they've done nothing . . . ?"

"I wasn't lying when I said coming down here is like a drug." He frees both skulls. "For them, it is."

If Val were alive, she would've told him to screw himself. He lied plenty. They both did. I cast a remorseful gaze her way. "How long has this been going on?"

"Shhh." He tries to hand me the skulls.

I don't take them. I've been afraid to speak up my whole life, and I can't stay silent now—not when I have to convince him to help save it.

"If you want to power up these bones so badly, why didn't you just kill us?"

A muscle in his jaw twitches.

"You could've slit our throats as we slept." In fact, he protected us. Multiple times. He was willing to forego a viable escape route because he was afraid Val would drown. He killed a cultist who held a knife to my throat. It doesn't make sense.

He glances past me at Stefan and Luc, who bicker in hushed tones. Their masks cover their ears, so I bet they muffle sound as well as hinder their peripheral vision. Even though they're paying us no mind, Julien shoves the skulls into my arms and turns to the wall.

I begrudgingly shuttle them to Selena, who moves sluggishly, clamping her lips like she's trying not to be sick. When I return empty-handed, I pepper Julien with more hushed questions.

He ignores them all.

"Did you delete the footage on my camera?" I persist, clasping my hands behind my back so he can't hand me another skull.

Julien grabs my arm, twists my palm up, and slaps the skull into it.

"Why bother deleting proof if you wanted us dead anyway—"

"We're not doing this," he hisses inches away from my face. "Not with him right there." The pleading look in his eyes makes me swallow hard. He's terrified of Stefan.

He turns to jiggle a femur loose. But I can't give up.

"He knew your parents," I whisper, switching tacks.

Julien freezes. Aha.

"Were they involved in all this?"

He bows his head, arm still raised, gripping the end of the bone. "I never knew. They kept it from me."

"Until they died?"

"Until my father—" Julien shakes his head.

"How did they die?"

He doesn't answer, resting his head against the back of his hand, even though it's so close to all those bones. Then he seems to realize and jerks back, wavering on his feet. It reminds me of his reaction when we found those two thrones side by side, how he nearly fell to his knees before them.

"My God, Julien," I whisper. "We found them, didn't we? Those thrones—"

"*Shhhh.*" Grief curves his lips down, his eyes hooded with sorrow as he pulls out the femur. "They couldn't contribute to the restoration fund anymore."

"What's that?"

Julien peers at Stefan, who's busy barking orders at poor Selena. "Money for fixing what the city won't fix fast enough."

So *that's* how Stefan's lining his pockets. Cult leaders often scam their members—that much I know—and that banal drain work's likely nothing more than a front.

"A few years ago," Julien says, handing me the femur and chiseling a skull free, "the high Gardien passed away. He ruled for decades. Everyone loved him, but his son who ascended next was weak. Funds ran dry, and Gardiens were leaving in droves. The dead warned Stefan that with fewer Gardiens, the Seine would flood these halls worse than ever. Nobody believed him. But soon, it happened. The inner circle panicked and ascended Stefan instead. He cracked down, organized canal repairs, quadrupled dues. The Gardiens pay gladly; they know what's at stake. *Protect the bones, or Paris falls.*" He imitates Stefan in a hushed tone, as though it's his motto. "But my parents had nothing left. My father was in the inner circle, but wasn't as wealthy as the others. He'd given *everything* to ensure our family's salvation. And those who can't pay enter a lottery to bring the next assimilation. When Stefan drew my father's name, it was *this*"—he nods toward Val—"or himself."

I'm breathless. "So that's it? Pay up, or power up?"

Julien's dark gaze meets mine as he passes me the skull. "He chose his path. And my mother chose hers."

"And you chose yours," I rasp. None of this changes the fact that Olivia and Val are dead because of him. "Why not, I don't know, steal bodies from a morgue or something? Why *this*?"

"It's what the dead instructed."

I can only gape at that.

Remorse haunts his face as he clenches his jaw, pronouncing his cheekbones, making him look gaunt. "Listen . . . I had no choice. Without Stefan's support, my sisters would be homeless. And they need me alive. Otherwise they'll have to—"

He can't bring himself to say it: *They'll have to join. Then kill or be killed.*

He's trapped.

"There's always a choice," I say. "Why didn't you report him?"

"Because it's all true," he says, low and gravelly. "All of it."

"You don't really believe that."

"You've seen it yourself."

I think of the femur that remained intact in my hands while our attacker's scattered the ground in shards. "So? One bone was more brittle than another. That doesn't make any of this true."

"It *must* be if my parents were willing to—" He raises a fist to his lips.

I let out a rattled breath. A scam artist tricked his parents into deserting their children in the worst possible way, then love-bombed him, called him *son*, kept him and his sisters homed . . . all with the underlying threat that they'd be next.

Julien's eyes suddenly widen. "*Go.* He's watching."

I turn, carrying an armful of bones. Down the corridor, Val's body is covered, and once they square off the seat and build a backrest, Stefan will decide what to do with us.

Maybe I can convince Julien that saving us will redeem him. He can't truly believe in all this. He must know his parents and all the others died for nothing.

I rush back to him. "How many—"

"*Shhh.*" His mouth becomes a thin line.

But when he passes me the next skull, I try again. "How many—"

"Enough. I owe you no more answers." He starts to turn from me.

I grip his sleeve and tug him back. "You owe me *everything*." The words come out like a whispery snarl.

"I owe you *nothing*," he whispers with equal ferocity. "If you three hadn't shown up, none of this would have happened, and my sisters would be safe." He turns back to the wall to chip away at cemented mud between two skulls.

I seethe. He's the one who pressured us all to come down here. He got *himself* into this mess.

But if he let us drag Val away, Stefan would've sacrificed him instead. And if he only brought Val and sent the rest of us home, we'd have known he caused her disappearance. So he faced an impossible choice: entrap all four of us or doom himself and his sisters.

He chose to entrap us.

Then we got lost.

But if what Stefan said was true, before we took that shortcut we'd been close enough to the party—sacrificial ceremony, rather—for two fellow cultists, Marion and Paul, to spot us in that chamber with all those bones and Pierre's wet graffiti.

That's all so many of us want in the end, to leave some mark on this world.

Olivia's response to my musings on Pierre's glistening paint echoes in my mind. I'd said it felt like reaching through time to someone who'd stood in that exact spot centuries before and left his mark on the world. In that moment, Julien was about to lead us to our deaths. He'd stared, lost in thought, knowing *that* would be *his* mark—killing a bunch of teenagers who remind him of his sisters . . .

Oh my God.

"You changed your mind," I whisper. "In that chamber—"

He swivels, jabbing a finger at me without touching me. "No I didn't."

But he did. He heard Marion's and Paul's laughter behind us in his moment of doubt and panicked. He knew we couldn't return to the grate without running into them. So he tried to take us to another exit, down the well, claiming it was a shortcut.

"*Sometimes you have to go down to go up.*" I throw his own words back at him. He'd said it before we crawled through the crevasse to the moldy corpse. "But then Selena got lost—"

"Stop it—"

"When she ran into them, you knew they'd hunt us down—"

"*Shut up—*"

"And when they broke through those bones, you knew it was all bullshit—"

"That's enough!" Stefan booms.

My stomach drops, and I jump and tear my gaze from Julien. I expect to see Stefan storming toward us, but he's still with the others, nudging a column of bones within their new structure with his boot.

"It's disrespectful to leave it this way," Luc argues.

Julien's shoulder bumps against mine—intentionally, I think—as he passes me to survey their handiwork. Maybe thrones are exclusively for Gardiens who've attained the ultimate salvation or something, because they've constructed what resembles more like a lopsided bench. Its low backrest is flush against the wall, composed of three rows of skulls only two-thirds the width of the seat.

Val's under there.

I hope Selena closed Val's eyes. I hope she won't have to stare up at all those horrible skulls weighing down on her forever.

"We can come back and fix it later." Stefan scoops up his backpack, his mind made up. "After we deal with them."

Selena scuttles to my side, pale and drawn, and her shaking fingers find mine again. Burying Val like that must've been horrific.

Stefan signals to Julien with a quick flick of his wrist, and Julien digs the can of spray paint from his pack and sprays the wall above Val's tomb. As a skull symbol takes shape, the hissing sound slithers through the corridor like a snake. Stefan raises his hands and chants low in French, "We offer this blood to give you strength. May you summon your powers and protect those who have forgotten."

Once Julien haphazardly fills in the skull's keyhole-shaped eye sockets and the spraying silences, a different noise echoes in the distance.

An unmistakable *growl*.

46
Sean

"Don't forget to eat." Jeff sets a ham-and-cheese baguette and a cup of soup next to me.

I straighten, startled. I've been hunched over my laptop and didn't even notice him get up to grab food from the buffet table. The French onion soup's savory smell makes my stomach grumble, but I'm too queasy to chalk up a real appetite. "Thanks, but . . ."

He plunks himself down and takes a bite of his sandwich. "If I can eat, kid, so can you. And God *damn* it. Apparently I have no clue how to bake bread." He shakes his head, examining the baguette's crust. "Mine never pans out like this."

I chuckle. "Good?"

"It's fucking fantastic. Everything here has been phenomenal, and I shouldn't be able to enjoy a thing right now." He sits back with a huff. "This week I've learned I can't keep my daughter safe *and* I'm a hack. How're you doing?"

"Not that far off." My voice cracks.

He nods and wipes his beard with a napkin. "Ruby told me you're headed to West Point."

"I dunno. That's where Pop wants me to go."

"What do you want?"

I shrug. "I got into Emerson's film program."

"Hey, congrats. In Boston, right?"

"Yup. I wouldn't have to leave—" I almost say *Ruby*. It must be obvious how I feel about her, anyway.

Jeff leans his elbows on the table. "Well, if your dad gives you crap, you send him my way. Trying to force someone to fit your mold only makes them ooze all over the place. Just look what I did to Ruby."

"This isn't your fault," I say.

Aliyah slides into the seat next to me. "It's not anyone's fault besides that asshole who took them down that ladder." She, Alex, and Kyle have been sitting with Selena's parents, trying to keep their spirits up. She flicks the back of my laptop. "Anything new on the socials?"

I shake my head. "I wasn't looking. I've been reading up on recent missing persons cases in Paris. Debois said something the other day I can't get out of my head . . ."

"What'd she say?"

"Well, first she pretty much called me a selfish American."

Jeff snorts over his spoonful of soup.

I don't laugh. "Then she told me how lots of people go missing in this city every single week. I looked it up, and tens of *thousands* of people go missing in France every year. And hundreds of thousands in the US. Can you imagine how big that number is across the world?"

"It must be *millions* . . ." Olivia's mother mutters from the next table. The whole room has quieted to listen.

"So why this?" I motion to the intensive news coverage. "Why now? Why doesn't the world react like this all the time?"

"Cuz they're lost in the *catacombs*, dude," says Alex.

"Yeah," says Aliyah. "But also, they're four American teenagers from upper middle-class families. And three of them are white."

Her words sink like a dead weight in my chest. "Damn."

She gives me a tight-lipped smile. Yup. That's how the world works.

I glance back at the TV showing aerial footage of the Seine, with white tents dotting the shore near a few quarry access points and rescue workers bustling around. However grateful I am that so many people have dropped everything to find Ruby, I can't help but think of all the other people whose cases have faded into silent obscurity.

The people who've stayed lost forever.

47
Ruby

Stefan and Luc whip their heads toward the growling noise like gazelles hearing a lion's paw snap a twig.

I brace against the wall—the stone one, not the bone one—dizzy and weary from fear and thirst and hunger and all of it, half expecting some demonic beast like the Balrog from *The Lord of the Rings* to storm down the corridor, wreathed in flame, poised to eviscerate us. Honestly, maybe that'd be for the best. At least then this would all be over.

"Let's go," Stefan whispers.

Luc nods toward Selena and me. "What should we do with—"

Stefan raises a finger to his mask's bony grimace. "Bring them. There's no time."

Julien's expression remains impassive.

Stefan signals for all of us to gather our belongings. As we do, more muffled noises echo in the distance.

More growling.

A sharp bark.

That's no demonic beast. "Dogs," I gasp.

These barren corridors' acoustics are distorting the echoes. Hope swells in my chest as I envision leashed golden retrievers following our scent, pulling along their rescue workers, and Selena and I exchange a frantic look.

Stefan curses. "Come. Now." He grabs my arm, and I nearly trip as he yanks me down the passageway.

"But that's where they are," says Luc.

"I *know*," Stefan snarls. Maybe he doesn't know another way out.

I have to practically jog to keep up with his long strides. We quickly reach what seems to be a dead end except for a cleft at the bottom of the wall, which reminds me of the crevasse we shimmied through before vaulting over that corpse. Sure enough, it's another crawl space.

Stefan scans us over, then slides his headlamp up off his mask and hurls it at Julien. "You go first. Unlock the gate." He takes a key from his pocket and hands it over as well.

There's a literal gate. To the surface, I assume.

And once these cultists lock it behind us, the dogs won't be able to reach us fast enough. These men could drive us wherever, kill us, dispose of us, and no one would ever know for sure what happened.

"Then you—" Stefan motions to Selena, then Luc, then me. "I'll take the rear."

"I-I can't—" Selena whimpers, clutching her injured arm to her chest, pale and weak.

"Is there no other way?" Julien asks Stefan.

A dog barks. Louder now. It will be a race to this gate of theirs. Stefan curses at Selena, then digs for something in his backpack. "There's *this* way." He pulls out a pistol and points it at her. My heart bottoms out.

Selena raises her hands in front of her chest. "No, please—"

"Crawl or die here," Stefan threatens. "Your choice."

Julien approaches him. "If they find her *shot,* they'll never stop hunting us—"

Stefan clubs Julien in the face with the pistol. He lets out a sharp gasp and careens back, clasping his jaw. "Must you undermine me on *everything*?" Stefan snarls. "You're as insufferable as your father."

Julien straightens, balling his hands into fists. "My father gave his *life* to protect you. To protect this city."

"Your father lost his life because he *refused* to protect it."

Julien staggers back in shocked disbelief. "No. You killed him . . . ?"

"He gave me no choice," Stefan doubles down. "He threatened to expose us all."

Bile rises in my throat.

"But he was in the inner circle" says Julien. "There was a ceremony."

Stefan tuts. "As insufferable as your father," he repeats, "and as naïve as your mother. She didn't understand why she had to *beg* me to let her die."

I gasp. Julien's dad's self-sacrifice was a lie. When he refused to bring a sacrifice and threatened to expose them, the inner circle murdered him and told everyone he'd *chosen* death. Even his own wife believed it. And if one of the top dogs was supposedly willing to die, it probably bolstered the whole cult's belief that Paris is in real danger. Stefan tricked them all into paying the dues or paying with an impossible choice. A choice that led to victims like us.

Rage overtakes Julien, that same rage I saw when he pummeled that lone cultist to death, and he shoves Stefan hard. Stefan doesn't shoot him, but instead clocks him in the jaw again. Even as Julien fights back, he doesn't pull the trigger. Maybe he's afraid a gunshot would give away our location with those rescue dogs so close. Maybe he really has thought of Julien as a son. Either way, Julien's called his bluff.

As they wrestle and Luc tries to pry them apart, my pulse races. I have an idea. There's an infinitesimal chance it'll work, and I'll need to risk *everything*. But it's the only way I can think for at least one of us to survive. Resolve flows through me.

"Here." I tug Selena's good arm and try to give her my phone.

She resists. "What? Why?"

"It still has battery," I whisper. "Use the flashlight. When you get to the other side, *run*. Run away from the gate. I recorded Luc, and maybe what happened to Val." I don't know how much I managed to capture from the edge of my pocket. "Show it to the police. The passcode's your birthday." I never changed it. Maybe they can use some facial recognition software to find Luc. "Tell my father and Sean that I love them."

Selena jerks her gaze to the men. Luc has a palm on each Stefan's and Julien's chests, and they're all rasping at each other in rapid-fire French. "Why don't *you* run?" she asks.

"He wants you to go first. *Please.* I need you to tell them—"

She frantically shakes her head. "Tell them yourself. I'm not leaving you."

I choke back a sob. "I'm so sorry," I say, flinging my arms around her. "For everything." I wish we had more time. We didn't even have a chance to process Val's betrayal before pure chaos descended.

She hugs me back, shaking. "I'm sorry, too."

Even though I'm probably about to die, I smile through my tears. "I was wrong. It's not all for nothing. We're more than a pile of bones."

We're this moment. And the last. And every memory we've ever made. Every recording. Every note. Everything we've created and the lives we've touched. We're our choices, our bravery, our sacrifices.

We're forgiveness and strength and the tears we've shed. We're the friendships we've built and the love we've shared. Time might go on without us and our cells might wither to dust, but that doesn't diminish our existence. We all leave a mark on this world.

I slip my phone into Selena's—Olivia's—coat pocket. "Don't argue this. Just *run*."

Selena must feel the weight of it. "*No*, Ruby—"

Before she can try to give it back, Stefan yanks her by the hood, breaking us apart to shove her toward the crawl space. "Go ahead of her," he barks at Julien. "Pull her all the way through if you have to."

Julien guides Selena by the small of her back. "You'll be okay. It's not too long—"

"Don't coddle her." Stefan aims the pistol at them. *"Go."*

Julien narrows his eyes at Stefan as he slides off his backpack and chucks it into the crevasse before lowering himself to the ground.

Selena glances back at me. But if she doesn't follow Julien, we both might follow Val.

Go, I mouth.

She nods, steeling herself, then gets on her hands and knees and follows Julien into the crawl space.

Luc moves to follow, but Stefan pulls him back. *"I'll* go next. You take the rear." Probably to ensure he can threaten Selena with that pistol. But my plan can still work. If anything, this is better.

Crawling into the narrow space is worse than I imagined. After a few feet, I have to lower myself to my belly, raising myself on my forearms to shimmy forward. I shrink away from the stone grazing the top of my head, and my purse digs painfully into my hip bone. It's so dark; the light from Stefan's flashlight barely filters around his lithe frame, and behind me, Luc slides his backpack ahead of him, so his headlamp doesn't help much, either.

I hold still to reach for my pocket, twisting to extend my arm. My fingers close around Julien's switchblade as Luc's backpack thrusts into my boots. "Go!" he yells. I gasp and drag my arm back, hissing from the burning sensation that sears the edge of my hand as it scrapes over stone.

But I have the knife.

My pain is nothing compared to what I'm about to do to the monster ahead of me.

I hurry to catch up to him. Stefan crawls with reckless abandon, hips jostling, feet flailing, nearly kicking me in the face. I haven't heard any barks in a while, but I can't tell if my labored breathing is masking the sound. All I can do is hope they're close.

This whole plan hinges on hope.

I hope Julien will let Selena run.

I hope she'll outrun him if she has to on her injured feet and reach the rescuers.

I hope the police will find me. That Selena and I will get to reunite. That I'll get to tell Dad how much I appreciate him. That I'll get to tell Sean how I feel about him.

I hope I survive this, and I promise in this moment that if I do, I'll love without fear for how it could all fall apart.

The end of everything is inevitable, but I won't let it stop me from living. Not anymore.

"Good job," Julien says up ahead. Selena made it through.

I press the button to eject the blade, envisioning those dogs sniffing and searching, picturing them finding Selena, imagining her telling them to find me, too.

It's not like we can manifest ourselves out of here, Selena said days ago.

"Try me," I whisper.

I lunge forward and clamp Stefan's ankle, then plunge the knife as hard as I can into his calf. The blade sinks through cloth and flesh and muscle, and Stefan lets out a howl of surprise and pain.

"What is it?" Luc calls ahead. "What happened?"

I hope Selena's running for it.

Stefan tries crawling ahead, but I have to buy her more time. My pulse roars in my ears as I yank out the knife and plunge it in again. Even in the low light I can see deep stains darken his taupe pants. He curses and jerks around like he's trying to twist and point the gun at me, but the space is too cramped.

He changes tacks, kicking furiously. I burrow against stone and bury my head in my arms, trying to protect it. One kick lands on my left wrist, and I yelp as pain shoots up my arm.

Satisfied he's landed a blow, he inches forward again. I grab the knife and twist it deeper. He shrieks. I squint against a beam of light that flits across my face. Julien's peering into the narrow cavity, reaching for Stefan, but he's too far to grab Stefan's outstretched hand.

"Get her off of me!" Stefan yells as Luc drags me back by my ankles, finally understanding what's happening. I release the hilt, leaving the blade buried deep. Stefan's leg has seized up, and Julien's crawling back into the cavity to drag him out.

Which means he's not chasing Selena.

Mission accomplished.

48
Ruby

Luc only holds me back long enough for Stefan to slither from the crawl space, then makes me crawl forward again. My fingertips get sticky with Stefan's blood as I wriggle over streaks of it.

As soon as I emerge, Julien grabs fistfuls of my jacket and hauls me out.

I gasp sharply, my left arm in agony from Stefan's kick, but grit through the pain and scramble to get my bearings. A rusted iron gate stands to our left. To the right, a corridor extends into darkness.

Selena's gone.

Julien holds his clutch on my jacket, getting blood all over his hands, and glances anxiously at Stefan, who's on the ground, the switchblade next to him as he races to tie some fabric around his calf to staunch the blood flow. He's in no shape to give chase.

"Julien, please," I whisper. "Let me go."

His eyes meet mine. He let Selena go. He helped us all along. And now he knows the truth about his parents. He can't still want to be a Gardien. He can't still be loyal to Stefan.

Too late—Luc's clambering from the crevasse. Stefan motions for his help to stand, and once he's on his feet, he lunges at me and Julien. Before I know it, he's bracing me against the wall, jabbing his pistol into the delicate skin under my chin. "Bitch," he rasps in my face, his breath foul. I cringe, trying to merge with the stone digging into my back, squeezing my eyes shut.

"Don't shoot," says Julien. "They'll find us—"

"They're already going to find us," says Stefan. "The other one will tell them everything."

"You can use this one as a bargaining chip." Julien gestures to the gate. "Let's get her aboveground—"

Voices. Yelling voices. The echoes make the distance impossible to discern.

Stefan releases me and backs away, breathing hard, shaking his head in disgust. "I hope you die knowing Paris is lost because of you."

I can't help it—a skeptical scoff escapes my lips. "If Paris falls, that's on you. You're the one who turned your own people against you."

Not that I believe a word he's said.

But seeing his eyes widen behind those bulbous sockets makes it worth saying, anyway. He casts Julien a wary look, and Julien glowers right back, balling his bloodied hands into fists.

Luc snatches the key from Julien and crouches in front of the gate. I'm confused; the bars are cemented to the ground and ceiling. There's no door that can swing open.

Click. Click.

He's unlocked something close to the ground behind two of the bars and pushes them back. It's a trick gate with hidden hinges near the jagged ceiling. To anyone else, the path beyond would seem permanently blocked.

Luc holds the bars open for Stefan.

"Her first," Stefan growls, aiming the gun at me.

"No, wait—" I try, but Luc shoves me so roughly I fall to my hands and knees in front of the opening. I gasp and glance back, hoping to see light illuminating the end of the corridor.

But there's only darkness.

With a gun trained on my back, I scramble through the opening.

Selena's my only hope now.

The men lead me a short distance, going as fast as Stefan's and Julien's limping steps allow until we reach a ladder. I assume it leads up to a grate or manhole in the street. Instead, Julien opens a trapdoor into a basement.

Hopefully this will be the last ladder I ever climb.

By choice. Not because I'm dead.

Oh God.

Julien climbs first, and once I reach the top I take in my surroundings. Boxes clutter a wide, musty room lined with walnut bookshelves brimming with old books and stacks of papers and files. I'm out of the catacombs but feel no relief. This might be the last room I ever see.

A flight of wooden stairs against the far wall leads to a closed door, but Julien grips my good arm to keep me from running.

"Is this someone's house?" I whisper. "How can this lead right into the catacombs?"

"They drilled deep," says Julien, "even long ago. This house has belonged to the Gardiens since the late 1700s."

My heart races as Luc helps Stefan up the last of the ladder's rungs. I half expect Stefan to shoot me immediately, but he slips off his backpack and drops to the floor, legs sprawled out, leaning back against a bookshelf to catch his breath. Luc boosts himself up through the trap-door, then shuts and locks it behind him. Julien releases me to help unfurl a ratty rug over it.

I bolt toward the stairs.

All three men shout, but I ignore them, thinking only to get through that door, to find the front entrance, to sprint into the street where I can scream bloody murder for help.

But as I reach that first step, strong arms loop around my waist from behind and tug me back. I yelp as something sharp pierces my neck over Olivia's scarf.

"What are you doing?" Julien cries.

"Putting her down for now." It's Luc.

He releases me.

I clasp my neck as he sets a syringe on a nearby shelf. It feels like icicles are radiating through my throat.

It's hard to breathe.

Julien watches me with a horrified expression. I don't think he expected Luc to inject me with whatever the hell that was.

Stefan raises his pistol from where he slouches on the floor, aiming at Julien's back. I try to shout a warning but only manage a whimper.

"I should . . . both . . . now . . ." says Stefan. I wish he'd take off that ridiculous mask so I could make sense of him.

Julien spins and raises his hands. "Stop . . . didn't mean . . . happen . . ."

". . . never have . . . fool . . ."

Their words jumble, fragmented and nonsensical.

I consider trying for the stairs again. Nobody's holding me back . . . but the room's . . . going . . . fuzzy . . .

Julien's pleading, ". . . all a mistake . . ."

"Doesn't matter . . . don't you understand . . . finished . . . your fault . . ."

I strain to make sense of them, leaning against a bookshelf.

Dizzy . . . so dizzy . . .

Everything is a blur.

A haze.

Like trying to peer through a cloud.

Like whenever I try to remember my mother.

But you can't remember what you never saw.

Shouts.

Frantic shouts.

I fall to my knees.

A shot.

A scream.

The world goes dark.

49
Sean

"Something's happening," says Olivia's mother. I snap my gaze to the TV in time to see the BREAKING NEWS graphic soar across the screen.

Selena's father snorts. "They claim there's *breaking news* every ten minutes . . ."

The next shot shows a cordoned-off area in the middle of a street I don't recognize. A circular metal cover is on the ground next to a gaping manhole. Police officers are keeping onlookers at bay as several men wearing yellow vests set up some sort of contraption with a pulley system and what looks like a harness.

The room bursts into chatter.

"Are they pulling someone out?"

"Where is that?"

"Why didn't the detective call us?"

I practically launch myself at the TV, unable to hear the reporter over the din. Jeff and Aliyah circle around the table to join me, but even up close, we can't hear.

"Quiet," I yell.

The din simmers down.

". . . are reporting that one of the missing girls is about to be lifted from this shaft. The rescue teams have located . . ."

A cacophony of cheers and shouts explodes around me. I can't even move; it feels like the air's being sucked from my lungs as my heart tries to eject itself from my chest.

They found them.

They *found* them.

Jeff grasps my shoulder and covers his mouth, and Aliyah races to Selena's stepmother to wrap her in a hug and jump around excitedly.

But there's something strained on the reporter's face, something frenetic about the way the rescue workers are assembling the pulley system behind her.

"Wait," I say. "She said *one* of the girls . . ."

Nobody's listening. Nobody but Jeff, who stiffens beside me. "Everybody, quiet!" he shouts, then nods toward the screen, crossing his arms. "There's our cop."

I recognize Debois heading toward the manhole, Garnier right behind her. Debois stoops next to it as some helmeted guy's head pops up to speak to her. If there's a ladder in there, why do they need that harness? He hands Debois something—something purple—and she nods at whatever he says. I can only see her profile, but her posture seems rigid. Grim.

My stomach sinks.

The man disappears down the hole again, and Debois straightens and stands there staring down at the purple thing. A phone. Then she says something to Garnier before they both stride off frame. An icy feeling floods through me, making my skin prickle. That flash of purple. Lavender. Like Ruby's phone case and laptop shell.

"Where the hell is this?" Jeff says in a low voice, his fingers shaking as he pulls up Debois on his phone.

"Hang on." I set a hand on his arm before he can place the call. He raises his brows. "I don't think we should distract her right now."

He tilts his head.

Something's terribly wrong. We won't help by interfering.

"I'm getting a call," Selena's father shouts behind us. "That other detective, Garnier." We all watch him press the phone to his ear. "This is Rafael."

His wife nudges his arm. "Put it on speaker."

"Hang on." He sets the phone on the table and taps the screen. "Go ahead." We all gather around that table.

"Mr. Rodriguez, I have an update." Garnier's voice is strained. Clipped. "We found your daughter—" Aliyah claps a hand over her mouth, and Selena's stepmother starts to squeal with delight, but several people shush her, picking up on his tense tone. "She's in stable condition but will need to be treated for exposure and injuries she's sustained to her arm and feet. Once she's lifted from the extraction point, you'll be able to meet her at Hospital Salpêtrière—"

"What about the rest of the girls?" Olivia's mother asks, clasping a necklace at her throat.

There's a long pause.

"Am I on speaker?" Garnier finally asks.

"Yes," says Selena's father.

"Where are the *others*?" Jeff asks.

"Perhaps it would be best if I came over there—"

"No." Olivia's father bends over to shout at the phone. "You tell us what you know, and you tell us *now*."

The next pause seems to outlast time itself. I'm pretty sure everyone in the room has stopped breathing.

Finally, Garnier says, "I don't think I should say this over the phone . . ."

But that's as good as saying it.

A low-pitched buzz fills my ears as my fingers go numb. Val's mother staggers back into her husband's arms, and Olivia's mother lets out this awful wail I know my brain will play on loop for the rest of my life. "Oh my God," someone else says.

"We think Ruby is still alive," Garnier says quickly.

My heart shoots into my throat. Ruby's *alive*.

But that confirms Val and Olivia aren't.

Garnier goes on. "Selena keeps telling the rescue workers, 'They have Ruby. You have to get Ruby.'"

Jeff and I exchange a horrified glance.

"They?" I say. "Who the hell is *they*?"

50
Sean

As we stream out of the police van—me, Aliyah, Selena's parents, and Jeff—it feels like I'm submerged in a cold vat of jelly, all numb and hazy. Rescue workers just extracted Selena from the shaft, and we've beaten her to the hospital.

They have Ruby.

Reporters and bystanders swarm under the emergency vehicle overhang, buzzing with tense energy.

They have Ruby.

We hurry past them. At least this mob's not as bad as the vultures crowding the hotel entrance, vying for footage of the grieving parents.

They have Ruby.

All Garnier would tell us was that Selena said the girls ran into members of some sort of cult. He remained at the extraction point to question her once she surfaced, but Debois and her team have been racing to make sense of footage on Ruby's phone, while more rescue workers are continuing along the route where Selena described last seeing her.

I'm trying not to get my hopes up.

The higher your hopes soar, the more disappointment can crush you. And the weight of this one would be catastrophic.

The group of us hover in the lobby, tucked away from the cameras. Selena's parents radiate with relief and excitement, but Aliyah's pacing back and forth near me and Jeff, wringing her hands like she still has something to be skittish about.

"You gonna make it?" I say.

"Sorry." She flaps her hands. "I'm nervous for Ruby. And for you. And to see Selena . . ."

"Garnier says she's stable." Though I have no idea if there will be any long-term effects from hypothermia or her injuries, not to mention the trauma she's endured. That'll probably last the rest of her life.

"I know, but . . . gah." She flaps her hands again. Maybe she's just anxious for their reunion.

I'd give anything to be anxious about that.

The crowd outside starts cheering.

"Oh my God," says Aliyah.

Through the doors' windows, we watch the ambulance pull under the overhang. A minute later, there she is, being wheeled inside by a pair of paramedics, conscious and covered in a shiny thermal blanket.

"Selena!" Her parents swarm her first. Everyone's a blubbering mess of tears. Aliyah hangs back next to me and Jeff, giving them a moment, clasping her mouth and trembling so hard I can see her fingers quivering at her lips.

When Selena sees her and calls her name, Aliyah bounds over and throws her arms around her. "Ew, you reek." But she kisses Selena anyway.

I'd give anything to be kissing Ruby right now.

But I'm happy for Aliyah. I'd be losing my mind if not for her. Seeing them reunite reminds me that no matter what happens next, everything we've done to help—all the rules we've broken and the commands we've eschewed—hasn't been for nothing.

Selena spots me and Jeff over Aliyah's shoulder as they hug again, Selena's face sparkling with tears. She releases Aliyah with a sob. Doctors have taken over for the paramedics and are saying it's time to take Selena into the ICU.

"Wait." Selena reaches out for Jeff, who takes her hand in both of his. "Ruby told me to tell you she loves you. She loves you so much."

Jeff's face bunches in anguish, and he shakes his head, trying not to lose it.

"They'll find her, Jeff," Selena's stepmom says, rubbing his back.

Selena's gaze shifts to me. "Sean."

Jeff releases her hand, and I inch forward.

We've never exactly been friends—more like acquaintances who happen to be in the same class every so often. I don't know what went down between her and Ruby, but whatever it was crushed Ruby. So I didn't have the best impression.

I clear my throat awkwardly. "I'm glad you're okay."

"Thanks." Her eyes well with fresh tears, and one streaks down her cheek. "Sean . . . Ruby told me to tell you she loves you, too."

51
Ruby

Darkness, then light.

Silence, then sounds.

Crash. Crash. Crash.

The black void returns.

I strain to make sense of it.

Maybe my eyes are already open. Maybe they'll never open again.

It makes no difference.

Nothingness consumes me.

And then it's over.

52
Sean

I never thought waiting could feel so endless.

Seconds bleed into minutes posing as hours.

Sometimes life has felt like one long stretch of waiting. Waiting for high school to end. For my career to start. Like I can't even start fulfilling my purpose until that happens.

Ruby gave time meaning. Suddenly what I did in the here and now mattered.

Now I'm waiting again. Waiting with the rest of the world.

Even in humanity's company, even though it doesn't take long, time creeps like watching paint dry, only it can't dry, so you watch forever.

And then it's over.

53
Ruby

I squint into the light.

So there is an afterlife after all.

I want to look for my mother, but my feet aren't grounded, so I can't walk. It feels like I'm floating on something fluffy—

"Here she is," says a familiar voice. "Welcome back."

Someone's here to greet me. A sense of peace trickles through me like soothing hot chocolate. My grandfather, maybe? He passed away years before my mother joined him. I turn toward his voice, but my neck's incredibly stiff.

I didn't think I was supposed to feel pain up here.

The cloud I'm floating on has white rails. Heaven looks awfully clinical—

Oh.

I'm in a bed.

A hospital bed. Those bright lights are fluorescents.

A warm, calloused hand takes mine. Dad's blurry smile comes into focus, his eyes watering. My heart swells. "Daddy?" I croak.

"Hey," he says, smoothing back my hair. "You're okay."

I try to respond, but a sob surges up my throat and my voice sticks.

"It's okay. It's all okay." He stands and stoops over me to wrap me in his arms. My left arm's in a cast and sling, but I hug him back with the other and cry into his shoulder, getting his plaid sweater all wet.

"I'm sorry," I finally say. "I'm so sorry."

"You have nothing to be sorry for."

"I have *everything* to be sorry for." Olivia. And Val. And—

"Selena," I gasp. "We have to find Selena—"

"She's fine," says another voice. "She's down the hall." I glance over, frantically blinking away tears. Someone's leaning against the windowsill, arms folded. When I meet his steel-gray eyes, I think my heart might explode.

"Sean," I whisper, releasing Dad, who steps away and gives Sean an encouraging nod. As Sean crosses the space to my bed, I stretch out my fingers, wanting so badly to touch him, to hold him, to make sure he's real, even though Dad's standing right there. I thought I might never see him again, and now here he is. I'm dizzy with relief—or maybe that's from whatever Luc injected me with.

A stabbing pain in my neck.

Stefan pointing that gun at Julien.

A shot in the darkness.

I gasp again the moment Sean's fingers brush against mine. "Oh God. Julien. And Stefan. What happened—"

"They cannot hurt you," says a voice accented with French. "You're safe here." I turn to see a sharp-looking woman standing in the doorway, her brunette hair in a tight bun, dressed in a dark navy uniform.

Sean clasps my hand. "Ruby, this is Capitaine Debois." I raise my brows. They seem acquainted.

Suddenly I'm elsewhere, clinging to a ladder, surrounded by crickets, sucking in dank air as I press my palm to that crusted manhole cover, wondering if Sean's searching for me, knowing he's up there some-where, *so damn close* yet so damn far.

Just in my mind.

Only in my mind.

I squeeze Sean's hand, never wanting to let him go again.

The police officer . . . detective . . . *Capitaine*—whatever—approaches and extends a hand, which means I do, in fact, need to let go of Sean's hand to shake hers.

"Hi," I say. "I'm Ruby."

"I know," she says with a light chuckle. I blush. "It's a pleasure to meet you."

"You, too . . ." I trail off. My mouth feels like it's full of cotton, and I release her hand to cough into my fist. I'm thirsty, so thirsty, even with an IV dripping fluid into my veins.

Dad bounds for the plastic carafe on a side table and pours me a cup of water. I slurp it all down, and he fluffs my pillow so I can sit straighter. "Maybe you can come back later," he says to the officer. "She just woke up."

"Of course," she says. "I was passing by and noticed she was awake, so I wanted to say hello. Selena's filled us in on most of it, but, of course, Ruby, whenever you're ready, we'll want to hear the story from your perspective." Selena didn't hear everything Julien told me, so I'll have to recount all that.

"Where *is* Julien?" I throw a wary look at the door. "And the oth-ers?" Logically I know Stefan won't barrel in here in that ghastly mask, but I can't help imagining it. Can't help fearing it.

"It's okay." Sean sets a comforting hand on my shoulder. "Those bone worshippers can't hurt you anymore."

"So you know . . . ?"

"Selena told us," Dad says.

I look between him and Sean. "They think bones have *magical powers*." They shake their heads incredulously. "Did you arrest them?" I ask the officer. Maybe I imagined the gunshot like I imagined those heavenly lights. That injection messed me up.

She purses her lips. "Luc has been taken into custody, and Stefan's in surgery. You did quite a number on his leg." She looks impressed. "My colleagues are interviewing the others we found in that house now. Though they're not saying much."

"What about Julien?" I wonder if Selena also surmised Julien had a change of heart. She figured out the cult's purpose the same moment I did.

"You're arresting all of them, right?" Dad asks. "They're accessories to kidnapping. And murder."

"No, wait," I say. "Did Selena tell you Julien changed his mind? He was trying to take us out another exit so we wouldn't run into any of them, but we got lost after Selena fell down a well. He kept saving us from them, and when Stefan found us, he tried to convince . . ." I trail off when I notice their wary expressions. "Oh, don't worry, this isn't Stockholm syndrome or anything, I just think he'd be willing to turn on the others. Stefan killed his parents."

Sean and Dad exchange a perturbed look.

"What?" My pulse quickens.

The officer sets her hand on my shoulder. "Ruby . . . Julien suffered a gunshot wound."

My breath hitches. That gunshot *was* real. "He's dead?"

"No. He's still in surgery as well. But he lost a lot of blood."

She thinks he's going to die.

Nobody offers any condolences. Why would they? If it weren't for Julien, Olivia and Val would still be alive, and none of this would've happened. But Stefan murdered his parents, then tricked him into becoming a Gardien. And his poor sisters. Holy hell. I don't know what to think. I have a feeling my heart will be a jumbled mess over this for a long time.

I let out a shuddered breath, desperate to change the subject. "How did you find me?"

The officer's demeanor relaxes. "Some of my colleagues have been investigating Stefan for fraud and passport violations. Their investigations turned up his cult—well, he insists we call it a *secret society*. Les Gardiens des Morts. They've been around since the eighteenth century, almost like a more intense, religious brand of cataphiles, but they were peaceful for ages. In fact, their last leader was a well-respected philanthropist. Their criminal activities only seemed to begin once Stefan *ascended*. I get updates on that case during briefings and have seen their symbology, and when I saw those skull masks in your video, and Selena told us their names, I had my colleagues pull his address. It was fairly straightforward, all things considered." She shakes her head. "Now he's in for a hell of a lot more than passport violations . . ."

"Passport violations?" I ask.

"Forgery, essentially." She waves it off like I shouldn't concern myself. I wonder if Stefan was stealing and selling the identities of the people he killed to make it seem like they were still roaming around, living their lives. Another way to line his pockets, too.

"He said the catacombs have been flooding more and more," I say, "and that the city has been doing nothing to fix it. He said buildings would start collapsing; that's how he took money—" A sharp pain zings my neck.

"You can tell me everything once you've rested," says Debois. "Just know that whatever that man told you is a lie. The city regularly maintains the drainage systems; there's been no more flooding than usual. And one more thing before I go." The officer nods at Sean. "Without this young man's help, we might not have found you in time."

I peek at him. "What do you mean?"

"He helped us narrow down your location."

"How?"

Sean reddens. "Uh . . . I might've snooped on your laptop." He rubs the back of his neck. "You forgot it in my room, and—anyway, the picture you took of that toad graffiti synced to the cloud, and the folder popped up."

I totally forgot I took that photo. I hadn't even considered that anyone might find it, that it might help.

They quickly fill me in on the rest—how Sean filmed the side street we'd disappeared on, how he tripped over the loose grate, and the next day, during our class's catacombs tour, he realized we might've been down there. Though the officer recounts most of it, I can't tear my eyes from Sean's. My fingers itch to grasp his hand again. Hearing how he kept searching for me, even when Debois apparently kept telling him to back off, makes me want to do things with him I absolutely should not be thinking about in front of Dad.

I flush and cough awkwardly into my palm.

"More water?" Dad guesses, pouring me another cup.

"Sure." I take it, grateful for something to hide behind.

"Anyway," says the officer, "I'll let you rest, but I'll be back. You have my number," she says to Dad. "If the hospital releases her before I return, please let me know."

"You bet." He shoves his hands into his jeans pockets and . . . oh my God, is he *blushing*?

"Thank you," says the officer. She gives him a slight smile before heading into the hall.

I clamp my lips to stifle a laugh and exchange an amused look with Sean as Dad watches her go.

"Dad?" I say.

He spins around. "Yup," he says way too fast.

"Okay if I have a minute with Sean?"

"Absolutely." He claps his hands. "Let me know when you need me. I'll be . . ." He jabs his thumb at the hall, then backs into it, closing the door behind him, for once giving me space when I've asked for it.

I blow air between my lips. "I think my dad has a crush on a French police officer." Sean laughs as I face-palm. "How would that even work?"

"No idea."

A meaningful look passes between us. If Sean ships off to West Point this summer, we'll be long-distance. Even more so whenever he goes on tour. Maybe it'll end us. But as we devour each other with our eyes, silken honey oozes through my veins, making my heart swell and my cheeks burn. I won't resist this out of fear I'll eventually lose him.

Neither of us makes a move, though.

As usual.

I've pulled away from him so many times, I can't blame him. But I'm kind of stuck in bed, hooked up to a machine as liquid drips down a tube and into my veins. It has to be him.

I can tell him how I feel, though.

"I'm just going to spit it out, Sean." I take a deep breath. "I've liked you for ages. But I was scared. Losing you would be horrible, and I thought if we took things further, that pain would hurt even worse when you left for West Point. So I kept pulling away." If that machine were beeping along with my heart rate, it'd be short-circuiting, sparks flying everywhere. "But living in fear like that is ridiculous. I really, really like you. Like, a *lot*. And if you don't kiss me right now, I'm going to lose my entire mind."

He seems to have stopped breathing. "Wow."

"Yeah."

He lets out a husky chuckle, then sits on the edge of my bed and cups my face, staring into my eyes for another long moment before gently touching his lips to mine.

Despite the lightness of his touch, sparks ignite inside me so intensely I think my very soul might catch on fire. I slide a hand around his neck, over his cropped hair that feels like silk under my fingertips, and pull him closer, deepening our kiss. His lips are warm and soft, and they mold against mine, moving in perfect unison like we've both imagined this countless times and now it's finally happening.

It's everything I imagined and more.

I never want it to end.

"Ruby," he whispers, his eyes glassy as he breaks our kiss to press his forehead against mine, still holding my face like he never wants to let me go. "I thought . . ."

"I know."

I thought we'd lost each other, too.

The future doesn't seem limitless—neither of us are invincible, and there are no guarantees—but it exists past this moment.

And I'll make the most of every moment we get.

EPILOGUE

Ruby

THREE DAYS LATER

The four of us—me, Sean, Aliyah, and Selena—mosey into the square in front of Notre Dame. Selena's on crutches, her left foot well enough to walk on, her right arm bandaged under her coat. My left arm's still in its sling. Dad and Selena's parents trail us, refusing to let us out of their sight until our flight home in the morning. I don't blame them. Besides, their presence is soothing, like aloe on fresh sunburn.

I entwine my fingers with Sean's and breathe in the crisp dusk air as we pause to admire the Gothic cathedral bathed in the warm, orange glow of the setting sun.

The two towers flanking the main entrance stand tall and proud, and intricate biblical carvings adorn the ornate arched façade beneath a row of saintly statues spanning the building's entire breadth. Above the statues, I'd guess at least two dozen weathered gargoyles are watching us. It's hard to believe that stone from those dark, dank tunnels could've created something so majestic. I vaguely wonder if the stained glass windows are usually illuminated from within, and whether they will be once the cathedral reopens to the public. Now they're eclipsed in darkness.

"I can't believe it almost burned down," says Selena.

"I can't believe it didn't," I say. "Did you know the towers were literally minutes from collapsing? The firefighters got control of the fire just in time."

"A miracle," says Aliyah.

I'm not sure I'd call it that. This cathedral survived to the credit of the firefighters' skill and determination, like how we survived thanks to Sean's smarts, the police's speed, and all those rescue workers and cataphiles who raced to help find us.

And maybe a bit of light maiming on my part.

It's no miracle we survived.

A shudder tears through me at the memory of that switchblade sinking into Stefan's leg. The media has been calling me a hero, but I don't know about that. I mean, logically, I know if Stefan managed to sneak us out and got away with it, his cult would've continued sacrificing people. But what I cared most about in that moment was getting Selena out alive. And I know that *sounds* heroic, but—oh, I don't know. Many people aided our rescue. Just like no single snipped mooring thread can unravel an entire web, no single thread can save it.

Sean puts his arm around me as a cool breeze sweeps back my hair, making me shiver again, and I snuggle close.

That's when I notice the crepe stand.

My breath hitches. "Selena." I motion to it. "Look."

"What about it—" Her eyes widen. She remembers, too.

It's Julien's favorite place in Paris. He'd get a warm, gooey crepe right outside Notre Dame and enjoy the view and crisp air.

Now he's in a coma. His doctors aren't optimistic.

I wonder if this is the same stand he loved.

My stomach clenches with unease.

"Want one?" Sean suggests, following my gaze.

"Uh . . . sure," I say. Selena nods. We exchange a morose look but say nothing. This story is just for us. Nobody else would understand. Nobody else was there.

We get in line, and the people ahead of us recognize us and offer their well-wishes, like so many have all day. As grateful as I am that so many people care and stepped up to help, forcing a smile on for strangers over and over is taxing. I'm mourning Olivia and Val—even after everything she did—and the grief is so raw it's almost unbearable. At least these strangers aren't asking for a selfie. Most people have been respectful enough not to, but getting even this much attention is overwhelming.

In that sense, it's a blessing Stefan's already stolen the limelight. The media quickly shifted their coverage from us to Les Gardiens des Morts, a secret society sworn to protect the Empire of the Dead that morphed into a necromancy doomsday cult in Stefan's desperate attempt to maintain numbers and power. I saw his face for the first time on social media—his high, chiseled cheekbones, thick eyebrows, pasty complexion, and full lips curved into a scowl. Liar. Murderer. I can feel his biting stare slice into me every time I scroll past him.

After the rescue teams recovered Val's and Olivia's bodies—and the cultist who drowned in the snake-shaped pool near Olivia—they started searching for the others. The sacrifices. So far, they've recovered the remains of a teenager from Spain who'd vanished during a weekend getaway, a young American woman last seen getting into an Uber at the airport, and one other unidentified woman. None of the cultists have confessed to how many sacrifices they've made, brainwashed, protecting their mission. They believe extracting the remains will squelch the ossuaries' protective powers.

All our phones trill or vibrate at once.

A news story just broke. Kyle sent the link to our class's WhatsApp chat.

"Oh God," I breathe.

"They found him," says Selena.

The man we stumbled across. A forty-three-year-old film producer named Sam Browning, found in the same cavern as the unidentified woman. His identification was in the backpack that had been propped under his head.

Our first night in the hospital, I hobbled down the hall to visit Selena, and we found his video someone had recovered and uploaded. As Julien and Val had recounted, you could hear a shriek in the distance before Sam spun and booked it. Many early commenters brushed it off as a hoax, mocking anyone who took it seriously, but we noticed how uncanny valley their profile pictures were. We dug deeper and, lo and behold, they were clearly AI-generated headshots for otherwise inactive accounts. Sock puppets. Likely Gardiens tasked with concealing the truth. And since the video did seem like something out of a low-budget horror film, it never took off.

But Julien knew it was real.

He *knew* that scream came from one of his cult's sacrifices.

"Whoa, check this out," Aliyah says, then reads aloud, "'Investigators have disclosed that Browning, a filmmaker, had been scouting locations for an upcoming documentary on urban explorers, intending to cover the secretive lives of cataphiles. Based on a recording recovered from his camera,' yada yada yada . . ." She scrolls down. "Ah, here. 'Browning overheard one of Les Gardiens des Morts's sacrificial ceremonies and fled, leading him to become panicked and disoriented. After a failed attempt to retrace his steps, he likely wandered into one of the cult's dens and perished due to dehydration. According to reports, a nearby cave-in kept the cultists from returning to the area. Authorities are awaiting the results of an autopsy report.'"

"Yikes," says Sean.

"So he wasn't a sacrifice himself," says Selena.

"We already knew that, right? He wasn't *assimilated*." I make air quotes.

"But someone else had been in that den."

Yeah. That putrid smell hadn't *only* been him. I bet she was in the pulpit.

The line for crepes inches up, but I have zero appetite. "Ugh, can we stop talking about this?" I say. "I just want to enjoy tonight."

"Yes, please," says Selena.

Aliyah nods and puts her phone away, and Sean kisses the top of my head. I order a crepe after all—one with strawberries and Nutella. Even Aliyah gets one made with buckwheat. Selena's dad rushes over to pay for all of them. My dad's chatting with Selena's stepmom. He promised me a backpacking trip across Europe this summer; he claimed the food here has blown his entire mind and he wants more inspiration for his restaurant.

I know he just wants to spend time together, though. I'm good with that.

It's nice to see him talking to Selena's parents again. After Selena and I fell out, Dad knew not to pry, saying, "I'm sure you've learned your lesson, whatever it was. And I'm sure she'll come around."

But she couldn't accept an apology she never saw. I still can't wrap my head around Val's note switcheroo. She was a real friend to me over the past ten months, or so I'd thought. And now she's gone. She apologized in the end, but Stefan stole any chance she had to redeem herself, any chance I had to forgive her.

I showed her goodbye message to her parents. I hesitated, though—she never got to re-record it, and it was so guilt-trippy, I wasn't sure whether seeing it would hurt or help them. But maybe if they hadn't ignored her so much, she wouldn't have sabotaged other people's relationships nor accepted a stranger's invitation to a secret party to feel wanted.

My crepe's ready first, and Aliyah hands it to me with a warm smile. One silver lining in all this has been getting my best friend back. And I've made a brand-new friend in the process. I have a feeling we'll all be spending a lot of time together, at least until graduation.

Before we search for an empty bench facing Notre Dame, Sean holds my crepe so I can snap a photo of the crepe stand with my good hand.

Selena nods at my camera as I take a seat between her and Sean. "Think you'll keep it up? The YouTubing?"

Thinking about anything past tomorrow makes my head spin. "I'm not sure," I say. "All I know is I want to travel and see the world. But I don't know what that looks like yet."

"Your channel would definitely take off now," says Selena.

I shrug. I'm wary to pursue something I was willing to do something so foolish for. I wanted views for Ruby's Hidden Gems, but what we went through wasn't worth exposure. Besides, the first thing on my to-do list is to recover—both physically and mentally. Not only did we just endure a trauma that will haunt me for years, but I need therapy for all the abandonment issues I've been quietly grappling with my whole life. I've already discussed it with Dad, and he's made appointments—both for me and for himself.

"It's okay if you're not sure," says Aliyah. "You don't need to have your whole life figured out tomorrow."

"Thanks," I say, then bite into my crepe. The edges are crispy and sweet, the insides warm and gooey, exactly how Julien described it. It makes my tongue sing and my stomach sink at the same time.

I can't reconcile how I feel about him. He initially wanted to kill us, but out of desperation, to save himself and his sisters. And in the end, *he* may have sacrificed himself for *us*. Yet Olivia and Val are dead because of him, and round and round it goes, fury and empathy swirling my mind into muddled stew. At least his sisters are safe—Capitaine Debois assured me they've been located and moved into France's child protection services.

"What are your plans after graduation?" I ask Aliyah.

She snorts. "Well, I got into Boston University's performing arts program for acting and I'll get a free ride since my dad's a professor there. But, you know, I've liked running Gavel Club even more than acting. I might switch to directing or production management, or maybe be a professor, I dunno. I have until junior year to declare a major, so I'll take some time, see what classes I like. How 'bout you?" She chucks a rolled-up ball of crepe at Sean. A pigeon attacks it the moment it hits the ground. "You're shipping out to boot camp or something, right?"

He chuckles. "Military academy. And nope."

I freeze midchew. "What do you mean, 'nope'? I thought West Point was basically a done deal."

"Nah. At least, not after I tell Pop I'm not going." He holds my gaze, and my heart does a little cartwheel.

"Why, though?" I hope he's not giving up on his future for my sake.

He shrugs. "Debois kept being all like, *Sean, you'll make a fine inspecteur someday.*" He imitates her French accent, reminding me of our first video together, how he'd shouted in French that the grocery store was big and had bananas. I smile at the memory. "And it got me thinking."

"So you want to be a detective?" I ask.

"That, or maybe a documentarian or something. I got into Emerson. Their film program."

I beam. "Seriously? Holy crap, congratulations."

"Thanks." He grins back. "Maybe that's what I'll do. Make documentaries on things like cults, unsolved missing persons cases, human trafficking that goes on all over the world . . . stuff like that." I love that idea. "We can figure it out as we go."

We. Together.

We might not have an expiration date after all.

I smile as he puts his arm around me and pulls me close again.

"What about you?" Aliyah pokes Selena's arm. "Still want to hurl yourself into space?"

"Abso-freaking-lutely," Selena says with a full mouth. After pausing to swallow, she tips her head back to see the stars. "All that wide-open space up there seems fabulous now."

I quirk my brows. "But most of the time—"

She chortles. "I know. Most of the time you're in a teeny-tiny rocket or space station or whatever. I'm kidding. Even if I never make it to space, I want to work at NASA. I want to make it happen. We only have this one life, this one shot to go after our dreams. It feels like we both got a second chance, doesn't it?"

A rock lodges in my throat as my gaze meets Sean's, so close his nose nearly brushes against mine. "It really does." And neither of us will let fear hold us back anymore. My eyes water as I look back at Selena. "I'm proud of you."

Selena smiles. "I'm proud of you, too."

"All right, all right," says Aliyah. "That's enough cheese for now."

"Cheesiest thing I've ever witnessed," Sean teases.

Selena and I exchange a tearful grin before finishing our crepes and taking in our surroundings—the looming Gothic towers, the smattering of stars twinkling near the crescent moon, the street performer playing the violin on the corner, the sugary smell wafting from the crepe stand, the tourists milling about. A sense of peace washes over me—

The ground shakes, and I feel the bench vibrate.

I gasp and jerk my head from Sean's shoulder, gripping the wooden slat beside my right leg.

"What is it?" Sean asks.

Baffled, I shake my head. "I don't know . . ."

What if Stefan was right?

I dart a glance toward the street, bracing to see the crowd disperse in a shrieking frenzy as a crack spiders through the square, splitting the earth in two.

But it's just a bald man rolling a massive cart behind us. The wheels rumble over asphalt before crunching over gravel beside the bench.

In the square, all remains peaceful.

A young woman in a pink wig dips a thick rope into a bucket and lifts it straight up, letting the breeze blow enormous bubbles into the air. Several children encircle her, eager to lunge and pop them before they can burst of their own accord.

I grin despite the chill slithering up my spine. "Never mind. I felt the cart, and I'm just jumpy, that's all."

I probably will be for a while.

I rest my head on Sean's shoulder again as he holds me close. But beneath the smile I plaster on my face, I have so much healing to do under the surface.

We all do.

At least we'll go through it together, whatever comes next.

ACKNOWLEDGMENTS

Thank you for being here. For having hope. For enduring these past few years, for picking up this book and giving it a shot, hoping you'd enjoy it. I hope you did. Your support means the world to me, whether you're a casual reader, bookseller, librarian, book influencer, or teacher. You matter so, so much.

Writing this story gave me the pleasure of working with the most wonderful team an author could ever hope for.

Ruta Rimas, my genius editor, I'm not sure I can ever fully express how grateful I am to you for this one. Thank you for your guidance as we ripped this story apart and put it back together . . . twice. This book simply wouldn't exist in its current form without your brilliant brain. Simone Roberts-Payne, your feedback was also invaluable, and I'm so thankful for your brilliant mind as well, and for all your help shepherding this to publication.

Jim McCarthy, my stellar agent, again, I'm struggling to convey the depths of my gratitude. You believed in this one for *years*. Now here we are. Thank you, a million times over, for advocating for me and this book. I'm so lucky to have you in my corner.

Jeremy Enecio, who illustrated the cover's artwork, and Kristin Boyle, the cover's designer, thank you endlessly for so beautifully capturing Ruby and Sean's plight! Thanks also to Danny Ride for illustrating such a cool map of Ruby's harrowing journey through the catacombs.

The Penguin Random House team—thank you to publisher Jen Klonsky; managing editor Jayne Ziemba; production editors Sola Akinlana and Misha Kydd; copyeditor Dani Moran; proofreaders Kaitlin Severini and Tricia Lawrence; French authenticity reader Marie-Christine Payette; marketers Felicity Vallence, Shannon Spann, and James Akinlana; and publicist Tessa Meischeid. I so appreciate all the time you've all spent making this book sparkle and getting it into readers' hands.

To all the authors who took the time to read and blurb this book: Karen M. McManus, Kathleen Glasgow, C. L. Herman, Josh Malerman, Krystal Marquis, Ginny Myers Sain, Megan Lally, Eva V. Gibson, Wendy Heard, Keely Parrack, Rebecca Mahoney, and Alex Aster, thank you so much. I'm humbled by your kindness.

To my ride-or-die author friends: Mike Chen, Wendy Heard, Hannah Reynolds, Jessica Olson, Sophie Gonzales, Alechia Dow, J. Elle, Jennifer Iacopelli, I could not survive this industry without you, and I treasure our friendship. Erin, Jess, Tess, Brigid, Janella, Mara, Laura, Karen, Dan, and everyone in the Bridging the Gap Discord (*insert flaming Elmo GIF*), thank you for always being there for a chat, a laugh, a vent. It's such an honor to be part of the author community.

To the creators who inspired and entertained me while writing this book, thank you, especially Taylor Swift (OF COURSE you released

"Paris" while I was writing this), Imagine Dragons ("Whatever It Takes" has always been my theme song for this story), and BioWare (*Mass Effect* kept me sane each day after spending hours trapped in the catacombs alongside Ruby).

My parents, Mark and Lorri, thank you for believing in me every step of the way since the beginning of everything.

Kitty, thank you for being the comforting fur ball in my lap during all those claustrophobic days writing this book.

Bryan, my wonderful husband, thank you so much for your endless love and support and for taking me to Paris way back when and igniting my obsession with the city and its catacombs. I can't wait for all the other adventures we'll have together.

I know some people read the acknowledgments before reading the book, so if that's YOU right now, this is your warning to stop here. Spoiler ahead.

This book is a work of fiction, and I took artistic liberties with the layout of the Paris catacombs and the existence of a cult dwelling in its depths. Despite that, the catacombs and the fact that people have gotten lost down there, sometimes for days, are real. If this book inspires you to venture into the real-life labyrinth, please do so safely by visiting the official Les Catacombes De Paris museum or taking a tour with a reputable guide or tour operator, such as those listed at catacombes.paris.fr.

Speaking of which, thank you to my catacombs tour guide, David with Viator tours. Thanks also to documentarian Francis Freedland for the catacombs segment on *Scariest Places on Earth* (2000) and the YouTubers and bloggers whose posted firsthand accounts helped during my research—Messy Nessy, Night Scape, Kristen and Siya from Hopscotch the Globe, Exploring with Josh—as well as Paris Musées for making part of the catacombs accessible to the public.

If you enjoyed this book, please subscribe to my newsletter at DianaUrban.com/newsletter (you'll get an invitation to my Facebook group and Discord server) and consider leaving a review on Amazon and Goodreads. I'd so appreciate any kind words you'd have to share. And again, thank you.